continued . . .

CAUSING HAVOC

LORI FOSTER

BERKLEY BOOKS, NEW YORK

THE BERKLEY PUBLISHING GROUP
Published by the Penguin Group
Penguin Group (USA) Inc.
375 Hudson Street, New York, New York 10014, USA
Penguin Group (Canada), 90 Eglinton Avenue East, Suite 700, Toronto, Ontario M4P 2Y3, Canada
(a division of Pearson Penguin Canada Inc.)
Penguin Books Ltd., 80 Strand, London WC2R 0RL, England
Penguin Group Ireland, 25 St. Stephen's Green, Dublin 2, Ireland (a division of Penguin Books Ltd.)
Penguin Group (Australia), 250 Camberwell Road, Camberwell, Victoria 3124, Australia
(a division of Pearson Australia Group Pty. Ltd.)
Penguin Books India Pvt. Ltd., 11 Community Centre, Panchsheel Park, New Delhi—110 017, India
Penguin Group (NZ), 67 Apollo Drive, Mairangi Bay, Auckland 1310, New Zealand
(a division of Pearson New Zealand Ltd.)
Penguin Books (South Africa) (Pty.) Ltd., 24 Sturdee Avenue, Rosebank, Johannesburg 2196,
South Africa

Penguin Books Ltd., Registered Offices: 80 Strand, London WC2R 0RL, England

CAUSING HAVOC

A Berkley Book / published by arrangement with the author

ISBN-13: 978-0-7394-7930-8

BERKLEY®
Berkley Books are published by The Berkley Publishing Group,
a division of Penguin Group (USA) Inc.,
375 Hudson Street, New York, New York 10014.
BERKLEY is a registered trademark of Penguin Group (USA) Inc.
The "B" design is a trademark belonging to Penguin Group (USA) Inc.

PRINTED IN THE UNITED STATES OF AMERICA

CHAPTER 1

A dull ringing reverberated through his brain, and for only a moment, Dean Conor relived that instant the night before when a meaty fist had connected with his temple. He'd almost passed out.

Almost.

But even as shadows crowded in, he'd maintained his hold on his opponent's knee, hyperextending the joint, using the very last of his strength . . . and two seconds later the ref was there, calling a halt.

At first, Dean had protested. He wasn't done for. Not by a long shot. Dean Conor never gave up.

Then the cheers sank in.

Rather than take real damage to his leg, his opponent had tapped out. Dean had submitted the number one contender with a knee bar. He'd walk away from another fight as the winner—and this time he knew it was as much luck as skill and strength and speed.

That persistent ringing sounded again, followed by low voices. What the hell?

Dean opened his eyes and immediately regretted it. Bright morning sunlight cut through an opening in the curtains to slice painfully into his brain.

He felt like his head would shatter.

He felt like his guts would come up through his nose.

Groaning, he turned away from the light, and this time, barely peeked. Yeah, he was in his own room. How he got there, he didn't remember, but he was thankful all the same. With a slow, careful query of his body, he knew he was still whole, but aches and pains screamed for attention. His head, his shoulder, a rib. That Russian bastard's punch had the force of a tank, and he kicked like a deranged mule.

Jesus. At twenty-nine, Dean felt too old to continue competing. Already he'd fractured his collarbone, broken a wrist, dislocated an elbow, and put more kinks in his nose than he cared to contemplate.

Not that he'd quit. Fuck no.

He lied to others, but never to himself.

The urge would return, as it always did. The cheers of the crowd, the satisfaction in getting bloody, in conquering a worthy challenger. . . . It was like a drug in his veins, his one and only vice. As long as the management called him to fight, he'd keep at it.

Luckily he'd have plenty of time to recoup before going back on the mat. He'd need every minute.

As Dean forced his throbbing body into an upright position, he heard his front door close. So he had a guest. But who? The last thing he remembered was getting the heavyweight belt strapped around him, his corner roaring in pleasure, and then the trip to the hospital.

A small crowd of groupies, both male and female, had tagged along with his trainer and members of his camp.

They wanted to party.

He wanted to pass out.

The doc had given him some pain meds that dulled the worst of it. He'd been iced, stitched, taped, and released to head home for rest.

Everything after that was sketchy.

Glancing down, Dean realized he was buck-ass naked. Not good. But then again, it could mean nothing.

Instead of feeling like a first-rate fighter in his prime, a heavyweight champion with a score of first-round knock-outs to his credit, his joints and muscles strained like that of an old man.

Shit, he'd hate for anyone to see him now.

After locating boxers in the middle drawer of his chest—he wasn't up to putting on any more than that—Dean pushed the bedroom door open of his temporary apartment. He tried to stand straight and tall as he made his way to the kitchen where there seemed to be some activity. He took his time, working out the kinks along the way. Then he stepped into the open archway and saw a woman cooking at his stove.

She wore an official SBC fighting shirt that didn't quite cover the nicely rounded cheeks of her ass. Long blond hair hung down her back, and she swished as she turned pancakes on his stove.

A damned groupie.

Dean had a vague memory of her begging for his signature right before he'd fought. As he'd made his way down the long aisle to the spotlight, she'd stuck out an impressive bared rack and handed him a black marker.

Playing to the crowd had made him a fan favorite, so he'd scrawled his fighting name over her left breast. The roar of the audience almost drowned out the hard-rock music blaring throughout the events center.

It had been one hell of a night.

Propping his shoulder against the wall, as much for support as attitude, he said, "Morning."

She spun around. "Havoc! You're awake! Finally."

If he didn't miss his guess, she was naked beneath the tee. "I'm awake." He cocked his head at her, racked his brain, but couldn't come up with a name.

She laughed as if she could sense his problem. "Tiffany," she offered.

"Right." Never in a million years would he have guessed correctly. "So, Tiffany, how'd you get in here?"

She turned coy in an instant. "I brought you home."

"Simon allowed that?" His trainer-slash-manager-slash-agent was so watchful that Dean couldn't imagine him sending him off with an unknown broad bent on screwing him to death. Most of the more successful fighters had a team of people working for them. Dean had Simon Evans. He didn't need anyone else.

"He was here, too. But he couldn't stay. Something about live interviews on your fight."

Yeah, that made sense. He hadn't been in any shape to be interviewed, so naturally Simon would take up the slack. "And you're still here because . . . ?"

Her smile slicked up a few notches. Strutting toward him, making sure that everything bounced just so, she said with a purr, "I couldn't rouse you last night."

"But you tried?"

Her laugh rubbed up his spine and wormed into his aching brain. Obviously rudeness wouldn't make a dent in her determination.

"Forget I asked." Dean had a vision of her molesting his drugged and down-for-the-count body.

To his surprise, the thought stirred him even as it disgusted him.

She stopped right in front of him—and cupped her hand over his crotch.

Uh-oh.

The corners of her soft mouth lifted with satisfaction. "Let's hope I'll be more successful today."

Self-preservation kicked in and Dean grabbed her wrist. "I need a shower."

"Want me to wash your back?"

He thought about it, considered tossing her out, then decided what the hell. He hurt, but not bad enough to turn down her offer. After all, he wasn't dead.

"Yeah." As he turned away, still holding that slender

wrist, he noticed the envelope on the table, and belatedly remembered the ringing doorbell. "What's that?"

"Just a letter." She cuddled up close to his side and rubbed herself against him. "It came special delivery."

Which explained the bell and voices. While Tiffany plastered her boobs to his back, Dean lifted the thick envelope.

Seeing the return address sucked all the air out of his lungs.

In the twenty-one years since his parents' deaths, he hadn't received a single card or note from that address. For him, Harmony, Kentucky, had ceased to exist. Uncle Grover had taken him away, and he hadn't been given the opportunity to look back. Ever.

"Hold up." He pushed the blonde away and started to open the envelope . . . but he hesitated. God, had something happened to one of his sisters? That thought annoyed him. Hell, could you call someone you hadn't seen or heard from in over two decades a relative?

He slipped a finger under the envelope flap and tore it apart.

"Havoc," Tiffany complained. "Can't you read that later?" To punctuate her impatience, she took a stinging love bite on his back.

"Ow, damn, leave off, will ya?" He shrugged Tiffany away.

In thick tones of petulance, she whined, "But I have to leave soon. I have work."

While unfolding several sheets of paper, Dean said absently, "Something's come up. I need you to go."

A huff nearly parted his hair. "I made you pancakes!"

He glanced at the still warm stove top. Oh yeah. But he hadn't invited her in, damn it. Groupies were like that: pushy, outrageous, and looking to add another notch to their bedposts.

"Thanks." And he meant it. The breakfast would be good. Then he held up the letter. "But this is important, so how about a rain check?"

Her bottom lip stuck out and she pouted—for about two seconds. Then she turned calculating. "All right. If you'll also get me ringside tickets to the August fight in Atlantic City."

Those tickets would go for about six hundred a piece—if bought now. In a few weeks, they'd go for double that. "Sure." He turned away, already distracted again. "Write your name and address down. I'll see that you get them."

"You'll be there, too?" She trailed a finger down his spine to the waistband of his shorts. "For the rain check?"

Lying through his teeth, Dean muttered, "Wouldn't miss it."

She squealed, went on tiptoe to put a wet, sucking kiss on the nape of his neck, then whispered, "You won't regret it."

"I'm sure you're right." His attention back on the letter, he noted a three-month-old date in the upper left-hand corner. So his mail had been following him around for a while?

He glanced at the feminine handwriting.

Dear Dean,
I hope this letter finds you well. I know it's been a lifetime and I regret that. Aunt Lorna always said there was no way to reach you. But I finally did some research when Uncle Grover died. That's how I found your address.

Dean flipped the page and skimmed to the bottom of the next sheet. It was signed, *Hopeful, Camille.*

His sister, Cam. She'd be . . . what? Twenty-three now. And Jacki would be twenty-one. The image of them both as babies—Cam a toddling two-year-old, Jacki still an infant—sent a melon-sized lump into his throat.

They were grown women now, well past the age of needing a big brother. If they'd ever needed him.

A pain clenched in his chest; it was unlike the aches rippling through his bones and muscles.

It was fucking worse.

Knotting his hand in the papers, Dean tried to make

himself toss them away. But he couldn't. His teeth locked. His eyes burned.

Slowly his fingers opened again.

"Here you go, sweetie."

He glanced up to see Tiffany dressed in jeans and sandals, with the same shirt now knotted at the side. She'd brushed her hair and put on lipstick.

Still radiating "come and get me" vibes, she put a card on his table and grinned. "See ya in August."

"Right. August." Dean dismissed her from his mind. He barely registered the sound of his front door opening and closing. But he felt the new stillness of being alone.

Again.

Which was just how he liked it.

Heart pounding in what felt like rage, but was probably anxiety, he sat down at the small table and smoothed the papers out again.

I'd love to see you. Can you come for a visit? Please?
There's so much to tell you, and so much I want to ask.
I want to explain everything. I want to get to know you.
I want you to know me. I want us to be family.

Dean grunted. People in hell wanted ice water; that didn't mean they got it.

But he couldn't keep from reading the rest, more of the same, more entreaties, more . . . desperation. Yeah, somehow the desperation was there, woven between the lines. Subtle, but detectable.

Or maybe it was his friggin' imagination, brought on by too many knocks on the head.

When Dean finished the note, he sat there, numb, undecided. Torn. Anxious.

And damn it, as hopeful as Cam claimed to be. Not that he'd ever admit it to anyone. But again, he didn't lie to himself.

Amazingly enough, he forgot his bruises and cuts. Unsure what to do next, he went to the stove and picked up the platter of pancakes. He covered them in syrup, and still standing at the stove, shoveled them down by rote.

At least Tiffany was a good cook.

Refusing to think any further than the here and now, Dean finished off the breakfast, then indulged in a long, hot shower. Some of his stiffness eased. A good scrubbing left him refreshed and removed the last of the dried blood. After he'd toweled off, he found his pain pills and popped one, then shaved and brushed his teeth and . . .

He gave up.

As Cam requested, he'd go home. He'd talk to her. He'd talk to Jacki. But nothing had changed and he'd be sure they knew that. They had nothing in common anymore, beyond blood. And when it came right down to it, blood didn't stand for much.

If it had, they would have been raised together instead of on opposite sides of the country.

If it mattered at all, one of his sisters would have contacted him before now.

Within four hours of deciding, Dean finished a dozen phone calls, packed up his belongings, turned in the key on his week-by-week rental, and booked a flight.

Simon was pissed. But he'd get over it. Dean didn't go into details on why he needed to make the sudden trip on top of being beat to a pulp, and Simon didn't press it. He had Dean's cell number, and Dean promised to call him when he got settled in Harmony.

It wasn't like he had to be training three times a day now, the way he did in preparation for a fight.

With recent trips to Europe, the UK, and Boston, he was up on his PR. He had offers pending from other sponsors, but they could wait. He deserved a few months off.

He deserved to see his family.

And more than that, he deserved a chance for retribution.

STANDING on the interior balcony, her bare arms folded over the cool steel railing, Eve Lavon watched the line dancing below. In so many ways, Roger's place was the perfect setting for a bachelorette party. The low-key honky-tonk offered drinks, dancing, private rooms, a festive environment . . . but God, she detested Roger. She didn't want to do business with the swine.

Blindly Eve reached for her longneck beer sitting on the tiny round table beside her. She finished it off, then turned to head for the bar to get another.

The sight of a tall man, roughed up and rugged, standing in the doorway, stopped her in her tracks.

He perused the area with a jaundiced eye, lip curled in disgust, body set in lines of weariness. Obviously Roger's place wasn't quite what he'd expected.

From the outside, Roger's Rodeo looked like any other small-time bar. From the inside, it boasted a disco atmosphere with an open first floor that overlooked the basement below by way of a balcony that circled the entire floor. Both levels provided a bar, and each floor had a smattering of private rooms. But the action happened downstairs: line dancing, mechanical bull rides, billiards, pinball machines.

Two-seater tables lined the balcony, with enough space between to accommodate spectators. Tonight Eve had come to watch, to make a decision on whether or not to organize an event in one of the private rooms in the basement. Harmony, Kentucky, didn't have a lot of options, and most of what it did have, Roger owned. The group hiring her wasn't interested in going out of town, so . . .

The hunk locked eyes with her.

Eve's heart skipped a beat. It seemed her all-business night was about to include pleasure.

As he started forward, he looked . . . way too intense. And really beat up. But sexy, too. Rock hard and ripped, all machismo and confidence despite the bruises.

To Eve's surprise, when he got right in front of her, his mouth lifted on one side—and he stepped around her to peer over the balcony.

Playing hard to get? Amusement and interest unfurled

inside her. Turning, Eve took up her position against the railing again. "First time here?"

Without taking his gaze from the dancers below, he rumbled, "Probably my last, too."

Nice, deep voice. A flutter stirred in her belly. "Not if you plan to be in Harmony long. Roger's Rodeo is about the only decent place to drink socially."

One thick shoulder lifted. "Drinking alone has its perks."

"Those being?"

"Less noise." He turned toward her, and his gaze boldly searched every inch of her person. "You drinking alone tonight?"

"Not anymore." She saluted him with her empty beer. "So did a bull stomp all over you, or did you forget your parachute when you jumped from the plane?"

He stared at her mouth. "It was a Russian bull, and mean as hell."

"I take it the bull won?"

"Actually, no."

"Ah. Well, looks are deceiving."

His gaze came back to hers. "I hope not."

Those three words dripped sensual suggestion. Eve almost sighed. How could one man possess so much appeal? It had been a very long time since she'd felt this drawn. She wanted to get closer to him. She wanted to touch him.

Even in the crowded bar, with the smell of liquor and sweat hanging in the air, she could detect his scent. Rich and reminiscent of the outdoors, it suggested that he'd had a long drive, probably with the windows down. She liked that.

His mussed, light brown hair nearly matched the mellow color of his expressive eyes. He stood easily six-four, towering over her by damn near a foot. His worn jeans and black T-shirt hung loosely on his frame, but solid muscles shown anyway. Whatever he did, he kept his body shredded, without a single ounce of fat.

Eve glanced behind her, saw an empty nook, and said, "Wanna grab a seat?"

His gaze searched hers. "Is a seat my only option for now?"

Lord help her, she wanted to melt. Instead she donned a cocky smile. "For now."

Both sides of his mouth lifted. "Then, yeah, I'll take a seat, especially if it comes with a beer."

Finally having a good excuse, Eve wrapped her fingers around his wrist on the pretense of guiding him to the room. He had thick bones, hot skin, and crisp hair. The fact that her fingers couldn't completely encircle his wrist got her heart pumping double time.

Along the way to the semiprivate alcove, Eve paused at the bar to say, "Bring us some beers, will ya, Dave?"

"Be right there."

"Thanks." They reached the room just in time to head off another couple. "Sorry," Eve said, and slipped in before them.

Once inside she had to release him, but she held out her hand. "I'm Eve, by the way."

He looked at her outstretched hand, but didn't accept the handshake. Instead he captured her wrist, lifted her palm to his mouth, and put the gentlest of kisses there. Still holding on to her, he whispered, "Hi, Eve."

Get a grip, Eve told herself. She sucked in a deep breath and leaned close as if sharing a confidence. "I'm already sold. You can ease up now."

His thumb teased over the inside of her wrist. Slowly he shook his head. "No, I don't think I can."

"Really?" Damn it, she squeaked. Clearing her throat, she said, "Try, okay?"

"How about one taste first?"

"One taste?" Yeah, sounded like a hell of an idea. "You mean . . . ?"

With one small tug, he had her up against him. His free hand flattened on the small of her back, but not in restraint. She in no way felt forced.

She felt . . . seduced.

And wasn't that a unique thing?

"A kiss," he told her, and his breath brushed her lips. "Just a small one."

Would she be able to control herself? Doubtful. Harmony did not have men like him. Her experience was limited. She'd never encountered—

Hot, damp heat touched her lower lip and her thoughts shattered. Lightly he traced the tip of his tongue to the corner of her mouth and back again, and sure enough, her lips parted.

He didn't overpower her with the kiss. In fact the contact of his mouth on hers was so light that he somehow lured her into leaning into him, trying to get more.

His head tilted the tiniest bit, his tongue pressed in, touched the edge of her teeth, slicked beyond to meet her tongue. . . . And he retreated.

Breathing hard, Eve finally realized that he'd released her. Her eyes fluttered open to find him watching her with so much force, she felt snared.

"Wow."

Something flared in his light brown eyes, an inferno exploding, and she knew she'd just sealed her fate—at least for that night. "So." She tried to gather her thoughts. "How about—"

Someone grabbed her arm from behind. Taken off guard, she stumbled back and almost fell.

The hunk reacted with incredible reflexes. Within a single second, she was free, upright, and somehow behind him.

She heard Roger sneer, "I guess I'm interrupting?"

Oh shit. Double shit. How could she have forgotten about Roger the Repulsive?

She ducked to the side of her hunk to meet Roger's seething condemnation. A glance at the hunk showed no expression at all. He didn't look angry. Or concerned. He didn't look like a man who'd reacted instinctively to a situation with lightning speed.

"Sorry about that."

"Save your excuses," Roger bit off.

"I wasn't talking to you." She stepped between the men,

putting Roger at her back. "I can't imagine how," she said with a smile, "but I forgot that I'm meeting Roger tonight to discuss business."

"Business, huh?"

"He owns this joint. I'm an events coordinator." She lifted her shoulders to share her predicament. "The town doesn't boast a lot of options, so I'm forced here on a regular occasion."

"Forced?" Roger snarled. "Without me, you wouldn't have a business."

Now that was too over the top. Eve prepared to blast him, but he beat her to the punch.

"Find your manners and introduce me."

"Right." She really shouldn't go out of her way to provoke Roger. He was right that without him and his establishments, her business wouldn't be nearly so lucrative. "Roger Sims, proprietor." She gestured toward the hunk. "And you are?"

He smiled.

Roger gave a caustic laugh. "You don't even know his name? Now why doesn't that surprise me?"

They both ignored Roger.

Propping one shoulder against the wall, the hunk said, "Most people call me Havoc."

"Seriously?" How odd. Sure, he'd caused havoc to her system, but that couldn't be his given name. "Oh wait. Is that like a fighting label?"

Roger pushed himself closer. "I hope you're joking."

Havoc winked at her.

Fascinating, Eve thought. And, somehow, the name suited him. "So how come Havoc? I mean, why not Mayhem? Why not Destruction?"

"I didn't choose it. You fight, you get dubbed. When a name sticks, it sticks."

"It's idiotic," Roger said.

Havoc's gaze flicked to him, dismissed him as insignificant, and came back to her. "How long will your meeting be?"

Their lack of attention didn't sit well with Roger. "It's going to take a while so you might as well forget it."

In the most emotionless voice imaginable, with no expression whatsoever, the hunk said to Roger, "I don't like you very much."

"Is that supposed to bother me?"

"Just stating a fact."

Roger bunched up. "Are you trying to pick a fight with me?"

Eve barely swallowed a groan. Roger was such a bully that he often egged some poor schmuck into throwing the first punch. Then he'd turn around and have the guy arrested for starting a brawl—a brawl that Roger usually finished.

But Havoc just said, "Nope."

That threw Roger, but only for a moment. "You're a fighter who's afraid to fight?"

Havoc laughed. "No."

"Then—"

Taking Eve's arm, Havoc pulled her a few steps away from Roger. After gently tucking a strand of hair behind her ear, he asked, "So how long will you be?"

Elation rose. Finally someone who didn't give a fig what Roger thought. Someone rational who wouldn't be pulled into an idiotic pissing contest. Havoc could be her knight in shining armor.

Was he moving to Harmony? She sure hoped so.

"Not long at all." She turned to face Roger. "I'll take the night we already discussed. The price you gave is fine. Seven hours, from eight P.M. to three A.M. Three private rooms. Exclusive use of the mechanical bull." She held out her hand. "Deal?"

Roger locked his teeth. "You need to sign the contract." Rather than accept her hand, he encircled her wrist in a fist. "We can go to my office now to take care of that."

As usual Roger's grip was too tight. Eve winced, half expecting her knight to intercede.

But he didn't.

His restraint amazed and thrilled her. Attempting to free herself, Eve strained away from Roger. "Since when do I need to sign a contract on the spot?"

The more she tried to pull away, the tighter his fingers clenched. "Summers are busy, you know that. If you want me to hold the time for you, you need to sign." Determined to have his way, Roger tugged her forward a step.

Eve didn't mean to, but she winced.

Havoc straightened from his lazy position. As if discussing the weather, he said, "No offense to your liberated soul, but do you need any help?"

Glaring at Roger, Eve said, "No, because he's going to let me go right now."

Instead Roger jerked her forward another few inches. "If you want—"

"Sorry, but I can't take it." Again Havoc's movements were fluid and fast. Everything seemed to happen at once. His hand circled Roger's wrist and squeezed.

On a grunt of pain, Roger's fingers opened, freeing Eve. Almost at the same time, Roger yanked hard against Havoc's hold—and Havoc just let go.

Probably because he wasn't expecting that, Roger stumbled backward. He fetched up against a table, lost his balance, and fell on his ass. The table tipped onto him, causing an awful clatter.

Good thing Dave hadn't yet brought their beers or they'd be broken on the floor.

Inside Eve laughed at Roger's predicament. Outside she mimicked Havoc and pretended disinterest. While Roger struggled to right himself, she asked Havoc, "Did you mean for that to happen?"

"I meant for him to let you go."

"I could have handled it."

He lifted her arm and lightly brushed his thumb over her skin where red finger marks showed. "Before or after he bruised you?"

"It's a complicated situation."

"Yeah?" Leaning against the wall, he asked, "How so?"

Before she could answer, Roger regained his feet. Red faced and shaking with fury, he said through his teeth, "I want you out of my place. Now."

With regret Havoc faced her. "I don't suppose you're ready to go?"

How she wished she could. "Sorry, no."

"Get out."

Going on tiptoes, Eve crowded into Roger's space. "Back off, Roger. You caused this and you know it."

"He attacked me."

"Because you had your hands on me. Again."

His nostrils flared. "And any other man's hands are fine, just not mine?"

Eve could barely breathe. She didn't understand Roger and never would. "One way or another," she promised, "I'm going to make Cam see the truth about you."

"I could say the very same thing." His shoulders straightened. "If it wasn't for Cam, I'd tell you to find another place for your functions. Be very glad that she's your friend." Those words were still hanging in the air when Roger turned on his heel and stalked out.

A little embarrassed by her outburst, Eve peeked at Havoc. He stood fixed behind her, his face a mask, his gaze piercing as he stared at her.

In some indefinable way, he suddenly seemed very, very different.

"Well." Eve clasped her hands together in regret. "I have no idea how I always end up in these awkward predicaments, but at least that should take care of my scene for the day."

"Who's Cam?"

Havoc's tone and stance indicated boredom, but his eyes told a different story. They blazed with emotion.

Was he angry with Roger and hoping to hide it? How could she know, when she'd only just met him?

"Cam Conor. My best friend."

He gave a small nod, then asked, "What does she have to do with Roger?"

Eve rubbed her forehead. "Unfortunately Roger wants to marry her. He's asked her a couple of times now. And although Cam hasn't said yes, she isn't really saying no, either."

Loud music and a cacophony of voices couldn't drown out the sudden stillness between them. Havoc watched her with unwavering attention, leaving her a little intimidated.

Eve tried a laugh. "But that's my problem." Seeing a way to ease the tension, she asked, "So what do you think of Harmony so far?"

"Not much."

Damn but she wished he'd smile just a little. "And me?" Eve tipped her head at him. "Have I made an impression?"

"You lead an interesting life."

With relief she chuckled at his teasing observation. "Not really. For the most part, I manage to get along with Roger. Not because I like him, but because Cam might marry him. So I bite holes in my tongue, try to keep my opinions to myself, and—"

"Fend off his advances?"

Now he was way off base. "I wouldn't call them advances as much as unnecessary interest. I've always assumed it's because I'm Cam's friend. Like maybe he's just going out of his way to make friends with me because Cam and I are so tight."

"No."

She made a face. "Then who knows? I've never been able to understand Roger."

Done with that topic, Havoc asked, "So now what?"

Eve looked at her watch and wanted to curse the fates. "I'm afraid my coach is about to turn into a pumpkin."

"Let it. I have a rental right outside."

The man was far too tempting. "Look, I don't usually pick up guys in bars. I never pick up fighters named Havoc." Her laugh went flat. "Roger was right about one thing. I'm not on my best behavior tonight. The only upshot is that I'm not likely to ever see you again, so I don't have to worry about your opinion of me."

"Is that so?"

"Yes. And that being the case . . ." She crossed the two-foot space separating them and reached for him.

Shamefully practiced, he scooped her in to full body contact and without missing a single beat his mouth was on hers. This kiss had no similarity to the first. Bold, hot, devouring, he kissed the strength right out of her bones and left her pulsing pleasurably in too many places to count.

Dazed, wishing with all her heart that she had the time and the demeanor to indulge in a quick fling, Eve said, "Wow again."

His big hand cupped her face, his thumb brushed her jaw. "About not seeing me again?"

Please, please, ask for my phone number. Eve said hopefully, "Yes?"

He grinned, and that grin did indeed cause havoc. "Don't count on it."

Confused, utterly mute, Eve stood there while he walked away. And damned if he didn't look as good from the back as he had from the front.

Chapter 2

DEAN drove slowly down the street. Memories seeped in, unpleasant, stirring, bombarding him with mixed emotions. So many things looked different—and yet still the same. Twenty years should have obliterated any remembrance of his former life. But he saw the manhole cover in the street and remembered getting caught under it. He saw the tree at the corner of the block and winced, remembering a fall that had knocked the wind out of him.

And he remembered his mother, beautiful, distracted, teasing. Busy with things other than her children. She would laugh at nothing, or at least, nothing that he understood. They had a variety of babysitters-slash-housekeepers around full time, and whenever possible, his mother delegated to them.

He remembered that his father was usually gone. He worked a lot, and when he got home, he wanted to relax. That meant soaking in the pool without kids to bother him or golfing with his buddies. Whenever his mother and father were near each other, they argued.

Day in and day out, the routine hadn't varied much. Even after Camille and Jacqueline were born, his mother and father hadn't slowed down or become more domestic. They were unhappy together, but not apart.

Then they'd died in a car wreck, and Dean's routine world had shattered.

Pulling past the driveway, he parked at the curb and turned off the engine. For a few minutes, he just sat there, looking at the house he'd lived in for nine years. It looked the same. White wood siding. Green shutters. Gray roof. Red front door.

The landscaping was out of date but well kept. Some trees had matured, others were gone. Nothing much had changed.

Then he took a closer look. The shingles on the roof looked a little shabby. The painted wood siding peeled in places. Cracks marred the driveway and sidewalk. The gutters showed patches of rust. Maybe it was his expertise in home repairs, but he saw every small flaw, every indication of neglected upkeep.

Before Dean even realized it, he was outside his rented car. Arms crossed atop the roof, he soaked in the sight of the house and yard and the sensation of seeing it all as an adult.

Damn, but it felt funny to be "home."

He'd played ball in that front yard with other neighborhood kids. He'd damn near drowned in the pool out back when he'd slipped on his way in. Once he'd chased Jimmy Barker around the house, until Jimmy tripped and knocked out a front tooth. Beyond the backyard pool were woods where he'd often hung out when he wanted to be alone.

Some things hadn't changed; others had changed irrevocably.

What would his sisters look like now?

Would they appear as deteriorated and run-down as the house? Did he even care?

He pushed away from the rental, locked the doors with the remote, and pocketed the keys in his jeans. Reflective sunglasses shielded his eyes as he strode up the walkway to the front door. Lead rested in his chest and an invisible fist squeezed his throat, but he didn't hesitate. He was many things, but not a coward.

He knocked and waited.

And waited some more.

Had he come all this way only to find an empty house? Should he hang around for a while or come back later?

After a minute, Dean thought he heard a splash from the backyard. Maybe everyone was out back, enjoying the summer day by the pool. With his fingers tucked in his front pockets, he left the porch and wandered around the side of the house. There were a lot of weeds in the yard, but the mowed lawn kept them mostly hidden.

Halfway around the house, he detected feminine chitchat.

More specifically, he detected Eve's husky voice.

The lead started to burn, and the fist opened on his windpipe to allow deeper breaths.

Ripe with curiosity, he rounded the corner—and found two women lounging poolside. They were perpendicular to him, facing the sun, and very distracted.

One woman wore a big floppy hat and sunglasses, with a blue, one-piece tank-style suit. Somehow he knew it was Camille in that conservative swimsuit. He felt it like a great gnawing ache, and for a few seconds, he couldn't pull his eyes away from her.

His sister—all grown up, slim, tall, and obviously modest given her choice of swimwear.

An unfamiliar ache, similar to longing, tried to expand. Dean ruthlessly tamped it down and transferred his gaze to the other woman.

Eve.

She wore a skimpy black bikini, showing off a lot of cleavage, sun-kissed skin, and a tantalizing belly button ring that glinted in the bright summer sunshine.

"You won't believe what I did last night."

As Dean watched, she slicked back her dark hair. She

was still wet, thin water rivulets trickling along her throat, her belly, and her thighs.

Predatory instincts kicked hard, curling Dean's mouth into a smile. This feeling he understood. It was lust. The love of the chase. Carnal excitement.

Meeting his sisters alone would be awkward. Having Eve around would blunt the impact. He couldn't have planned this better.

"With you," Camille said, "I'll believe it. Now give."

"I met a man."

With her hat pulled low over her eyes, Cam laughed. "Yeah, so?" She stirred just a little, shifting one long leg. "You tend to meet men everywhere you go. Nothing new in that. You're like a magnet."

"You get your own share of looks."

"Maybe. But not the same kind of looks you get."

Dean could believe that. Eve had a sensual charisma that he hadn't encountered with too many women. Last night she'd drawn him on every level. If only that ass Roger hadn't interrupted.

Eve's toes curled. "Yeah, well, this time . . . I looked back."

"So?"

"And . . . I did more than look."

Cam became more alert. "Like?"

For one moment, Eve covered her face, then with a groan she dropped her arms wide. "I was bad."

"Um hmm. *How* bad?"

Not bad enough, Dean thought. But he stayed silent, listening. Putting off the inevitable meeting with Cam.

Grinning, Eve turned her head toward his sister. "Outright scandalous."

As Dean moseyed closer, his feet made no noise on the lush lawn and the women didn't notice him. Given he was the topic of their chatter, that suited him just fine. He parked himself against a warped railing around the back deck and settled in to listen.

Cam laughed again—not the little-girl giggle that Dean

remembered from long ago days, but a woman's laugh. "Scandalous, huh? Did you sleep with him?"

"No! Of course not. I'd just met him." Eve hesitated before admitting, "But I wanted to. If Roger hadn't butted in, I think I might have."

Dean *knew* she would have. Hell, she'd given off signals that a blind man couldn't have missed. And when he kissed her . . . He still felt scorched, remembering it. They would have ended up in bed. He knew it. She knew it. But maybe she didn't want to tell Cam that.

"Then you should be glad Roger butted in, huh?"

"Maybe." She closed her eyes again. "But Cam, he was the most gorgeous hunk of man I've ever seen. And it wasn't just his looks."

"Keep talking."

"I don't know. There was just something about him. He was so macho, without throwing it around, ya know? And ohmigod, he smelled so good."

Dean puzzled over that. He smelled good?

"I just . . . I wanted to eat him up."

Shit. Much more talk like that and he'd have a boner. Maybe now was a good time to announce himself. He started to do just that, when Cam spoke again.

"Tell me you got his number."

Eve groaned. "I was hoping he'd ask for mine, but he didn't, and even though I'm ballsy, and even though he was the hunkiest hunk I've ever seen, I'm kind of glad I won't ever run into him again."

"Why? You sound totally smitten."

"I was totally in *lust*. I flirted. I kissed him." She bit her lip. "I made it clear that I was interested. And that's just it. I behaved like a . . . a shameless hoochie." Eve covered her face again. "That's a tough act to back away from."

Seeing his intro, Dean smiled and asked, "Was it an act?"

The resulting female screeches could have peeled paint off the house. Both women scrambled fast to their feet. Cam pulled on a terry cover-up.

Eve didn't have a cover-up, thank God.

She stared at him, her eyes an even more startling blue beneath the hot afternoon sun. Her cheeks flushed; her breasts heaved.

Yeah, he could eat her up, too. Just not yet. But soon.

Dean turned to his sister. "Camille, right?"

"Who are you?"

Eve gasped. "He's the guy. . . ." She floundered, gulped, and went all breathless. "The guy from last night. The one I was just telling you about."

Immediately Cam stepped in front of her friend. "What are you doing here? You're on private property." She'd gone from sweet to Amazonian in a heartbeat. Even with the big-framed sunglasses concealing a good portion of her face, Dean could see her frown warning him away. "How did you know where to find her?"

So she felt protective of Eve? Nice, not that Eve needed her protection. But he liked it that his sister had a backbone.

"Actually I was looking for you, not her." And to Eve, Dean said, "You're just a very nice bonus."

Both women stared at him, mute.

Sighing, Dean reached into his pocket and pulled out the crumpled letter. "You wrote me. Back some months ago, I know, but I was traveling and it took a while for my mail to catch up to me."

Cam pushed her glasses to the top of her head. "I wrote you?"

Rather than try to explain, he stepped forward and extended her the letter. She stood about five-eight. Tall, like him, though he still topped her by more than half a foot.

Shaking, Cam accepted the wrinkled pieces of paper. She held them in both hands and stared at them, eyes blinking, lips caught in her teeth. When she looked up at Dean, her eyes were liquid with tears and that twice cursed hope.

Shit, shit, shit. Dean prepared himself. Or at least he thought he did. But how the hell did a man prepare for a long-lost sister?

"Dean?" Her voice went all high and silly. "It's . . . it's really you?"

He didn't get a chance to reply. The next thing he knew, she had him clutched in a ferocious, unbreakable bear hug. He couldn't remember the last time a woman had plastered herself to him in a platonic way. Even before his mother died, she hadn't been a demonstrative woman. A pat on the head, a tickle beneath his chin . . . but not this full-body contact warm with emotion.

Their housekeepers had been kind, but not forward enough to show so much affection. He'd had a few caring schoolteachers, known women while working construction, met his buddies' wives, his uncle's one-nighters. But . . . none of them had treated him like a treasure, like something more than a friend.

None of them had held him like a lifeline.

Even through his numbness, Dean made note of so many things. The chirping of birds. A gentle breeze. Eve's acute attention and Cam's softness, the pleasure of her scent. He closed his eyes and inhaled.

His emotions rioted, but in a wholly unfamiliar way. Cam wasn't a frail girl, but her strength was puny in comparison to his. Her embrace felt . . . good.

Really fucking good.

Deliberately Dean kept his arms at his sides and struggled to block the sensations of comfort. As one of the most celebrated mixed martial-arts fighters in the world, he sure as hell didn't need comfort. Not like this.

Not from her.

Looking for a quick distraction, he turned his gaze on Eve.

Mirrored sunglasses shielded his expression from her, but Eve didn't have the same advantage. He saw her shock, her embarrassment, and something more. Red faced and wide eyed, she stared at him.

Her lips parted, her breathing came fast. Taking his time, Dean looked her over. Compared to Cam, Eve was downright petite, at least in height. But she had curves galore, and in all the right places. She'd spoken as if her brazenness of the night before might have been an anomaly. She wasn't a shy woman, but she'd reacted to him differently.

He wouldn't let her forget the chemistry between them. He wouldn't let her retrench. One way or another, he'd have her—on his terms.

Finally Cam pushed back from him, but only a little, enough to look at his face and smile as if the world had just solved all its problems.

Sniffling and laughing at the same time, she attempted to apologize. "I'm so sorry, Dean. I don't mean to cry all over you." She absently smoothed her hands over his chest, sort of feeling him, absorbing him. "In my mind, I rehearsed this moment a thousand times. I prayed that my letter would find you and that you'd come home, but I just didn't . . ." Her voice broke and she had to clear her throat. Twice. "Ohmigod, *it's really you.*" And she started laughing again.

Feeling like a dope, Dean said, "Yeah," because he had no idea what else to say. He'd rather fight three undefeated maniacs, *for free*, than deal with this sentimental crap.

Cam clasped his shoulders. "Eve's right. You're so very handsome. And big. I thought Jacki was tall, but . . . look at you."

Jacki, his youngest sister. Was she taller than Cam? When would he see her?

Inside Dean's instincts rioted. Outside he felt rigid enough to break. He locked his teeth and let Cam chatter.

She went on tiptoe to run a hand through his hair. "We have the same color hair." She sounded delighted by that fact. "Eve, did you see?"

Still mute, Eve nodded.

"Oh, Dean, it is so good to have you here." And Cam squeezed him again.

Dean didn't know what to think. Cam was so damned familiar with him, touching and hugging as if she knew him or something. As if they'd actually grown up together. As if he were the typical big brother, instead of an absent stranger.

"Where are my manners?" she asked no one in particular in a voice still high and a little too excited. "Let's go inside and I'll get us something to drink. There's so much catching up to do." She hooked her arm through his and started dragging him toward the house. "Did you have to travel far to get here? Where were you when you got the letter? Where do you live?"

So many questions at once. Dean looked over his shoulder at Eve. She appeared planted to the spot, but with his attention on her, she suddenly unglued her feet and darted past them, mumbling, "I'll just go inside and dress."

As she went past in that perky little half-run, he watched with interest. He was an ass man through and through, and though Eve was slender, she had a generously rounded behind that balanced a nice C-cup up front. Before he left Harmony, he'd know that killer body intimately. That reality helped to soften the others as he faced his past.

"I'm sorry," Cam said again. "I'm attacking you with questions. You must think I'm nuts."

He didn't know her well enough to pass judgment on her mental state. "It's okay."

"One at a time, I promise. So . . . where were you before coming here?"

Dean shook off his reserve. If Cam could be so at ease, then so could he. "When I got your letter I was in Vegas. Before that, I'd been out of the country."

"Where?" she demanded playfully. "Someplace exotic?"

"Europe mostly."

She pretended a half-swoon. "*Europe.* I'm *so* jealous."

"I travel a lot. It's not a big deal."

"It is to me. I've never even been out of Kentucky."

"Never?" Eve had gone in so fast, she'd left the sliding doors open, and Cam urged him into a cool breakfast and family room combination that opened into the kitchen. He glanced around, reacquainting himself with his childhood home. "You're kidding, right?"

He'd watched morning cartoons in this room, stretched

out on the sofa in his pajamas. He'd played with two-year-old Cam on the carpeted floor. Things were different—pieces of the furniture, the window treatments, even the wall colors. But it was also the same.

"Nope. After school I attended a local college for awhile, but . . ." She rushed past that topic with nervous haste, as if embarrassed that she hadn't gotten a degree. "What would you like to drink? Soda, tea, coffee?"

Dean eyed her. "Got a beer?"

She blanched. "Sorry, no." After a quick glimpse at the clock on the wall, her fingers tangled in a fretful way.

Did she consider two in the afternoon too early to drink? "Is there a problem, Cam?"

"No, it's just . . ." Her shoulders lifted. "I'm sorry, but Aunt Lorna doesn't believe in drinking. She forbids alcohol in the house."

Grover had told him a lot about Lorna, including what a pious, judgmental bitch she could be. Because of her, he didn't know his sisters. Lorna had forbidden any contact.

Was she due home soon? Is that why Cam checked the clock?

Unwilling to make an issue of it so soon, Dean shrugged. He trailed her into the kitchen area. "Unsweetened ice tea then, if you have it."

"Of course." Cam pulled out a chair like a gallant knight. "Please, sit down. Make yourself comfortable. Are you hungry? I could make you a sandwich."

"No, thanks."

"Soup? We have some left over from yesterday. Or I could make you—"

He cut her off, saying, "I'm not hungry." Good God, Cam could talk a mile a minute. He supposed some of that was excitement.

At seeing him.

Fuck.

"Then how about a cookie? Homemade. I baked some fresh this morning. Oatmeal and raisin."

Protective, with a Martha Stewart inclination? His sister was an interesting paradox. "I don't eat sweets very often."

He might have said he had two heads, with the way she reacted to that. "You don't? Why ever not?"

"I have to stay in shape."

With a half laugh, she scoffed at him. "You're in shape, all right." Plopping her hat and sunglasses on the counter, she strode to the refrigerator to get his drink. "Just look at you. You're all bulging muscle."

Dean didn't want her thinking him a fanatic, so he explained. "I'm a fighter, Cam. My diet is an important part of my lifestyle."

Drawing to a halt, she turned to gape at him. "A *fighter*?"

Unsure if her look meant revulsion or intrigue, he said nothing.

"No cookies, but beer is okay?" Suspicion brought her brows down and she propped her hands on her hips. "How's that work?"

He realized she was teasing, and he smiled with her. "Hey, I have to draw the line somewhere. No way am I going to give up *everything*, and I'd rather watch the sweets. But I limit my drinking to the times in between fights. When I'm training, I cut out the alcohol, too."

"You must have amazing willpower. I try, but I'm a sugar junkie."

It didn't show. Cam had a trim, athletic figure. He supposed that was part of their gene pool. He remembered his mother as a slender woman and his father as leanly muscular.

As Cam filled the glass with ice and tea, she kept glancing at him. "You're a professional fighter? Like a boxer, you mean?"

"Not exactly a boxer." Rather than continue to hide, Dean removed the mirrored sunglasses and laid them on the table. When he looked at Cam this time, she saw his eyes—and immediately jumped subjects. Again.

"Dean! We have the same eyes, too. Isn't that amazing?"

He couldn't help but grin. Cam amused him with her overload of enthusiasm. "Are you always this upbeat?"

Eve strolled back in. "Yeah, she is. Sickening, isn't it?"

Swiveling in his seat, Dean looked at her. She avoided meeting his gaze, but he didn't mind. They both knew how she felt, just as they both knew what would come of it.

She'd pulled her wet hair into a ponytail, emphasizing high cheekbones and a stubborn chin. Short jean shorts showed off her ass almost as good as the bikini bottoms had. A thin tank top advertised her lack of a bra. Her bare legs were beautiful.

While checking out every inch of Eve, Dean said, "Cam and I might share coloring, but our dispositions are polar opposites."

Cam laughed. "Meaning you're a bear? I don't believe it. Look at how you've put up with me already."

"I believe it." Eve went on tiptoe to reach a glass, then helped herself to the tea. "His fighting name is Havoc." She tipped the glass at him in a salute. "That oughta tell ya something, right?"

Now this was familiar. Sparring with an attractive lady, cultivating the sexual tension. Much, much easier than that . . . that sentimental mishmash Cam kept slinging his way.

Relishing the new game, Dean made sure Eve saw him eyeing her breasts before saying, "They call me Havoc because, to some, I appear a disorderly fighter." His gaze came up to meet hers, and he caught her arrested, flustered expression. He smiled, just to let her know he knew what she felt and what she thought. "Most guys have a technique that can be pegged. It gives other fighters something to study, to prepare for. But I'm unpredictable. I change from one fight to the next." Boldly staring, he explained, "I do whatever I have to do to win."

Eve's eyes narrowed. "Is that a warning?"

"Absolutely."

Oblivious to their sexual banter, or willing to overlook it, Cam pulled out a chair and sat opposite him. "Do you win a lot?"

"Yeah. I do." Damn it, he had no reason to feel so proud when telling her that. What Cam thought of him shouldn't matter one iota. But still he said, "Often enough to be the main event on the SBC card the last four fights."

"What does SBC stand for?"

"Supreme Battle Challenge. It's a combat sport with a variety of disciplines like jiu-jitsu, judo, karate, boxing, kickboxing, or wrestling—usually a combination of all of those."

"It sounds confusing."

"It's not. Competitors strike using hands, feet, knees, or elbows. You grapple for submissions, chokeholds, throws, or takedowns. There's no one single discipline that does better than another."

Eve joined them at the table, sitting at Dean's right. "Huh. So if you're that good," she taunted, "how come you're so beat up?"

Cam looked put out by Eve's question, but Dean didn't mind explaining. "I don't fight pansies, that's why. Only the best contenders earn the right to challenge me. Besides, a few bruises don't count as beat up. Not when the other guy got the worst of it."

Cam winced. "What could be worse?" Then she rushed to add, "Not that I doubt you. But you do look like something ran over you. I hadn't planned to say anything. I didn't want to be rude. But since you brought it up . . ."

The thought of Cam trying to ignore his stitches, cuts, and bruises almost brought Dean to laughter—and he hadn't expected that. "Most of what I have is superficial. But cuts that bleed enough to impair vision or pose a threat to the fighter's health can cost him a win. Broken bones, dislocations, and torn muscles can keep him from competing for months."

"*Broken bones?*"

Dean rolled a shoulder. "Serious injuries are rare, but

I've seen them all." And had most of them himself—not that he'd share that little tidbit with his sister. "I won that last fight with a knee bar."

"What's a knee bar?"

"A Brazilian jiu-jitsu submission technique. It's one submission used to win, though most SBC fighters know a dozen or more."

"So what does a knee bar do?"

When he'd imagined their meeting, he hadn't even considered talking about the SBC. Cam's interest surprised him, and though he'd like to deny it, he admitted to himself that it pleased him. "The basic concept of all leg-lock submissions is using leverage and control of joints." Stretching out his own leg, Dean gave a basic idea of how the move would work. "You lock the joint out, and with the right amount of pressure, you can submit anyone."

Cam's eyes rounded. "Because if he doesn't submit, something would dislocate or break."

"That's about it."

"Fascinating." Eve ran a finger through the sweat on her glass. "Sounds a lot like barroom brawling to me. Do men actually pay to see that now?"

Dean leveled a look on her. So she felt snippy, did she? And just because he'd overheard her mooning on him. Good. He liked a woman with a little fire.

Settling back in his chair, Dean folded his hands over his abdomen. Eve's gaze followed the movement, then flitted away.

"Unlike barroom brawls, this is one man against one man. No weapons. And the matches are supervised. Scoring is based on athletic-commission approved definitions and rules. They take place before live crowds in Nevada, California, New Jersey, Massachusetts, and Florida. The SBC features experienced fighters, many of them Olympic champions. Competitors come from Brazil, Russia, Japan, Holland, England—pretty much everywhere. More often than not, the tickets are sold out, with prime seats going as high as a grand a piece. The basic concept is that two men go into a fenced-off area and fight until one of them gets knocked out or taps out."

Cam grew more interested by the second. "What does that mean, to tap out?"

"Like crying uncle, sort of. If you know your arm, leg, knee, or ankle is about to shatter, you can give up. Some guys get choked out—meaning they black out from lack of oxygen—or they tap out because they know they're about to black out. Occasionally the decision goes to judges, but no one wants that."

"Yeah," Eve said, "God forbid the fight end without a broken leg."

This time Dean couldn't hold back the laughter. "The fighters are well trained and intelligent, and doctors are on hand."

"Intelligent?" She nodded in facetious agreement. "Yeah, they sound really bright."

"Eve."

So now Cam had switched alliances? She wanted to defend him against Eve. He shook his head. "It's okay, Cam. Where the SBC is concerned, women come in different sets. You have your groupies who are turned on by the celebrity of it. Women who turn their noses up at it before understanding it. And those who are genuinely interested in it as a sport." He tipped his head. "Which are you, Eve?"

But she was frowning at him now, hoping to turn the tables on him. "When you say groupies, you mean women who throw themselves at you, right?"

"That's right." He stared into her eyes. "At the last fight I signed a pair of breasts, and she ended up following me home."

Cam choked on a laugh, but Eve went stiff as a broomstick. "Just like a puppy." Her voice emerged as a near growl. "Imagine that."

"She was young," Dean conceded, with more good humor, and then with a knowing smile, added, "But old enough."

Cam leaped into the sudden tension. "If all the fights are in the States, why do you travel so much?"

He let Eve off the hook—for now. "Different reasons. It helps to get experience with the best, and that means traveling to different camps to train. And I have sponsors everywhere, some promotional tours, stuff like that."

Cam looked suitably impressed. Eve kept her attention fixed on her glass of tea so he couldn't measure her reaction.

"I do most of that in my off time. When I'm preparing for an event, there's no extra time. I train up to six hours a day or more. You can never learn too much. Nearly every fighter I know has studied martial arts as a lifelong vocation."

"You included?"

In younger days, he'd trained as a way to rid himself of anger. Grover had encouraged it, but Dean paid for it himself, and made sure it didn't interfere with the work schedule. The same applied to his extended education. "I've always enjoyed competing. I got into it more in college, after Grover died. That's when I found out about the SBC. One of the SBC sponsors saw me fight, and he offered to back me if I'd compete. Those first few wins helped pay for school."

"You juggled school and fighting?"

Cam made it sound like a big deal. "Most of the competitors are college educated. Some of the younger guys are still in college. Others are businessmen or professionals of some sort."

"The two don't really seem to go together."

"A dummy wouldn't get far in the SBC. It's as much a cerebral competition as it is physical. You have to be able to think fast under pressure and to outwit your opponent."

Cam accepted that as truth. "It makes sense. But I still think I'm going to worry about it."

Why the hell would she worry? Certainly she had no reason to worry for him. She barely knew him. "It's an intense sport, but doctors are at every bout to ensure fighter safety."

Eve wrinkled her nose. "It still sounds gruesome."

"I think it sounds fascinating." Cam reached across the table and touched Dean's bruised cheekbone. "This is from your last fight?"

"Yeah." Luckily his hair hid the worst of the stitches high on his forehead, near his temple. "I got your letter the morning after I'd competed." His gaze shifted to Eve. "And won."

"I wish I'd known. I could have watched." Cam beamed at him with pride. "When do you fight again?"

"Not for awhile. I'm taking some time off." To visit her, but Dean didn't say so. "The next fight for me won't be for months."

"You make your living at fighting?"

"Yeah. But I also flip houses in my spare time, and that's pretty lucrative, too."

The women looked at him in blank confusion.

"I buy run-down houses cheap, fix them up, and sell them for a profit."

Eve brightened. She sat forward, ready to say something, but Cam quickly hushed her.

"Do you enjoy traveling?"

They'd just covered up something, but Dean had no idea what. "I always have. Grover did construction all over the world. Now I'm on the go for competitions and promotional purposes." What had Eve wanted to say? And why did Cam not want her to? "That's enough about me. What is it you do?"

For whatever reason, it embarrassed Cam to have the focus on her. "Nothing as exciting as being a professional fighter who travels the world." She laughed a little self-consciously. "I'm a manager at Roger's motel."

At the mention of Roger, Eve closed down again.

"The same Roger you might marry?"

Cam turned to Eve. "You told him about Roger proposing?"

Eve shrugged. "After good old Rog tried to pick a fight with him, we did discuss him a little."

"Oh, Dean, I'm so sorry." Cam let out a long sigh. "Roger struggles with some issues of insecurity."

Dry as dust, Dean said, "Really?"

Hoping to convince him, Cam nodded. "It's so ridiculous, given all that he's accomplished. But he forever feels like he needs to prove himself. I hope it wasn't too much of a problem."

"No problem at all."

"Luckily," Eve said, "Dean turned him down on the offer." She propped an elbow on the table and studied Dean. "And now that I know more about you, I have to wonder why you did that."

"Idiots challenge me all the time. It's nothing new." He finished off his tea in one long guzzle. Just the thought of Roger left a bad taste in his mouth. But it wasn't his business. If Cam decided to marry him, what did he care?

Eve didn't let it go. "Most guys would feel pressured to accept, to prove their capability or whatever. Macho pride and all that nonsense."

"I'd have killed him," Dean said. "I don't need that on my conscience."

Cam stayed silent, but Eve looked provoked. She put both elbows onto the table and leaned in close. "You never know. You're big, but then Roger's not a small man, either. Did you know he played college football?"

Dean shrugged. He didn't give a shit what the idiot did.

"He was a star running back. Probably would have gone pro if a knock on the head hadn't caused him long-term impaired vision."

"Good for him." Dean mimicked her posture, closing the space between them until their breath touched and he could see the thickness of her lashes. "He still wouldn't have stood a chance against me. He doesn't have the bearing of a fighter, the reflexes of a fighter, or the brains of a fighter."

"Sounds like he's lacking quite a bit, doesn't it?" Cam teased. "Should I be insulted on Roger's behalf?"

Damn. Recalling himself, Dean retreated. "No insult

intended, just stating facts. But you should tell Roger to keep his hands off other women."

Eve's eyes sank shut in dread.

Cam's eyebrows shot up in question.

And into the silence, another female voice said, "Someone could have warned me that we had company."

Dean turned, and there stood a tall girl with ratty, bleached-blond hair sticking out at odd angles, likely due to an overload of gel followed by a rough night of tossing and turning. He guessed her to be five-ten, at least, lanky, long limbed, and . . . his baby sister.

As Dean surveyed her, his heart gave an odd, erratic thumping. By look, stance, and overall attitude, she screamed *trouble*.

For some insane reason, that delighted Dean.

So his youngest sister had grown up to be a hell-raiser. If he didn't miss his guess, that'd make her dead opposite of Cam. And although Cam would only be two years older, she seemed far more mature than Jacki.

An earful of silver hoops in varying sizes glinted from the sunshine pouring in through the kitchen window. Jacki turned toward him, and he saw a wicked tattoo on her hipbone, displayed by a cropped shirt and super-low-slung cotton pants that, despite her long legs, managed to drag the floor.

Cam blurted, "Jacki, you're up early." She jumped to her feet and went to the younger woman. With an enormous smile, she said, "Hon, this is our brother, Dean."

CHAPTER 3

WELL, Eve thought, this ought to be interesting. Dean scrutinized Jacki as if well acquainted with rebellious twenty-one-year-olds. And Cam, poor thing, looked caught between pleasure at announcing Dean and dread at what Jacki might say or do.

Typical of Jacki, she blinked eyes smudged with black mascara and said, "You're shittin' me."

Cam scowled. "Watch your language."

"What did I say?"

Dean laughed. "It's nothing I haven't heard before."

"Amen," said Eve. Personally she understood Jacki's attitude a lot better than she did Cam's. The sisters hadn't had an easy time of it lately.

Because it was obvious Jacki had just gotten up, Dean glanced at his watch. "Have a late night?"

Jacki pursed her mouth, looked Dean over from head to toe, and then turned to the coffeepot as if long-lost brothers were nothing out of the ordinary. "Killer party. My head's splitting. Cam, you don't have coffee made?"

"Take a seat before you fall down and I'll make some."

Eve watched Dean as he encountered the dynamics of his family. It didn't take a genius to figure out that Cam mothered Jacki, and Jacki soaked it up.

"So." Dragging herself over to the table, Jacki dropped into a chair, and after an inelegant yawn that showed her tonsils, smiled at Dean. "Aunt Lorna is going to have a cow."

"Jacki," Cam warned, without interrupting her coffee preparations. "I'll tell Aunt Lorna. Don't worry about that now."

"Sure, but *what* will you tell her?" Jacki slouched lower in her seat. "She's going to wonder why the prodigal son has returned." She turned to look at Cam. "I take it you invited him?"

"Yes."

"Of course you did." She turned back to Dean. "And you accepted the invitation, obviously. But why? Did we find out we have money after all and no one told me?"

Cam froze.

Even Eve felt shock at such a blatant dig. Jacki was always outrageous, deliberately so, but that was over-the-top sarcastic, even for her.

Dean didn't even flinch. "Prodigal? Not quite."

"Huh." She raised her eyebrows. "And the money?"

"You wanna compare bank accounts?" He did a quick once-over of the old appliances in the kitchen, the faded wallpaper, and the marred countertops. "I'm pretty sure I'd come out ahead."

"Really? So I've got a well-to-do brother. Better and better. But that doesn't explain why you're here. Aunt Lorna always said we'd never see you."

Something snagged around his heart. "Did she ever tell you why?"

"Yeah." In a high-pitched, phony voice, Jacki said, "Men are all no-account bastards who only care about themselves."

"That's enough, Jacki." Cam finished the coffee preparations with haste. "Put the claws away right now."

Jacki grinned. "I sounded just like her, didn't I?"

Eve started to say yes, but Cam said, "No, you did not. You sound like an ill-behaved child. Now knock it off."

"Yes, Mama."

Dean laughed.

It relieved Eve that he hadn't taken offense, but Jacki appeared more confused than ever at his sign of humor.

"What's funny?" She propped both elbows on the table-top. "Or do I even want to know?"

"You're trying a little too hard, that's all."

Eve noticed Dean's relaxed smile and the gentleness of his eyes. He really was a devastating man in many ways.

"And if you're not careful," he unwisely continued, "those skinny shoulders are going to break under the weight of that gigantic chip you're carrying."

Uh-oh. Of all the insults Dean could have dished, call-ing any part of Jacki skinny probably hurt her the most. Eve waited for the fireworks. They weren't long in coming.

Jacki shoved out of her chair. "Hey, I changed my mind about the coffee." She saluted Dean, bowed at Cam. "I'm going to go shower and dress."

Cam took a rigid stance. "I wanted us all to get ac-quainted."

"I already have plans with friends." And with that, Jacki stalked out.

Cam offered a hasty apology. "I'm so sorry, Dean. She's not at her best in the morning."

"She's hungover. That can make anyone grumpy."

"Jacki doesn't drink."

It was beyond obvious that she'd tied one on the night before, but Dean didn't debate the point with her.

Eve appreciated his restraint.

"If you'll just excuse me, I'll . . ." Cam's voice trailed off, and she dashed after her sister.

"Way to go," Eve told him, as she watched Cam's exit. "You managed to trip right into the thick of things. Real es-tate, drinking, and female figures—you touched on all the hottest Conor family topics."

She could almost feel sorry for Dean, being this had to be awkward for him. But as she brought her gaze to his, she didn't see discomfort at the turn of events.

No, she saw a sudden inferno of heat. And intention. "Uh . . ."

He pushed out of his chair and stepped around the table toward her.

Eve's heart shot into her throat. "What are you doing?"

With one hand braced flat on the table and the other on the back of her chair, he closed her in. "I'm going to kiss you."

The way he said that, with his voice so rich and deep, made her shiver. "Not a good idea."

He stared at her mouth. "It's a great idea, and you know it." As he leaned down more, he murmured, "You said it yourself. Things clicked last night."

"Last night I didn't know you were Cam's—"

His mouth settled over hers, warm and firm, and oh-so-delicious. She sank like a dead weight.

When his tongue licked into her mouth, she welcomed it with her own. A rumbling groan vibrated up from deep inside her, and he moved away a scant inch to look at her with those golden brown eyes.

Oh boy. If only he'd left the reflective sunglasses on, this would be easier. Eve sighed and, sounding breathless, whispered, "Don't you dare start something you can't finish."

Awareness flared in his eyes. "Trust me, honey, I can finish it."

Lord help her. "Right." Eve cleared her throat—and held him back when he would have kissed her again. "I'm pretty sure you can. But you see . . . I have to leave in twenty minutes. I'm meeting a prospective client."

"Have dinner with me tonight."

She shook her head. "That's impossible. You just met your sisters. Surely they want—"

"I want *you*. The sooner the better."

He certainly knew how to make a point. "Be fair, Dean.

What if Cam is already making plans? I'm her best friend. I can't infringe on that."

"I'll spend the day with her until dinner."

"She has to work, too." Seeing that he wasn't about to give up, and knowing she didn't even really want him to, Eve thought fast. "I'm having dinner with my folks. But afterward . . ." Her voiced dropped off as his hand curved around her neck. His fingertips teased along her sensitive nape.

"Give me an address and a time." His voice went low and gruff and his lips lightly touched hers. "I'll be there."

Given how she felt now, all hot and trembling, she'd never survive until then. If she didn't love her parents so much, she'd cancel on them. "Eight o'clock?"

After one small nod, he took her mouth again, and somehow, in the next few seconds, she ended up standing and pressed against his hard body. One hand still clasped her neck, keeping her in close, and the other coasted down her back to cup around her behind. He stroked, squeezed, then groaned softly.

"God, you have a great ass."

Using his hold on her there, he snuggled her up close against his lower body. Eve caught her breath. The man was solid muscle, sizzling heat, and restrained power. Pressed against him so tightly, she felt every inch of him, and got a tantalizing glimpse of how it'd be.

She would have groaned, too, but he didn't give her a chance. Suddenly, through no effort of her own, she was back in her seat, confused and cold, and he was in his, looking bored.

What in the world . . .

Cam strode back in. She had her mouth open to say something, but she looked at Eve and snapped her teeth together. Drawing to a halt in the middle of the kitchen floor, she looked at them both suspiciously.

Eve knew she should say something, but all she managed was a smile that she knew came off rather guilty and insincere. How had Dean heard Cam's approach? She'd been only aware of him, of his taste and muscular frame and hot, stirring scent.

"Everything okay?" Cam asked.

Dean answered for her, saving her from trying to find her voice. "I take it Jacki was unaware of the letter you sent me?"

Now Cam flushed. "Yes. I'm sorry. The only one who knew was Eve."

Grateful for a neutral topic, Eve jumped in. "But I didn't put it together when you showed up at the bar last night. Cam wrote that letter a while ago."

"And you didn't tell Lorna about it?"

Cam shook her head.

"Because she never wanted you to contact me."

Cam shared a look with Eve. Wishing she could reassure her friend, Eve smiled. "Lorna never talked about you, Dean. Cam was so young when you left—"

"When I was taken away."

Cam seemed frozen, unable to respond.

Eve, however, had no such problems. "What do you mean?"

"I didn't leave on my own. Hell, I was only a kid. I had no choice in the matter. Grover took me because Lorna refused to have all three of us."

Cam shook her head. "No, that can't be right."

"How do you know, if Lorna never spoke of me?"

Blindly Cam groped for a chair. "But . . . you see, I barely remembered you."

"You mean you quickly forgot about me."

Dean said that without any emotion at all, but still Eve winced. What awful misconceptions did he have? Probably none worse than Cam's.

Shaking her head, Cam reached for his hands and squeezed tight. "I'm sorry, Dean, but I was only two. Still a baby. So much happened, our parents dying, the funeral, friends and neighbors coming and going. Everything was strange and different. You were just . . . gone, like Mom and Dad, and Lorna made a point of not talking about you."

Watching Dean, Eve saw the tightening of his jaw and the telling way he eased his hands from Cam's grip, as if he couldn't quite bear to be touched while discussing this particular topic.

They were both hurting so much, Eve wished for a way to help them.

Cam drew a calming breath. "When I was sixteen I found some old albums in the attic." Her smile flickered and was gone. "There were photos of you holding Jacki and me, playing with us, spraying me with a garden hose, and kissing Jacki's head. . . ."

"We were siblings. Things like that happened." Dean looked more remote than ever. "What's your point?"

"I was curious about you, so I asked Lorna. It upset her that I found the album, and I realized then that I never saw photos of us before our parents died. There were pictures taken after that, mostly by friends or neighbors, but there weren't any of me as a baby and none of Jacki as a newborn. And . . . none of you at all."

"I guess when she got rid of me, she got rid of every trace of me, too." He narrowed his eyes. "What about our parents? Have you seen photos of them?"

Cam shook her head. "Not many. At least, not before I found that album."

Dean smirked. "If Lorna had known that album existed, she'd have thrown it out, too."

Cam stared at nothing in particular, lost in her confusion. When she looked at Dean, her need to understand was plain. "You're saying she never intended for Jacki or me to know about you. We'd have grown up as sisters, unaware that we had a big brother, too."

"That's obvious, isn't it?"

"But . . ." Cam frowned hard. "I don't understand why she'd do that."

"She didn't want any reminders, I guess."

And, Eve thought, Cam would have grown up sensing that something was missing from her life, without knowing what. For a certainty, Lorna never would have told her.

Seeing the stark pain on Cam's face, Eve knew her friend had already realized it, too.

As if trying to soften the blow, Dean told her, "I have pictures if you're curious about our parents."

Cam stared at him. "I'm curious about *you*. I want to understand all this. I want to know you."

Dean's jaw tightened. "If you want," he continued, ignoring Cam's plea, "I can get them sent here. Or I can make you copies."

Confusion shone in Cam's expression. "How is it that you have photos when I don't have any?"

"When Grover took me, he also took two albums and some of the framed pictures that were sitting around." Dean tugged at his ear. "He didn't steal them or anything. Lorna didn't want them."

"She told him that?"

He shrugged. "Grover said because it'd be a painful reminder to you and Jacki of what you'd lost."

With an absent nod, Cam accepted that explanation. "I suppose that could have been her motivation."

"Maybe."

Straightening with new resolve, Cam again took his hands. "She didn't lie to me, Dean. When I asked her about you, she told me you were my brother. But she said you wanted to go with Grover. She said you wanted the adventure. . . ."

"Then she did lie, didn't she?"

At Dean's statement, Cam looked so lost, so wounded, that Eve put her arm around her. Dean made note of the gesture and looked away from them both.

"Do you really think," he said, "that at eight years old, after just losing both my parents, I wanted to leave everything that was familiar to me? My friends, my belongings? You really think I wanted to leave my life?" He turned back to Cam. "Lorna lied to you."

Dean's voice never wavered; it didn't go higher or deeper.

He'd carefully, and skillfully, masked his expression—
except that Eve read the truth and hurt in his eyes, even if
Cam didn't.

"Why would Lorna do that?" Eve asked. It didn't make
any sense.

"Like I said, I was just a kid." Dean nodded at Cam.
"But Grover talked about you and Jacki all the time, almost
as much as he talked about Lorna. So I have my theories."

Eve decided it was a good time to get on her way. After
giving Cam's shoulders another squeeze, she rose from the
table. "You two need to talk, and I need to go home and get
ready for a meeting. I'm running late as it is."

Dean stood when she did. "I'll walk you out."

With Cam sitting there looking wounded and unsure
of herself and her life? Eve shook her head. "No. That's
okay."

"I still need your address."

Well. That certainly distracted Cam. She watched them
with keen interest, and Eve almost blushed. "Right." As familiar in Cam's home as she was her own, Eve went to a
drawer and pulled out a pen and paper to scrawl down her
information. "Here you go. I put my cell number down,
too, in case you need it." Maybe to cancel on her, if things
smoothed out with his sisters.

Cam looked from one of them to the other. "You two
are going out?"

"Yes," Dean said.

"No," Eve corrected. She walked over to the door and
slipped her feet into a pair of thongs. "I mean, *maybe,* but
not until later and not if it interferes with your plans. I
know you and Dean have a lot of catching up to do." She
gave Dean a meaningful look. "I don't want to get in the
way of that."

Dean stared right back at her. "I'm seeing her tonight.
Isn't that right, Eve?"

"Not," she said, making her tone firm, "if Cam has other
plans."

"Umm . . ." Cam bit her lip. "I was hoping you'd have

dinner with us, Dean. And Eve, of course you're invited if you want to—"

Eve shook her head. "I've already got dinner plans."

Finally Dean turned to Cam. "I need to get going, too. There are some things I have to take care of today. But I'd like to see a little more of the town, so why don't I take you out to dinner tonight? Jacki, too, of course. Can you suggest some place nice?"

Relief loosened Cam's shoulders. "That'd be great, if you don't mind eating early. I have to be at work at seven."

He glanced at his watch. "I could pick you up at four-thirty."

"Perfect."

"Will Jacki make it?"

Cam's eyes narrowed. "She'll be there."

"Well." Eve opened the patio doors. "I guess I'll be on my way."

Dean reached for her elbow. Eve noticed that, unlike Roger, his hold wasn't tight. But somehow she was far more aware of Dean's touch than she'd ever been of Roger's.

"I'm walking you out," he said.

"No." She nodded toward Cam, hoping he'd get the message. "That's not necessary."

"Yeah, it is."

Eve tugged experimentally, but while Dean's hold wasn't abusive, it was unbreakable.

"I was ready to go anyway." He picked up his sunglasses and nodded at Cam. "Thanks for the drink. I'll see you in a few hours."

Cam hesitated, uncertain, then she launched herself at Dean. He released Eve while being choked with Cam's warm affections.

"I'm so glad you're here," she told him. "Somehow we'll work all this out."

Eve noted Dean's lack of participation; he didn't hug Cam back. No, he just suffered the embrace, cold and distant. Not that Cam seemed to notice. She stepped back, smiling, happy, and hopeful. "See you tonight."

Dean nodded, and as if grateful for a reason to escape, he said, "I don't want to make Eve late. See you later."

DEAN got Eve all the way to her car before she began protesting.

Sounding very disgruntled, she said, "I can't believe you're just walking out on her like this."

"Who?"

She pulled up short, rounded on him, and scowled with incredulous disbelief. "Your sister!"

Dean still felt unsettled from Cam's warm welcome, not to mention her mind-blowing disclosures.

She hadn't known about him.

Before actually seeing her and talking to her, he'd had some lame plan to rebuff her every gesture, to let her know that he hadn't needed her then, and he sure as hell didn't need her now.

But everything was different: the situation, his sisters, and his own feelings toward them both.

"I'm coming back to see her tonight." And because he wasn't ready to think about that too much yet, he dismissed Eve's attempt to chastise him. "Don't worry about it."

Eve jerked free of his hold. "Don't worry? She's my best friend, as close as a sister. You could tell that she didn't want you to go. She invited you here for a reason. You two could have talked. You could have explained these theories of yours instead of leaving her to—"

Dean bent and kissed her. Even when bitching at him, Eve had the softest, sexiest mouth he'd ever encountered.

She tilted out of reach, looked at him through heavy eyes, and without much conviction, whispered, "Stop."

"No."

She didn't argue. Instead her eyes sank shut again in blatant invitation, and Dean settled his mouth over hers.

Despite her earlier antagonistic attitude, her lips parted under his. He'd had easy women. He'd had women with ulterior motives. He'd had interested women.

But he'd never had a woman melt for him like this.

While backing her up against her car door, Dean turned his head to find a better fit and sank his tongue past her teeth.

Damn, she tasted good. She felt good, too, like the perfect counterbalance to the emotional upheaval Cam's attention had caused him. When he touched Eve, he could almost obliterate awareness of his sisters and everything that came with reacquainting himself with their lives.

Anticipating the evening—along with Eve—Dean opened his hands on her narrow back. He thought about getting her alone, naked, under him. . . .

Gasping for breath, Eve turned her head away.

Dean took advantage of the moment to softly warn her away from overstepping herself. "Keep your nose out of my business with my sisters, okay?"

Eve's mouth fell open. Stunned at his admonishment, her brows snapped down, she gathered herself to give him hell—and Dean kissed her again before she could say a single word. Groaning, she leaned into him. . . .

For about two seconds.

Then she exploded. Or tried to explode, but he had her snuggled in close and other than freeing her mouth, she really didn't accomplish much with her huffing attitude.

"Now, Eve," he whispered. "Don't get mad."

Straight-arming him, she said, "Back it up right now, mister."

Another unique trait. Far as he could recall, no other woman had ever given him hell.

Enjoying her, Dean held up his hands in surrender.

Once freed, Eve took a moment to draw in several calming breaths before meeting his gaze. Her expression bordered on hostile. He kept his merely curious.

She drew one more needed breath. "Did you seriously just tell me to butt out?"

"Yeah." Damn, she was cute. "Is that going to be a problem?"

"A problem?" she sputtered. "Yes, it's a problem. You

can't come into my best friend's life, only to walk right back out again."

"I said I was going back."

"And you used *me* as an excuse to walk out. How do you think that made Cam feel?"

Dean shrugged. "I wouldn't have hung around there all day anyway."

As if he hadn't spoken, she continued on her tirade. "And then you seriously expect me to keep quiet and not have an opinion about it?" She ended all that on a high, shrill note. "What is *wrong* with you?"

"I hope that's a rhetorical question, that you don't really expect me to bare my soul."

Her eyes nearly crossed in confusion. *"What?"*

Dean laughed. "I'm a flawed man, Eve. Accept it. I have. I'm here with a lot of doubts and misgivings. I have no idea how much I want to know about my sisters or how much I want them to know about me. Getting involved would be a mistake on your part. So I'm telling you nicely: Stay out of it."

"Good God." She dropped back against the car in flagrant shock. "I can't believe you said all that with a straight face."

"It's the truth."

She folded her arms under her breasts. "Oh, I believe you're flawed."

Unsure if he liked her agreement, Dean lifted a brow. "Is that so?"

"But I also saw you with your sisters."

He did *not* want her to go there. "Well hell. You're not going to psychoanalyze me are you?"

His sarcasm didn't put a dent in her resolve. "You want to be a part of them, Dean. You *are* a part of them— whether you want to admit it or not. I saw it in your eyes."

What he admitted to himself and what he'd admit to her were two different things. "I barely spoke to Jacki before she hightailed it out of there, so whatever you thought you saw—"

"You hid it better than Cam," she told him, still undaunted, "but then, Cam doesn't try to hide it. She wears her heart on her sleeve, always has. From the moment she found out about you, she's cared. You could have shown up as an ogre, and Cam would still love you."

"Oh, for God's sake," he complained. But he was half-afraid Eve was right.

"She might not like you, but you're her brother, and that means a lot to her." Eve touched his arm. "Luckily you're a nice guy, not an ogre. And I think being her brother means something to you, too."

Knowing he couldn't stop her, not yet anyway, Dean stared up at the sky.

"So I know you don't mean to hurt her feelings. I know you'll do what you can to make it up to her." Eve moved closer. "Right?"

Dean wasn't about to let Eve manipulate him, even if what she said made sense. Propping one forearm on the roof behind her head, he diverted her off that particular topic and onto another. "Why did you blanch when I mentioned Roger groping you?"

Her gaze scuttled away. "He didn't *grope* me."

"He damn near squeezed bruises into your arm."

"It wasn't personal on his part."

"It was damn personal, and you know it."

Given the way she huffed, Eve didn't like being corrected. "Roger manhandles everyone. It's just his way. Something about being a football player." She gave him a calculated look. "Most of the athletes I've met are a little dense that way."

Dean didn't take the bait. "There's dense, and then there's abusive, and neither has anything to do with sports. The guys I know in the SBC are family men. They care for women, they treat them carefully, and with respect."

"Even the groupies?"

He grinned at the snide way she said that. "It doesn't matter who the woman is. Only an insecure jerk uses his size and strength against someone smaller or weaker." He propped his other arm on the roof of her car so that he caged her in. "And for the record, the groupie who followed me home didn't get what she came for."

Eve's mock surprise looked adorable. "Don't tell me your scruples got in the way?"

Her time under the warm summer sun had amplified her scent. A breeze teased it past his nostrils and stirred his insides. "I'm not sure I have scruples where sex is concerned."

"At least you're honest."

"I'll always be honest with you." Her dark blue eyes really were beautiful. But then so was her mouth. And her body. "The truth is, I was too beat up to accommodate her. Then the next morning I got Cam's note and . . ." He shrugged. "I sent her home with the promise of free tickets to the next event."

Dean waited to see what she'd think of his sacrifice, but her reaction almost laid him low.

Shaking her head, Eve placed her fingertips on his chest and smiled with derisive pity. "And she accepted that? What a fool. If you ask me, she got the short end of the stick."

Dean drew in a necessary breath. "You are such a tease."

"Not usually." She slipped her hand up to his neck. "Now I really do have to go. I think you've made me late."

"We're still on for tonight?"

Her attention went to his mouth, and she nodded. "Yes. But you better be worth all this bother."

"Damn woman." He put his forehead to hers and laughed. "I do love a challenge."

And with one last searing kiss, he let her go.

CHAPTER 4

❧

WHEN Cam opened the door to his knock, Dean knew right away that something was wrong. Her apologetic smile told him so. The nervous twisting of her hands told him so. The negative energy in the air had him looking past her—and he saw not only Jacki, but also a prickly, rigid woman nearing sixty.

Tight faced with disapproval and, if he didn't miss his guess, barely disguised apprehension, the older woman stared at him.

Bringing his gaze back to Cam, Dean asked, "Lorna?"

Cam's taut expression said better than words that she expected a scene. "Yes."

Regardless of all the lectures Dean had just given himself about keeping his emotional distance, he didn't want to cause her worry. "She's going with us?"

"When she found out you were here, that is, when I told her Jacki and I were going to dinner with you—"

Dean cupped her shoulder and moved her out of the

doorway. "No worries. It's fine." He stepped into the house past Cam, and she rushed into introductions.

"Aunt Lorna, this is Dean. Dean, our Aunt Lorna."

No one would miss the way Cam stressed *our* aunt. While Dean hoped to ensure a peaceful evening, he did not intend to claim Lorna as a relative. Cam could forget any thoughts along those lines.

Dean couldn't even bear to touch Lorna, not after what Cam had told him about her wiping him from her memory. To keep her from offering her hand—if she'd intended to—Dean kept his distance and nodded. "Lorna." He didn't bother with a smile. "So you're joining us for dinner."

A surprisingly firm chin elevated. "I feel very responsible for the girls, and we don't know anything about you. Of course I'm coming along."

"I already know quite a bit about him," Cam corrected. "After Dean and I talked, I looked him up on the Internet. He's famous."

Dean swallowed back his groan. "I'm known within a niche audience, but I'm hardly famous."

"Don't be modest, Dean. You're paid to endorse dozens of products. You have a big fan club. The SBC has created T-shirts with you on them."

She had him there. The SBC actually had a whole line of apparel with his face or name on them. "Okay, true enough."

Cam smiled at his reluctant agreement. "There, you see, Aunt Lorna. We're probably safer with Dean than without him. He's well known *and* very capable." Good manners had her adding, "But, of course, we're thrilled that you're coming along. I'm sure you'll want to get to know Dean, too."

Rather than listen to Lorna choke over that, Dean turned his attention to his youngest sister. "So, Jacki, you can make it after all?"

Jacki gave a negligent shrug. "Cam twisted my arm."

"I did not!"

Seeing how easily Jacki riled Cam, and how much she enjoyed doing it, made Dean laugh.

"Relax, Cam." Jacki tossed back her hair, now styled bone straight with an occasional skinny braid here and there. "He's not taking me seriously."

With her coal-lined eyes and funky outfit, Jacki looked wickedly teasing. Dean wondered if she was a handful when younger. He'd bet his next fight on it.

She wore a metallic brown halter top that tied behind her neck and super low jeans with holes manufactured into the knees, across one thigh, and over a hipbone. Her tattoo showed through, but he couldn't quite make out the design.

"I'm relieved to see we're not dressing up." He'd worn his own holey jeans and an untucked Grateful Dead T-shirt. He'd half expected to catch a little grief for his super casual wear, but Cam, dressed in white slacks and a turquoise shirt, was too pleased to be anything but bubbly.

Lorna, however, made her disgust apparent with a searing look.

"This is as dressed up as I get," Jacki told him. "But Aunt Lorna wouldn't be caught dead in jeans, especially any as comfortable as ours."

From her styled light brown hair, fake fingernails, designer dress and heels to her aloof attitude, Lorna Ross was everything Dean had expected. Uncle Grover hadn't exaggerated one bit.

"Some of us," Lorna said, in a frosty tone, "care about our image."

Their aunt was so cold that Dean almost felt pity for his sisters. Grover hadn't supplied a cushy life, but at least he'd known how to laugh and occasionally cut loose with a beer and a few raunchy jokes.

Sticking his hands in his pockets, Dean tilted his head at Jacki. "I've never really given a shit about image, but I'd say yours is young, fun, and casual."

"Right on, brother." Jacki high-fived him before turning to Cam with satisfaction. "Told ya he wouldn't care what I wore."

Dean stood still. That simple touch, that brief moment of unity, left him flummoxed.

Until he saw Lorna scrutinizing him. Then he shrugged off the novelty of siding with a sibling and gestured for the door. "Everybody ready?"

Cam hugged his arm. "I hope Italian is okay with you."

"Anything's fine." They left the house and strode down the walkway. The sun still beat down, making the day hot and humid. "I'm not picky, as long as it doesn't require a suit. Like Jacki, it takes a lot of coercion for me to spiff up."

He opened the back door for Lorna and she slid in without a word. Jacki followed her, leaving Cam to sit up front with him. After the ladies were all seated, he rounded the hood and got behind the wheel.

"This place is totally casual," Cam assured him, "but they have the most incredible pasta and breadsticks and—"

Lorna's icy voice cut through Cam's enthusiasm. "What about your sister's wedding? Will you 'spiff up' for that?"

Cam turned in her seat. "Aunt Lorna, for crying out loud. Nothing's been confirmed, yet. Roger and I are still discussing things."

"Meaning that you're dragging your feet when you should be pouncing on his proposal."

Jacki slouched in her seat. "I think she should keep dragging her feet for another decade."

"Nobody asked you, young lady."

Leaning forward again, Jacki said to Dean, "If I end up stuffed in some hideous bridesmaid dress, then you're going to have to bite the bullet and wear a tux."

Dean felt that damn constriction around his windpipe again. They all spoke as if his attendance to a family wedding was a given. Maybe he should discuss it with Cam. . . . No. Who she married was none of his business, and he wanted to keep it that way.

Glancing in the rearview mirror, he saw Jacki watching him, waiting for his reaction. "Buckle up."

She hadn't expected that. "I never wear a seat belt."

Such a rebel. "My car, my rules."

"Is it your car?" Lorna asked, and he heard her skepticism.

Did she consider a nice sedan beyond his means? Dean wondered. Or did she assume he'd have something rich and sporty, as most of the other fighters did? He'd already told her, image wasn't one of his major considerations.

"It's a rental. Back home I have a truck that's probably as old as you." Lorna gasped at that dig, but he didn't give her a chance to voice her insult. "It's not much to look at on the outside, but it gets me where I'm going. I don't get to drive it that often since I'm so seldom home. I end up with a lot of rentals or sometimes leases. I looked at a few cars today and I think I've found one I want." He started the engine, but didn't put the car in gear. "We're not going anywhere until *everyone* buckles up."

Full of impatience, Cam looked at Lorna, and she gave up and latched the seat belt into place. "You do realize that some people have died because they wore a seat belt."

"Far more lived because of them." Dean pulled away from the curb. "So where to?"

Cam gave him quick directions. "It shouldn't take more than ten minutes or so to get there."

Silence reigned for about fifteen seconds, then Jacki asked, "So what type of car are you getting?"

"Nothing too fancy. Just a Sebring Convertible. Here, take a look at this." He lifted the trifold color brochure off his dash and handed it back to Jacki. "I like the red one."

"Wow." Jacki studied the photos. "Nice."

"There's a good short-term lease."

"Short term?" Cam asked.

Dean honestly didn't know how long he'd hang around. "It has the option to buy later."

"Must be nice." Jacki handed the brochure back to him. "I have to get rides from other people, and it sucks."

Cam rolled her eyes. "Like you don't have a dozen guys just waiting for a reason to give you a lift."

"It's not the same as having my own car."

"So why don't you get one?" Dean asked.

"Some of us," Lorna informed him, "aren't made of money."

"Aunt Lorna," Cam warned. And then to Dean, "We can't afford it right now, not with college and everything else."

Given Jacki's appearance that afternoon, he thought she'd either skipped college or gotten a two-year degree. "What's your major?"

"Elementary Education."

Dean almost choked, but he managed to hold it in. "You're going to be a teacher?"

"That's the plan. But the way things are going, I won't get my degree anytime soon."

Had he tripped into another touchy subject with her? "If you're having trouble with your classes . . ."

"Trouble paying for them, not passing them." The sarcasm came through loud and clear. "Money that *should* have gone for college got diverted elsewhere."

Dean was thinking that he didn't want to know about their financial situation, so no way in hell would he ask, when Lorna snapped, "You listen to me, young lady. Despite what your sister tells you, the world doesn't revolve around you."

Tension crackled in the air. Cam turned in her seat. "Well. Now that we've aired our dirty laundry for Dean, do you think we can all concentrate on having a good time?"

Jacki snorted. "Oh, sure. Count on it."

Dean knew women well enough to know that Cam was mortified, and Jacki was hurt, and that's what decided him. Between loans and a job, Jacki should be able to handle her tuition. "Where do you work?"

She leaned closer to the window, so close that her nose almost touched the glass. "I don't have a job."

"You don't . . ." The idea of a twenty-one-year-old adult *not* working had never occurred to him. "Seriously?"

Like a mother hen, Cam pounced on him. "I wanted her to concentrate on her grades. I know how hard it was for me, working and studying."

"Hard work never killed anyone." Dean caught Jacki's

gaze in the rearview mirror. "I worked my way through college. Sounds like your sister did, too."

"You're wrong." Cam laced her fingers tightly together. "I dropped out without finishing."

Dean grunted in disbelief. He wasn't well acquainted with all of Cam's traits, but he'd have put money on her being stubborn and proud. "I thought you said you attended a local college. How expensive could it have been?"

"There were . . . other expenses, too."

Dean noticed that Lorna kept herself silent, and he wondered at it. She didn't strike him as the type to hold back invective.

Don't ask, he told himself. Stay out of their finances. No good will come of it. But despite the orders he gave himself, he said, "I'm not following you. What other expenses?"

No one answered him. And that nettled. Maybe they didn't want him involved any more than he wanted to be.

"Forget I asked. It's none of my business."

"No," Lorna agreed. "It isn't."

Cam jerked around to glare at Lorna over the seat. Neither said a word, but Cam's expression clearly told Lorna that she didn't like her behavior.

Dean marveled at his sister. One minute she seemed like the head of the household and the peacemaker. But once or twice, she'd looked far too vulnerable and too alone.

Cam settled back in her seat, all business. "You're my brother, Dean. I don't want to keep anything from you. It's just that some things are complicated, so it seems best to save them for later, after we've talked more."

In other words, she wasn't going to explain. "Right. No problem." He sure as hell wouldn't coerce her into sharing secrets, especially since they all three seemed to have a boatload.

They finished the ride to the restaurant in an uneasy silence. By the time they arrived, the sun had retreated behind darkening clouds and a brisk wind stirred the humid air.

"Looks like rain," Cam noted in a pathetic attempt to lighten the mood.

Dean didn't reply. He got out and walked around to open the passenger side doors. Cam stepped out first, and as Jacki left the car, a gust of damp wind blasted them. Dean's shirtsleeve blew up, revealing the edge of a tattoo circling his biceps.

"Aha!" Jacki lifted the short sleeve further. "So you're into tattoos, too?"

"Tattoo. Singular." He held the door for Lorna, who took the time to tie a scarf around her hair. "You have more than one?"

"Not yet, but I'm considering another."

Dean eyed her. "They aren't cheap." And she'd just been involved in a discussion about tight finances.

The moment he said it, he regretted the words. Jacki slicked on a smile. Touching her hipbone, she said, "This was a birthday present from a friend."

"Some friend."

She propped her hands on her hips. "Oh, good Lord. Are you going to start playing concerned big brother, now?"

"Hell no." He was *not* that kind of brother. "I was just making an observation."

"We're going to get drenched if you two don't stop standing here discussing idiotic things." Lorna hustled past them for the restaurant entrance, and Jacki fell into step behind her.

He looked at Cam, who scowled at him.

"She's not had an easy time of it, Dean."

"You don't say." Wearing his own insincere smile, Dean nodded. "But that's probably one of those complicated things better saved for later." He gestured for Cam to precede him to the entrance.

Instead she put her shoulders back. "Look, anything you want to know, I'll tell you. But not out of order and not at inappropriate times."

"Meaning?"

She inhaled a deep breath. "Give me a little time, please."

Dean felt like an ass. "Take all the time you need." And, again, he gestured for her to get a move on.

She remained tight-lipped until they were seated, given menus, and had ordered drinks. Then, after a fleeting look around the table, she visibly girded herself. "Okay, here's the thing."

Jacki groaned. "Don't tell me you're going to start spilling your guts before dinner."

"She brought him here," Lorna said, with venom. "*Against* my wishes, all for the purpose of telling him things that are none of his business. What you or I think doesn't matter to her. Of course she's not going to change her mind now."

"Hey." Jacki held up her hands in a show of denial. "Don't group me with you, Auntie. I don't give a damn what she tells him; I just don't think he'll care. But if she wants to lay it all out, that's her business."

Bristling with irritation, Cam shot out of her seat. "Both of you will be quiet."

Other patrons glanced up. Lorna and Jacki stared at her. After a few seconds of silence, Dean couldn't help but grin. He lifted his water glass in a toast and said with facetious good humor, "So nice to be welcomed into such a warm and loving family. Thank you."

Cam sank back into her seat, held her head in her hands, and let out a long wearisome sigh.

Looking from Dean to Cam and back again, Jacki tried to make amends. "Hey, sorry, Dean. I didn't mean—"

Lorna snapped, "Don't you dare apologize to him, Jacqueline Conor. You owe him nothing. *Nothing.*"

Dropping one hand while keeping her head propped on the other, Cam addressed her aunt. "Now that's where you're wrong, Aunt Lorna, and you damn well know it."

Lorna said, *"Do not—"*

"Too late." With all the poise of a woman facing the gallows, Cam straightened and turned toward Dean. "I didn't plan to do this right now, but there's no time like the present, and I'm tired of dreading it." She stared right at him and said, "We're probably going to have to sell the house."

Detesting all the theatrics, Dean narrowed his eyes at her. "Yeah, so?" He agreed with Lorna: It had nothing to do with him. Unless . . . did she expect him to bail her out? Had she invited him here to take care of her financial woes? Like hell.

"So it's part yours."

An eerie dread crawled up his spine. "How do you figure that?"

Jacki laughed. "This is great." When Dean glanced at her, she laughed some more. "Hate to tell you, Cam, but he's not only untouched by the gesture, he almost looks offended."

Touched? What was there to be touched about? More annoyed by the second, Dean said, "Forget it. I've got my own house. Make that plural: *houses.* I don't want or need yours."

Impressed, Jacki asked, "You've got property? Cool. Where at?"

Before he could answer, Lorna huffed.

Cam sent her an evil look that silenced her. She turned back to Dean. "Whether you need the house or not isn't the point. It's as much yours as it is ours. One third of the monetary value belongs to you. The thing is, there's not any equity in it."

Dean didn't want anything from her, but the businessman in him had to know. "Why's that?"

She cleared her throat. "It had to be used to keep us afloat. I'm afraid that, even after the sale, I won't be able to give you your share of the house's value."

Teeth locked, Dean said, "I wouldn't have taken a dime anyway."

"So you said." Cam's fleeting smile went flat. "Still, it didn't seem right to even consider selling it without contacting you first. Legally and morally, it's your inheritance, too."

Dean started to speak, but she quickly cut him off.

"*However,* I now realize that you don't want anything from the sale." She reached out to touch his forearm. "I'll accept that—for now. But that still leaves some memorabilia. Perhaps something of sentimental value that you'd like? I've decided, and Jacki agreed with me—"

Jacki laughed. "Like I had a choice."

Ignoring her, Cam continued, "—that you should have anything from the house that you want."

Dean closed his eyes. God, this was getting worse and worse. He could feel the cut of Lorna's glare. Her dislike of him was almost as strong as Cam's warped need for justice.

He had no intention of accepting a single thing from the house—but he wasn't quite heartless enough to tell Cam that.

"Not that there's much," Jacki suddenly pointed out. "Some of mom's jewelry. Dad's coin collection. A bedroom set. Some knickknacks." She shrugged. "Anything really valuable is already gone."

Lorna slammed down her napkin. "It's obscene that you're airing our private business to him."

Oh, he understood Lorna's objections. Because somewhere along the way, she'd squandered a lot of money. Dean couldn't put the responsibility of fucked finances on Cam or Jacki. He doubted they even knew how much had been left to Lorna for their care.

Certainly there'd been enough to send both his sisters through college. Had Lorna blown it all? And if so, on what?

Fed up with the intrigue of it all, Dean waved the table to silence. "Business can wait. Are we ready to order? I'm starved." He raised his hand for a waiter, who hurried to the table. "Lorna, would you like to start?"

CHAPTER 5

❧❧❧

CAM watched Dean devour his food. The awful silence at the table didn't bother his appetite at all. Whereas he'd already eaten a plateful of pasta and two garnished chicken breasts with a salad and breadsticks, she'd barely touched her salad at all. She envied his confidence, his bearing.

His independence.

Her brother was an amazing man, and she was so proud of him. Nothing rattled him. He'd walked into the unknown with them and presented himself admirably.

She, on the other hand, tended to chatter, fret, or lose her temper. There was so much to explain to him, but how could she when all she really wanted to do was hug him and tell him she'd missed him, when she hadn't even known about him? Truth be told, she wanted to lean on him.

She had no one else.

But that'd be grossly unfair to him. Dean hadn't asked for any of this. And now she knew how badly he'd been cheated. *Rejected from his own home.* God, it hurt her to even think of it. She and Jacki had been young enough that they'd quickly adjusted to the life-altering changes. She'd never known anything else and hadn't understood the difference in what she had compared to other kids until she was older.

But Dean had been at an age to suffer each loss and rejection.

And still, despite that, he'd grown into a man so strong and kind, she wanted to tell everyone about him. *Her brother.*

Already she loved him. But then she'd started loving him the second she found out about him. Somewhere deep inside her was a kernel of memory, a hint of closeness that had never died.

More than once she'd heard Lorna talk about their uncle Grover. By all accounts, the man was crude, irresponsible, and without concern for others.

Yet he'd raised Dean.

Had his life been horrible? Had he thought of her, of Jacki, and missed them? Had he wished to come home, but known he wasn't welcome?

The questions ate her up, and finally, she couldn't take it anymore. "Dean?"

"Hmm?" He looked up from his plate. "Would you like dessert?"

"No." She wanted, needed, to talk. She had to explain the inexplicable. If Aunt Lorna had deliberately kept them apart, she wanted to know and somehow apologize.

"I'm going to order tiramisu." He laid his fork on his plate and folded his hands over his hard abdomen. "Love the stuff, and what the hell, tonight is special, right? I can indulge. Jacki, how about you?"

To Cam's surprise, Jacki nodded. "I'm partial to the zabaglione, but it's pricey so we can't usually afford it."

He flashed her a fat smile. "I can afford it."

She laughed. "Hey, if you're buying, I'm eating."

"Knock yourself out." He winked at her, then turned to

Lorna. "What about you, Lorna? You up for something sweet?"

"Thank you, no."

"Watching the figure, huh?"

Lorna looked ready to leap across the table to cut out Dean's heart. Why was there so much animosity there? Okay, so Cam knew Lorna was a man-hater. Early disappointments in romantic involvements had left her very bitter. She and Grover had never gotten along because their personalities were too dissimilar. But that shouldn't include Dean. He'd done nothing to her.

Knowing things had gotten way out of hand, Cam gave him a light kick under the table.

Incredulous at her audacity, he said, "Was that to get my attention?"

"Yes." Cam could feel her face heating, but she wouldn't let him rile her. She sat a little straighter. "We have more to talk about, and it'll be better accomplished if you aren't baiting Aunt Lorna."

"Why don't I just cut to the chase?"

Uh-oh. Had he been stewing the whole time he ate? It looked like it. "Okay."

"I don't want your house. Do whatever you want with it; it's not my concern. I don't want anything in the house. Divide it up, sell it, throw it in the trash."

Jacki said, "Well, that's harsh."

"Sentiment clutters the closets. Who needs it?"

"I'll take his share."

Cam glared at her and Jacki said, "What? You're not seriously going to trash it, right?"

Dean paid no attention to her. "It's just one more thing to store, to move when I move—and I move a lot. Believe me when I tell you, there's absolutely nothing of the past or the present that I want. Let it go."

He couldn't mean that, Cam thought.

But he looked like he did.

"Now, with that settled, you sure you don't want dessert?"

Jacki elbowed her. "Come on, Cam. Eat the dessert."

Head pounding, Cam declined. If she put a single bite in her mouth, she'd gag. "No, thank you. I'll take a coffee though."

"You got it."

The waiter had just departed with their orders when Dean looked up—and his gaze became fixed on something across the room.

Seeing him so enrapt, Cam turned in her seat to look, too, and found Eve and a man at the bar. They were both dressed nicely, shoulders touching, in close conversation.

Oops.

Gone was Dean's expression of careless disregard. He looked . . . She didn't know. Not happy. But then, she hadn't seen him look happy, yet. Distant, that she'd seen. Polite, amused, even a little wary once or twice. But excesses of emotion were not his forte.

"Probably a client," Cam told him.

He narrowed his eyes but didn't look away. And when Cam twisted around again, she saw Eve suddenly stiffen and slowly pivot on the stool to look in their direction. Her gaze locked on Dean's and even from the distance separating them, Cam could have sworn she saw sparks snapping in the air.

Interesting.

The seconds ticked by and they continued to eye each other. Never before had Cam seen her friend so instantly enamored with a man. Eve was the original free spirit. She did not get infatuations and she couldn't be charmed. She spoke her mind and disregarded polite flattery or practiced come-ons.

But even so, Cam could see the flush climbing Eve's face. Embarrassment?

Cam didn't think so.

Eve turned to say one last thing to her companion. All smiles, they shook hands, apparently sealing a deal, and the man took his leave. After watching him go, Eve knocked back the rest of a mixed drink and left her stool.

Dressed in a satiny white camisole with a black skirt and very high heels, Eve started toward their table.

Dean didn't so much as blink. He tracked Eve's every step. Right before she reached them, he pushed back his chair and stood.

In static silence, they stared at each other.

Taking up the challenge, Cam smiled. "Eve, hello. I didn't realize you were here tonight."

Watching Dean, Eve said, "A business meeting, that's all." She finally drew her gaze away from him to greet everyone else. "This is nice. A family outing. Wish I had my camera."

Jacki snickered.

"Since your meeting is over, why don't you join us?" Cam looked at Dean with encouragement. "You could get another chair."

"She has plans."

Smile tight, Eve agreed with Dean. "Yes, I do. My family's waiting dinner on me. I only wanted to stop by and say hello."

Dean murmured, "Hello," and he sounded dark and sinful as he looked down at Eve.

Eve's color increased. "Hi."

With so much sexual chemistry clogging the room, Cam wanted to fan herself.

Tucking in her chin, Jacki said, "Jesus. Turn it down a little, Dean. I'm too young to see this."

Lorna swatted at her with her napkin. "You have absolutely no decorum at all."

"Me? Dean's the one seducing Eve right at the dinner table. Why aren't you bludgeoning him with your linens?"

Eve smirked. "Trust me, Jacki, I'm not seduced. But I am late, so I'll be on my way. Enjoy yourselves."

As Eve started to turn away, Dean caught her hand, drew her back, and planted a soft, quick, oh-so-familiar kiss right on her open mouth. "See ya in a bit."

Again flushed, Eve nodded. "Right." She licked her lips. "See ya."

She was barely out of hearing range when Lorna started in on her. "As usual, that girl has shown disgusting behavior."

Jacki propped both elbows on the table and stared toward Dean as he reseated himself. "I'd have called it educational."

"It was a lewd public display likely brought on by too many drinks." Lorna was so pinched, she looked in pain. "Eve is a bad influence on you and your sister."

Praying Dean wouldn't feel the need to defend Eve, Cam nodded. "So you've often said, Aunt Lorna." To the point that Cam was sick of hearing it. Lorna disliked anyone and everyone who wasn't of her own choosing. Sure, Eve was different. She was *free*. That's what Cam loved most about her.

Rather than get defensive, Dean pointed out, "She's hardly a girl. She's what? Midtwenties?"

"Twenty-five," Jacki told him. "And good thing or you'd be labeled a perv for thinking what you're thinking."

Exasperated, Lorna tossed her napkin into her plate. "That's it. I've had enough. There's no controlling you these days."

"What?" Jacki asked. "What'd I do now?"

Ignoring Lorna, Dean smiled crookedly. "Now, Jacki, you really are too young to have any idea of my thoughts, perverted or otherwise."

"The desserts are here," Cam announced. Perfect timing, too, she thought. While Lorna looked ready to storm out, Dean and Jacki seemed to be bonding more outrageously by the moment. They shared a similar wit and irreverence that Cam envied.

On the one hand, Cam didn't want to deliberately irritate her aunt. Lorna hadn't been perfect, God knew, but she had altered her life to raise two girls that weren't her own. She'd made sacrifices, and Cam honestly believed that she'd done the best she knew how to do.

She couldn't help it that she wasn't maternal.

On the other hand, it was nice to see Jacki relating so easily to Dean. Once, not that long ago, she and Jacki had been very close. But lately Jacki had changed so much, growing dreary and sarcastic. Her cheerful, smiling baby sister was long gone, and Cam didn't know what to do to help her find her way back.

"So," Jacki said. "How long have you had a tattoo?"

Accepting the change of subject, Dean shrugged. "I think I was around fourteen when I got it."

"Fourteen?" Cam couldn't believe that. "They let children do that?"

"They do in Thailand."

Her mouth fell open, and when Dean noticed, he paused from eating his dessert. "I told you that Grover and I worked all over the world."

"But . . . how?" She knew so little about him. "Thailand of all places. It's so exotic."

"Not when you're in construction, it's not. Grover's boss took government jobs. Grover was foreman."

Lorna sipped her coffee. "And he dragged you around with him? Lovely. But, then, I would have expected no less from him."

"Don't."

That single word, issued in a near whisper, cut through the air with razor sharpness. Dean stared at Lorna, furious and not about to hide it.

Back snapping straight, Lorna set down her cup with a clatter. "I beg your pardon?"

"Make slurs at me if you want, Lorna. Act snooty. Show your disdain. I don't give a shit and I figure you can't help yourself. You're just being you." His voice lowered even more. "But Grover is off-limits. If you speak of him, it'll be with respect."

At either side of her saucer, Lorna's hands curled into fists. "How dare you dictate to me! He was my brother, and I'll speak of him any way—"

Startling everyone, Dean launched out of his chair. His palms smacked flat on the tabletop, and he loomed over Lorna with burning aggression. "You disowned him just as you did me, and if you're smart, you'll let it go."

Doing her best to hide her intimidation, Lorna asked, "Or you'll do what?"

Dean's smile made many promises, all of them ugly. "I'll tell them things you don't want them to know. Sooner rather than later."

Them? Cam wondered. Them *who?*

"Meaning you intend to tell them anyway?"

"They have a right to know."

Cam said, "Who are you talking about?"

When Lorna clamped her lips together and flicked a guilty peek at her and Jacki, Cam knew exactly whom he meant.

What could Dean possibly have to say to her that would stifle Aunt Lorna?

Uncharacteristically tactful, Jacki spoke into the silence. "So you got a tattoo in Thailand? Cool. It looked like vines to me."

The seconds ticked by with the precision of a time bomb. Cam held her breath, her gaze bouncing from her brother to her aunt and back again.

With icy control, Dean pulled away and finally seated himself again. "It is. Just vines, that's all." He dug in to his tiramisu.

"Pull your sleeve up," Jacki ordered. "I want to see it better."

He hesitated, so Cam joined in. "Me, too, please."

After a heated glance at Lorna, Dean reached for his right sleeve and tugged it above a bulging, rock-hard shoulder. Three vines, two of them delicate with rosebuds, one thicker and with thorns, wrapped around his bulging biceps.

Propping his elbow on the table made his muscles more pronounced still. Cam had already acknowledged his size and strength, but it startled her to realize that her brother was an extreme male specimen. She couldn't recall ever seeing arms like his.

Roger, whom she'd always considered physically intimidating, seemed average in comparison.

After a glance at the tattoo, Dean shook his head. "I was young and dumb when I got it."

"I agree with the young part." Cam looked closer. "The colors are still so vibrant."

"Thai tattoo artists are usually monks. Instead of the machines they use here in the states, they go old-school."

"How's that?" Jacki asked.

"They have this special tool they use, sort of like a long brass tube with a pointy rod that runs down the inside. The way the rod pierces your skin, the colors are more deeply imbedded, so they last longer."

"Dear God." Cam put a hand to her throat. "It sounds worse than what Jacki did."

"Yeah," Jacki said. "And I thought mine was bad. Heck, I broke down and cried while getting mine."

Dean relaxed enough to indulge a half smile. "It hurt like hell, sort of like a slow grinding sewing machine, and it took forever. You can't rush a monk." He shook his head and dropped the shirtsleeve. "If Grover and half the crew hadn't been there cheering me on, I probably would've been in tears, too."

Hearing him say that made Cam want to bawl. She envisioned a motley crew of sweaty workers egging on a young boy to prove his manhood. "They encouraged you?"

"One thing you should know about men, they're always trying to talk one another into doing something totally dumb ass."

"You weren't a man. You were a child."

"I was male, that's all that mattered." He grinned at some memory, then said, "Grover once told me that one male has a brain, two males have half a brain, and three males have no brain at all."

Thankfully Jacki's laugh overshadowed Lorna's snide agreement.

"I'm not sure females are any different. I've been talked into some pretty dumb things." Still studying his tattoo, Jacki added, "It looks different from what I usually see."

"That's because it's created with lines of dots rather

than a solid line. And each tattoo is unique. You tell the monk what you want, and he designs it right on the spot. There aren't any duplicates."

"I like it." Cam tilted her head. "Does it have any significance?"

For a moment there, Dean blanched. Then his expression went carefully neutral. "Yeah. It reminds me how gullible I was at fourteen." He nodded at Jacki. "So what do you have on your hip?"

To the accompaniment of Lorna's groans, Jacki came out of her seat and rounded the table to stand by Dean. Hip jutting out, she showed him her tattoo.

"It's a rose overlaying a tribal design," Jacki gushed unnecessarily. "Cool, isn't it?"

"Pretty." Dean looked up at her. "Okay, let's hear it. I can see you're dying to tell me the significance."

Laughing, Jacki sauntered back to her seat. "Well, I used to think it represented the loss of my innocence. And Aunt Lorna, before you start freaking out, I'm not talking about my virginity."

That pushed Lorna right over the edge. She shoved back her chair and announced, "I'm going to the ladies' room. I hope when I return, you'll have finished with this absurd conversation."

"Better take your time then," Jacki told her.

Lorna marched away.

"Jacki." Cam wanted to admonish her sister, but she ended up smiling instead. To be honest, she was grateful for the moment of peace. "You're not helping."

"Sure I am. Look at Dean's grin."

With both sisters looking at him, Dean tried to wipe it away, but he ended up chuckling. "You're a real brat, Jacki."

Seeing that look of amusement on his face, hearing his honest humor, filled Cam's heart. Leaning closer to Dean, she confided, "She always has been. And some days are worse than others."

"Oh, I see how it is," Jacki teased. "With Lorna gone, you'll take aim at me. Well, dish it out, guys. I can take it."

Indulgent, Dean folded his arms on the table. "You were talking about lost innocence?"

"Yeah." A little sheepish now, Jacki pushed away her empty dessert plate. "You know how it is when you suddenly realize life isn't the way you thought it should be."

He shook his head. "No, I don't. How do you think it should be?"

"I don't know." Oddly serious, Jacki considered the question. "More fun maybe. More secure." Her thin shoulders lifted. "Fewer surprises."

Her sister's words sent a pang through Cam. She'd tried so hard to protect Jacki, to make her life easier, but she'd obviously failed.

Though Dean's expression didn't change, Cam felt him retreating again. He didn't want to hear of their recent financial woes, the way their lives had turned upside down. He might be their brother, and while she'd felt fully connected to him as soon as she'd laid eyes on him, he made it clear that he didn't share the sentiment. Not that she blamed him. They barely knew each other. Too many years had passed, and too many wounds existed.

Hoping to lighten the mood, Cam lifted her coffee cup in a salute. "Here's to surprises. How boring would life be without them?"

After a tense moment, Dean lifted his cup, too. "To pleasant surprises."

"Like long-lost brothers." Jacki touched her cup to theirs.

From behind them, Lorna snapped, "It appears we're done here." She drew her scarf out of her purse. "It's a good thing, too, because I'm ready to go."

Cam didn't want the evening to end, but already Dean had risen from his seat. Panic began to set in. When would she see him again? How long would he be in town?

Dean pulled back her chair for her. "I'm going to be busy for a couple of days. But I have your number, so I'll be in touch."

He didn't offer his own number in turn, and she didn't have the nerve to ask for it. "Thank you." Almost like a question, she said, "I'd like to spend more time getting to know you."

To her surprise, he lifted his hand and, for a fleeting moment, his fingertips touched her chin in a gesture of encouragement. "I'm not going anywhere."

"It's a good thing, too," Jacki said. "Because I've got dibs on taking your new car for a drive." She winked at Dean. "After all, discovering a hidden brother should come with some perks, right?"

Watching Lorna, Dean said, "Perks . . . and maybe some problems. We'll have to see how it goes."

ANTICIPATION rising, Dean dashed through the pouring rain from the car to the front door of Eve's small but well-kept home. It wasn't a new house, but it had lots of charm and a cozy porch that protected him from the storm.

Shortly after returning his sisters and aunt to their home, the skies had opened up. Lightning, thunder, and lots of wind accompanied the rain. He loved weather like this—filled with fury, so turbulent that he could feel it deep inside himself.

Slicking rain from his face, Dean knocked on the door and then looked around. Twin dormers, gables, and bay windows flanked the columned porch. In one corner, Eve had tucked a single white rocking chair. A cheery welcome mat lay at the base of the door. Potted flowers sat everywhere, filling the air with a sweet scent, amplified by the humidity.

On a cul-de-sac, her half-acre lot backed into a wooded area that provided privacy.

Surprising that a single woman Eve's age would own a house. But, then, from the moment he'd met her, Dean figured Eve to be driven, determined, and stubborn. If she wanted something, she'd get it.

Tonight she wanted him. He could hardly wait.

Mind-numbing sex was just what he needed to obliterate the conflicting emotional remnants of dinner with a family who didn't know him.

Thinking that, the second Eve opened the door Dean stepped in, hauled her up close, and stole her greeting by sealing his mouth over hers.

Sweet.

Hot.

A combination sure to make him combust.

He knew his wet shirt would get her damp, too, and he didn't care. Behind him, through the open door, thunder rumbled loudly enough to shake the ground.

Eve jumped, but Dean only tightened his hold and turned his head so he could deepen the kiss.

He'd have a hard time patiently working his way through foreplay when all he really wanted to do was strip her naked and take her down to the floor. And actually, since he didn't know the layout of her house, the floor wasn't a bad idea. Finding a bedroom would take too damn long. He dropped a hand to her ass to urge her closer—and she freed her mouth on a gasp.

"Dean—"

Realizing that she pressed her fists against his chest, Dean allowed a miniscule amount of space between them, but he cupped the back of her head, keeping her mouth within reach. "Let's talk later."

A male voice said, "But later I won't be here, and I'm too anxious to meet you to wait."

Shock stilled Dean's every motion, even his heartbeat.

Eve groaned and hid her face against his chest.

He didn't want to, but Dean looked up—and found himself facing a man at least twenty years his senior. Even worse, he had the look of Eve . . . as if he might be her father.

Well, hell.

Next to the man stood a woman and, beside her, a younger guy . . . maybe Eve's brother. They all smiled at him.

Not releasing Eve, Dean whispered near her ear, "Your family?"

In obvious misery, she nodded.

"I'm early?"

She shook her head, then suddenly pushed away and turned to confront them all with her hands on her hips. "They wouldn't leave, as I asked them to."

"She did ask," said the younger man.

"Repeatedly," added the woman.

"But they're stubborn," Eve said unnecessarily. And then to Dean, "I'm sorry. Really."

She sounded very disgruntled and not all that embarrassed, so Dean moved her to the side of him and stepped forward, hand extended. "Dean Conor."

"Better known as Havoc." The older man grabbed his hand and pumped it with enthusiasm. "I'm a fan, as is my son. It's a real pleasure to meet you."

A pleasure? Really? Even though he'd been about to molest his daughter? Dean didn't know what to make of that. But then, he didn't meet many fathers. The women he saw usually sought him out, and they sure as hell didn't drag Daddy along.

He glanced at Eve, but she kept her mulish expression frozen on her family. Even with her father standing there, beaming at him anxiously, Dean noticed the way Eve's dark hair gleamed, curling around her shoulders.

She'd changed clothes, replacing the crisp business attire with a cool and casual sundress. Spaghetti straps kept the snug bodice in place. The skirt ended just above her knees. No shoes, no bra. Where he'd held her to his chest, damp spots made the material cling to her breasts. . . .

Don't think about it, Dean.

With haste, he turned back to her father. "Thank you." And he lied, "Nice to meet you, too."

He didn't have much practice in dealing with a woman's family, but surely there had to be a way to rid himself of them quickly.

A woman as petite as Eve held out her hand. "Since my

daughter is busy casting evil spells on the lot of us, and my husband is too twittered to do introductions, I'll take care of it."

Dean accepted her hand.

"I'm Eve's mother, Crystal. You can call my husband Ted, and this is our son, Mark."

"It's nice to meet you." Dean wondered if indeed Eve was casting spells. If so, he hoped they worked. And fast.

"I know we're intruding," Crystal continued, "but the men are rabid fans of the SBC and the second Eve let it slip that you were coming over—mostly because no one was leaving fast enough to suit her—"

"*Mom.*"

"—they refused to budge without meeting you first. I just hope you like Eve enough to forgive them, because it'll be at least a half an hour before I can drag them away."

So no one intended to mention his faux pas in groping Eve? Her family didn't care that he'd been all over her, that he'd come calling with certain obvious expectations?

Apparently not.

He wanted to groan, but Dean kept his smile in place. After the family drama during dinner, he'd wanted nothing more than casual, uncommitted sex.

Instead he was stuck with more family.

It wouldn't be so bad if he knew anything about families. But living with Uncle Grover, and sometimes a crew of workers, hadn't prepared him.

"Not a problem." If chatting with them would get them on their way, he'd tell them whatever they wanted to know.

Mark, who looked to be close to Jacki's age, started the interrogation. "Who do you fight next?"

"Whoever they put in front of me." Eve's foyer opened into a great room with a ten-foot ceiling, and by silent agreement, everyone gravitated forward, taking seats. Dean sank into the corner cushion of a sectional couch. He watched Eve as she and her mother disappeared into the dining room, which he assumed led to the kitchen.

"Who do you want to fight?" asked Mark. "I know

Marsh has been talking a lot of smack. He says you're too undisciplined, that you lack technical skills—"

"He's just showboating," Dean explained, "hoping to build up interest. If enough controversy gets going on the fight, the organization will pair us. That's what he wants, so he's doing what he can to make it happen."

Mark's eyebrows shot up. "You don't care what he says?"

"No." Worrying about the opinions of others had never been his thing.

Affronted on his behalf, Mark scowled. "He's insulting you."

Dean just shrugged. "He's not the first and he won't be the last."

"Amazing." Ted shook his head in awe. "You could demolish most men, yet you aren't the least bit obnoxious about it."

"Whatever I have to prove," Dean told him, "I prove in sanctioned SBC fights where I get paid and where I won't get arrested. Outside the SBC, I've got better things to do with my time."

"But it wouldn't take you much time to annihilate him," Mark predicted. "You should offer to teach him a lesson. I'd love to see it."

"That's what he's hoping I'll do. But if I did, every upcoming fighter would try the same tactic. So I don't make requests or denials. I leave the matchups to the people who run the SBC. It's their jobs to know which fights will generate the most interest."

Mark couldn't let it go. "Marsh says that if he gets you in a fight—"

"He'll knock me out. Yeah, I know what he says. He spouts off every chance he gets."

"And?"

Obviously they wanted some assurances from him, so Dean placated them. "Marsh isn't a marshmallow. He has KO power. But to knock me out, he'd have to plant his big feet for the punch. If he did that, I'd take him down, and he sucks on the ground. No submission defense at all. He'd be tapping out within a minute."

That bit of boasting must have sufficed, because both Mark and Ted beamed at him.

But Dean didn't stop there. "Of course, he could catch me. It happens." Luckily it didn't happen to him often, and not in recent years.

"No way!"

"You never know. It only takes one mistake. Did you see that last fight?"

Ted nodded. "We watched it on pay-per-view. We never miss a fight."

Dean touched the colorful swollen bruise high on his cheekbone near his temple, remembering the numbing pain of the blow that landed there, a blow that had nearly knocked him out. "I damn near lost that one."

"Yeah, but Dima Cheslav is a freakin' monster. You're huge, but he's two inches taller than you and outweighs you by twenty-five pounds." Mark sat on the very edge of his seat. "And that tattoo! It's like Death or something on the back of his head and neck."

"He's a billboard for every asinine tattoo out there. He's even got a couple on his ass now."

Eyes wide, Mark said, "Seriously?" He barked a laugh. "Well, no wonder he came out so crazy—roaring and foaming at the mouth like he was really pissed off or something."

Dean half smiled. "He always carries on like he's berserk. The audience loves it. But outside the SBC, he's a regular guy."

"I don't mind telling you," Ted said, "thinking of Dima as a regular guy is tough. They say he has a hard time getting anyone to accept fights with him these days. But from the start of the fight, you looked as cool as ever."

"Against a man like Dima, you have to stay focused. Otherwise, you lose."

"You were focused all right." Ted shook his head in wonder. "He plowed his fist into your face, you went down, and I hate to say it, but I thought it was over."

For a moment there, Dean had thought so, too.

"Then in the next second you had him in a perfect knee-bar. It was like an automatic thing for you, just going with the momentum. He never saw it coming."

"Yeah." To Dean's surprise, he actually enjoyed the conversation. "Dima's so used to knocking people out in the first round, he tends to get cocky."

"Can I ask you something?"

Dean took in Mark's anxious expression, and he shrugged. "Shoot."

"You've fought with injuries. You've been knocked down, caught in submissions. You've gone up against guys known for doing real damage." Warming to his subject, Mark eased closer to him. "Does it ever scare you?"

With no hesitation, Dean shook his head. "No."

"Never?"

Not since he was a kid kicked out of his own home, sent to live with an uncle whom he didn't know, had Dean experienced real fear. In those early days, he'd learned that fear was a waste of energy.

"Being afraid doesn't change the circumstances. It only affects how well you deal with them."

"Well . . . yeah. But still—"

"It's counterproductive," Dean continued. "You get scared, and you make mistakes. You take your eyes off your opponent to flinch, and you can't see where the next punch or kick is coming from. You lose the offense and turn defensive, and any good fighter will take immediate advantage of it."

"The way you took advantage of Dima."

Dean nodded. "They dubbed me Havoc because when I first started everyone thought I didn't have a plan. It didn't take them long to realize that they were wrong. My plan is to win. One step at a time, whatever I have to do, however I have to do it. When the fight changes, I adjust. I couldn't do that if I let fear take over."

To Dean, it seemed a simple philosophy. Being afraid could never be part of his plan.

Yet . . . seeing his sisters had shaken up some strange sensations that felt too close to fear. He didn't want to admit it, not even to himself, but it did unnerve him that, despite everything, it would be so easy to get sucked into the family dynamics.

He didn't know jack about being a big brother or caring for siblings. He didn't know how to fit into an existing family atmosphere. He didn't know how to offer security or how to say the right things at the right time.

For Cam and Jacki's sake, as well as his own, he'd have to remember that he was an outsider, here for a visit.

Nothing less—and definitely nothing more.

CHAPTER 6

❧

"HOW big are your biceps?"
That question threw Dean, but one look at Mark, and he knew he was serious. "Hell, I don't know."

"You're kidding? You have guns like that and you've never measured them?"

Because Mark looked ready to hunt up a measuring tape, Dean added, "No, and I never will." Where the hell was Eve? He looked toward the arched doorway where she'd disappeared, but she didn't return.

Ted and Mark had an endless store of oddball questions, but at least they weren't prying into how much he made. More often than not, that question was the first. Most people considered the fighters celebrities, and while he couldn't complain about the pay, he worked damn hard for what he made. People didn't realize the amount of commitment and the hours of hard work that went into training. He more than earned every cent he made.

"You're a credit to the sport."

Again surprised, Dean looked at Ted. "Yeah? How's that?"

"You don't talk trash. You don't boast. You're respectful of the other fighters. You've got a quiet dignity instead of all that showmanship."

Dignity? Ted had to be kidding.

Rubbing his chin, Dean tried to figure out how to set Eve's father and brother straight. "Look, I don't sound off because I know there's always the chance I can lose. I say I'll do my best, and that's what I do."

Ted smiled. "There, you see? A class act all the way."

Oh God. The man was delusional. If Eve didn't show herself soon, he'd—

As if on cue, Eve strolled back into the room. "Here." She handed Dean a beer. "If we're going to have a social gathering, you might as well have a drink."

Dean noted that her family didn't harbor the same hang-ups about alcohol as his own. He accepted the longneck bottle. "Thanks."

She plopped down next to him, curled her bare legs up beneath the skirt of her dress, and leaned into him. To the casual observer, it would seem they'd known each other a lot longer than a few hours. Eve showed no reservations at all in front of her family, which meant she felt very comfortable with them. He liked that.

Ted sat forward with his elbows on his knees. "Do you know when you fight again?"

"Not for a while. I took a small leave."

Faces fell. "You aren't going to be in the bout with Canada?"

"No. Maybe not the one after that, either."

"I told you," Eve said. "He's here to get acquainted with Cam and Jacki. They haven't seen each other for years."

Dean slipped his arm around Eve's bare shoulders. Even in the cool interior of the house, her skin felt like warmed silk. "Actually it has nothing to do with them. I'd already decided to take a little time away."

"Why?" As Eve turned slightly toward him, her breast pressed into his ribs.

Dean forgot what he wanted to say. He stared at her. "Why what?"

Her smile flickered, then warmed. "Never mind."

"To think Cam had a famous brother and I never knew it." Ted shook his head. "She's practically part of the family. The girls have been friends for years."

"Since grade school," Eve admitted.

"But Cam's never mentioned you." Ted sounded very confused about that.

Dean went still, but only for a moment, then he forced a smile. "No, I don't suppose she did." He took a swig of his beer and tried to ignore that niggling of unease roiling in his guts again. *Cam hadn't known of him, so how could she have mentioned him—or missed him?*

"If I start dating Jacki," Mark asked, breaking the tension, "can I get free tickets to the fights?"

Eve tossed a round decorative pillow at her brother's head.

"It can't hurt to ask." Mark threw the pillow right back, nearly causing Eve to spill her drink on Dean.

Unused to sibling antics, Dean snatched the pillow away. "Sorry, Mark, but I'm not that type of brother."

Mark settled back with a grin. "Then I think I'll keep a safe distance. Truth is, Jacki scares me anyway."

"*Mark.*"

"Stop squawking, Eve." Her father frowned at her. "I'm sure Dean knows he's kidding."

Actually Dean didn't know what to think. At Mark's words, some strange disquiet squirreled through him. Mark was a decent-looking kid, tall and lean. Young and goofy. So why did Dean suddenly want to smack him upside his head? "What's scary about her?"

"She's outspoken," Mark explained. "You never know what she's going to do or when she's going to do it. She used to be different—well, she was never like Cam."

Dean knew he shouldn't ask, but what better opportunity would he get to find out more about his sisters? Cam and Jacki weren't here to mistake his curiosity for caring.

And he was curious—nothing unnatural in that. It didn't mean anything. "Like Cam how?"

"You know, private and quiet. Real . . . contained."

Using her fingertip, Eve traced a small circle on Dean's jean-covered thigh. "Cam's always been that way." She looked up at him, and he noted the darkness of her blue eyes, the thickness of her lashes. "I'm not sure why, but even back in high school, she always seemed more mature, more responsible and aware of things."

Beautiful eyes, Dean thought, full of emotion and, when she looked at him, full of attraction. He couldn't wait to see her lazy and sexually satisfied—thanks to him.

He cleared his throat, put his hand over hers to flatten her palm to his thigh, and said, "She's a mother hen." It hadn't taken him long to see the signs in his sister's behavior. Cam was maternal in ways Lorna could never be. "She probably feels responsible for Jacki."

"True enough," Eve agreed. She pulled her hand away from him, but rested her head back against his shoulder. "Cam was never young, ya know? I mean, for as long as I can remember, she's worried about things. The house, bills, Jacki, and even Lorna."

Dean didn't like to think of Cam with the weight of the world on her narrow shoulders. "Why Lorna?"

At first, no one answered. Then Eve shrugged. "She grew up with the realization that she and Jacki had been forced on Lorna, that her aunt had never planned to have children of her own."

"That's a tough pill for a young girl to swallow." Ted sounded as disgusted as Dean felt. "It left her guarded. Probably because she never quite trusted that Lorna would be around for the long haul."

Dean's muscles tensed. Lorna had a lot to answer for—more than these people, or his sisters, realized.

"But Jacki's just the opposite," Mark said. "Not a care in

the world, always the center of attention, no matter what's going on. She teases and flirts, and wherever she goes, there's a crowd around her. People gravitate to her."

"And that's scary?"

Mark shrugged. "No, not usually. Intimidating maybe, but . . . lately she's been really outrageous."

"Meaning?"

Mark started to speak, and Eve said, "Give it a rest, Mark." She turned those big blue eyes on Dean again. "Jacki's fine. Cam's always made sure of it. Right now, she's just going through growing pains or something."

Dean frowned. "She's twenty-one and nearly six feet tall."

"She's five-ten," Eve corrected. "And it's just a figure of speech."

"Either way, she's done growing. And that's not what your brother was talking about anyway."

When Eve started to speak, Dean hushed her. "No. I want to hear it from Mark."

Everyone turned to look at Mark, and his face went red in discomfort. "Well, that is . . ." He cast a quick guilty look at his sister. "Eve's right. I, uh, didn't mean anything by it."

"Now look what you did." Eve turned on Dean, playfully punching him in the shoulder. "You've got him shaking in his boots."

Dean's brows shot up. "I didn't do anything."

"Ha!" Her expression challenged and teased him. "You used that tone."

"What tone?"

"A tone that says you're feeling protective."

How many times did he have to tell people that he wasn't that type of brother? Her assumption irritated him, so he leaned closer to say, "I was *not* being protective. That's not it at all."

Ted quickly interrupted. "Hey, no big deal. Eve, quit fussing at the man."

"Yeah, Eve." Mark looked back and forth between the two of them. "Knock it off."

"Oh, for crying out loud." Rolling her eyes, Eve deliberately popped Dean again before saying to her father, "He's got shoulders like boulders, Dad. There's no way I hurt him."

Hurt him? Did she mean physically? Ready to laugh, Dean glanced up and saw that Ted actually looked concerned. "How the hell could *you* hurt me?"

Now she looked disgruntled. "By punching you. Heaven only knows what a big bad SBC fighter like you will do when riled."

Of all the idiotic . . . Dean knew what he wanted to do to her, and it had nothing to do with anger.

"You punched me?" he teased, pretending he hadn't noticed. "When was this?"

"Why you . . ." Feigning outrage, Eve swung again. But Dean automatically caught her wrist and pulled her off balance. She landed facedown over his lap and almost tipped off onto the floor.

Dean tried to catch her, but he held his beer in one hand and Eve was flailing, trying to find her balance. The skirt of her dress somehow ended up twisted to her hips.

For only a scant second, Dean got a glimpse of lacy, lavender panties.

With a yelp, Eve shoved herself away and tumbled onto the floor. Her face was beet red as she slapped down her skirt to cover herself.

Mark roared with hilarity. Ted snickered.

In walked Crystal. She took one look at her daughter and threw up her hands. "Eve, for crying out loud. What are you doing on the floor?"

Eve scampered back to her feet, threatened Dean with a shaking fist, and plopped back down next to him.

"Are you okay?"

She made a face at him. "With you smiling like that, your concern doesn't seem at all sincere."

"Sorry." Dean smoothed her tousled hair. "Want me to teach you a few moves so that it doesn't happen again?"

To his surprise, she nodded. "Yes, I do." And then to her

brother, "But you can wipe that look off your face right now, Mark. You're obnoxious enough already. You don't need special moves to make you more so."

Knowing Mark would press the issue, Dean asked him, "So what has Jacki done?"

He drew back. "Nothing." Face blank, Mark added, "Really."

Dean turned to Eve. "Give it up."

"Fine." Still flushed, Eve said, "If you must know, the police were called on her last weekend."

The police? "For what?"

"Unruly behavior, that's all. Some . . . stuff had happened, and I guess it bothered Jacki. She went out with a group of college friends, had too much to drink, and ended up dancing on the tables."

That didn't sound so bad to Dean. "The police came over that?"

"There were people sitting at the tables, trying to finish their drinks."

Oh. Dean did his best not to grin.

"The police only gave her a warning and called Cam to pick her up. Lorna swears the entire town is talking about it."

"It's mostly just the college set that knows," Mark added in an effort to contribute. "And really, no one was all that shocked about it. Not with Jacki."

Dean let that go. "So what upset her?"

Now Eve looked worried. "That's really something you should discuss with Cam."

His curiosity doubled in an instant. "I'm discussing it with you."

Crystal made a sound of impatience. "It's not like it's a secret, Eve." Then to Dean: "Jacki doesn't want to sell the house. Especially since there's no equity in it. They're only getting rid of it because the upkeep is too much, which is absurd. If the three of them had jobs, instead of just Cam working, they could easily make ends meet."

So Lorna didn't work, either? Why, that manipulative . . .

"It's the only home Jacki has ever known." Crystal seemed intent on gaining Dean's sympathy for Jacki. "Everyone knows that they're taking a big step down, from one of the nicer houses in the community to an apartment. Of course Jacki's unhappy about it."

"Mom, I don't think—"

"Why does Jacki care what the town thinks?"

Both women blinked at him, but it was Eve who spoke. "Well of course she cares what others think. Doesn't everyone?"

"I don't."

"You don't?"

Dean shook his head. Hell, he'd spent most of his life moving, so he'd never really known anyone long enough to be concerned with what they thought. Spoiled, that's what Jacki was. "She's falling apart because she has to move?" He grunted. "That's it?"

"She's not falling apart," Eve corrected. "She's just un-happy about leaving behind . . ." She hesitated, probably remembering Dean's circumstances.

"The familiar?" he finished for her.

She nodded, and slipped her hand into his. Trying to comfort him? Dean stiffened. He wanted several things from Eve, but sympathy wasn't one of them.

"If you ask me—" Crystal said.

"He *didn't* ask you," Eve quickly pointed out, but it left her mother undaunted.

"Lorna squandered a lot of the money left to those girls."

Dean figured as much. It was the only thing to make sense. But then, Grover had always assumed that would be the case.

She nodded to punctuate her statement. "Don't get me wrong. Lorna is a nice enough person. But Lord above, the woman doesn't have an ounce of sense when it comes to finances. And with that one, what she wanted or needed always came first."

Eve groaned and dropped her head into her hands. "I don't believe this."

Dean rubbed Eve's back, letting her know that Crystal's enlightening account of details didn't bother him.

"I still remember when Cam needed tap shoes for the sixth-grade school recital. The way Lorna carried on, you'd have thought they cost the moon. But did she stop getting her nails done? Did she skip a new spring wardrobe? No, she did not. Cam sure stopped participating in school events, though. I don't think she went to another party or dance until she got old enough to get a job and pay for things herself."

Dean didn't like the sound of that. From what Grover had told him, there should have been plenty of money for what Cam and Jacki needed, including new dresses and shoes for parties. His parents hadn't been without resources, and not only did an insurance policy pay off the house after their death, it also provided a nice chunk of change. Add that to the assets and bank accounts they already had, and they should have been set financially.

"I'm sorry." Eve peeked at Dean. "My mother is a world-class gossip. It's what she lives for."

Crystal swatted at her daughter. "He's their brother, so he has a right to know all about them. How else can he help?"

Dean locked his teeth. "I'm not here to help."

Crystal waved away his protests. "It's all right. Eve explained to me why we hadn't met you before now."

"Is that right?" So that's why the women were so long in the kitchen. And Eve called her mother a gossip?

"She asked," Eve said, in her own defense.

Not in the least self-conscious about snooping, Crystal shrugged. "Naturally I was curious about you. Both Cam and Jacki spent plenty of time with us while growing up. Our house was a second home to them. It seemed odd that they'd have a brother I'd never heard of."

"During the summer," Mark said, "it was like having three sisters. They outnumbered me in a big way. They were here more than they were at their own home."

"Not that we minded." Crystal smiled in fond memory.

"Both Cam and Jacki were just precious, and it broke my heart to think of them growing up without a mother."

Hadn't that been Lorna's role to fill? From what Crystal said, Lorna had been well compensated to do just that. "How old were they when you met them?"

"We moved here when Eve was eight. She's a year and a half older than Cam."

Which meant Cam would have been around six, already under Lorna's care for four years—more time than she'd spent with their birth mother.

Cam hadn't remembered him, so maybe she didn't remember their parents, either. What had Lorna told her about them, about their lives, and about their deaths?

Probably not the truth.

Dean thought about it, and realized both girls called her Aunt Lorna. Nothing more affectionate. Nothing more personal. Had Lorna insisted on the distinction?

For Dean, Grover had been his father, his uncle, his . . . entire family, all rolled into one. Grover was a gruff old bird, but never had Dean felt like an inconvenience. Never had he felt like an intruder in Grover's life.

Moving to stand by his wife, Ted put a hand on her shoulder. Though he hadn't witnessed it before, Dean automatically recognized the show of support. Grover had never settled with a single woman. He hadn't even dated, not in the conventional sense. Plain and simple, his uncle had brought women around for sexual purposes only. He hadn't been blatant about it, but he wasn't ashamed about it, either. It hadn't taken Dean long to catch on.

Grover liked the ladies, but he'd never shown an emotional intimacy or domestic companionship with any particular woman. The silent connection between Ted and Crystal had been missing in Grover's relationships.

"We're real fond of your sisters." Ted smiled at Crystal. "Both of them, but especially Cam because of the closeness she and Eve shared."

"Cam confided in me," Crystal said. "She came to me when she needed someone to talk to, someone she could trust. She asked me all those things a young girl usually asks her mother."

Dean wondered what those things might entail. Whatever they were, it bothered him that Cam had to go to a friend's mother. Lorna should have been there for her, in all things.

"You see, Lorna wasn't that approachable. She didn't understand your sisters. She expected them to be perfect at all times, to cause her the least amount of trouble. She didn't give them much room or opportunity to learn things on their own. And that made it tough for them, but especially for Cam."

As much to himself as to Crystal, Dean said, "Because Cam felt responsible for Jacki."

Crystal nodded. "She wasn't much more than a child herself when she started mothering Jacki, stepping up for her, protecting her and guiding her."

"Lorna suffocated them with rules and more rules," Eve said with feeling. "So when Cam got into trouble or got curious about guys or just plain needed to vent, she came home with me, and Mom would advise her."

"And in turn," Crystal said with pride, "Cam learned to be there for Jacki."

Dean brooded. He'd spent many years in foreign countries, on uncomfortable beds, without friends, dragging through one day after another. At night, he'd thought of his sisters, and he always assumed they lived the cushy life. After all, they'd kept everything—the house, the toys, the pool, the friends . . . everything a nine-year-old boy enjoyed.

He was the one booted out with only a few changes of clothes.

Did he really have it all wrong?

"Crystal is privy to information about the sale of the house because she's the Realtor who'll be listing it," Ted explained. "Free of commission, of course, since there's no money to be made. She's trying to help out where she can, to keep Cam from making any hasty mistakes."

Dean tightened his jaw, refusing to ask the question aloud. But in his head, where no one could hear, it echoed again and again: What hasty mistakes?

Why did his sister write to him now, and what did she want from him? What did she need so badly that she'd contact a long-forgotten brother?

It occurred to him suddenly that he had Eve's undivided attention as she waited for his reaction. He tried to smooth out his frown, but already Eve popped off the seat in a rush.

"That's enough from all of you. You've thoroughly embarrassed me. I'll be red faced for a year at least." Against her family's protests, she began herding them all toward the door. "If Dean doesn't make a run for it now, I'll be amazed."

Without haste, Dean pushed to his feet. "I'm not going anywhere." He and Eve had unfinished business, and he wouldn't leave until he got what he came for. Besides, he had a few more questions for Eve once her family got out of the way.

"Good," Crystal said. "Then you can join us for dinner tomorrow night."

Eve winced and immediately complained, *"Mom."*

It was a novel thing for Dean, dealing with pushy parents, but he found it interesting, too. Eve wore one persona when with him alone, another in front of his sisters, and yet one more with her parents.

No matter how she reacted, he found her appealing. "Sorry, Crystal. I appreciate the invitation, but I'm going to be busy."

Undaunted, Crystal asked, "Doing what?"

Before Eve could start groaning again, Dean explained, "Checking out property. I was hoping you could give me some leads."

Crystal perked right up at that. "Leads for what?"

"Anything that's in need of cosmetic repair. I want something that I can fix up and sell for a profit."

That deflated her. "You're not moving here?"

"No." He could feel Eve's tension as she shifted

restlessly beside him. "I move around a lot, so I don't really settle in any one place."

Accepting that, Crystal asked, "You're experienced in flipping houses?"

"It's what I do when I'm not training for a fight."

After digging into her purse, Crystal handed him a business card. "Come by the office tomorrow, say around noon? I'll have some spec sheets ready for you to look over, maybe see if anything appeals to you."

Sliding the card into his back pocket, Dean nodded. "Thanks. I'll be there."

"Where are you staying in the meantime?" Ted asked.

"The Cross Streets Motel."

Mark made a face. "That's another of Roger's properties. He's involved with Cam."

"We've met." But Dean hadn't realized that Roger owned the motel. He wasn't sure if it mattered to him or not. He'd have to think about it more when he wasn't edgy with lust.

Both Crystal and Ted looked ready to launch into more discussions, but Eve loudly announced, "Time to go," and began shooing her family to the door and out into the storm.

They left with some good-natured ribbing, more invitations, and a few laughs. All in all, Dean found them to be friendly and familiar, as if the love they shared gave way to certain liberties.

Eve turned on a porch light, then waited at the door as her family raced through the rain to the car. After they all settled inside the vehicle, she waved one last time, closed the door, and locked it.

"Sorry about that." She rested back against the door. "My family isn't usually so intrusive."

Dean felt new tension in the air, and this time it was sexual. "Do you really expect me to believe that?"

She laughed. "No." Avoiding his gaze, she pushed away from the door and headed toward the kitchen. "They can be a real pain, but they mean well. I hope they didn't put you off."

"Not a chance." He watched her pick up two empty beer bottles on the way out of the room.

Over her shoulder, she asked, "So if you're buying property, you can't be planning to rush off anytime too soon, right?"

Dean refused to paint himself into a corner with statements that he might regret later. He didn't yet know enough about his sisters, about what problems Cam might have or why Jacki rebelled, to make any final decisions. Until he figured things out, he didn't know what he wanted to do. Buying a house to flip seemed a good delaying tactic until then. "Maybe. I haven't decided yet."

"I hope you do stick around for awhile." She went to the sink and rinsed a dish.

"Yeah?"

"Cam and Jacki could really use your help."

Dean came up behind her. With his hands at her waist, he leaned down and nuzzled behind her ear. "For the last time," he murmured, "I'm not that kind of brother."

Going stiff, Eve glared over her shoulder at him. "Then what kind of brother are you?"

"Right now, being a brother is the furthest thing from my mind." He enjoyed the feel of her through the soft cotton of her sundress, the way her breath caught, how she trembled the tiniest bit.

Touching another damp kiss to the side of her neck, Dean whispered, "Tonight, I'm more interested in you."

CHAPTER 7

THE time of reckoning, Eve thought. She'd teased Dean, led him on—and now she'd get the payoff. Oh boy. She just hoped she could handle him.

Pasting on a smile, she said, "Dean," and started to turn. She didn't get very far.

One big warm hand settled on her belly and his hips moved in closer to her behind, pinning her in place against the counter.

"Yeah?" The whisper of his breath in her ear sent shivers down her spine. "Do you know I've been thinking about this, about you, all day? I've been damn near obsessed. I've been half-hard. I've had a hell of a time concentrating on anything or anyone else." His fingers contracted, sort of stroking her stomach, kneading her.

Eve stared out the kitchen window over her sink, not really seeing the storm or the bending trees or even the violent flashes of lightning.

On every level, in every nerve of her body, she sizzled with awareness of him. "Me, too."

"Good to know." He skimmed his lips along the nape of her neck to her ear, caught the lobe between his teeth and teased with his tongue. Her eyes felt heavy before she closed them completely.

But shutting out her sight only heightened her other senses to his nearness and to his obvious intent to devastate her.

By aligning his long legs outside hers and crowding closer, he surrounded her with his strength and size, his indescribable scent. Masculine heat touched all along her back, making her muscles weak. He kept his hands busy with casual but enticing strokes.

Eve felt enclosed by him, wary of his potent effect on her. At the same time, she wanted more, of his touch, of his kiss, of *him*.

Resting her head back on his chest, her heart thumping madly, Eve admitted, "This is very odd, Dean."

"How's that?" His fingers on her belly continued to cuddle her, teasing, threatening to move lower without actually doing so.

It was diabolical on his part, because now she could only think of how to get him to touch her when moments before she'd been pondering ways to hold him off.

Using his free hand, Dean lifted her hair away, baring more of her throat before cupping his hand over her shoulder in a very gentle bond.

He opened his mouth over the delicate skin where her neck and shoulder met—and sucked on her.

"Oh God."

"Do you taste this good all over?"

The way he asked that, his voice rich and deep with insinuation, had Eve groaning. He was good. Too good. She couldn't understand him or her reaction. "How are you doing this?"

"This?" Trailing his tongue along her neck, he left a damp, sizzling path to her ear, where he dipped inside, then breathed softly, "Or this?" He pressed his fingers lower—so close—but stopped short of actual satisfaction.

Damn it, she wasn't a timid woman. She wasn't a woman afraid to address her own needs. In past relationships, she'd been plenty vocal—without near the results.

Right now, with very little effort on Dean's part, he had her primed, as if they'd been indulging in the most intimate foreplay for an hour. "This is insane."

"Because you enjoy me touching you?" He slipped his other hand over her shoulder, down her upper arm, and onto her breast.

She sucked in a startled breath. "Yes."

"Just relax, Eve."

"I'm relaxed."

His husky laugh teased along her nerve endings. "No, you're not. You're fighting me."

How the hell could he tell?

Dean held her breast, but he wasn't actively involved in exciting her. That is, he wasn't groping, prodding, exploring. Her nipple puckered tightly against the soft material of her dress, but he didn't rub her, didn't even seem to notice or care. He just left his hand there while he continued to kiss her shoulder and neck and throat.

He showed such a complete and utter lack of haste that she began to have a few doubts.

Until he pressed a solid erection against her derrière. "You are so petite."

He somehow made that sound like a smooth compliment. "Dean, wait."

Rather than argue or press her, he said, "Okay," and propped his chin on the top of her head. "Do you want to talk?"

Damn him. Eve could barely breathe and it wasn't fair. He sounded totally unaffected. But she knew he couldn't be. Maybe it was time for her to regain some control. "Yes, talking would be good."

"I'm okay with that. What do you want to talk about?"

She needed something to throw him off stride, something that he wasn't expecting. She went with an honest concern. "Where's this headed?"

For only a brief instant, his arms hugged her in a way that seemed wholly affectionate. "With any luck and a little cooperation on your part, I'd say a screaming orgasm."

Oh God. Eve had the feeling he needed neither luck, nor her cooperation, to make it happen. Not with the way she felt right now.

Needing to regain herself after his bold statement, she closed her eyes. When she thought she could speak with a modicum of strength, she replied. "I meant . . . all of this. Not just the sex."

Becoming thoughtful, Dean tilted his head down to see her profile. "It's probably too soon to say. Where did you want it to go?"

She swallowed. He'd just put it all back on her. "I don't know, either. But I'm not in the habit of jumping into bed with men."

"Then I count myself lucky."

She ignored that. "It's just that you've taken me by surprise and I'm not really being myself. That is, I usually don't let things move so quickly."

"Hmmm." He propped his chin back atop her head. "So what habits do you have with men?"

She couldn't quite bring herself to turn and face him. He had to be annoyed with her about-face. Never mind that he sounded merely curious. He *had* to be irate.

"Dating." Yeah, that sounded reasonable. "I just met you last night, Dean. We haven't even socialized beyond a little small talk with other people around. There's so much I don't know about you."

Something changed in his voice. "Are you asking me to leave?"

"No." She'd collapse in disappointment if he walked out on her right now. "But . . ."

"But you want to date, to get to know me better. After tonight, that is."

It sounded so dumb when he said it. But she wouldn't back down now. "Yes."

"Okay. I can handle that." As if hoping to soothe her, he kept his hands still. "How about a movie tomorrow?"

His easy compliance blew her away. "A movie?"

"Yeah." His thumb coasted over her nipple and she nearly jumped out of her skin. He kept stroking, maybe to ensure he'd get the answer he wanted. "There any movie theaters in this little redneck town?"

The light movement of his thumb over her nipple, so casual and almost . . . careless, made coherent thought nearly impossible. "Yes."

"Anything good playing?" Both hands settled on her breasts, heavy and warm, and Eve had to stiffen her legs to support her own weight. "By good, I mean something kick-ass or scary. No chick flicks. I can't stand them."

Eyes closed and hands clenched, Eve shook her head and said, "I don't know."

"I'll check into it. Maybe we could do dinner, too." His mouth touched her temple, and using both hands, he tugged gently on her nipples. "I can't dance though. Chalk that up as another of my many flaws."

Why wouldn't he just shut up and let her enjoy the way he made her feel?

"You know, Eve, I'm not sure you're really listening to me."

Eve could hear the teasing in his voice, and she knew that he toyed with her on purpose. It infuriated her.

She mustered up the strength to put him in his place, and he whispered, "I think I know why." He kissed her cheek. "You need release, don't you?"

Every muscle in her body clenched in expectation. She couldn't answer. She couldn't even nod.

"Do you want to come now, Eve?"

A moan must have been answer enough for him.

His right hand pressed between her legs, and the pulsing of building pleasure bloomed.

Dean made a hungry sound as he cupped her through the material of her dress and panties. Fingers searching, he explored her—and pushed her closer to the edge at the same time.

"Very nice, Eve. I can feel how hot you are." He trailed his fingers in and up, and even through her clothes, he found her swollen clitoris. After a throaty growl, he whispered, "This dress isn't much of a barrier, and I doubt that your panties are either. But I'd rather there be no barriers at all."

She'd prefer it that way, too.

Reaching down, he caught the hem of her dress and lifted it. In the next second, his hand slid inside her panties. "Hot—and wet. You really are ready, aren't you, honey?"

Her hand clamped around his wrist. Not to draw him away, but to ensure he wouldn't pull back on her. She was so close that nothing else mattered just then.

"Shhh. Easy now." He held her so carefully, cradled against his body, supporting her, hugging her. In the slightest of movements, he rocked her. He kept kissing her. And his rough fingertips played over her with perfection.

"I don't believe this." Her voice was high and weak, but she couldn't breathe. Deep inside her, a wild trembling started. Everything closed in around her.

Another minute would do it.

When cool air touched her fevered skin, she realized that Dean had somehow lowered the straps to her dress.

Her breasts were exposed.

"So damn pretty. And so sensitive." As he moved his hand from one breast to the other, circling each nipple with the edge of his thumb, he added, "I can't wait to taste you. But for right now, this position is working out pretty good I think."

Eve gave up. No longer caring what Dean might think of her behavior, she adjusted her stance to open her legs, and felt his smile against her cheek.

"Now no more talking," he told her, as if he weren't the one carrying on a very one-sided conversation. With one hand on her breast, the other between her legs, he said, "All you have to do is trust me and enjoy."

Trust him? She barely knew him. The thought came and

went so fast, Eve couldn't grasp it. Between the fingers rasping over her nipples and those gliding easily between her legs, the awesome power of the body supporting her and the gentle, damp kisses to her throat and nape, coherent thought remained well out of reach. Sensory overload blocked everything but the pleasure.

Somehow Dean knew when to apply just the right amount of pressure, in the most perfect of places.

Marveling at his ease, at how well he knew her body— better than she knew it, in fact—Eve relished the building orgasm. The things she felt now, the things he made her feel, were stronger than she'd known possible. Sweeter. Tighter.

And coming so fast, she could hardly believe it.

To help ground herself, she dug her fingertips into his thighs. She didn't plan it—she was well beyond planning anything—but she pressed back into him, moving against his erection, wanting all of him, everything.

He never made a sound, never wavered from the rhythm he'd set, but his heartbeat hammered against her shoulder blades, and heat came off him in waves.

Just when she needed it most, he eased one finger slowly, deeply into her, and she heard herself moaning, but didn't care. He caught her nipple between finger and thumb, gently tugging, tugging. . . . It inflamed her more.

"Time to let go," he whispered. His teeth closed on her shoulder in a soft love bite, and as he ordered, the last of her control spiraled away.

The orgasm rolled through her, making her internal muscles clamp around his finger. With a hungry sound of appreciation, he pressed in harder, further. Legs stiff, head thrown back, Eve came—and Dean never missed a beat. He kept her there, in the clench of nearly painful pleasure, for what felt like forever.

Finally he eased his touch and the feelings began to dim. Her legs would have given out, but Dean scooped her up into his arms.

"Where's the bedroom?"

Trying to understand what had just happened, Eve stared at him. She wasn't a nymphomaniac who got off on a simple touch. Like with most women, a blinding orgasm was an elusive thing for her. Hell, *any* orgasm was elusive. Not that she hadn't enjoyed sex before. But . . . she couldn't call this sex.

She didn't know what to call it.

He smiled. "You okay?"

She was . . . foggy and limp, and *very* sated. A pleasant tingling continued in her limbs, ebbing out, pulsing. Her stomach felt both heavy and as light as air.

Dean's smile widened. "Eve?"

In utter amazement, she stared at him. Words wouldn't come, so she cupped the side of his face, touched a bruise on his high cheekbone, another on his rigid jaw.

He was a most remarkable man.

"Damn, woman, you're killing me here." Leaning forward, Dean kissed her parted lips hard and fast. "Where's your bedroom, babe? Or should I find it on my own?"

Awed by his control, her gaze dropped to his mouth. She sighed.

His expression sharpened more. "Never mind. I'll find it on my own."

But he started in the wrong direction so she forced herself to speak, albeit a little breathlessly. "Back through the family room, then to the left of the front door."

"Got it."

He carried her as if she weighed nothing, but then to a macho, bulked-up, superathlete like him, Eve supposed she didn't. After resting her head against his shoulder, she felt compelled to say, "You're good." She knew that wasn't the right word, but stupendous, breathtaking, and out-of-this-world all seemed like overkill.

"Good, huh?" His good humor was inexhaustible. "Well, you can't make that judgment." He glanced down at her with hot eyes and a resolute expression. "Yet."

Languid fulfillment evaporated as new desire sliced into Eve. Her pulse fluttered anew; her lax muscles tightened.

Dean's confidence was almost enough to bring her back to the boiling point. "I'm not sure I can take much more of this."

"Trust me." He narrowed his light brown eyes on her; his arms tightened around her. "You can and will."

Oh, *wow.* The way he spoke, she probably should have been a little worried. He had such a domineering nature, yet . . . he didn't dominate. She knew, because she'd seen him with Roger.

And with Cam.

So far, his personality was so complex that she didn't have a clue what to make of him. But one thing was certain: The sexual chemistry was enough to melt her bones.

At least it was for her. But what about him?

Without removing the comforter, Dean lowered her to the mattress. The designer set had cost a fortune, but when he pulled off his shirt, Eve decided she didn't care.

Lord have mercy.

Could men really look so perfectly sculpted? So incredibly sexy? Even covered in bruises and a few old scars, Dean Conor's bare torso was worth a dozen designer bedding sets.

Knowing he was hurt and seeing it, were two different things. Filled with sudden concern, Eve rose to an elbow. "Dean. Are you sure you're okay?"

He glanced down at the bruises as if he'd forgotten them. "It's nothing."

Sure looked like something to her. Big splotches of purple and green mottled one side of his rib cage and around one shoulder. Low on his left side, more colorful bruises dotted the top edge of his hipbone.

Compassion nearly smothered her. "That has to be painful."

"Right now," he whispered, "I can't feel a thing." He stared at her naked breasts and kicked off his shoes. Showing no reservation, no modesty at all, he opened the fly to his jeans and shoved them down and off, ridding himself of his boxers at the same time.

Ah, so he wasn't unaffected at all. He wanted her. In a *big* way.

Lifting herself on both elbows, Eve savored the sight of him. The obvious battering only made Dean more masculine and larger than life. Most men would still be in bed, nursing their wounds.

Not Dean Conor.

He treated the signs of battle as nothing.

Being so near him played havoc with Eve's peace of mind. She could feel herself falling fast, and blast it, it wasn't just his incredible physique and rugged good looks. She'd known attractive men before. She'd dated plenty of them. Okay, so they weren't as impressive as Dean.

Dealing with mere physical attraction would be an easy thing compared to the mélange of feelings bombarding her now.

The outward packaging was a bonus, but it was his attitude, too, the way he moved with such certainty, and the way he treated her—naturally, without reserve, but also with gentle admiration and acute anticipation.

She'd never felt quite so . . . desired. She'd never been intimate with a man like him.

And the way he'd teased Jacki, how he'd let Cam hug him, even though platonic hugs clearly weren't within his comfort zone. Everything about him appealed to her.

And for now, tonight, he was all hers.

Standing at the side of the bed, Dean smiled down at her—not with amusement, but with sensual promise. "Do you know, Eve, you have a very deep, thoughtful expression going. What are you thinking?"

Oh God, she could add mind reader to his many other attributes. Licking dry lips, she looked him over again. "I'm thinking that you're the most devastating man I've ever met."

For whatever reason, her compliment made him scowl. "If you want to get dreamy on me, at least let me give you reason first." So saying, he caught her knees and parted them enough to let him step between her legs.

Excitement jolted through her again.

Dean's body hair was a shade or two darker than the light brown hair on his head. Her brother had claimed that a lot of the fighters waxed off their body hair to show off their tattoos and muscles.

Not Dean. Running her hands along his chest, she said, "I'm glad you left your chest hair alone."

His brow shot up, as if she'd finally taken him by surprise. He snorted. "I don't have time to fool with that crap."

"Good."

Muscles flexed as he moved, bunching and stretching. The man was so ripped that he couldn't have a single ounce of fat on him anywhere. And everything on him was . . . big. Hands, feet, shoulders, biceps, chest.

Erection.

He saw the direction of her thoughts and murmured low, "Not so fast this time."

Eve dropped her head back and closed her eyes in disbelief. Fast? He called that excruciating teasing in the kitchen *fast*?

Smoothing his big palms from her knees to the tops of her thighs, then over her hips, Dean caught the waistband of her panties. He dragged them down as far as they'd go, given that he stood between her parted thighs.

But it was far enough.

While he stared at her, he trailed his fingertips over her stomach, her hipbones, from one thigh to the next. It might have been a tickling touch, except that she was too aroused to be ticklish.

He brushed his fingers between her legs in one brief, tantalizing stroke.

Suddenly he stepped back and stripped her panties down to her ankles, and off. "How do I get this dress off you?"

She forced her eyes open. "There's a zipper in the back."

That sexy, crooked smile appeared again. "Then over you go." And that easily, he flipped her onto her stomach. But instead of opening her zipper, he paused, and a second later, Eve felt his breath at the base of her spine. "You have such a sexy ass."

With no more warning than that, Eve felt him kissing her there, all over. She knotted her fingers in the comforter. "Dean . . ."

He gave one last nibble to her cheek and raised himself again to tackle her zipper. Once he had it open, he turned her back over and she helped him strip away the dress.

Expression taut, he stood there looking at her naked body. Without taking his gaze from her, he reached for his jeans and found a condom. "You on the pill?"

He was so calm and matter-of-fact about everything. "Yes."

"Good. Can't be too careful these days." He rolled on the condom and came down over her, his hips settling between her legs. As if his patience had run out, he took her mouth in a devouring kiss.

But he didn't enter her, and he didn't move except to kiss her senseless. The man knew how to kiss. He knew how to consume.

And she was starting to feel desperate again. The second he freed her mouth, she said, *"Dean?"*

"How about bowling?" He rose to his elbows, surveyed her breasts, and bent to lick her left nipple.

Eve inhaled a startled breath and rasped, *"Bowling?"*

"You don't like to bowl?"

How could he talk, or expect her to talk, while he did that? She moaned instead.

"Is that a yes? I thought we could make that our second date. I'm a good bowler. Not great, but I can hold my own."

He had to be kidding. But if that's how he wanted to play it, so cool and detached, she'd give it a go. "Bowling is good—" He latched onto her nipple and began sucking softly.

Forgetting all about his fresh bruises, Eve gripped his back and arched into him.

When he lifted away to switch to her other breast, he said, "Great. Bowling the day after tomorrow," and then he drew on that nipple, too.

He was so leisurely yet so thorough that within minutes Eve was nearly mindless again. She writhed against him, ready to insist that he stop playing and get on with business.

"I was thinking—"

"Shut up, Dean."

"I'm serious. Maybe we should get to know each other better."

Eve grabbed his face and held him close. "Knock it off, Dean." *Please.*

He moved to the side of her and rested one hand low on her belly. "No, I'm serious. Tell me something about yourself."

He *looked* serious, damn him. After grinding her teeth in frustration, Eve asked, "What do you want to know?"

"Everything." He stared into her eyes and lowered his hand between her thighs. "But let's start with whether or not you like oral sex."

Clever fingers slowly searched over her, then into her. Deep, then pressing deeper still. Withdrawing, circling, sinking in again.

He tormented her on purpose, but she couldn't bring herself to protest. *"Yes."*

"You do like it?"

She nodded. "Yes. I . . . *Yes.*"

Watching her, keeping her caught in his probing gaze, Dean pressed into her again. When her hips lifted off the bed, he said, "Ah. Right there, huh?"

Exactly right there.

He brought his thumb into play, gliding ever so lightly over her already supersensitized flesh. Again, then again—until she moved her hips against his hand, trying to increase the pressure.

Voice deep and rough, he asked, "Giving or getting?"

Not understanding, Eve shook her head.

"Do you like being kissed here, Eve?" And he pressed his fingers into her while rolling his thumb over her in a deliciously provoking rhythm.

A great pulsing started inside her, and she knew she would come again. Very soon.

"Yes," she whispered, trying to hold back, wanting to feel his mouth on her now that he'd mentioned it and gotten her imagination all hyper.

Somehow, without his expression changing at all, she saw his pleasure and a new heightened level to his own arousal.

"Just what I wanted to hear." He bent over her until his mouth touched her rib cage. As he moved off the bed to kneel on the floor, he trailed his tongue down her abdomen, and then to her navel.

Eve was rigid, her breath held, her heart pounding.

"You smell so damn good." He nipped her hip bone with his teeth. She jumped, then squeezed her eyes shut and again clenched her hands in the bedding.

The cool silk of Dean's hair drifted over her inner thighs as he opened her legs more, urging her to bend her knees, to bare herself to him completely. She did so—and held her breath.

For three heartbeats, there was utter stillness in the room, and Eve knew he was looking at her. It must not have been enough for him, though, because he parted her with his fingers, too. Just when she thought she couldn't take another second of his silent scrutiny, he made a small, rough sound and she felt his breath, his mouth, his tongue.

The intense intimacy of it drew her tight, making her muscles spasm. She arched, twisting against him, then away from him because it was almost too much.

Dean obviously didn't know how to be timid about *anything*. He hooked his arms around her legs. The hold kept her still so that she couldn't retreat from the overwhelming pleasure. Within seconds, another orgasm racked her. Dean didn't withdraw.

He continued to eat at her, insatiable, relentless.

Tangling a hand in his hair, Eve moaned. "No more." His tongue moved over her again, and she cried out. "Dean, it's too much. Please."

Leisurely, he licked his way back up her body to her mouth. He treated her to small kisses and a few warm nuzzles that were somehow as erotic as everything that had come before them.

Tears blurred her vision. "I feel shattered."

He raised himself up enough to look at her, his expression tight, dark. Expectant. His jaw clenched. He cradled her face in his hands.

And in one long, deep thrust, he entered her.

Eve cried out with the shock of it, the pleasure of having him finally fill her.

His gaze burned her. No more smiles. No more teasing. "I'm glad that woke you up." He tilted her chin up and kissed her more thoroughly. Against her lips, he murmured, "You taste so fine."

She should have been embarrassed—to have done the things they had so soon after meeting and then to have him comment on that intimacy in such carnal terms.

But . . . Dean began a slow, easy yet deep rhythm, and somehow, in some outrageous way, Eve felt herself responding again. Amazing. So amazing that she just couldn't muster up the strength to blush.

"You . . . overwhelm me, Dean."

His fingers tunneled further into her hair, and he put his forehead to hers. "Good." He spoke without breaking his slow, driving rhythm. "Because from the second I saw you in that back-ass bar, you've been under my skin."

Even through the sensual fog sifting around Eve, that sounded nice. Really nice.

This time, Eve kissed him. When she started to smooth back his hair, he winced, and she saw stitches high on his forehead. So battered. So strong and capable. So damn sexy. "I'm sorry."

"It's nothing."

Did he make light of all personal injury? Probably. For

whatever reason, that seemed very endearing to her. And sad. And . . .

"No, you don't," he rasped, and he thrust a little harder, rocking her on the bed, making her catch her breath. "Stay with me, Eve. I need you here."

How did he know her thoughts so easily? "I am here," she answered gently.

Holding her gaze, he lowered one hand to cup her breast. His fingertips played over and around her puckered nipple before carefully capturing the very tip and applying a tantalizing pressure.

She gasped, not with pain but with a jolt of red-hot pleasure.

"Better," he whispered.

Turnabout was fair play. And after climaxing twice, Eve finally felt capable of following through. She started by wrapping her legs high around his waist. Given the intensity of his gaze, he liked that.

Smiling, she put her hands on his shoulders, away from any bruises or scratches. "Dean?"

His jaw clenched. "Hmmm?"

"I do like oral sex."

For only a brief instant, his eyes closed. "Yeah, I figured that out."

She saw that he was close but holding back. "Giving," she whispered low, "as well as getting."

An arrested look of pure, hot lust darkened his face. His big body tensed, and he pulled back, only to reenter her harder, faster. "Good to know."

He left her breast to scoop a hand under her bottom, tilting her hips up so that each forward thrust took him impossibly deep.

Her lips parted on a sharp inhalation.

His fingers contracted on her bottom. "Okay?"

She managed a nod. With Dean, she'd just learned things about herself that she hadn't known before—like how pleasure and discomfort could combine into an irresistible lure.

Her nails bit into his shoulders again.

Dean didn't complain, but he did study her face. "I don't want to hurt you, Eve."

His concern warmed her. He started to ease from her, and she locked her ankles. "You're not. Just the opposite."

He studied her a moment more, then took her mouth in a hungry, wet kiss. Against her lips, he murmured, "Good. Now come for me again."

Again? She couldn't possibly. . . .

"Again, Eve."

The position he held her in ensured that each slick glide stroked along her clitoris while also touching deep inside her, and Eve thought . . . well, maybe she could.

When his body stiffened, all his muscles bunching taut, she held him, closed her eyes, and joined him in release.

Some time later, through the blur of exhaustion and satiation, Eve's head began to clear. It had taken her longer to recuperate this time, but since Dean made no move to leave her, she didn't mind. Against her breasts, she felt the continued pounding of his heart. He was still inside her, but not so much now.

Sweat had melded them together—their stomachs, thighs. Each breath filled her lungs with his scent, intensified from their lovemaking.

Numb, astonished, maybe even thunderstruck, Eve stared into nothingness.

Three times.

Who knew?

Okay, so she'd read about it in books. She thought they were lies because it had never happened to her. She'd never imagined . . . never dreamed. . . .

One thing was certain—after this, after time with Dean, she'd never be the same. Since Dean intended to hightail it out of Harmony sooner rather than later, that was a pretty unsettling thought.

Because she knew, she just knew, no other man would ever measure up to him.

CHAPTER 8

⊱❧⊰

DEAN heard Eve sigh, a long, melodramatic sound that he didn't understand at all. Every time he started to relax, she started pondering things. What things, he didn't know. But he didn't like it when she turned too thoughtful and got that wary look in her blue eyes.

Maybe women had come too easily to him before now. He'd never really thought about it. But looking back, all the way to when he'd been no more than a teen, he realized that whenever he'd wanted sex, a willing female was easy to find.

He wasn't a man to fool himself, so he had to admit to the possibility that part of his attraction for Eve was her emotional distance. Physically she didn't deny him. Even after they'd disagreed about his sisters, she hadn't shut him out, hadn't used sex to try to manipulate him. It wouldn't have worked anyway, but . . . she couldn't have known that.

Was she just too honest to play those games?

Just as Dean didn't like fooling himself, he didn't like

brooding. Life for him was clear-cut. Black and white. Plain and simple.

Or at least it used to be.

Dean lifted his head to look at her, then couldn't resist kissing her. And once he started, he didn't want to stop. For her part, Eve didn't move, didn't even pucker.

It didn't discourage him. He'd exhausted her, and he knew it. She knew it, too. He deepened his kiss, his tongue in her mouth, his possession complete when he'd never before thought about anything as barbaric as possessing a woman.

When he finally felt her stirring, he rolled to his back beside her. She wasn't ready to give him one hundred percent again yet, and that's all he wanted. All he'd accept.

Letting out a long breath, Dean stared at the ceiling. He felt pleasantly sated, a little sweaty, and . . . unnerved. A first for him. Sexual encounters did not leave him feeling like this.

Apparently sexual encounters with Eve did.

As he lay there, he could practically hear her thinking. He could feel her heat. He could smell their combined scents and the scent of sex.

Damn, but he felt attuned to her, and he didn't really like it. Now that he'd had her, shouldn't some of his edgy awareness be gone? Shouldn't he be able to look at her with less . . . appetite?

Dean turned his head to test that theory, but instead of detachment, he noticed Eve's closed eyes, how her arms rested limply at her sides, palms up. She looked really soft and warm and cute, despite her tangled hair and smudged makeup.

More than anything, he wanted to start again, to make her scream a few more times, to show her . . . *what*?

Running a hand over his face, he contemplated his own obscure motives. He'd really been the show-off, when usually he didn't care about proving anything to anybody.

So he was a hell of a good lover?

So what?

His teeth locked. So he wanted Eve to know it, that's what. He wanted her to remember him, always.

But why? Sure, he liked satisfying a woman. In fact, he insisted on it. Any man worth his salt would see to a lady's orgasm first. He'd always enjoyed those female sounds of pleasure, feeling the way a woman would curl her body around him in her excitement, the way satisfaction darkened her eyes.

But he couldn't recall ever pushing a woman so hard before. Hell, if Eve hadn't started talking about oral sex—which his brain had visually and graphically equated to her giving him a blow job—he probably would have pushed her over the edge a few more times before letting himself come.

Foolish. And irresponsible. And delicious and carnal and . . .

He was still recovering from his last fight. He wasn't in the best of shape, certainly not in shape for a sexual marathon.

Yet he wanted her again. Right now.

And short of that, he wanted to touch her. To pull her against his side. Snuggle with her.

Shit.

Dean put his hands behind his head, and he'd damn well keep them there.

Eve shifted beside him. With a sleepy, luxuriant sound, she rolled to her side and gazed at him dreamily.

Dean waited for her to compliment him, to admit to his exceptional lovemaking skills.

She yawned. "It's getting late."

Dean's brows crunched down at that not-so-subtle hint. The way things had gone, he figured he'd be welcome for the night.

Damn it, he didn't want Eve to dismiss him. And he sure as hell didn't want to get up and leave—which was a major first. He generally liked to end the night alone in his own bed, wherever his bed might be at the time. No commitments. No misunderstandings.

Not that he used women. He took, but he also gave. He was generous. Eve could vouch for that.

But tonight, right now, her bed suited him just fine. He was already comfortable. And damn tired.

Pretending he hadn't gotten the hint, Dean glanced at her. "Tell me something about you."

"Other than my sexual preferences, you mean?"

Despite his exhaustion, his dick stirred, prompting him to say, "Up to you."

She laughed, then put her hand on his chest and stroked lightly over some deep bruises. "I don't know. You go first."

"I saved an old lady once."

That surprised her.

It damn near floored him.

Bragging? Since when did he brag? *Never.* He detested braggarts. So why had he brought it up? To convince Eve that he was some kind of hero?

He felt asinine.

Eve propped herself up on an elbow. "What do you mean, you saved her? Her life?"

Too late to pull back now. "Yeah." Dean shrugged to make light of it. "Not a big deal really."

"Wow." When he didn't continue, she nudged him. "Tell me."

Disgusted with himself, Dean stared at the ceiling. "She was about sixty-five, I think. One second she was gabbing up a storm, then she keeled over. Heart attack or something like that. Everyone stood around looking at her, trying to decide what to do."

"Where was this?"

"At an outdoor arena in California. I was signing autographs with some other SBC fighters. We'd been there for hours. The lady was in my line, about ten people back. I noticed her because I don't normally get women that age wanting my autograph. It's mostly guys of all ages and younger women."

Her eyes narrowed over the "younger women" comment, but she said nothing.

"Anyway, one second she was fine, then boom—she hit the pavement like a bag of wet cement. I remember the sun was really bright that day, and I could see her turning blue."

"Oh my God. How awful."

"Yeah." Dean scrutinized Eve's expression. She looked appropriately appreciative of the situation, so maybe telling her wasn't such a lame idea after all. "There was all this immediate chaos. The woman she'd been talking to started screaming and crying, and folks were trying to calm her down. One of the guards at the event called nine-one-one, but he was so excited, he wasn't making much sense. Someone tried pouring water on her face, but she didn't stir at all. After that, no one did anything. They just looked at her and fretted."

"Except for you?"

Dean made a face. "I asked if anyone knew CPR, and got all these blank, horrified stares in return, so I did what I could."

"You resuscitated her?"

"I guess. When the paramedics got there, I was still working on her. I started to get out of their way, but they told me I was doing fine and to keep it up while they got out a gurney and med kit and some other stuff. Then the lady started sputtering and gagging and I backed up real quick."

Eve grinned at him.

"Once she was breathing, the EMTs took over and within a few minutes the ambulance was on its way to the hospital."

"You know for sure that she made it?"

"I called the hospital and checked." A reluctant smile pulled at him. "A few months later, she came to one of my fights, and Simon, my manager, brought her around back to meet me."

"She must have been excited."

He shook his head, remembering. "She'd brought me flowers."

"No kidding."

"Big yellow roses." Simon had put the stupid things in water and toted them along when they left the arena. They'd lasted nearly a week. "She claimed the paramedics told her that she would have died without me. I don't know if that's true, but she seemed to believe it."

Eve tenderly smoothed his hair away from the stitches. "It's a good thing you knew CPR."

"I didn't."

She froze, her eyes widening. "Then how—"

"Like most people, I'd seen it done in movies. And I figured she was dying anyway, so it wasn't like I could hurt her by trying." He shrugged. "That night, after I won the fight, I brought her up on the mat and had the photographers take a few photos for her. She blushed like a schoolgirl—but she loved it."

"That was so sweet of you."

Dean frowned. "It wasn't sweet. It's just that she'd been in my line for an autograph when she collapsed."

"So you felt responsible?"

"No. But I figured giving her a little attention was the least I could do."

Eve looked at him with awe and with some softer emotion that Dean couldn't nail down. He didn't know if he liked it or not. And that made him uneasy.

"It's funny how most people will stand there, waiting for someone else to do something, instead of trying." Her gaze tripped down his body and back up again. "But you're not that type of man, are you?"

Oh hell. She sounded all mushy now. "I'll tell you one thing, I still catch crap from the guys."

"Why?"

"Are you kidding? I gave an old lady mouth-to-mouth. At the time, no one was laughing. But now? Some of them insist that I molested her, that she was breathing just fine before I took her to the ground. Others claim she was faking, and I fell for it." They'd said other, more crude things, but Dean didn't share those. They were said in jest, and he had a feeling Eve wouldn't appreciate the humor.

"Gee, why am I not surprised?" She rolled her eyes. "I mean, men are all so mature."

Dean laughed. "Your turn. Tell me something about you."

She leaned over and kissed him. Then, uncaring of her nudity, she flopped onto her back. "The problem is that I've never saved anyone or done anything half as interesting as professional fighting."

"Well, hell, I hope not."

"Let me think about it for a minute."

After a sideways look ripe with impatience, Dean left the bed and went into her private bath. Outside he could hear the storm still raging, with rain and wind lashing the windows.

When she still said nothing, he decided to help her along. "You attended college?" he prompted through the open door.

"Locally. I majored in PR and later attended a tourism and hospitality management program."

"You ever been anywhere else?"

"Just on vacations. Never any place exotic."

"No desire to move, to maybe see the rest of the country?" As he spoke, he cleaned up, ridding himself of the condom and again wondering if Eve would make him leave in the storm. If that's what she planned, he wouldn't make it easy on her.

"Harmony is home. My family and friends are here. I wouldn't mind visiting other places, but I can't imagine living anywhere else."

He stepped back into the bedroom in time to see her finish smoothing back the comforter. The moment she saw him, she hustled back into the bed and under a sheet.

Dean didn't wait for an invitation; he stretched out on his side facing her, propped on one elbow.

Eve raised a brow.

Grinning, Dean reached for the sheet, pulled it back, and tossed it to the bottom of the bed. Eve didn't move, except to stiffen.

He looked at her body, from her shapely, lightly tanned

legs to her dark pink nipples, which were now soft and very tempting. His gaze went back to that little belly-button ring. He rested his hand on her stomach, relishing the warm silk of her skin.

She clamped her hand over his. "No way, Havoc. Forget it. I'm done. Finished."

He brought his gaze to hers, wondering if he should test the theory.

Eve drew back. "Seriously." Her fingers tightened on his. "After three . . . Well, I never realized . . . I mean, good God, *three*."

"Yeah."

She let out a long, shaky breath. "I'm definitely done."

Dean felt both charmed and challenged, but he tamped down the urge to show her how easy it'd be for him to change her mind. He smoothed her hair from her face and said gently, "All right."

What looked remarkably like disappointment clouded her blue eyes, but she didn't remark on his easy agreement. "Thank you."

That made him laugh. "You're naked. I'm naked. If we're going to refrain, we need to talk. So tell me, you're what? Midtwenties, right?"

"Twenty-five."

"So in twenty-five years, what has Eve . . ." It suddenly struck Dean how little he knew of her. With as bland an expression as he could muster, he said, "Out of curiosity, what is your last name?"

Eve groaned. "Oh my God, this is sad. I'm naked in bed with a stud who doesn't even know my full name."

"You gotta live life to the fullest."

With absurd formality, she offered him her hand. "Eve Lavon."

Dean accepted the handshake. "So Eve Lavon. What have you been up to during your life?"

"Nothing worth talking about, really." She frowned in thought, gave him an impish smile, and said, "I guess I could tell you how bored I usually am with men."

"Usually?"

"Yes." She laced her fingers with his, probably to ensure his hands didn't wander. "But you don't bore me, Dean. Not at all. I guess because I've never known anyone like you."

He waited, wondering if she'd expound on that.

"Now, don't get skittish," she teased. "I'm not going to ask you to move in or anything."

Dean pulled his hand free so he could cup her chin and turn her face toward him. "I'll admit that we don't know each other that well, but you'll soon discover that I don't get skittish. Ever."

"You don't?"

"No. You're confusing me with someone else. Probably someone who was an idiot—if he got skittish."

She laughed. "If I told you that ever since I was twelve I've wanted a husband and a dog and three kids, maybe even four, in a tidy house with a white picket fence, would that make you skittish?"

"No." Talking with her this long in a bed, both of them buck-ass, had worn on him. But laughing with her had affected him, too. He didn't often laugh with women. Not really with men, either.

And then there were her smiles. And her teasing. And her scent . . . Dean lowered himself over her so that he half covered her and her mouth was only an inch away. "I'm not skittish, but I am relieved that you haven't yet found a guy to fit the bill."

"Oh."

Taking her bottom lip between his teeth, he stroked her with his tongue—and then released her. "So tell me, what about these men bored you?"

She stared at his mouth and breathed heavily. "I'm not sure."

Dean smiled. Yeah, it'd be real easy to change her mind—that is, if she hadn't already changed it on her own. "Maybe they weren't strong enough for you."

Her brows came down. "Strong enough?"

"I bet you crooked your little finger, and they came running. Right?"

At first, she didn't answer. But her frown smoothed away and her chin lifted. "With you, I didn't even have to crook my little finger." Her smile taunted him. "Now did I?"

Dean put one leg over hers, trapping her on the mattress. "Is that how you saw it? And here I thought you were chasing me, not the other way around. Especially after hearing everything you said to Cam."

When he bent to kiss her, she flattened both hands on his chest. "Now wait a minute. I've never chased a man in my life."

Dean nearly laughed—until she added, "But speaking of your sister, I want to know when you're going to see her again."

It was his turn to frown. "I thought we agreed you'd butt out of my business with Cam."

"Nope." She stubbornly shook her head while continuing to hold him at bay. "Not even close. You ordered, and I ignored."

"Leave it alone, Eve."

"No." She pulled him down and kissed him hard—*almost* distracting him. "So when will you see her? I know she's anxious to get to know you and she has so much to tell you. And I'm worried about this storm because her roof—"

Pushing his hand down between their bodies, Dean cupped his fingers over her—freezing her in midsentence. "I have an idea."

"Forget it." Her eyelids sank down. Her voice became ragged. "I mean it."

No, she didn't. "Instead of trying to piss me off, why don't you invite me to stay the night?"

Her eyes opened and she stared at him. "Why would I do that?"

"So we can go for number five."

Her mouth fell open, then closed with a snap. "*Five?* You're kidding, right?"

"No." He began nuzzling his way down to her breasts.

"But . . ." A soft moan escaped her. "What happened to four?"

He reached a nipple, licked a circle around it, and said, "It comes before five. But I'm not fond of even numbers, so I can't stop there." At the same time, he eased two fingers into her.

Her body lifted into his, her arms came around his neck, and her protests died a quick death. In a mere breath of sound, she whispered, "All right. You can stay the night."

JACKI sat at the back booth of the bar and finished filling out the application. Now that she was twenty-one, her employment choices weren't so limited. And Dean was right—she needed to work whether Cam liked it or not.

A wicked crack of lightning flashed across the big window at the front of the bar, followed seconds later by the deep rumble of thunder. She sighed. No doubt, the roof was leaking again. And that meant tomorrow Lorna would complain nonstop about not getting enough sleep and about Cam's hesitation in selling the place.

For sure, Roger would hire her. But she didn't want to work for Roger. It was bad enough that Cam did and that Cam was even considering him for a husband.

Jacki shuddered just thinking about it.

If she got a job here waiting tables and serving drinks, she would probably make a killing in tips. She could help with the expenses and maybe they could keep the house.

Maybe Cam would stop thinking about tying herself to Roger.

The pay sucked, but the hours would work with her class schedule. And how hard could it be to serve drinks? Lots of laughter, lots of fun, many of her friends hanging around. She could handle that. It'd be like a nonstop party.

Jacki finished the application and started toward the front, wending her way around tipsy men and flirting women. Halfway there, she caught sight of a massive man striding up to the bar.

Mouth hanging open, Jacki absorbed the impressive sight of him, tracking her gaze over him from head to toe and back again.

Jeans dark with the rain molded to legs as thick and sturdy as tree trunks. Longish black hair clung to his forehead until he ran a hand through it, slicking it back. A snowy white T-shirt, soaking wet and mostly transparent, glued itself to his upper body, showing off the ample chest hair beneath.

Jacki couldn't get her feet to move. Hell, she could barely keep her heart beating.

He had to be six and a half feet tall, and probably weighed no less than two hundred and fifty pounds—all of it rock-solid, rippling muscle. A variety of tattoos twined around colossal biceps, disappearing into the sleeves of his shirt.

Thickened ears and a few faded scars along the side of his face in no way detracted from his looks.

But his size and outward appearance alone didn't dominate the room.

His booming voice helped.

As did the jovial confidence he reeked.

Along with a quiet determination that had men quickly removing themselves from even his peripheral vision.

Fascinated, Jacki finally got her feet unglued and eased up behind him. The application hung limply in her hand, all but forgotten.

The object of her attention rested his forearms on the top of the bar and stared at Dickey Webster, the night manager and bartender. "I'm looking for Havoc."

Though the thick walnut bar separated them, Dickey took a step back, frowned, and shook his head. "We don't want any trouble here."

The giant grinned. "I don't want trouble, either, my man, so relax. Havoc is a . . . friend."

Dickey didn't look the least bit relieved. "I don't know anyone by that name."

Jacki did. Her heartbeat picked up pace.

"Ah well," said Goliath, "whether you heard his name or not, if you saw him you'd know it. And I have it on good authority that he was heading this way. Knowing Havoc as I do, a bar would have been his first stop."

Huh, Jacki thought. Perhaps he didn't know Dean as well as he thought. While the bartender muttered a quick reply, Jacki glanced at her watch, saw that midnight had long since come and gone, and she shrugged.

This was too interesting not to share.

She pulled out her cell phone and dialed Eve.

After six rings, Eve picked up. Her voice was huskier than usual, a little breathless. "Hello?"

Jacki raised her eyebrows in surprise. "Hey Eve, it's Jacki."

"Jacki?"

Almost laughing, Jacki said, "Yeah, Cam's sister."

"I know who you are." The phone was muffled, she heard some shuffling and muted whispering, and then Eve said, "It's really late, Jacki."

"I know."

"Is something wrong? What is it?"

"Nothing's wrong." Jacki strove for a quizzical tone. "Am I interrupting something?"

"No! No, not at all." More quick shuffling and low whispers. "So . . . uh, what's up?"

Now Jacki did laugh. "Well, I was going to ask if you had Dean's number because I need to talk to him. But seeing as he's right there with you—"

Eve groaned and a second later Dean took the phone. "What is it?"

Well, well, well. Apparently, big brothers didn't like interruptions. "Hey, bro. You don't have to bite my head off."

She heard a long annoyed sigh, then: "I'm not." And in a more even voice, he repeated, "What's going on, Jacki?"

"You know, I'd say nothing and let ya get back to it, really I would."

"Jacki . . ."

Eve's laughter sounded in the background.

"But you see, there's a guy here asking for you. And I sort of thought you should know about him."

More alert, Dean asked, "A guy *where*?"

Oh yeah. "I'm in the Roadkill Bar."

Two seconds of silence passed. "You're kidding."

The bar's name often got that reaction. "Nope. It's a little local place, only about fifteen minutes from my house." She winced. "That is, I mean *our* house."

He let out a long breath, but didn't debate the point. "Partying again?"

In sugary tones, Jacki replied, "Not that it'd matter to you, right?"

His annoyance practically vibrated through the receiver. "Who's asking for me?"

"I don't know, but he's a big sucker. Bigger than you even. And he asked for Havoc, not Dean. He's got shaggy black hair, a mild case of cauliflower ear, some mean tattoos, a few scars—"

"Who's he asking?"

Obviously Dean recognized the description. "Well, it was just the night manager, who's also the bartender, but he didn't know anything. I take it you haven't been in here yet?"

"Eve told me the only bar in town was Roger's idiotic Rodeo Bar."

Jacki chuckled. It didn't surprise her that Dean had the same impression of Roger's joint that she had. "Yeah, well, this isn't exactly the kind of place Eve would visit or remember."

"Yet you're there."

Cutting right past that, Jacki got to the point of her call. "So anyway, right now your friend is making his way around the room. And I don't mind telling you, he's spooking everyone. Some people are picking up and leaving as fast as they can."

Another long sigh. "Let me talk to him."

Holding the phone away, Jacki stared at it in disbelief. Dean had to be joking. She brought it back to her ear. "You want me to go to him, then give him my phone?"

"He'll give it back, brat. Don't worry. Just tell him I'm on the line."

Somehow, the way Dean said "brat," made it sound like an affectionate nickname instead of an insult. Glancing up, Jacki caught sight of the big man and, strangely enough, anticipation squirreled through her.

A reason to approach him. To talk to him.

To make him notice her.

"Yeah, okay, I can do that." Really. She could. "Hang on a second."

Summoning up a core of bravado, Jacki sauntered over, tapped the giant on his . . . well, not quite his shoulder, because his shoulder was *way* up there. She considered herself tall, but her fingertips landed on his shoulder blade.

Startled, he flashed only a brief glance toward her. Then his shoulders straightened and, slowly, he turned back again to give her a more thorough perusal.

His bold scrutiny made Jacki feel buck-naked.

His smile made her heart jump.

His manner both alert and carnal, he took one step closer and stared down at her with chocolate brown eyes. "Hello, darlin'."

On the outside, Jacki smirked at the slick show of interest.

But on the inside, everything fluttered and heated. He had the darkest eyes she'd ever seen, heavily fringed by girlish lashes.

And he had a deep honeyed voice and a way of speaking that . . .

Get a grip, Jacki. She struck a comfortable, slouching pose, one hip jutting out, limbs relaxed. "You want to talk to Havoc?"

Clutching his heart, he made a ridiculous face of torment. "Ah, now, honey, please don't tell me that son of a bitch claimed ya first?" He snatched up her hand, carried it to his mouth, and pressed a damp, warm, *very provocative* smooch to her palm.

Jacki stood there like a frozen lump of female awareness.

A smile made his dark eyes twinkle. "I can promise ya I'm better." Voice going even deeper, he said, "In all ways."

The phone almost dropped out of Jacki's free hand. Her tongue stuck to the roof of her mouth. Then she felt his thumb stroking the heart of her palm, and she yanked her fingers away. "It's not like that."

"No?"

"No."

"Well, thank you, God. I can't tell you how happy I am to hear it." He nodded toward the phone. "'S Havoc on there?"

"Yeah."

"All righty then, business comes first. But once it's out of the way, you and I need to become much better acquainted."

Appalled at her lack of wit and retort, Jacki shoved the phone toward him. "Here. Take your time."

Needing some space, Jacki started to turn away, but then she heard him say into the phone, "Gawd almighty, Havoc. The cutest little wet dream just strutted up to me and—what's that?" His voice lowered to a growl. "You're bullshitting me, you bastard. You don't have a sister."

Jacki turned to look at him, but he didn't notice.

He paused, and with his voice raised again, he blurted, "*Two?* No fucking way."

Jacki grinned.

A sour expression crossed his face, and he winced at whatever Dean said.

Running a hand roughly through his already tousled hair, he barked, "How the hell could you have sisters and no one know about it?"

Deciding she didn't want to give him any privacy after all, Jacki strolled back and leaned against the wall beside him. When he glanced at her, she smiled.

His gaze automatically started to drift down over her, then he caught himself and snapped it back up to her face. Appearing chagrined, he scowled and propped a fist on his hip.

Whatever Dean said to him, the giant listened intently. "Right. Hang on." He turned to Jacki again. This time he went ahead and quickly looked her over before pinning her in place with a mesmerizing stare. "I don't suppose you got a pen and paper on ya, do you, darlin'?"

"For what?"

"I need to write down Havoc's address."

She waggled her fingers for the phone, the big guy handed it back to her, and Jacki asked, "Where're you staying, Dean? Yeah, I know where that is. I can give him directions."

Dean said, "Good. You do that. And then why don't you think about heading home instead of hanging out there any longer?"

Lip curling, she taunted, "What's the matter, bro? Worried about me?"

"Not even a little. But with Gregor there—"

"Gregor? That's his name?" Jacki looked up—and got snared in that piercing dark gaze again. She swallowed. "He doesn't look like a Gregor."

Without releasing her from the invisible snare, the giant tipped an imaginary hat. "Gregor *'The Maniac'* Marsh. At your service, sugar."

Maniac? "I take it you're a fighter, too?"

He said, "The best."

Dean snorted. "Whatever he tells you, Jacki, don't believe him."

Jacki nodded. "Right. He's a liar. Got it."

Gregor roared with laughter.

"So," Dean said, "will you be heading home now or not?"

"Actually, I will, as soon as I can find a ride." Now that she had a job taken care of, there were other priorities at home. Like a leaking roof. And probably a clogged pool pump. And—

"What do you mean, find a ride?"

Suspicion dripped from Dean's tone, prompting her to explain. "No car, remember? But the bar is packed so I'm sure there's someone here I know."

Much aggrieved, Dean let out a long breath. "Everyone there is drinking."

"I'm not drinking." She started to add that she seldom drank, despite what he might think, but she got sidetracked when Gregor held out his gargantuan arms, offering himself like a sacrifice.

"I haven't had a drop, either, love. Tell your damned brother that I'll see you get home."

Dean must have heard him, because he said, *"No,"* a little too loudly and way too fast.

Keeping the phone at her ear, Jacki looked at Gregor. The name grew on her. So he was a hulk. And a fighter. And far too chauvinistic, with his corny endearments.

Overall, he seemed harmless enough. Going through all the considerations, she said to Dean, "Why not?"

"Yeah," Gregor seconded, "why not?"

The sound of grinding teeth came through the phone. "Jacki, for God's sake, you don't even know him."

"But you do," she reminded him.

Gregor chuckled. "And therein lays the rub."

"Shit." Another long sigh, a hesitation fraught with ripe frustration, and finally Dean said, "Stay put, brat. I'm coming to get you myself."

Jacki's mouth dropped open. Dean had to be kidding. It was late. He was with Eve. He had absolutely no obligation toward her at all. "But . . . that's crazy."

"I'll be there in a few minutes."

"Dean, wait. If I can't find a ride, then there's a bus stop only two blocks away—"

"Do *not* move," Dean demanded. "I mean it."

Her temper flaring, Jacki said, "Now wait one damn—"

And Dean hung up on her, just like . . . a very serious and overprotective big brother.

Huh. Imagine that.

Jacki wasn't sure if she liked Dean's attitude or resented it. For sure, it'd take a little getting used to. She closed the phone and slid it into her pocket.

Pretending to pray, Gregor asked, "So, what's the verdict, darlin'?"

"Sorry." She lifted her shoulders. "Dean's coming to get me himself."

Crestfallen, he muttered, "That rotten SOB."

He gave the insult so dramatically, Jacki couldn't help but laugh. "Look at it this way. It'll take him twenty minutes to get here."

Gregor's expression brightened. "And that'll give us twenty minutes to get familiar with one another." Flashing another sexy, confident grin, he said, "I see a nice private booth there in the back."

Jacki shook her head. "No way. Besides, I have to turn in my application."

"Application for what?"

"Work." As she started away, she explained, "Two women just quit on them, and they're desperate. The night manager already said I qualify, so I'm hoping he'll hire me on the spot."

"To start *tonight*?"

She wished. But obviously the big guy didn't feel the same. Was he really that anxious to spend some time with her? She hoped so. It had been a long time since any guy had intrigued her this much. "He said I'd start the following Monday."

"So you only have to hand in the paper?"

"That's right." She glanced back at him—and caught him staring at her tush. Since her behind boasted the only female curves she had, Jacki didn't mind so much. But if he decided to start eyeing her nonexistent chest, they'd be in trouble.

She paused, their gazes met, and new heat burned in his eyes.

His smile came easily. "And when that's done?"

"We can sit up front, where there are plenty of lights."

She got her feet moving again. "It'll be easier for Dean to spot us that way."

Trailing her, the giant grunted. "Like he could miss me, wherever I sit?"

He had a point. But Jacki wasn't ready to isolate herself with him. And besides, much as she relished his admiration, she wanted a real clear view of Dean when he got there.

Because she'd never witnessed it before, she wanted to see what a worried big brother looked like.

CHAPTER 9

❧

SHE got the job.

Dickey Webster, the very grizzled and grumpy night manager who also tended bar, barely glanced at her application before saying, "You start Monday, eight to two A.M. That work for you?"

It worked just fine, perfect in fact. As a natural-born night owl, Jacki couldn't have chosen better hours for herself. All servers wore the same style apron, supplied by the bar, so she didn't have to worry about a corny or revealing uniform. Jeans and tees would work just fine.

Her days would be Monday, Thursday, Friday, and Saturday, leaving her plenty of time during the week for her new classes.

Contributing to the family income should afford her some say in financial decisions. Relief and excitement at the prospect of finally being heard almost outshone Gregor's presence.

Almost.

Dean's friend had an awesome sense of humor, an infectious laugh, and so much sex appeal, Jacki felt bludgeoned by it. For the eighteen minutes that they sat together, not once did the patrons of the bar, men and women alike, stop staring. The men watched Gregor with wary interest, but the women ogled with prurient greed.

"You sure draw a lot of attention," Jacki commented.

"Honey, that's the pot callin' the kettle black." He took a drink of his cola and then leaned forward with his elbows on the table. "I'm bettin' you get eyeballed everywhere you go."

Jacki shrugged. A fair share of looks came her way, but it didn't change the fact that she was too tall, bone thin, and lacking in the upper works. "Men are easy. For them, it's like a habit. Any female in their line of vision gets checked out. It doesn't mean anything."

He gave her a sly side smile. "Playing coy, huh? Okay, I dig it." He reached for her hand. "Do I need to rhyme? Maybe get on my knees? Play soft music?" He held on to her when she would have snatched her hand away. "Flowers? Chocolates? What's your thing, baby? You tell me, and I'll make it happen."

"I don't know what you're talking about."

"Sure you do. I'm talkin' about wooing you."

She just shook her head, making him smile.

"I take it you're not the romantic type, huh? Great. I gag on all that sappy shit anyway. How 'bout I just cut to the chase and say how delicious you are? Mouthwatering even. So damned sexy that I'm practically—"

"For crying out loud. Knock it off, will you?" She glanced around the room at their oh-so-rapt audience. "Someone might overhear you." Embarrassed, Jacki again tried to tug her hand free—and that's how Dean found them.

One second her brother wasn't there, and then in the next, she felt him breathing down on them.

Gregor must've felt it, too. An arrested expression came over his face. Seconds later, anticipation replaced it. He kissed her knuckles with a flourish before turning toward Dean.

"Damn, you got here fast, Havoc. And here I thought I'd need a pack of hounds to hunt you down. Who knew pursuing your little sister would do the trick?"

"Jacki's nearly six feet tall," Dean pointed out, sounding droll, maybe even bored. "Not really what you'd call little."

"Next to me, she's small." Gregor copped a ridiculous look of surprise. "But wait. No one knew you had a sister, right? We all thought you'd hatched in some damn lab as part of a mad-science project gone bad. So how could I have known she was the trick to getting your ass in gear?"

At Gregor's teasing words, a sick feeling of dread entered Jacki's stomach.

Oblivious, Gregor smiled at her again. "But now I'm on to you. You not only have a beautiful sis but you're a vigilant guardian as well."

"You're an idiot, Gregor."

He snorted. "You were rushing to her rescue. And now you'll have her thinking you don't trust me."

With the weight of a wrecking ball, comprehension crashed down on Jacki: Gregor's pursuit had more to do with irking Dean than winning her over.

He'd out and out used her.

And she'd been stupid enough to let him.

Slouching back in her seat, she waited to see how Dean would handle the situation.

He said to Gregor, "I'm here to give her a ride, that's all."

"Because I offered her a ride, and you don't want your baby sister around me."

Dean slashed a hand through the air. "I'm not that kind of brother, damn it."

"Is that right?" Gregor left his seat. He stood toe to toe with Dean, but he had a couple extra inches in height. "So what kind of bro are ya? I'm askin' for future reference, you see. Bein' as I'm smitten and I plan to stick around town awhile."

Jacki stared. Gregor actually expected to keep on using her?

Over her dead body.

Needing him to know that she was on to him, Jacki waited until she had his attention, and when she got it, she said, "Asshole."

Gregor's brows shot up, and he roared with deep laughter. "By damn, Havoc, she *is* your sister." And even with that, he somehow managed to look charmed instead of insulted.

But Jacki wouldn't let him fool her again.

"You're wasting your time," Dean told him. "You can't provoke me, so stop trying. If you want a fight, take it up with the SBC officials."

"You know, I'd do exactly that, but they're more inclined to listen to you."

"That's too bad for you, then, because I'm not telling them shit." Dean turned to Jacki. "Let's go."

She nodded and pushed herself out of the booth. "Believe me, I'm ready."

They turned to go, and Gregor muscled his way in front of her. Jacki noted that he moved fast for a gargantuan jerk. "Hold up, darlin'."

"I am *not* your 'darlin'.'" He started to speak, and she stopped him by taking a step closer. "I'm not your 'honey' or your 'love,' either. My name is Jacki, and if you ever speak to me again, you ought to remember that."

He went from surprised to conspiratorial. "Ah." He glanced at Dean before nodding at her. "I take it havin' big brother around changes things."

Dean snarled, "I am *not* that kind of brother, damn it."

Both Jacki and Gregor ignored him. "Actually, no. Dean has no influence on me. But how dumb do you think I am?"

"I never said—"

"Anyone can see that your real interest is in egging Dean into a fight."

"No, I—"

"You just passed the time with me in the hopes of getting him to agree. You *used* me."

Gregor smashed two fingers against her lips. "Facing off with your irritating brother is definitely an interest, dar . . ." He cleared his throat. "*Jacki*. But now that I've laid eyes on you, it's not the only interest."

"Yeah, right. Whatever you say." Jacki rallied a believable show of scathing disdain. "Now go bug someone else."

Gregor again blocked her path. He no longer looked so amused or charmed. "Now wait just a damned minute, woman. You have me all wrong."

So near to her back that Jacki could feel his heat, Dean said, "Get out of the way, Gregor."

Caught between both men, Jacki actually felt petite, and wasn't that a first? But she had no time to indulge the novelty of it. "I'm a good judge of character," she told Gregor. "And you're lacking it."

He puffed up with indignation, making himself taller, somehow bigger. To Jacki's surprise, he said to Dean, "A little help here, Havoc?"

"What the hell am I supposed to do?"

"You could start by tellin' the gal that I'd never use her to get you in a fight. That'd be chickenshit and we both know it."

Dean pinched the bridge of his nose, then gave in with a sigh. "He's not chickenshit, Jacki. He's obnoxious and he has a big mouth. And he lacks skill on the mat, as well as patience, but—"

"I said to *help* me," Gregor reminded him dryly, "not crucify me."

"I'm still feeling my last fight. I haven't had enough sleep all week, and you interrupted a very pleasant evening." With each word, Dean crowded closer against Jacki's back. "So tell me, Gregor. Why the hell would I want to help you when I'd rather you just go away?"

Jacki would be deaf for days with the way Dean had just yelled in her ear. And blast Gregor, he looked satisfied with Dean's rising temper.

He even dared to make a tsking sound of reprimand. "Havoc, Havoc, Havoc. I've never known you to lose your cool. You sure you're not feeling protective toward the baby bird here?"

Baby bird? Jacki sucked in air, fueling her outrage. What an insufferable oaf! Using both hands, she shoved Gregor hard. Because he'd been looking at Dean, she took him by surprise and he stumbled back.

Not far, but it gave her enough room to storm away. And she did.

Behind her, she heard Gregor shout, "Darlin', wait." And when she only moved a little faster, he added, "There goes my heart, Havoc. Your little sister just ripped it clean outta my chest."

Dean said, "You don't have a heart, you miserable prick."

A second later, her brother was at her side. He kept pace with her as she left the shelter of the bar's overhang and stomped out into the rain.

"Jacki?"

Mortification kept her from acknowledging him.

"Did anyone ever tell you that you shouldn't physically assault trained fighters who are easily twice your size?"

She couldn't help it. She said, "Ha!"

"And that means . . . what?"

"You were there," Jacki snapped, and she kept walking. Her footsteps were so forceful that puddles splashed up around her.

Dean caught her arm and swung her around. "So you expected me to fight him for you?"

He looked so irate by that possibility, Jacki half-expected steam to rise off his head.

She rolled her eyes. "Of course not. The big idiot wants to fight you in the ring, not in a bar. I just meant that seeing the two of you together assured me he wasn't the type to manhandle women. If he was, you wouldn't have been having a casual conversation with him."

"Why?"

"Because I don't think you'd associate with abusive bullies."

"You can't assume that about me. Hell, you don't even know me."

For only a moment, Jacki touched his jaw. "You're my brother, Dean. I dunno. It's nuts, I agree. But I *do* know you."

Dean scowled at her, propped his hands on his hips, and glanced beyond her—at nothing much. Just more street, noise, and human congestion. His gaze came back to her face. "Where do you think you're charging off to?"

She had no idea. She'd only wanted to put distance between herself and the source of her embarrassment: Gregor. "Your car?"

Very slowly, his gaze measuring her, Dean nodded. "You were headed the wrong way."

He seemed totally unconcerned with the rain, but then, she hadn't noticed it either till just then. Now she felt the chill sinking into her bones, and her hair began to drop in wet clumps over her shoulders.

All because Gregor had infuriated her.

"You can take the lead."

"Gee, thanks." Turning in the opposite direction, Dean started off at a long-legged clip.

Following him half a block up, Jacki saw where he'd parked by the curb. After opening her door and waiting for her to be seated, he circled the hood and got behind the wheel.

Jacki was feeling chilled, wet, and pretty damned stupid until Dean said, "So you think I have some standards when it comes to who I'll associate with? That's what you meant?"

Jacki smiled to herself. For a big tough guy, Dean sure had a hard time accepting that his honor was as apparent as his muscles. "Yup. I may not have known you long, but I can't see you putting up with that nonsense. You insulted Gregor, and you sounded impatient. But you didn't sound sickened by him or anything."

"Sickened?" He scowled at her with grave offense. "I don't get sickened."

"What? That's not macho?"

His expression darkened even more, but he said nothing. He started the car and flipped on the heater. Reaching over the seat into the back, he located a windbreaker and handed it to her.

He put on his seat belt and pulled away from the curb. At that hour, the streets were all but deserted. Harsh wind drove the rain into the windshield like bullets. The wipers could barely keep up.

After a minute, Dean glanced at her. "You're okay?"

"I'm okay. I just feel like an idiot, that's all."

"How come?"

Sighing, she put her head back and stared at the black windshield. "I should have known he wasn't really interested."

"Because . . . ?"

Feeling worse by the second, Jacki slumped lower into her seat and wrapped her arms around herself. Thanks to the rain, she could feel her eye makeup sliding down her face. Her hair hung in heavy clumps to her shoulders. She had mud on the hem of her jeans.

Inside and out, she felt unappealing. And she didn't want to talk about it.

But Dean didn't let it go. "Jacki?"

So much had happened recently, too much for her to handle. She and Cam were scrapping at each other all the time. Little by little, they were losing their house. And now a long-lost brother . . .

Fed up, she fired at Dean, "What do you care anyway?"

He looked startled, but like a pot boiling over, she couldn't stop herself.

"You're not big brother material, remember? You don't care about me." Her shaky voice turned to a sneer. "Or are you worried about Gregor?"

Struggling with herself, Jacki sucked in fast breaths—and finally felt the difference in Dean. He sat right next to her in the car, but his cold distance put miles between them.

Oh God, her awful temper. The sound of tires on wet

pavement and the rage of the storm couldn't drown out the roar of her guilt. "Dean . . ."

"Forget I asked, all right?"

For the first time since meeting him, Dean seemed unapproachable and forbidding. Because of her. He'd come as soon as he got Cam's letter. He'd left Eve's bed just to drive her home from the bar.

It didn't matter what he said, his actions were loud and clear.

A great flash of lightning cut through the concealing blackness of the storm, lighting up the interior of his car.

Jacki wished it hadn't. She wished she hadn't seen his face, so remote and deliberately blank and . . . wary.

What to do? No options came to her—other than honesty. So Jacki curled her legs up onto the seat and turned toward him. He said nothing, didn't even acknowledge her.

"You know I've never dealt with a brother before."

He ignored her, but Jacki refused to be intimidated.

"Naturally I'm going to botch it here and there." Tears swelled in her throat, causing her voice to break. And that pissed her off. She hated nothing more than being a wimpy girl. "You're going to have to give me some time, damn it."

A new emotion—something like awful dread—sucked the air out of the car. Dean glanced at her, then away. "Swear to God, Jacki, if you start crying, I'll pull over right now and put your sorry ass on the curb."

Such a terrible threat to make. But Dean didn't sound like he meant it. He sounded desperate.

Jacki gargled a hideous, weepy laugh. "Yeah, right."

"Try me." He leaned over and opened the glove box to hand her a box of tissues.

"Thank you."

"They came with the rental."

That made her laugh again. And while they were on a high note . . . "It's because he's a big, gorgeous hunk."

"Who is?"

To go from crying to laughing was an odd thing, but

maybe big brothers were good for that sort of thing. "Gregor."

Looking more appalled than she'd thought possible, Dean said, "Don't make me puke."

And with that, she fell into the giggles. Dean suffered her, just rolling his eyes when she'd try to collect herself, only to lose it again.

They were only minutes from her house when he said, "Are you done being hysterical?"

"I wasn't. It's just that you're funny."

"Yeah, and that's why they named me Havoc."

Grinning, Jacki reached over to punch him in the shoulder. "Such a comedian." She studied his handsome profile. "Thank you. I appreciate the concern."

"No problem." Silence reigned for another minute. "I take it we're done talking about Gregor?"

"Definitely." No way would Jacki discuss her insecurity about her boobs with Dean.

He accepted that with a shrug. "So, you go to that bar often?"

"Not really." Half a box of tissues helped to clean up her ruined makeup, but there wasn't much she could do about her hair. "I've been there a couple of times. The other day I noticed a HELP WANTED sign, so I put in an application."

"Why there?"

"Why not there?"

Exasperation showed in the way he adjusted his hold on the steering wheel. "It's a bar, probably overflowing with men who've had too much to drink."

"And here I was thinking it was your kind of place."

"Exactly."

Yep, her brother was a regular joker. "I've thought about what you said."

He groaned. "What'd I say?"

"You know, about working and going to school both. I can do it. I know I can. It's just that Cam has always insisted I shouldn't, and it was easier to let her have her way than to do what I know is right."

"It wasn't my place. I should have kept my mouth shut."

Jacki was glad he hadn't. "You made perfect sense, Dean. All the financial pressure shouldn't fall on Cam." She hid her grin when she added, "And now I can use you as backup when Cam has a fit, because I've already been hired."

As Dean turned down her street, his headlights cut across the wet landscape. They'd driven out of the worst of the rain. Now only sprinkles remained, with the low rumble of thunder off in the distance.

Dean's expression didn't change, but she felt his consternation. "Jacki—"

"I know, I know." She patted his shoulder in understanding. "You're not that type of brother. Don't worry about it."

She heard him mutter, "Shit," real low, and then, "Couldn't you have applied at a dress shop in the mall or something?"

Jacki snorted. "Yeah, right. For minimum wage? Thanks but no thanks." They'd be home soon. She regretted it. It was kind of nice, talking with Dean like this. "I'll get two bucks more an hour at the bar, plus the tips are great. And in case you haven't noticed, I'm hardly the mall clerk type."

A brief smile appeared before Dean asked, "What is a mall clerk type?"

She didn't have to think about it. "Perky."

"You're not perky," he agreed.

"Most of those dippy girls in the mall are ex-cheerleaders, real into designer duds and flirting and fashion." She looked out the passenger window. "Too much of that and I'd go nutty."

Dean actually laughed. "Yeah, it'd make me a little crazy, too."

She turned back to him, wanting his support, though she didn't know for sure why. "The late hours at the bar suit me. Unlike Cam, I'm not a morning person. And it's part-time so it won't interfere with school. It's close enough that getting a ride there and back shouldn't be a big problem. But when it is, there's a bus stop only a few blocks away."

"A bus stop," he repeated without much enthusiasm. He nodded, chewed his upper lip. "You mentioned that on the phone."

"Before you hung up on me."

Again his fingers tightened and then loosened on the steering wheel. "Listen, I'm not playing protective older brother or anything like that."

Yeah, he was, Jacki realized. But she said only, "Got it."

"Do you think it's a good idea to be walking around down there alone at night? It didn't look like the best section of town to me. Two blocks away is far enough that if you got into trouble, who'd hear you if you called out for help?"

"I won't get into trouble." She hoped. But damn it, now Dean had spooked her. The area wasn't that bad, but it also wasn't well lighted or very busy in the evening.

"I don't know . . ." Their eyes met, he studied her for a brief instant, then shrugged. "But hey, you're an adult. I'm sure you know what's good for you."

He didn't sound at all convincing.

They pulled up in front of her house. "I'd like to make one suggestion—" Dean stalled midsentence. His face went blank with disbelief. "No fucking way."

The sudden expletive took Jacki by surprise. She leaned forward to look through the front windshield. She followed Dean's gaze, and saw . . . her sister on the roof!

"Damn it." Jacki quickly undid her seat belt and opened her door. "The stupid roof must be leaking pretty bad for her to be up there right now."

"No way." Dean shook his head. "Your sister is not on that roof in the middle of an electrical storm. Wait a minute. What the hell is she doing? Is she holding . . . *plastic*?"

Jacki left the car. "Yeah, she is. Sometimes when it rains this hard, the upstairs leaks, especially the ceiling in Aunt Lorna's room. I better go help her." She leaned into the car, wondering how mushy she ought to get. She settled on saying, "Thanks for picking me up, Dean. I really enjoyed our chat."

"Oh, no you don't."

For the first time, Dean looked outright furious, more like Havoc than the man he'd shown her so far.

It was something. Impressive. A little scary.

And confusing.

Jacki pulled back. "Is something wrong?"

With nothing more than a dark expression, he turned off the car and got out. His slammed car door sent an echo along the wet, empty streets. Jacki winced.

Still muttering, Dean made a beeline through the rain-soaked yard to the side of the house where Cam struggled with a sheet of plastic.

Jacki hustled after him.

He stopped just below where her sister worked. Standing back far enough that he could see Cam from the glow of the streetlamp, he propped his hands on his hips and bellowed, "Just what the hell do you think you're doing?"

CHAPTER 10

C AM nearly fell off the roof.

She'd been so intent on wrestling with the stupid plastic against the wind and rain that she'd barely noticed when the car pulled up out front. In the back of her mind, she'd assumed a neighbor had just gotten home. Not for a single second had she expected such a late-night visit from Dean.

What was he doing here?

She called down, "Dean?"

Jacki answered. "Hi, Cam. Dean gave me a ride home."

Cautiously approaching the side of the wet roof, Cam peered down at her brother and sister.

Brother and sister.

Damn, it struck her again. Despite the current circumstances of being stuck on the roof in a storm, happy tears leaked into her eyes. From the moment she'd met Dean, she'd been fighting off a good cry.

A happy cry.

But neither Dean nor Jacki seemed sappy about it, so she refused to let them hear her weep.

It was dark enough that they wouldn't notice, and with the rain pelting all three of them, the tears were likely hidden anyway.

So frustrated and cold that her teeth chattered, Cam gripped a fistful of the thick plastic and concentrated on making her voice steady. "Where were you, Jacki?"

Throwing up his hands, Dean laughed in disbelief. He stomped two steps closer to the house and glared up at her. "What the *hell* does that matter right now?"

Cam's knees started to shake from her awkward positioning on the slanted roof. "I didn't know she was out."

As if she were too stupid to realize it, Dean slowly and precisely growled, "You're on the roof, Cam. In a storm." And then his back stiffened in added horror. "Are you in your *nightgown?*"

His nasty tone nettled her. She'd pulled on a housecoat. But once the rain started pouring into the house—as she'd known it would—what else could she have done? Taken the time to dress? Waited until the next day, after more damage had occurred?

She didn't have the money to call someone for repairs. She didn't have anyone she could ask for help, except Roger, and he'd helped far too much already.

The stupid plastic caught on the wind and twisted around her legs. She pushed wet knots of hair from her face. Lips stiff and voice crackling, she said, "I have to finish tacking this down. If you two want to go inside, I'll be right there to make some coffee."

For a second, Cam thought Dean might somehow fly up to the roof and throttle her. He appeared more than capable of it. And it was odd, because not much light reached them at that corner of the yard, but she had not a single doubt as to his feelings at that moment.

Then suddenly he calmed. "Where's the ladder?"

Cam didn't know what to make of his new mood. "Around back. Why?"

"I want you to come down from there." He walked away before she could explain she wasn't finished.

Cam carefully freed herself from the restraining plastic and inched her way back to the point of the roof where she thought most of the rain entered.

A minute later, a big, warm hand circled her elbow. "Enough, Cam. You'll go down the ladder and into the house. Dry off, then go ahead and make coffee if you want. Or better yet, have Jacki make it."

How the heck had Dean gotten up there so quickly? And he wasn't stooping, the way she did, trying for better balance. He stood straight and tall.

She shook her head. "Jacki doesn't know how. She's never made coffee."

"Then it's about time she learned. She's not an idiot. She can read the directions on the can. Tell her to do it and she will."

Cam blinked at him. And her shivers of cold turned to trembling annoyance. "I can't go in just yet. I still have to—"

"No, you don't. I'll take care of it."

More than anything, she wanted to say, "Okay," and get inside where it was warm and dry. But she'd been independent too long to let a beloved brother come on the scene and order her around. "Thank you. That's very nice of you. But I can't—"

"Yes. You can." That odd steel thickened his words. "You will."

Her brows crept down. "If you really want to help, since you're up here anyway, that's fine. But I've only got one hammer and a small pack of tacks with me."

"That's all I need."

He could be right. "You could hold down the plastic while I tack it in place. We'd get done quicker that way." The idea of working with him pleased her. "Between the two of us—"

"You'll be in my way."

Somehow, without her even realizing it, he'd managed

to urge her over to the ladder. Jacki stood at the bottom, waiting for her.

"This is my . . ." Her words trailed off. Arguing that it was her roof, after she'd spent dinner convincing him the house was partly his, didn't seem like the best tack to take. "It's my responsibility."

"Not anymore." Dean held her arm tightly. "Careful now. The rungs are wet."

He waited for her to get on the ladder.

The soaked nightgown and housecoat clung to her knees. The sneakers she'd tied on in haste squished with every step she took.

Seeing no hope for it, she got on the top rung, but then hesitated. "What are you going to do?"

"Find where it's leaking, first."

"I already did that. I was covering the leaks with plastic."

He glanced back at her lumpy layers of plastic. "I don't think so."

"But—"

"Most leaks come from lost or loose shingles or cor-roded metal flashing, especially around the chimney. Some are from open joints."

He didn't understand. "I was using the plastic to cover the places where the water is coming into Aunt Lorna's ceiling."

His long sigh sent hot breath across her chilled cheeks. "You don't know what you're talking about, Cam. I'm sorry, but you don't. Where it comes through the ceiling doesn't usually have much to do with the location of the leak on the roof. Water can travel on the underside of sheathing or down roof rafters before dropping off in one or more places inside."

"It does?"

"Look, the longer I stand here explaining it to you, the wetter I'm getting and the more likely we both are to slip off here and break our asses."

She'd never had anyone talk to her like that. For some

reason, it made her want to grin. She pinched her lips shut and nodded.

Suspicious, he stared at her. "Just trust me. I know what I'm doing."

"Okay." She really did trust him. And that in itself felt remarkably good. "Be careful."

"You think?" The words no sooner left his mouth than he shook his head and dropped the sarcasm. "Go on. I'll be down in a few minutes."

He held her secure as she maneuvered into position on the ladder, then released her as she lowered herself.

Cam wanted to thank him or . . . something. But she didn't know what to say, and Dean had already turned away to get to work.

She climbed down, walked past her wide-eyed sister, and went inside.

Compared to the stormy night, the house felt almost muggy and too warm. God, she hoped that didn't mean the air was on the fritz, too. One more catastrophe and selling the house wouldn't help. They'd be too far in debt.

Knowing she was alone, and with the lights off, Cam removed her wet night clothes and sneakers, dumped them into the laundry room, and dashed upstairs to dress.

Seconds later, Jacki cracked her door open and slipped in. While Cam towel dried her hair, Jacki stood there against the closed door, looking anxious and edgy.

"Is something wrong?"

Jacki blurted, "This is weird as hell, that's all."

"Weird?" Setting the towel aside, Cam slipped into slacks and a loose top. "Dean showing up and insisting on helping, you mean?"

"Yeah." Jacki came in and sat on the edge of Cam's bed. She faltered a moment before announcing, "I got hired on at the Roadkill Bar."

Cam had just started to drag her wide-toothed comb through her tangled hair. But at her sister's statement, she brought her head up sharply. "You did what?"

"Don't bitch, Cam. Dean was right. I need a job, and that's the job I want. I start Monday."

Is that how Jacki saw her concern, as bitching? A little hurt, Cam nodded. "I see."

"The thing is, Dean found out I was there and he insisted on driving me home."

"How did he find out?"

All quiet and conspiratorial, Jacki leaned forward. "He left Eve to come get me."

"Eve?" How had Eve gotten involved in this convoluted story?

"They were . . . you know"—Jacki's eyebrows bobbed and her mouth curled—"having a good time."

Her hair forgotten, Cam took a seat on the bed beside Jacki. "How do you know?"

"I called Eve to see if she had Dean's number, since he didn't give it to either of us, but we both saw them connect at dinner. Right?"

Connect seemed like a mild word compared to how Dean and Eve had sexually collided. "Right."

"So I called her, and when she answered, I could tell she hadn't been sleeping."

"Wait, back up." Prying into Eve's personal life didn't feel quite right. She needed a moment to assimilate things. "Why did you want Dean's number?"

"It's a long story that I'll be happy to share later. But you see, Eve didn't tell me Dean's number." Jacki leaned closer. "She just handed the phone to him."

"What time was this?"

"Not more than an hour ago. And Dean didn't exactly try to hide the fact that I'd interrupted."

It all seemed like too much to take in. "Dean was rude to you?"

Jacki laughed. "Considering the situation, he was fine."

Eve and Dean, intimate already? Well, Eve had made it clear how Dean affected her, but still . . . Cam shook her head to clear it. "Why didn't you call me for a ride?"

Jacki flopped back on the bed. "How did I know you'd ask that?"

"I'd like to think we're still close."

Jacki groaned. "So we're not going to talk about Eve and Dean?"

It wasn't any of their business, but . . . "Maybe later." Right now, emotional and physical exhaustion pulled at Cam. She couldn't think clearly. "I would have come for you, Jacki."

"I know. But you had a full day. Why should you be responsible for me?"

Fierce protectiveness reared up inside Cam. "You're my sister."

"Yeah, sure. But I'm twenty-one, not twelve. Only a few years younger than you." Jacki rose up on her elbows. "Do you realize that just because Mom and Dad died, you treat me like I'm fragile?"

Did she? Cam bit her lip, knowing that she did. But she loved Jacki so much that she didn't ever want her to feel alone.

The way she often had.

"Dean's a hoot." Jacki bounded back off the bed and paced the confines of Cam's midsized bedroom. As a night owl, Jacki was more awake now than at any other time of the day. "Talking to him isn't like talking to other guys, though."

"He's your brother." Cam gave up on her hair and pulled it into a damp, snarled ponytail. "We've never had any male relatives around and no close male friends. Naturally, Dean's interaction with you would feel different from other men."

"Right. I get that. But he's a brother who doesn't know us, Cam. He can't possibly care about us."

Cam didn't know about that. After all, she barely knew him, but she cared. A lot.

A sudden hammering on the roof had them both going still.

"He found the hammer."

Jacki grinned. "Sounds like. And I'd say he's not cautiously tapping in tacks the way you do."

They both winced when heavy footfalls sounded across the roof, and then more hammering.

A door banged open in the hallway. "*What* is going on?"

Jacki rolled her eyes. "Here we go with the drama queen."

"Behave." Pasting on a smile, Cam opened the door and stepped into the hall to greet her aunt. "I'm sorry we woke you, Aunt Lorna."

At one end of the second floor, her aunt had the largest bedroom with her own private bath. Jacki and Cam had smaller rooms connected by a bathroom that they shared, at the other end.

Just outside her door, Lorna looked from one sister to the other, and her frown of anger turned to one of confusion. "If you're both here, who's on the roof?"

"Dean."

Lorna's face pinched, making her look . . . ridiculous. She slept with her hair in a cotton turban to protect her salon style. Expensive cream left her skin shiny, and small pieces of what appeared to be tape concealed the worst of her wrinkles.

Cam tried not to stare, she really did.

Jacki wasn't so discreet. "Aunt Lorna, did you cut yourself shaving?"

Lorna's tense gaze went to her. "What are you talking about?"

"You have little strips of surgical tape all over your face."

Like a fresh pasty, Lorna puffed up. "*Imbecile.* A woman does not shave her face."

Cam hid her grin. With the tape between her brows, over her upper lip, and at the corners of her eyes, shaving did sound absurd.

Jacki just frowned in mock concern. "Then why are you all taped up?"

"It's a wrinkle treatment."

Hoping to intercede before her aunt got truly angry,

Cam stepped between the two of them. "Name-calling is childish, Aunt Lorna."

An explosion seemed imminent.

Before Lorna could give voice to her anger, Cam added, "And you don't have wrinkles, so why would you need that stuff?"

Lorna deflated suitably. "Don't try to distract me. I want to know why that man is here."

Jacki leaned around Cam. "That man is our brother."

"Not that he cares! He made it clear that he—"

"That's enough." One way or another, Cam was determined to have Lorna accept Dean.

"No, young lady, it is not." Lorna stormed down the hall toward Cam. "Why is he here at this ungodly hour?" she demanded. And before Cam could answer, she added suspiciously, "What is he telling you?"

"Telling me?" Her aunt made no sense.

Lorna shook a fist. "He's here to meddle, to cause trouble, I tell you. You should never have allowed him into our lives. He'll only—"

That did it. *"He's on the roof,"* Cam shouted, charging forward three big steps. "In the rain, making repairs so that *your* bedroom doesn't flood!"

"Well!" Lorna drew herself up. "You already put out a bucket to catch the drips. There was no need for him to do a thing. And why didn't you call Roger instead? In case you've forgotten, he's your fiancé."

"Not yet, he isn't," Jacki insisted. "You keep forgetting that Cam hasn't made him any promises at all. In fact, you're the only one—"

Again trying to avoid a full-fledged argument, Cam caught Jacki's arm and started for the stairs. "Go back to bed, Lorna."

"I'm not done talking to you."

Cam said over her shoulder, "Yes, you are." Still dragging Jacki, Cam neared the open stairwell overlooking the main living area. Dean stood at the bottom of the stairs.

Dripping. Listening.

Oh God.

He sized Cam up in a single long look. "And I was worried that I'd make too much noise."

He must have heard Lorna, not that Dean would show any reaction to it. As usual, he looked calm and in control— while she'd just been in a shouting match with her aunt.

Cam was so tired of false smiles, but she drummed up another one. "Dean, I didn't realize you were done. I'll have the coffee ready in a minute."

His light brown eyes—eyes identical to her own— shifted over to Jacki. "I thought she was going to make it."

"She and I were talking."

Jacki slipped down the stairs past Cam. "I'll do it." When she neared Dean, she leaned in and said, "But if you lose all your chest hair from drinking it, you have no one to blame but yourself."

He smiled.

Until he looked at Cam again. "You and I need to talk."

"Of course." He'd pushed his wet hair back and re- moved his sodden shoes, but his shirt clung to his wide chest. "You need to dry off first though. Let me get you a towel. And if you want, I can put your shirt in the dryer."

He caught her arm before she could rush past him. She turned automatically and saw his cold gaze directed up the stairs—clashing with Lorna's.

Now what?

"Show me where the leaks are in the house."

Oh boy. "They're, uh . . . mostly in Aunt Lorna's room."

"All right." He started up the stairs and since he still held her, Cam could either cause a bigger scene by pulling away or go along with him.

She chose to go along.

Only Lorna didn't move. She blocked the top of the stairs, and Cam didn't know what would happen.

Dean stopped in front of her. Even one step below Lorna, he towered over her. He waited two heartbeats, then said, "Move."

And she did just that.

Grumbling and complaining, Lorna sidled out of the way, but followed directly on their heels as Dean compelled Cam along, going the wrong direction in the hall.

She dug in her heels. "That's where my and Jacki's rooms are. Aunt Lorna's room is this way."

He glanced back at Lorna and smirked. "You took my parents' room?"

"It was empty." As if she immediately regretted those words, Lorna put a hand to her forehead. "It seemed best not to unsettle Jacki and Cam any further. They'd just lost their parents. Their rooms were familiar to them."

Dean paused, looking toward the forth bedroom upstairs—across from Lorna's room.

Realization brought a lump to Cam's throat. She put her hand over his, where he clasped her arm. "That was your room?" The room that had been familiar to a nine-year-old little boy who'd also lost his parents.

It hurt so badly for her to think about it. How must it feel to him?

"Yeah." Dean shook off the sentiment as if it had never been there. "Show me where the leaks are."

Lorna trotted to get ahead of him. She stationed herself at the door, barring him from entering. "I don't want you in my room."

"Tough." He turned to Cam. "Do you want the leaks fixed or not?"

"Fixed? As in actually repaired?" Surely he wasn't offering to—

"Patching them every time it rains hasn't helped, has it?"

Not even a little. Cam shook her head, but had to ask, "You saw my patches?"

Real humor lifted Dean's mouth, and for a second there, he looked as if he might laugh. "Yeah. Pretty pathetic." Then his gaze shifted to Lorna, and the humor vanished. "But at least you tried."

"It doesn't matter," Lorna insisted. "We're selling the house anyway."

Dean chose to ignore her and instead turned back to

Cam. "You need to reshingle the whole roof. It should have been done five years ago." His eyes narrowed. "Of course, you were only eighteen then, probably still in high school."

He deliberately baited Lorna, and Cam knew from experience where that'd go. "Everything seemed to break on the house at once."

"That's usually how it is, especially if no one maintains the property with regular upkeep."

Propping his shoulder on the wall beside Lorna, Dean continued as if she didn't stand there in a turban, wrinkle tape speckling her face, guarding her door against him.

"There are already two layers of shingles on there, and they're in pretty bad shape, so we're probably going to have to take them off."

Surprise put a stranglehold on Cam's throat. "We?" she squeaked.

"I need some physical activity to keep me in shape. And Jacki's new sweetheart can help."

Whoa. The squeak left in a hurry. Hands on her hips, Cam straightened. "Jacki has a sweetheart?"

"She didn't tell you?"

"She said she had a story that she'd have to share with me later."

"That's probably it."

Dean smiled again, and Cam got distracted with how handsome he looked when he let himself relax.

"Gregor 'The Maniac' Marsh," he told her.

"Oh my God."

Dean laughed. "He's a fighter, Cam, like me."

"Like you?"

"In the same organization but not as good as me. Since he's trying to court me into a match, and trying to court your sister for the obvious reasons, we should be able to finagle his help."

Cam went blank. So much to think about! Dean and Eve were having an affair; her sister was seeing someone called "The Maniac," and her brother wanted to help her with her roof.

She opened her mouth, but nothing came out.

"That is totally unacceptable!" Lorna screeched. "It's a ridiculous waste of money to do anything to the roof since we're selling the house anyway." She shoved herself away from the door. "Cam, you listen to me—"

The moment Lorna moved, Dean opened her door and moved inside her bedroom.

He'd barely taken two steps when he drew up short. A long, shrill whistle conveyed his shock.

Cam gave an apologetic shrug to her aunt and slipped inside, too. Dean stood staring at the fat bubble in the ceiling.

Since Cam had last seen it, it had doubled in size. "Wow. It's like the blob, growing and growing."

Dean looked down at the five-gallon bucket already half-full and shook his head. "You're going to need something a whole lot bigger than that. And you're going to need it fast."

"Bigger?"

"A lot bigger. Like a tub or something. That bubble is getting heavier with water." As Dean spoke, he picked up the bucket to empty it in Lorna's bathroom. "It's not going to hold much longer."

Cam watched Dean disappear into her aunt's bathroom. She looked back at the ceiling bubble, now as big as a basketball. Not good. Dashing out of the room and racing down the stairs, Cam headed for the kitchen.

Jacki said, "So you're finally ready to join me?"

"Not yet!" She went into the laundry and rummaged around until she found a ten-gallon bucket. But nothing else appeared. "Jacki, find a bucket. Or two or three. Hurry. The ceiling is going to burst."

"Lorna's ceiling?"

"Yes."

Jacki snorted as if she didn't care.

"Jacki!" Cam paused to glare at her sister. "Dean is alone with Aunt Lorna in her bedroom."

"Oh shit." Jacki went past Cam, through the laundry

room, and into the garage. She came back with two more buckets. Nothing too big.

It'd have to do.

A sudden uproar had them both cringing. They recognized Lorna's shout of pure outrage.

But that other sound . . .

The sisters stared at each other for a split second before they dashed up the stairs, down the short hall, and into Lorna's room.

They spotted Dean against the far wall, roaring with hilarity. He laughed so hard, that he couldn't stand upright and instead slouched into the corner, the now-empty bucket dangling from his hand.

In the middle of the floor stood Lorna. She was soaked to the skin, her turban askew, her wrinkle tapes barely hanging on.

A nervous laugh escaped Jacki before she slapped a hand over her mouth.

Cam stared. "What happened?"

Dean couldn't stop laughing long enough to answer.

Lorna, however, saw nothing humorous in the situation. She rolled her eyes toward the ceiling, and snarled, "Dean was right." Turning her back on them all, she sloshed toward her bathroom. "The ceiling blew."

CHAPTER 11

THE knock sounded just as Eve zipped up her favorite halter dress. It was flowery and feminine, made of soft georgette fabric that showed off her every curve. She stepped into her high-heeled sandals and, as she dashed to the front door, slipped her earrings into place.

It was too early for most people to come calling, so she opened the door with curiosity, then smiled in delight at her visitor. "Hey you."

"Hey." Dressed in jeans and a snowy white cotton T-shirt, Dean looked beyond her, ensuring they were alone. When none of her meddling family appeared, he slipped one arm around her waist and drew her close for a long, leisurely kiss. "Damn, woman, you taste even better than I remembered."

Everything inside Eve went soft and jittery. "You, too." Assuming he'd follow her in, she stepped away from the door. "But I'm sorry to say you caught me at a bad time. I have to be out the door in ten minutes."

"That's okay. I can't stay anyway." He trailed her into

the kitchen. "I just wanted to apologize for running out on you last night."

"You're kidding, right?" She lifted her coffee cup for the last drink. No way could she start the day without caffeine. "I want you to spend time with your sisters, remember? In fact, I was hoping—"

He held up his hands. "Don't go there."

"Come on, Dean." Smiling, feeling very giddy, Eve set her cup in the sink, went to him, and cupped his gorgeous, bruised face. Even freshly shaved, he looked tired—and so sexy she wanted to cancel her appointments and stay home with him. "I'm Cam's best friend. You and I are sleeping together. It's going to come up."

His hand slid boldly onto her behind, nudging her into intimate contact with his body. "Now that you've told me what I wanted to know—that we didn't just have a one-night stand—it's already up."

Laughing and swatting at him, Eve tried to wiggle away. He countered her every move with ease. "Dean," she only half-complained.

"Eve." Nuzzling her cheek, her jaw, he whispered, "I need to cancel our date for tonight."

Disappointment crowded in. "I see."

"I could come by tonight." His damp tongue touched her ear, making her shiver. "Around nine or so."

A cold dash of ice water wouldn't have been so startling. He *had* to be kidding. Eve shoved back to see his face.

He looked serious enough. Of all the nerve!

Equal parts furious and hurt, she stated, "To get laid?" She curled her hands into fists. "That's what you meant, right?"

His smile caused chaos to her already roiling senses. "Call me optimistic."

Somehow his leg got between hers, and the next thing Eve knew, they were belly to belly, solid chest to soft breasts. Her heartbeat galloped in excitement.

Dean looked at her mouth. "You know you want me, too."

She did, but pigs would fly before she made this easy on him. "Not happening, big boy, so forget it."

His gaze came up to hers. "Wanna bet?"

Oh God, he sounded so damn sure of himself! Probably with good reason, too. Not that she'd cave. "Absolutely. How can I lose?"

"Hmmm." He eyed her breasts displayed by the deep V of the bust-enhancing cups. "So what should we wager?"

To distract herself from the way he so easily seduced her, Eve said, "Whatever. You name it."

Another dazzling smile. "All right, I will."

She could get used to seeing him like this.

She could get used to him, period.

And here he was, already pulling away from her after only one night.

He pressed a soft, quick kiss to her mouth. "But first, I have to cancel because Cam's roof is ready to cave in. Patching it isn't going to help her this time. I'm heading to the car dealership to pick up my new lease, and then I'm heading to the hardware store to rent some tools and buy new shingles."

Her lips parted in surprise. "You're going to do the work?"

That odd, indifferent mask fell over his face. He lifted one heavy shoulder in a negligent shrug. "Why not? I used to do all kinds of construction with my uncle. I'm as good as she'd get if she hired it out, without costing her an arm and a leg. And since I've got some time off, I can have it done in a few days as long as the weather holds out."

Touched by his caring, Eve snuggled closer. "That's so nice of you."

He grouched under his breath, then said, "It's not a big deal, so don't act like it is."

So touchy about being nice. Eve hid her smile in his shoulder. "Dean, I hate to say this, but right now, I'm not sure Cam can even afford the shingles."

His fingers slid lower on her bottom, along the back of

her thigh, then up and under her skirt. "She shouldn't have to. Lorna had provisions for these things."

"If you're hoping for Lorna to pay you, you're delusional. That woman never—"

"Shh." His fingers encountered her panties and teased along the leg band. "I'm taking care of it."

Breath catching, Eve closed her eyes and concentrated on getting control of herself. Dean had just taken a giant step into his sister's life, and she wanted to talk to him about it.

But she couldn't, not with his hand there, doing scandalous, wonderful things to her. "You need to . . . to stop that."

"Okay." Her feet touched the floor, Dean walked her backward, and suddenly her backside bumped into the wall. "You still have five minutes, right?"

"Only five."

He smiled, and insinuated his hand right back in that tantalizing spot.

It was downright cruel to do this to her. "Five minutes might work for you, buster, but it wouldn't—" He shifted his fingers, and she gasped. "Oh God, how *do* you do that?"

His mouth touched her temple as his fingers moved over her, in her. "Relax, okay? Let me have a little quick fun."

Eve could barely keep still. The play of his fingers was both gentle and very determined. A building ache threatened to take hold. "But, Dean . . . I don't have time to redress."

"You won't have to." He interrupted his sexual torment long enough to tug her panties down over her hips. They dropped to her knees, then to her ankles.

"Step out of them."

She couldn't. "You'll get me all messy and everyone who looks at me will know what I've done."

His soft laugh affected her like a lick. "No one will know, I promise." Bending to one knee, he urged her out of the panties, then kissed a path up her thigh to her hip bone. When he stood before her again, he looked into her eyes and Eve was a goner.

"I can't believe I'm doing this."

"Believe it." He cupped his right hand between her legs, and with his left, he opened his jeans, then handed her a condom. "Get a move on, woman. We're running out of time."

Staring down at his thick erection, Eve's mouth went dry. He'd barely kissed her. Her breasts were still safely tucked behind fabric. He'd done so little to prepare her—but somehow, that only made it more exciting.

She glanced at the sliding doors to her right. Her backyard was private, but it still seemed risqué to do this here, in the light of day, mostly dressed.

She couldn't resist.

After locking her gaze with Dean's, Eve used her teeth to open the condom packet. New urgency sparked in his eyes. "Tease," he accused.

"Look who's talking." Her hands shook when she cradled him in her palms. So warm and firm . . . She stroked once, twice, let her thumb slide over the silky head, spreading a warm drop of sleek fluid.

Dean's breath caught. "Get on with it."

"Hush." Taking more time than necessary, Eve rolled the rubber onto his erection. His eyes closed and he gave one ragged groan, and then his mouth was on hers, kissing her long and deep as he maneuvered their positions, lifting her against the wall, helping her to wrap one leg around his waist.

"Hold on to my shoulders."

Eve did—and he sank into her. *"Dean."*

Covering her mouth again, he used his tongue to mimic the rhythmic thrusting inside her body. Lights sparked behind Eve's closed eyelids. Tension coiled, surprising her at the fast approach.

Dean tilted her hips upward, adjusting her so that with each in and out stroke, his erection made contact with her clitoris. Her nails bit into his shoulders; he held her tighter to him, and a climax ripped through her.

She freed her mouth to cry out, aware of him watching

her, taking pleasure from her loss of control. It didn't matter. Nothing had ever felt like this. It was too much. Too incredible.

Way too easy and overwhelming.

As the pleasure faded, she had to suck deep breaths to keep from crying. She felt so . . . lax and drained.

So . . . *addicted.*

Last night had been phenomenal and she'd thought about it, about him, ever since. But today proved that Dean Conor had a unique effect on her, that he did things to her no other man could. Whether he had half the night or a mere five minutes, he could turn her to mush, make her forget all her convictions, probably even her pride.

He almost scared her. Almost. "You're a wizard or something, right?"

Dean had his face resting in the crook of her shoulder, his hot breath pelting against her throat. "I have one minute left, honey. Let me use it to catch my breath, please."

She smiled easily, charmed by his casual attitude toward things carnal and awed by his powerful machismo. He slumped against her and spoke in a raw whisper, and still he seemed more of a man than any man she'd ever known.

Eve drifted her fingers through his thick, light brown hair. "You should probably be in a bed."

"With you? Hell of an idea."

She laughed as she shook her head. "No. Recuperating."

"Now what fun would that be?" He straightened, searched her face, and kissed her again before allowing her legs to slide down until she stood on her own. "You need a trip to the bathroom?"

"Um, yes." Seeing her panties on the floor between them, Eve shooed him away. "But you go first." She wasn't sure her legs would work yet.

He cupped her face and brushed her cheek with his thumb. "All right." He shucked up his jeans and went back through the house to the powder room.

As soon as he'd left, Eve retrieved her underwear and dashed into the connecting laundry room to refresh herself. It shook her, how easily he turned her on. Like he had a magic switch he flipped. A button that he knew exactly when to push.

If she were smart, she'd put some distance between them.

Dean reappeared. He managed to look both cocky and vulnerable. "So, nine tonight is good for you?"

Secret places in her body quaked at just the thought. "You still want to? I mean, after we've just done . . . this." Surely he was satisfied now.

"Yeah. I still want to. Maybe more now than before."

Because that was exactly how she felt, Eve let out a sigh of relief, and smiled. "Okay then."

His mouth twitched into a grin. "You realize that means I win the bet."

Her confusion turned quickly to comprehension. "Now wait a minute—"

"Can't. You're going to be late." With two big steps, he reached her. "But don't worry. You'll enjoy paying up."

"Dean—"

He kissed the denial from her lips and left her standing there, mute, annoyed, and filled with scalding anticipation.

DEAN drove to the car dealership by rote. He'd only been there once, but luckily his subconscious knew the way, because his brain sure as shit wasn't on directions.

When he'd gone to see Eve, it hadn't been for a quickie. Just the opposite. He'd planned to cancel on her, and leave it at that. Whatever happened, happened.

But he'd taken one look at her, heard her, breathed in her fresh-from-the-shower scent, and his plans went haywire.

He didn't know if he should be annoyed, bemused, or embarrassed. Jesus. If he kept up like this, she'd think he was a sexual control freak. Not that he minded controlling her. Hell no. He loved it.

And that was the problem.

After leaving her the night before, he'd thought of her at least a hundred times. Jacki said something ridiculous, and he thought about telling Eve. Cam climbed up on a roof in a rainstorm, and he wanted to rail to Eve about it.

Lorna treated him like a damn parasite, and he wanted to go to Eve to . . .

No.

He didn't. He wouldn't.

So why the hell had he told Eve that he intended to fix the roof? Come to that, *why* was he fixing the goddamned roof? It wasn't his problem. It had jack shit to do with him.

Stopped at a red light, Dean squeezed his eyes shut and purposefully cleared his mind. He'd fix the roof and be done with it. Period. As he'd told Eve, it wasn't a big deal. He could afford it, and then when he left again, he wouldn't have to think about a woman—didn't matter if the woman was his sister—*any woman* standing on a roof that was in dangerous need of repair.

He pulled away with the flow of traffic and, minutes later, arrived at the car lot. On his way in, he noticed a used Ford Focus. Clean. Good tires. And the price was reasonable. . . .

Damn it.

Keeping his stony gaze straight ahead, Dean stormed into the office and completed his business with no questions asked about the other car. He had his Sebring; he didn't need another car.

And fixing a roof was more than enough charity on his part.

After the storm the night before, the fresh morning air felt good. Dean put the convertible top down and drove to the address Eve's mother had given him. He wanted to stop in to let Crystal know he couldn't look at any property today after all. Soon, though.

Crystal's workplace had an upscale feel to it. The building was new and professionally landscaped. As Dean opened the etched glass entry doors, he pushed his mirrored sunglasses to the top of his head. A friendly receptionist directed him down the hall to Crystal's office.

Halfway there, he heard a man's raised angry voice.

"This is absurd. It's a waste of her money and you know it."

Crystal said, "Look, Roger, it's none of my business. You'll have to take it up with Cam."

Roger. Great. Someone else Dean *didn't* want to see.

"Sell me the damn property now, and Cam won't have to bother with repairs."

"Sorry," Crystal said. "It's not mine to sell."

An angry silence crackled in the air before Roger bit off, "Do—the damn—paperwork."

Dean reached the end of the hall just in time to see Crystal come out of her chair and around her desk. Her pose showed obvious annoyance. "I will when Cam tells me to, and not a second before that."

"I've tried to call her, but she's not answering her home phone or her cell." When Crystal shrugged, Roger took a step closer to her. "You know damn good and well I'm her only buyer, and I don't want the roof fixed."

Lounging in the door frame, Dean asked, "Why not?"

Roger spun around, first startled and then, when he recognized Dean, furious. "What the hell are you doing here?"

"Not that it's any of your business, but I'm here for the same reason you are."

Anger colored Roger's face, until Dean clarified. "I'm thinking of buying some property."

He took an aggressive step forward. "The Conor home?"

Dean sent him a *hell no* look, then said to Crystal, "Good morning."

Crystal greeted him with relief and a hearty hug. "You're early."

"Sorry about that. My plans had a few changes." And to Roger, he said, "Cam is probably still sleeping. She was up late fighting roof leaks."

Eyes narrowing, Roger asked, "And how would you know that?"

"I helped her fix them."

Again Roger started forward, and Crystal said, "I take it you've met Cam's brother, Dean?"

That brought him to a standstill. "Her brother?"

"That's right." And with a puzzled frown, he added, "You didn't know?"

Roger was so transparent that Dean could see his every thought and intent.

"No," Roger said. "We met, but I didn't realize . . ." Undecided on which tack to take, Roger waffled between bullying anger and a slicker façade that might aid him in prying.

He decided to try slick.

"I understood from Eve that you weren't sticking around." Hands in his pockets, Roger avoided offering a friendly handshake. "She was wrong?"

"No." Dean turned back to Crystal. "If you have any addresses for me, I'll take them now and check them out when I can."

"Sure thing. I have them right here." She handed Dean a multipaged printout, safely tucked inside a folder for the sake of privacy.

Frustration darkened Roger's eyes, though he tried to keep it out of his voice. "If you're not sticking around, why are you buying property?"

"Investment." Dean glanced at the addresses, nodded, and said to Crystal, "Thanks. I owe you."

"After the way the men chewed your ear the other night? I'd say I'm still behind."

Roger again tried to gain Dean's attention. "You're into real estate? Me, too. It's a smart man's move." He watched Dean with speculation. "I don't know if your sister told you, but I own quite a few enterprises here in Harmony."

"Actually Eve told me."

"I see." A muscle ticked in Roger's cheek. "So you two are an item?"

Rather than answer, Dean closed the distance separating him from Roger. When he stood only a foot away, he smiled. "It's my turn."

Roger's gaze shifted to Crystal and came back. "Your turn for what?"

"The interrogation. I'll start with asking why you don't want Cam to have the roof fixed."

It was a struggle for Roger, but he didn't back away. At six-two, he probably wasn't used to anyone standing over him. But Dean not only topped him by a couple of inches, he had a more powerful physique and a lot of practice intimidating people.

He used both to his advantage now.

Why he wanted to break Roger down, he didn't know. But he had an instinct on some things, and on a basic gut level, he loathed and distrusted Roger.

Keeping his annoyance under wraps, Roger shrugged. "Your sister and I are engaged."

"Really? I heard that was still up in the air."

Roger's expression tightened. "Cam and I have yet to finalize our plans. In the meantime, I don't want to see her stressing about unnecessary things. I'm buying the house, and I don't give a damn how the roof is."

Dean slowly nodded, but he didn't trust a single thing Roger said. "You claimed you're her only buyer. Why is that?"

"Who else would want it?" Roger laughed. "You've seen the roof, but maybe you don't know that the plumbing is faulty, too, and the windows are so warped that they're nearly useless. On any given day, half the damn circuits will overload or short out. The heat pump is shot and needs to be replaced. The—"

"Strange," Dean interrupted. "It seems the pool is in perfect working order. Why would Cam let the house fall apart, but maintain the pool?"

Crystal snorted. "Lorna uses the pool, that's why."

Dean couldn't credit such a thing. "Lorna wears a swimsuit?"

"No." Crystal actually shuddered over the thought of that. "But she does a lot of entertaining out there. Little club parties and such."

That explained why they had such nice outdoor furniture, too.

"When the pool pump broke at the beginning of the season, Roger fixed it for Lorna." Crystal stared between the two men. "At his own expense."

"Real generous of you." Dean wondered why Roger would assist Cam with one thing, but not another. And why had Cam let him help? From what he'd seen of his sister, she was too independent and far too proud for her own good.

"The girls like to swim, too," Roger defended. "And it didn't cost that much."

Of course they liked to swim. They grew up with a customized pool in their backyard. He could still remember his own days of summer, before his parents' deaths. Lounging in the pool all day, swimming and playing until he was too exhausted to do more than eat and nap. Nothing, not even hard work, tired a person more than sun and water. It was a good tired, though. The kind that took away tension and made problems seem less severe.

Just like that, Dean made another decision. He refused to ponder it too long, to dwell on his murky motivation. His dislike of Roger proved to be enough reason for anything he chose to do.

Turning to Crystal, Dean said, "Don't sell the house until you hear from me."

Roger snorted. "What are you talking about? You have no say in this."

"Actually I have the final say."

Crystal's eyebrows shot up, so Dean explained to them both at the same time.

"Cam told me the house is part mine. The fact that I wasn't around much doesn't change anything." He clapped Roger on the shoulder. "And I just decided I don't want to sell it."

"That's ludicrous." Incredulity left Roger's face color-less. "Cam and I have a deal!"

"But you and I don't." Done with explaining himself, Dean saluted Crystal with the file of addresses. "Thanks again. I'll be in touch."

Dazed by the turn of events, Crystal nodded. "Yeah, I'll be waiting with bated breath to hear from you."

Dean strode out on Roger's swelling tirade. He felt like he'd just tossed a heavy weight off his shoulders. The whole day looked brighter.

Time to get things under way. Taking his cell phone off the clip on the waistband of his jeans, he dialed Gregor's number.

On the third ring, breathing hard and fast, Gregor answered. "Yeah?"

Had he caught Gregor at an indiscreet moment? "I gather you're either screwing or working out."

"Havoc? How are you, you son of a bitch?"

"Breathing easier than you."

Gregor laughed. "It'll disappoint you, 'cuz it sure disappoints me, but you're not interruptin' anything more ex-citin' than a jog. What's up?"

Dean came right to the point. "I have a proposition for you."

"Interesting. Let's hear it, buddy boy."

To guard against the bright morning glare, Dean slipped on his sunglasses. He looked up at the clear blue skies. Not a cloud in sight. But how long would it last?

"I could use a hand with something. If you help out, I'll spar with you."

"Spar? Shit, man, I want a sanctioned fight."

"Sparring first, and then we'll see." Dean opened the door of his new car and slid behind the wheel. "But the sparring comes after we finish up a job. For every day that you work with me, I'll spar with you for two hours. What do you think?"

"I think you've got me by the balls, you bastard."

Excitement deteriorated Gregor's language. "But fuck, yeah, I'm your man. Whatever you need, you tell me."

"For starters, I need you to clean up your language."

"What the fuck do you care?"

Gregor could be such an idiot. "I'm going to reshingle my sister's roof, and she'll probably be around. She doesn't need to hear your foul mouth."

A heavy pause, ripe with anticipation, followed Dean's statement. Then, as if savoring the words, Gregor murmured, "Oh, yeah. Little sister."

Dean rolled his eyes. "Don't say it like that, you ass."

"Like what?"

"Like she's a buffet dinner, and you're a starving man." Wading into unfamiliar territory, Dean tossed out his first bit of brotherly caution. "Keep in mind that she's my sister, okay?"

Gregor laughed at that. "Hell, man, knowin' little sis will be around, I'd have done this without the promise of a payback. Too bad for you, you've already given me your word."

"It's hard work," Dean warned him. "And it's going to take a few days."

"Yeah," Gregor said with satisfaction. "The longer, the better. Because I'm going to enjoy every second of it."

CHAPTER 12

LATER that afternoon, when Dean walked around to the backyard, he saw Gregor's hulking form already taking up a good deal of space on the deck. He must have raced right over, Dean thought, in the hopes of seeing Jacki. Gregor was a real ladies' man. But Dean had never seen him have to work at it before.

The bonus to having Gregor help him with the roof was getting a front-row seat to his pursuit. Dean instinctively knew that Jacki wouldn't make it easy on him. She was a real pistol, with a few issues of her own, so Gregor would have to go forward carefully.

At that moment, only Cam and Eve were available to keep Gregor company. Did that mean Jacki was deliberately avoiding him or was she unaware of his presence? She liked him, Dean could tell. So what held her back?

As Dean approached, he watched Gregor pouring on the charm, smiling down at both Eve and Cam. His manner with them held no resemblance to the territorial, almost barbaric way he'd behaved with Jacki. Because of their close relationship to Jacki, Gregor wanted to win them over.

It wasn't working.

Cam stared up at him in something akin to horror. As always, she tried to be polite, but she kept blinking. And looking at Gregor's ears, fattened from too many solid punches during fights. And his tattoos, meandering all over his upper torso.

And his bare chest, which most women would find intimidating.

Dean would have said something about Gregor's lack of a shirt, except that his attention strayed to Eve, standing beside Cam.

She'd changed from her sexy dress to even sexier shorts and a halter top that left a strip of bare soft skin exposed above her waistband. He could see her little belly-button ring, and it entranced him.

Unlike Cam, Eve didn't appear nearly so distressed at Gregor's ponderous appearance.

Dean's armload of tools dropped to the ground with a clatter.

Gregor turned, saw it was Dean, and his charm turned to complaints. "Damn it, Havoc, your little sister is dodging me."

"Can't say as I blame her." Dean looked at Cam. "Where is she?"

After two tries, Cam found her voice. "She, ah, volunteered to make a quick run to the grocery store for me."

"For lunch," Eve explained to him. "We figured we'd grill some hamburgers and hot dogs. What do you think?" As she spoke, she approached Dean with a smile. "Are you hungry?"

"Always." And with her, that wasn't a stretch. He'd just been inside her a few hours ago, and already, his body turned taut and twitchy again, just because she stood within reach.

Gregor tugged on an earring. "So how long do you think little sis will be?"

Looking hopeful, Cam said, "Jacki shouldn't be too

long." And with the obvious desire to escape, she added, "I'll bring out some iced tea for everyone. How's that sound?"

"Awesome." With his giant mitt on Cam's slender back, Gregor started her toward the house. "I'll help you, and you can tell me more about Jacki."

Denying him wouldn't be polite, so her expression both dismayed and resigned, Cam went along.

As they disappeared into the house, Eve grinned. "Mighty colorful friends you keep, Havoc."

"He's more an anxious contender for the title than a friend. But he's all right. Just overzealous about things."

"Your sister being one of those things?"

Dean grinned. "She knocked him on his ass. I swear he was ready to spout poetry to her. The thing is, Jacki doesn't seem to know it. She thinks he's using her to get to me."

"But you're sure he's not?"

"Gregor doesn't work that way." Dean thought about it and decided to put the question to Eve. "You got any idea why Jacki would second-guess his interest?"

"Nope. As far as I know, she's had a lot of boyfriends. You heard my brother. Jacki draws people, male and female alike. With her caustic wit, she's very charismatic."

"Maybe." But Dean didn't buy the façade. He'd seen too many flashes of insecurity.

It was Eve's turn to study him. "You know, when you first met Jacki you sort of stomped on her one obvious vulnerability."

Dean wasn't an idiot; he well remembered the moment Jacki had walked out on him. "Her height and thinness?"

"And what comes with it. Or rather, what doesn't."

"Ah." So that was it. *Women.* Why did they persist in thinking men judged them by the size of their boobs?

Shaking his head, Dean said, "So she's not stacked. That really bothers her?"

Eve gave him an exasperated look. "It'd bother most women."

"Shouldn't. We males aren't nearly as shallow—or one-dimensional—as women try to make us out to be. Sex, in the nude, with the lights on. A few laughs. Lots of moaning. And no inhibitions." He winked. "That's all we want."

Because he'd gotten exactly that with her, Eve blushed. Dean touched her chin, grinned again, and kissed her quick and hard. "If Jacki would give Gregor a chance, I'm sure he'd show her how little her bra size matters to him." Now that he saw that Gregor was actually interested, and not just out to score, Dean wouldn't mind seeing him succeed. Jacki could use the boost.

Eve cleared her throat. "I'm dying to find out how he met Jacki already."

"It's a boring story."

"So bore me."

Shrugging, Dean said, "He was asking around town about me, and Jacki overheard him." He couldn't help himself; he bent and kissed Eve again. "You're done with your appointment?"

"Mmmm." Eve licked her lips. "Free for the afternoon. I couldn't resist coming by to watch you sweat. It's bound to be a spectacular sight." Her smile couldn't quite hide the worry in her eyes. "Are you sure you're up to hard work in this heat?"

Women had never looked at him with concern. From the fairer sex he got lust, manipulation, and in the case of fans, blind admiration. Eve's worry both unmanned Dean and made him want to cuddle her.

He blew off both sensations by teasing her. "By now you should know how *up* I can be."

She didn't laugh. She smoothed her fingertips over the bruise on his cheekbone, brushed his hair back to see the stitches on his forehead. Dean felt her gentle touch everywhere, in places he'd never thought about before.

Like his heart.

Forcing a laugh, he stepped out of her reach and stripped off his shirt. "If you want to do some stroking, I've got better places I can direct you to."

"You do have an awesome physique, no two ways about

that." She locked her fingers together. "But if I start touching you, I won't want to stop. And now's not the time."

Damn. It was so easy for her to get to him. "Hold that thought till tonight then." After tossing his shirt on the back of a lawn chair, Dean gave Eve a more leisurely kiss, and then turned away to inspect the tools he'd need for the job. Because they had to strip off the old shingles, he'd arranged the delivery of a large Dumpster in the driveway. They'd toss the old shingles in there to make it easy to haul them away.

Later that evening, the hardware store would deliver new shingles right atop the roof.

Eve followed close behind him, and Dean felt her gearing up for something. If she thought to back out on him tonight, just because she'd lost the bet . . .

"My mom said you don't want to sell the house."

Dean relaxed. He could handle her nosiness. "That's right."

"So . . . what do you plan to do?"

"Talk to Cam first. I don't want to blindside her with this." He raised a brow. "You haven't mentioned it to her, have you?"

She shook her head. "I figured you could do that. It'll be a good chance for the two of you to talk more, maybe get better acquainted."

"Right." Thinking of the job at hand, Dean walked a circle around the supplies, taking a mental inventory to ensure he hadn't forgotten anything. Two shingle scrapers, rolls of tar paper, boxes of galvanized nails, strips of roofing edge, aluminum flashing, and two hammer tackers.

So that he and Gregor could finish faster, hopefully before more rain moved in, he'd gotten duplicates of each tool. With any luck, they'd have the roof prepared by the end of the day.

"When are you going to tell Cam?"

Dean sent Eve a fleeting look. "You keep pushing for us to bond or something. But it's not going to be like that, so get it out of your head."

Suspiciously agreeable, Eve said, "Of course it's not." She seated herself on the lawn and pretended to examine a patch of clover. "But it won't hurt for you two to discuss a few . . . things."

Placating him? Dean didn't like it. For some strange reason, Eve had relegated him to the role of close and caring big brother, when she didn't know him well enough to make that assessment.

He had no intention of allowing Eve to dictate to him. But at the same time, he didn't want to disappoint her, either.

Standing over her, Dean crossed his arms and willed her to look at him. When she did, he almost got distracted with how bright her blue eyes looked in the glaring afternoon light.

"Before I do anything, I need to see how many repairs the house needs in order to turn a profit."

"You're going to sell it?"

He didn't know for sure, so rather than lie, he just shrugged. "From what Roger told me, it's all but falling down."

"He exaggerated." Visibly distraught, Eve plucked a blade of grass and slid it between nervous fingers. "But not by much."

"So it is that bad?"

Her bare shoulders lifted, drawing his eyes to her smooth skin and delicate bone structure.

"I'm not sure what the costs will be, but the house has been neglected. Cam tried to keep up with everything, but she has a tendency to take too much on herself. And Lorna never offers any help." She looked away again. "It's still home to them, though. Neither Jacki nor Cam wants to sell."

Her insinuation was loud and clear. "No one should keep what he can't afford."

"But maybe with just a little help, they'll be able to afford it now. I heard that you convinced Jacki to get a job."

Eve had braided her dark hair. Thanks to the heat and humidity, small, damp tendrils had escaped around her ears and clung to her nape. Why that made him hot, Dean couldn't say.

Hell, everything about her, even her damn meddling, had a singular effect on him. "I had nothing to do with that."

"Cam has always encouraged Jacki to skip work in favor of concentrating on her studies. You said she should be able to do both. And now she's taken the initiative and gotten herself employed." Pure satisfaction sounded in Eve's statement. "I'd say you had everything to do with it."

To keep her from slapping a halo over his head, Dean decided to clue her in on a few facts. He dropped down to sit beside her. "Before I get any credit or blame, you should know that Jacki will be working at some sleazy bar. I think she said it's called the Roadkill Bar."

Thick lashes lifted in surprise. "I've heard of it."

"But you've never been there?" Sitting so close beside her, Dean breathed in the scent of summer-warmed skin and flowery shampoo, a scent fast becoming familiar to his libido.

"It's not exactly my kind of place."

Dean couldn't keep his hands to himself when he was this close to her. He brushed the backs of his fingers over her cheek. She was so damn soft.

When Eve turned her head and kissed his knuckles, Dean withdrew.

It was either that or advertise a boner to his sister and Gregor. "She'll have late hours, staying on till two in the morning."

"Ouch. That is late." Eve caught a blade of grass between her thumbs, cupped her hands, and lifted them to her mouth. Eyes twinkling at Dean, she blew hard into her hands.

An ear-splitting whistle sounded. Dean grinned with her. "Your talents abound."

"Dad taught me that when I was six." Drawing her knees up and resting her crossed arms there, Eve surveyed him. "What kind of stuff did your uncle teach you?"

By rote, Dean tried to deflect the personal question.

He'd spent a lifetime keeping people at a distance, well out of his private business.

Looking toward the house, he said, "I wonder what the hell's keeping Cam so long."

Almost on cue, Cam came out. She looked around until she spotted them and then waved. "I had to make some more iced tea. I'll have it ready soon."

Animated cheerfulness had replaced Cam's skittish reserve, making Dean suspicious. "Everything okay, Cam? Gregor's not getting on your nerves, is he?"

"No. Not at all." Her smile should have warned him. "He's telling me all about your history in the SBC. And he said he'd get me an official T-shirt with you on it, and some autographed pictures of the other fighters. He's really a very nice man. I like him." She turned and went back inside.

Bemused, Dean watched her go. "God only knows what he's saying."

Eve shoved his shoulder. "Who cares? It can't be bad or Cam would have tossed him out."

Her and what army? "Eve? Did you happen to notice how big Gregor is?"

Eve shot back, "Did you happen to notice how delighted Cam is to have you here? She's not going to let anyone bad-mouth you."

No, Dean thought, she probably wouldn't. He scowled at the house. He didn't feel deserving of Cam's defense.

But he liked it just the same.

"Now come on." Eve nudged him again. "Tell me about your uncle and your relationship with him. Surely he taught you stuff."

Dean thought about it, then decided, why not? Stretching out in the warm, sweet grass, he crossed his arms behind his head, closed his eyes, and let the sun soothe his still-aching muscles. "Grover taught me how to build things the right way."

"Like what?"

"Everything from putting on a simple addition to constructing an entire house. He told me too many people take

shortcuts these days, and he'd take it as a personal affront
if I didn't do the work right. He put me with the crew as
soon as he took me in. If I could hold a tool, he let me use
it. Hammers and drills and power saws." He smiled with
the memory. "Sometimes the tool weighed as much as me.
But I managed."

"It's a wonder you didn't hurt yourself."

"Or someone else." Dean could still picture his uncle
standing over him, supervising, patiently explaining.

Just . . . being with him.

Which was something his own parents had never done.

"Later he told me that he wanted to keep me busy so I
wouldn't dwell on my parents' deaths and my new life. He
figured if I worked hard enough during the day, I'd be too
exhausted at night to feel sorry for myself."

Very gently, Eve asked, "Did it work?"

It hadn't, but he didn't want Eve to know that, any more
than he'd wanted his uncle to know. "It made me independent. And I liked being around the other men. They were . . .
rough."

"With you?"

"No, just in their manners. The only adjectives they
knew were curse words. They drank too much in the evenings. A couple of times a week, they fought with each
other." Sometimes Dean missed those days. "I learned
from them, too."

"What did you learn?"

Where to start? There were things he couldn't tell her,
but most of what he'd learned from his uncle's crew had
been harmless. "They showed me how to repair just about
everything from watches to car engines. If it runs, I can
probably fix it."

"That'd go a long way in being self-sufficient."

"Yeah." Dean relaxed a little more. "They taught me
how to play poker, too, and how to cheat without getting
caught." He smiled. "I can pick a lock, start a fire from
scratch, cook dinner, and sew a hem."

"I take it none of these men were married?"

Laughing, Dean said, "No sane woman would have had any of them. Not long-term anyway. What they needed done, they did themselves." There'd been women, but not the marrying kind. Making an admission, Dean said, "They taught me to be the same."

"You'd be handy to have around then."

Except that he never stayed long. Dean opened one eye to see Eve leaning over him. His heart thumped a little faster. "Are you inviting me to stick around?"

Her mouth twitching, Eve laid one hand over his bruised ribs and, though she didn't realize it, his bruised heart.

"Actually, I was thinking of Cam and all the stuff that needs to be done on the house."

He groaned. Damned frustrating woman.

"Seriously Dean, with you helping her on repairs, and Jacki contributing financially, she might be able to keep it."

The sooner he got the issue of the house out of the way, the better Dean would like it. Closing his eyes again, he shut out the sight of Eve and her blind faith in his charitable goodness.

But his awareness of her remained. Not just the physical awareness, but also the idea of who and what she believed him to be.

Before he had time to think it over, Dean heard himself say, "I'll get everything in working order."

The words no sooner left his mouth than he wanted to take them back. He started to lower his arms, intent on sitting up and getting to work. But he'd barely moved when Eve's mouth touched his, urging his eyes open again.

So close that he could see a few freckles on the bridge of her nose, Eve said, "You are one terrific man, Dean Conor. Do you know that?"

Infuriated more with himself than with her, Dean moved fast, catching Eve's shoulders and turning to tuck her under him. He half covered her, pressing her into the thick lawn. "You're delusional, Eve."

"No."

His jaw locked. "You don't know shit about me."

She put her hands at either side of his face and smiled with too much emotion. "You want to know what I think?"

For some reason, tension pulled at him. "Probably some idiotic romanticized nonsense." When her confidence didn't falter, he made a sound of disgust. "All right, go ahead and tell me."

"I think you're the one who doesn't know shit about you."

Her words sucked the breath right out of him. He opened his mouth to correct her—how, he didn't know— and a squeal sounded behind him. Rolling off Eve and onto his feet in one agile move, Dean faced the intrusion, only to catch sight of Jacki hurrying to him.

"What now?" he muttered. The women of Harmony, Kentucky, were going to be the death of him.

"You got the car!" Grocery bags in both arms, Jacki rushed to him, her long legs eating up the distance in record time. An ear of corn bounced out of one bag, but Jacki didn't stop to retrieve it.

"It's awesome, Dean. Even better than the photo in the brochure. I love it." Pleasure brought color to her cheeks and added an impish twinkle to her eyes. "I know you're busy now, but you *have* to take me for a ride later."

Dean shook his head in wonder. For God's sake, it wasn't an expensive car. Not even a particularly sporty car, especially when compared to what other SBC fighters drove. Gregor had parked his new Saleen Mustang convertible right behind the Sebring.

But maybe Jacki didn't realize it was Gregor's.

Or . . . maybe she did.

She stood in front of Dean, all smiles, several silver earrings in her left ear glinting in the sunshine. She wore her too-blond hair twisted up into some super-funky do, and her light brown eyes looked huge with all the dramatic makeup.

Like Eve, Jacki had dressed for the warm weather. A crop top left most of her midriff bare. Low-slung shorts put her tattoo on display. She wore cheap rubber flip-flops on her feet. She looked more like a teenager than a twenty-one-year-old woman.

Her animated chatter lightened Dean's mood. "I figured you'd be sleeping the day away."

Jacki rolled her eyes toward the house. "Yeah, I would have, except Goliath showed up bright and early." Her gaze swung back to Dean, now full of accusation. "And speaking of Goliath—he said *you* invited him."

"To help me with the roof."

"That's what he claimed. But c'mon, Dean. Why *him*?"

Fighting a laugh, Dean chucked her under the chin. "Because he's big. It might surprise you what asphalt shingles weigh. Even the cheapest grades go around two hundred and twenty-five pounds per hundred square feet." He looked up at the roof. "With two layers of roofing, and the size of this roof, I'd say all the old shingles should weigh in at more than six thousand pounds. That's over three tons, hon. And I know you didn't want me laboring on it all on my own."

Jacki skipped her gaze over his chest. "Right, not when you already look annihilated."

"I'm fine."

"Fine, huh?" She rolled her eyes. "Even tough guys need time to heal, you know."

Did she just scold him? "I wasn't—"

She wrinkled her nose. "Yeah, okay, so Gregor will come in handy." She glanced toward the house again. "I suppose I can tolerate him for awhile."

"Tolerate him. Torment him." Dean caught her chin to bring her face around to him. "Get to know him. You'll have a few days, so make the most of it."

A flash of something, maybe gratitude, shown in her eyes before she ducked her head.

"Speak of the devil," Eve said, and Dean looked up to find Gregor bearing down on them.

Still shirtless.

Which Jacki made obvious note of right away. She shoved the bags of groceries toward Dean, squared her shoulders, and met Gregor halfway.

CHAPTER 13

❧

DETERMINED to set Gregor straight, Jacki charged up to him. He was all smiles, as if thrilled to see her. And his blasted gaze roamed everywhere it shouldn't, lingering on her belly, studying her tattoo, sliding along the length of her legs. She felt scorched . . . until he zeroed in on her chest with extreme absorption.

What a joke. How dumb did he think she was? She barely had enough to see, much less enough to hold attention.

Quickly, Jacki crossed her arms over herself.

Gregor opened his mouth, and she said, "Don't start."

He went blank. With caution, he asked, "Start what?"

"With the 'honey,' 'baby,' 'darlin'' talk." His brows bunched together in a "put out by her attitude" frown, but Jacki wouldn't let him intimidate her. "If you actually want to get to know me, Gregor, fine."

Relief lifted the scowl. "Now you're talkin'."

"But," Jacki added in a hardened voice, "I will not be used as a pawn just so you can coerce Dean into fighting you."

The scowl snapped right back into place, more fierce than ever. "Forget your damned brother, will ya? He's got nothin' to do with it."

"Oh really?" Jacki imbued as much sarcasm in those two words as she could.

Slowly, deliberately, Gregor straightened to his full impressive height of six and a half feet. To make sure he wouldn't be overheard, he stepped closer, leaving no more than a breath between them. And good thing, because when Jacki glanced around, she saw that no one was making any bones about eavesdropping.

Her sister, Eve, and Dean all stood there watching the spectacle they made. That was pretty distracting.

Until Gregor said, "I want you, you stubborn little twit."

Twit! Jacki dropped her arms to prop her hands on her hips. "Is there any woman you don't want?"

"Yeah." His chest nearly bumped into her chin, he got so close. "Two of 'em are tryin' their best to hear us right now."

Oh. Chagrined, Jacki glanced at Eve, and got a smile. She looked at Cam, and felt her concern.

Knowing they needed to finish this in private, she said to Gregor, "C'mon," and grabbed his thick wrist to drag him to the far side of the pool.

He went willingly, almost . . . anxiously.

Out of hearing range, Jacki stopped to square off with him. "Now, first off I don't like being called a twit."

"Then quit actin' like one."

"I wasn't."

"Bullshit. I want you, and it doesn't have a damn thing to do with Havoc." Arms at his sides, posture challenging, Gregor said, "If for some asinine reason you doubt me, you should dangle your gaze a little south, and you'll see that you get me half-hard just by bitchin' at me. Or it might have been grabbin' my wrist. Or a combination of the two."

Jacki's eyes rounded—and stuck resolutely to his face. In a low whisper, she hissed, "Don't get a jones now, for God's sake. My sister will see."

"I can't help it." His voice went all seductive. "You do that to me."

She peeked, and wished she hadn't. After a heartfelt moan, Jacki covered her face. "Okay, so you're easily excited."

"By *you*." He looked too damn serious. "Hell, woman, you don't think every skirt that flits by gets this reaction, do you? If they did, I'd never be able to fight, because the audience always has its fair share of females beggin' for it."

Great. Just the image she wanted. Packs of women fighting for his attention.

"If I got a boner every time I saw a sexy broad, I'd never get a cup to fit—"

"*Stop.*"

"All right," he soothed, now that he'd gotten her to lose her temper. "But understand this, little girl—"

Her head snapped up at that idiotic bit of sweet talk. "I am not little."

"Yeah, you are." Cupping her face in his hands, Gregor smoothed his thumbs over her cheeks and waited until she tipped her head way back to meet his gaze.

And damned if she didn't feel downright tiny.

It wasn't an altogether comfortable feeling, yet it sparked a carnal awareness that had her breath coming faster and deeper.

Voice going gruff, Gregor murmured, "You're small and fragile and hot. I can't wait to get you naked."

Oh, wow. The man had a way with words that could be very convincing.

"But understand this, darlin'." He spoke over her when she started to protest. "I'm not a liar and I don't take kindly to being called one. You want me to drop the endearments, fine. I'm not makin' any promises because I am who I am, been that way for too many years to count. But for you, I'll give it a shot."

He made it sound like any effort on his part should be greatly appreciated. Jacki had no doubt that few women would ask him to change much. "Gee, thanks."

"But only if you stop accusin' me of things I haven't done. Like usin' you."

"So coming on to me has nothing at all to do with Dean?"

"Not a thing. Trust me, I'll get Havoc on the mat one way or another. He can't hold out forever, and if I have to work my way up through the ranks, breakin' heads left and right, that's what I'll do."

Jacki laughed. "Yeah, I can believe you're capable of that."

"Damn right." He bent to put his forehead to hers. "I'll take a shortcut if I can get it, but not by chasin' a gal who doesn't do it for me."

"So . . . I do it for you?"

His leer made her blush. "If you didn't, why would I be here? There are plenty of other women waitin' around to try me on for size, even here in backwater Harmony."

Jacki rolled her eyes—but again, she believed him. She'd seen for herself how the women in the bar had all ogled him.

"But they didn't grab me the way you did," Gregor continued. "If we didn't have that freakin' audience strainin' their ears to hear, I'd show you just how much you get to me. You see, darlin', I'm proportionate in size all over, if you get my drift."

She got his drift one hundred percent. Close as he stood, she couldn't have missed it.

"It tends to make any sexual interest on my part a tad noticeable." Discomfort replaced the leer. "As it is, I think I'm gonna need a dip in your pool to get things under control."

Jacki swallowed back a moan of interest, and said calmly, "I think I can help you with that."

Sexual heat flared in his dark gaze. His voice dropped lower still to an inflamed growl. "Yeah?"

"Oh, yeah." She laid both hands on Gregor's bare, broad chest, doing her best to ignore the sleekness of his skin, the rock-solid muscle with no give at all, the touch of crisp hair. She drew a stuttering breath.

And shoved.

Gregor shouted a surprised curse, but he couldn't stop the momentum. Arms and legs flailing in the air, he hit the icy water with an awesome splash.

Jacki heard her sister's laugh, Eve's gasp, and Dean's muttered, "Uh-oh."

When Gregor emerged, he used both hands to shove his shaggy dark hair away from his face. His lashes, now clumped together by the water, looked longer and thicker than ever.

Fighting off a chuckle, Jacki knelt by the edge of the pool and said in a sweet voice, "All better now?"

He wore a reciprocating grin. "Paybacks are hell, darlin'. And I always get even."

For the first time in a long while, Jacki felt lighthearted and carefree enough to indulge in a real laugh. "You deserved it for calling me a twit."

He tread water in the middle of the pool. "Is that what did it?"

"Yes. As for everything else you said . . ." Jacki hesitated, but what the hell? She liked Gregor. A lot.

So why did she suddenly feel shy, when everyone knew she didn't have a shy bone in her body?

"I'm waitin'," Gregor told her.

Jacki decided to go for it. "How about a movie tonight, after you finish working with Dean?"

Expression intent and filled with confidence, Gregor stroked his way toward her, reached the ledge, and held out a hand. "Deal."

Knowing exactly what he'd do, Jacki backed away. "Oh, no you don't." She grinned. "Our agreement will have to be a verbal one."

"Chicken," he taunted.

She didn't take the bait. "I'm not a fool, Gregor, and I'm not swimming until I've put on my suit."

"So put it on."

Jacki backed up another step. In her suit, it'd be more apparent than ever how few assets she had to offer.

Gregor watched her and mistook her hesitation. "Should I say please?"

"I'll swim with you another time—once you show me that you can behave."

He laughed, but the laughter stopped short as Jacki turned her back on him and strode away with a little extra swish in her stride.

She heard another splash and looked back to see Gregor had submerged himself again. Things were looking up. She had a job. She had the interest of a supreme hunk.

Now if only she could figure a way to keep the house.

TUNING out Lorna's incessant droning on about Dean Conor's intrusion into her life, Roger steered up to the curb in front of Cam's home and put the car in park. He saw the new Sebring and the sporty Mustang and felt bone-deep satisfaction at his silver SL55 AMG Mercedes-Benz.

Growing up poor, in and out of foster homes, had made him very aware of appearances. These days he reeked of success in every way.

Yet it wasn't enough. It would never be enough until he got everything he wanted, everything he damn well deserved.

In the worst ways imaginable, he'd been wronged. Yet the guilty people had never suffered the blame. They'd never taken accountability.

And that burned like acid inside him.

Because Cam hadn't suffered the same hardships as him, she wasn't into material things. But surely she would appreciate the difference in what he drove compared to what most men considered adequate transportation.

"Will you look at that," Lorna snapped. "Now that boy is up on the roof, doing work that shouldn't be done. And half-naked. He's a complete embarrassment. How am I supposed to explain him?"

Her complaints drew Roger's attention away from the cars to the top of the house. Sure enough, Dean stood there shirtless, sweating, bruised from one end to the other but not letting it slow him down.

"You should have told me about him sooner." If Dean and Eve hooked up, Dean might decide that the town had enough to offer to be his home. If he stuck around long enough, he could ruin all of Roger's plans.

That the bastard interfered with the house was hard enough to accept.

"I assumed Cam would tell you." Intentionally offensive, Lorna added, "For an engaged couple, you two aren't as close as I would hope."

Snippy bitch. But Roger wouldn't let her see how the observation cut him. "We're not officially engaged yet, Lorna." As Roger watched, Dean hefted a pile of shingles that had to be over a hundred pounds. Holding them as if they weighed nothing, he made his way to the edge of the roof and dropped them off the front of the house to a large metal Dumpster below.

"When will you get officially engaged, then?"

Roger had always prided himself on his strength and physique. After his football days had abruptly ended, he hadn't gone to fat. He hadn't lost himself in a bottle or drowned in self-pity.

He'd proved himself to be an incredible businessman, making money hand over fist.

But compared to Dean's fighting fame, Roger's life, his every hard-earned success, seemed about as exciting as watching fish swim.

And compared to Dean's capability . . . well, there was no comparison. In a physical contest, the only way Roger could defend himself against Cam's brother would be with a deadly weapon in hand.

"Roger?"

"I'm working on it," he snapped.

"Work harder," she snapped right back.

A second later, a towering shadow moved across the roof and another man came over the peak and into view. His jeans rode low on muscled hips, showing off a sculpted six-pack. A bandana around his forehead kept back longish black hair. Chest and shoulder muscles bulging, he toted his own massive load of shingles to drop into the Dumpster.

Roger stared in near awe. "Who the hell is that genetic freak?"

"What? Where?" Lorna squinted at the roof. "Why, I have no idea." She dug in her purse for her eyeglasses, looked again, and her jowls dropped. "Good God."

She sounded genuinely appalled.

"You don't recognize him?" he asked.

Wide-eyed and pale faced, Lorna said, "He's . . . *obscene.*" She continued to stare.

"Probably a fighter," Roger mused. And judging by his extraordinary size, likely a champion.

"I'm mortified. Absolutely shamed." Hand to her chest, Lorna rounded on Roger. "Going by the disreputable looks of him, he must be one of Dean's friends. But what could he be thinking to bring that criminal here?"

"You don't know that he's a criminal."

"Well he certainly looks like one!"

Roger considered that. The man was colossal and layered in solid muscles. He had an abundance of tattoos. He looked mean. He looked hardened enough to chew off the old shingles.

He would certainly provide excellent backup for Dean, *damn* it.

"Dear God, Roger. What if my neighbors see him up there on my roof, clomping all around?" Lorna sounded on the verge of expiring. "You have to do something. You're Cam's fiancé. Put a stop to this nonsense right this instant."

Doing his best to hide his hatred, Roger studied Lorna. As his only ally in the Conor family, he needed the old bitch.

But one of these days, hopefully soon, her usefulness would reach an end.

Roger's eye ticked, showing his irritation if only Lorna weren't too self-absorbed to notice.

"Well?" A web of wrinkles showed on Lorna's upper lip

when she curled it with venom. "Are you going to do something about this or not?"

"Yes." Roger glanced at the roof and the two men toiling there as if they owned the house. He returned his gaze to Lorna. Very softly, he said, "I'll take care of it."

A flash of alarm widened Lorna's eyes. But in the next instant, they narrowed with impatience. "Good. I think the first thing you should do is—"

Done discussing it with her, Roger opened his door and left the car. He wouldn't give Lorna a chance to grill him for details on his plans. Let the old bag wonder at what he'd do. He didn't want her digging deeper into his personal motivations.

The sky remained clear without a cloud in sight, so Roger didn't worry about putting up the top to his Mercedes. He opened Lorna's door for her, then suffered her grip on his arm as they made their way to the back of the house.

In numerous ways, he detected the intrusion of men to the Conor household.

Hard rock music from a CD player vied with the sounds of hammering, heavy boots, and the occasional curse. The scent of grilling meat drifted on the air.

At a nearby patio table, Jacki set out paper plates and plasticware onto a colorful tablecloth. Every few seconds, she glanced at the roof and sighed. Or frowned.

Or just licked her lips.

Roger gave her long, lean body the once-over. On a physical level, very little of Jacki appealed to him. He considered her too tall and lanky, and he disliked her skimpy clothes and glaring makeup.

But she was a Conor, and for that reason, Roger's morbid curiosity drove him to learn as much about her as he could.

Beneath the shade of a tall oak tree, Eve stretched out in a lounge chair. With her eyes closed, her body relaxed, she might have been asleep. But Roger noted the signs of tension in her face, the way her brows puckered, the press of her lips together.

Illness or fatigue?

Not that he cared, really.

Except that Eve made no secret of despising him and that wouldn't do. Cam valued Eve's opinion. That meant Roger had to value it, too.

And thinking of Cam . . . She stood at the grill, her trim hips swaying in time to the music as if she actually enjoyed it. Did she? He thought she preferred country music. He'd have to remember to ask her about it.

He wanted to know everything about her, all her likes and dislikes. Her worries. Her fears.

Sweet, naive Cam. He gazed at her as she turned hamburgers and hot dogs with that same attention to detail that he found so enthralling.

One day soon, he'd be the recipient of that attention—in bed. With them both naked. Hot. Sweaty.

Breathing deeper, Roger absorbed the sight of her and accepted the effect she had on him. Each day he grew more obsessed with her. More possessive. On his list of things to have, Cam Conor was number one.

That anyone dared to stand between them infused him with raw fury.

Roger glanced over his shoulder at the men on the roof—and found Dean staring down at him. His expression was inscrutable, but somehow Roger still felt warned.

Refusing to be cowed, Roger stared back until Lorna suddenly burst out, "And just whose outrageous idea was it to have a picnic?"

Everyone became aware of them at once.

Eve sat up from her reclined position.

Jacki paused in her attempts to set the picnic table.

Cam turned—and smiled at him. "Roger. When did you get here?"

That innocent smile never failed to do things to him, making him feel touched. Teased. Sexually primed.

The sun added blond highlights to her light brown, baby-fine hair. The humidity of the day combined with the heat of the grill put a dewy flush to her delicate skin. In many ways, she seemed younger than twenty-three.

Until he looked into her eyes. Or at her body.

Young or not, she had a woman's responsibility, a woman's sensuality.

Roger metered his breathing with effort. "We just arrived."

Today Cam wore a casual sleeveless blouse in a summery shade of pale green, with tan walking shorts. Such understated clothes—hiding such a provocative body.

He'd seen her in her bathing suit enough times to fantasize with accuracy. The sight of her small waist and long shapely legs was permanently burned into his memory. Unlike Jacki, Cam's breasts would fill his hands. . . .

Lust stirred deep inside Roger. For so many reasons, Cam often felt like an unattainable dream. But that was an illusion, and he'd prove it by making her his own. He *would* have her.

One way or another.

Separating himself from Lorna's abrasive attitude, he strode forward and greeted Cam with a light kiss to her mouth. She didn't dodge him, but she didn't exactly seem thrilled, either.

How could she continue to put him off with everything falling down around her? Despite her damned brother's intrusion, *he* was her savior. When the time was right, she'd have no choice but to turn to him.

For everything.

And then he'd get his due.

"I want someone to answer me this instant," Lorna demanded.

Roger barely managed to keep his frustration hidden. Lorna Ross had no sense of subtlety, no real discretion.

Cam put up a hand to shade her eyes. "I decided to grill out, Aunt Lorna. It's a beautiful day, and I'm sure Dean and Gregor are working up an appetite."

Lorna lowered her voice, but not enough. "Gregor? And

who is this Gregor person with all those disturbing tattoos? What do you know of him? Are you sure he's not a convict or some such?"

A smile twitched on Cam's mouth. "Of course he's not. He's a friend of Dean."

Lorna sniffed her disdain. "And on that recommendation you allowed this man to know our address?"

The blatant insult sent shock rippling through Cam. Roger started to intervene, but she didn't give him a chance.

"Enough." Pushing Roger aside, Cam stepped around him to deal with her aunt. She didn't lower her voice one iota. In fact, she might have raised it. "On that recommendation, I would move him in if asked."

On a deep gulp of air, Lorna prepared for a ripping tirade—when Dean's booming laughter erupted.

Everyone turned to look at him.

Shouting down from the roof, Dean said, "Cam, that's real generous of you. But there's no need for Lorna to get her girdle all twisted. Gregor's not staying on."

More outraged by the second, Lorna waited in vain for someone to defend her.

Everyone was too busy snickering.

When the old battle-axe realized that no one would speak on her behalf, she soured even more.

It took all Roger had not to laugh out loud.

Dean turned to the giant. "You're not planning to stay in Harmony, are you, Gregor?"

Raising a forearm to swipe the sweat from his face, Gregor said, "Nah." Biceps the size of cantaloupes bunched and swelled with his every movement. He dropped his arm and smiled. "Not unless little sister asks me to."

Everyone looked at Jacki.

Face coloring, she snorted. "You see, Aunt Lorna. There's nothing to worry about. He's not staying." Her chin lifted. "Not too long anyway."

Trembling with anger, Lorna addressed everyone in a sweeping glance. "That's enough from all of you!" She made

Cam the brunt of her anger. "And you. It's bad enough that you're willing to waste money we don't have on repairs we don't need."

"They're needed," Cam insisted.

"Bah. You should be signing papers to complete the sale of this money pit, and instead you're playing outdoors and celebrating with a picnic."

Dean muttered to Gregor, "Celebrating? Is that what we're doing?"

Fury turned Lorna's face crimson and her lips white. "I refuse to take part in such obnoxious, irresponsible behavior."

She turned to Roger for backup, leaving him without many choices.

Keeping his expression bland, Roger said to Cam, "I'll only be a moment."

She slanted a look at her aunt, but Lorna snubbed her. Cam sighed. "Thanks, Roger. I'll save you a burger." And with that, she turned back to the grill.

As if the contretemps had been nothing out of the ordinary, Dean and Gregor resumed their work.

Digging her artificial nails into Roger's arm, Lorna dragged him along as she marched into the house.

Along the way, Roger considered things. So, he thought, the muscle-bound monster wanted Jacki. Bad taste on his part, but more power to him.

Getting Jacki out from under Cam's wing would leave her less encumbered with responsibility—which would clear the path for Roger's ultimate goals.

The moment they were out of sight of the others, Roger rudely brushed off Lorna and then suffered through her glare of disbelief.

Stupid woman. With no more than the force of his anger, Roger backed her up to the sink counter. He could keep an eye on everyone in the yard and at the same time set Lorna straight on her bad judgment.

She shrank back. "Roger. What do you think you're doing?"

He was so annoyed, he wanted to choke her. "Instead of always reacting with your goddamned temper, why don't you try thinking for a change?"

She blinked hard in incomprehension, forcing him to explain.

"Jesus, Lorna." He rubbed his forehead, once again amazed that someone as gentle and clueless as Cam could have any relationship to a calculating evil bitch like Lorna. "How exactly do you expect me to handle this situation if you remove me from it?"

Never would Lorna admit to a mistake. "You weren't handling it at all. You just stood there."

"And you think your insults were productive?" Roger shook his head at her stupidity. "By now you should know your niece better than that."

"Oh, believe me, I know her. She's fanciful and full of herself."

"You're joking."

She paid no attention to his sarcasm. "But regardless, I didn't raise her to associate with men like Dean or that Gregor character."

No, Roger thought, but Lorna also hadn't been successful at influencing Cam with her own hatred and mistrust of men. Somehow she'd survived with an unrealistic enthusiasm that alternately bemused, annoyed, and encouraged him. "Cam is defensive of everyone she cares about. And she cares about her brother."

"She doesn't even know him!"

"She knows you kept her from him. That's something you ought to think about before you continue maligning him at every chance."

Lorna didn't want to hear it. She clutched her designer purse to her chest and scowled new wrinkles into her face. "That bastard is going to ruin everything."

No, Roger vowed to himself. He wouldn't let anyone destroy his plans. "You're distraught." Removing his wallet, Roger flipped off several twenties and pressed them into Lorna's hand. "Why don't you go to the salon, get a facial or a massage or whatever it is women do to make themselves feel better."

"Well . . ." Lorna counted the money carefully. "I suppose I could call a friend." She slanted a sly look up at Roger. "Perhaps lunch, too, while I'm at it. Heaven knows I have no desire to choke on charred meats off the grill."

Wearing a tight smile, Roger peeled off another forty dollars for her. "Excellent idea." Getting rid of Lorna was worth every penny.

"What will you do?"

No way in hell did he trust Lorna enough to give her the truth. If she knew about his background and why he wanted what he deserved, not only would she distort his purpose, but she wouldn't be able to keep her mouth shut, either.

"I'm going to go outside, visit with everyone," Roger told her. "I'll be cordial and hopefully get a lay of the land, so to speak. Once I see what's what, I'll figure out the best way to handle things."

"And you'll keep me informed?"

"No, I won't."

Her double chin jiggled with her indignation.

"The less you know of my plans, the better it is for you. I don't want to implicate you in any way."

Her expression grew more severe. "Dear God, what are you planning?"

Roger could barely credit her audacity. Lorna had squandered a lot of money without thought toward her nieces. She'd used them and their inheritance to lead a pampered life. More than once, she'd overstepped her legal boundaries to make financial decisions that served her interests alone.

Hanging on to her ill-gotten gains wouldn't be easy if Dean started digging.

Putting it simply, Roger asked, "Does it really matter how I handle the situation as long as it gets the issues resolved?"

She subsided, as he'd known she would. "No, I suppose not."

"Good. Then we agree. Now I should get back outside or Cam will start wondering what's keeping me."

Lorna dredged up a crocodile tear. "You're a good friend, Roger."

If she hugged him, he'd vomit. So he stepped out of reach and nodded. "Enjoy the afternoon, Lorna. You've earned it."

Head held high, Lorna started away with Roger's money crushed in her fist. "Yes, yes I have." She nodded more to herself than anyone else. "And then some."

Glad to have finished with Lorna, Roger strode to the sliding doors and surveyed the yard. He couldn't see the men on the roof, but he could hear their footfalls as they worked.

Once again, Eve dozed in the shade. It was very unlike her to indulge in so much idle time. On a normal day, she presented nonstop energy and drive. Even while seated, she somehow exuded vibrant life.

Had she spent a sleepless night with Dean Conor? Had they screwed all night long and into the morning? Roger wouldn't put it past Eve. She struck him as a very sexual woman.

He looked over, head to toes, her reclined body. Was Eve lure enough to keep Dean Conor in Harmony?

Possibly. And that meant that, somehow, Roger would have to deal with Dean.

Eve was so dissimilar to Cam that Roger often wondered how and why they remained friends. Thinking of Cam, his skin prickled with that familiar rush of warmth and awareness. From his position still inside the house, Roger looked at her.

After shooing away a bumblebee, Cam lifted a large platter in one hand and used tongs to remove meat from the grill. A variety of hungers stirred. It had been a long time since he'd eaten food prepared outdoors.

Food prepared by Cam.

Roger started to open the patio doors when his attention snagged on Jacki. She stood off to the side, close to the house, where the others couldn't see her. Roger watched her as she adjusted her top, trying to squish her small breasts together enough to create some cleavage.

A futile effort on her part.

Disgruntled, Jacki dropped her arms and stepped away from the house to look toward the roof. At Gregor? Likely so.

She compressed her lips in anger and, head hanging, started toward the house.

Roger slid the door open. "Hey Jacki. You got a second?"

Her head snapped up and she eyed him with suspicion. Her voice filled with accusation, she said, "I thought you left with Aunt Lorna."

Reading Jacki wasn't nearly as difficult as reading her sister. Cam was deep; Jacki was superficial. She might exude confidence, but deep down, Jacki's insecurities ran rampant.

"I believe your aunt is calling a friend to accompany her on a ladies' day out."

Her mouth twisted. "Good riddance."

If only Cam would adopt that attitude. Roger shook his head. "If you have a moment, I'd like to speak with you." He had an idea that just might advance his position with Cam, while assisting Jacki at the same time.

Hip cocked out, Jacki asked, "What do you want?"

"Just a word."

She resisted the invitation. "I need to get the potato chips and pickles. I forgot them."

"Perfect timing." Roger stepped back to give her entrance through the patio doors. "I can lend a hand and make a suggestion at the same time."

A noise sounded behind them and Jacki turned to see Gregor standing there. Sweat dripped down his shoulders and chest. The sun had added richer color to his naturally dark skin tone. An icy bottle of water dangled in his hand.

But his eyes reflected the most heat as he watched them like a hawk, making no effort to hide his burning jealousy.

And that seemed to make up Jacki's mind.

"All right." Smiling, she stepped in around Roger. "What kind of suggestion?"

A dangerous game, Roger thought, to incite the anger of that one. But with Cam as the ultimate prize, he put all other considerations out of his mind. With one last glance at the hulk staring holes through his soul, Roger slid the patio door shut. "A suggestion that I think will please you."

And in the long run, it'd please him, too.

CHAPTER 14

D EAN felt Gregor watching him as they finished prying loose the last strip of shingles. It had taken three
hours of hard, nonstop labor to remove them all. Not that
hard work was a problem. He'd never shied away from it.

But for the last fifteen minutes, Gregor had been stealing glances at him.

Dean wouldn't ask him why. He wouldn't give Gregor
the satisfaction. He'd just ignore him until they finished the
roof and—

"Hey, Havoc?"

Meddling son of a . . . So ignoring him wouldn't work.
He wasn't surprised.

Using his scraper, Dean ripped viciously at a stubborn
clump of leftover shingle pieces, removing a few twisted
roofing nails at the same time. *"What?"*

Silence.

Disgruntled, Dean sat back on his heels and in a more
moderate tone said, "What the hell do you want, Gregor?"

Gregor shrugged a shoulder sleeked with sweat and grime. "Never heard you laugh like that before, that's all."

"What?"

"Earlier. When you were snipin' at the old broad. You were really cuttin' up."

"So?"

"I don't think I've heard you that happy."

"Bullshit." Dean tossed the hunk of mangled shingles and nails onto the pile. "Don't go dramatic on me. You've heard me laugh plenty of times."

"Not like that. Not like ya meant it."

"The sun must be frying your brain." Dean stripped off a glove so he could clear the grime from his face. It gave him a solid reason not to look at Gregor. "Good thing we're ready for a break."

Gregor pulled off his gloves, too. "My brain is fine and you know it."

"Uh-huh."

He made a dry face. "For God's sake, Dean, don't get defensive. I was just curious—"

"Don't." To make certain Gregor understood, Dean replied sharply, "Don't be curious, and don't think to start prying." To make certain Gregor understood, Dean added a glare for good measure.

Meddling would not be tolerated.

Not the least bit bothered by Dean's mood, Gregor continued with his nosy interrogation. "You're diggin' the whole family thing, aren't you?"

"Go fuck yourself."

Gregor's eyebrows shot up, and his humor returned. "Now what fun would that be? You know I'd rather—"

Knowing exactly what he'd rather, Dean warned, *"Don't say it."*

Chuckling, Gregor pretended to zip his lip.

Shit. Somehow Gregor had egged him into giving himself away. Expression carefully blank, Dean looked at him. "You're an annoying ass, you know that?"

Gregor nodded. "Yeah. I've heard that before."

Dean assured himself that his reaction had less to do with being Jacki's brother and more to do with being hot, sweaty, and tired. "Instead of hassling me, why don't we get done here so we can eat?"

"Sure thing." But after a moment, Gregor started again. "You know, I wasn't judgin'."

Dean dropped his head back and groaned at the expansive blue sky. "Un-fucking-believable."

Gregor couldn't keep his grin at bay. "And I wasn't going to ride you about it or anything. Hell, Havoc, your family is real nice. Lots of good-lookin' women. Friendly. Sassy. I like 'em. All but that old one." He shuddered. "Nasty old coot, isn't she?"

"Yeah." Nasty and manipulative. Had Lorna ever told the girls *how* their parents had died? Not just about the car wreck, but the whole shebang? He doubted it.

Should he tell them?

"She must make Jacki and Cam miserable, don't you think?"

Dean tried to ignore Gregor—but he hit a nerve, damn it. For their part, Cam and Jacki seemed to take Lorna in stride, as if they were used to her acerbic attitude on life and expected nothing different.

And that bothered Dean more than anything else could.

"Why's the old broad so sour anyway?" Gregor asked. When Dean didn't answer, he tried prodding him. "Hey, Havoc? Got any ideas?"

Slowly, Dean laid down his scraper and gave Gregor his full attention. "Ideas? Yeah, I have an idea."

Gregor's back straightened. "Why do I have the feelin' that I won't like your idea?"

"Maybe because it has to do with me tossing your muscle-bound butt off the roof."

Grinning like a fool, Gregor peered over the side to the ground below. "I'd rather you didn't." He swung his gaze back to Dean. "You know, I outweigh you by more than thirty-five pounds, I'm taller, and you're beat all to hell and back already."

"So?" If Dean decided to toss him, Gregor *would* go over. No doubt about it.

"So little sis is down there, and she'll think I'm a pussy if I let you throw me over. Can't have her getting' the wrong impression, now can I? Besides, imagine the mess it'll make of their nice lawn. A mess you'd probably end up fixin' since you've morphed into a domesticated family man."

That did it.

Shooting to his feet, Dean took a hard, aggressive step forward. "How about you shut up and mind your own god-damn business? Or do I need to shut you up?"

"Hey, chill out, already." Holding up both hands in sur-render, Gregor waited for Dean to subside. "Jesus, man, re-lax, why doncha?"

Feeling like a raging idiot, Dean cursed and loosened his stance. "I'm relaxed."

Gregor grunted over that gigantic lie. "It's the truth, Havoc. I liked you better when you were laughin'." He gathered up the pile of shingles and crossed the roof to the front of the house to dump them.

Muttering to himself, Dean again wiped the sweat from his face and tried to ignore his prickling guilt. Gregor was a jerk, but he didn't deserve to bear the brunt of Dean's bad humor.

Luckily, unlike women, men didn't require apologies to let shit go.

When Gregor returned, Dean said easily, "Ready to eat?"

"Sure. If you think we're done here for now."

Dean surveyed the roof. There were still lots of tiny pieces of shingle stuck to the wood and many roofing nails that needed to be removed or pounded down. The plumb-ing vent stack had an old metal flashing around it, sealed with gobs of roofing tar. Before he'd lay the new shingles, he'd remove that and scrape off the tar.

But all that could wait.

"Yeah, we can get back on this after a break."

"Thank God. I'm so hungry, my ribs are clankin' to-gether." Gregor went halfway down the ladder and then jumped the rest of the way. The second his feet hit the ground, he looked for Jacki.

She was nowhere to be seen—but Dean did zero in on Eve, watching as she went into the house again. That was her third trip inside. Each time she came back out, she looked more listless.

He didn't like it.

Dean sat in the shade of a tree, drinking iced tea when Eve returned this time. She looked so uncomfortable, she didn't notice him, and that bothered him, too.

He sat his drink aside and met her halfway across the lawn. She seemed lost in thought, her head bowed, her pace slow. Dean halted her by putting the back of his hand to her forehead.

Surprised blue eyes lifted and locked with his. "What are you doing?"

Dean frowned. "You okay?"

Wary, she pulled away from him. "Yeah, why?"

She felt hot, Dean decided, but not really feverish. Still, she looked beat, not at all like the dynamic woman he knew. "Why don't you go on home and rest up? You should probably stay out of this heat."

A frown tugged at her brows. "I'm fine."

"You don't feel well."

Her shoulders squared in protest. "Says who?"

Why did she sound so prickly? Dean propped his hands on his hips. "I say."

"Well, you're wrong, because I'm not sick and I'm not going home. Not just yet anyway. After we eat, I do have to go home to change. I have an appointment early this evening."

"What kind of appointment?"

The way she pokered up, he might as well have demanded that she hand over her firstborn. "I'm an event coordinator, Dean, remember?" She slapped a lock of hair away from her face with more force than necessary, then crossed her arms. "I have to meet with a potential client."

Dean chewed over what she said, compared to how she

acted, and decided he didn't like it a bit. Taking her arm, he said, "Come with me."

Eve dug her bare heels into the soft lawn. "Come with you where? What are you doing?"

Dean kept walking, towing her along toward the back of the yard near the woods. As a boy, he'd gone there often just to be alone, to think. It afforded some necessary privacy.

Cam called out, "Dean? Eve? Where are you going? The food's ready."

Dean yelled back, "Give us a minute."

"I'm hungry, damn it." Eve trotted along, barely keeping up with his long strides. "Dean," she hissed. "You're causing a scene."

"So?" They reached the woods and Dean urged her behind a thick oak tree.

"Oh, that's right." Eve practically sneered. "You don't care what anyone thinks, do you?"

Dean sighed. Whatever bothered her, it must be something substantial for her to be so bitchy. He intended to find out what and then he'd fix it.

"Tell me what's wrong, Eve." When she just pinched her mouth together, he cupped her face and kissed the end of her very cute nose. "Come on, honey," he cajoled. "Talk to me."

Maybe the endearment did the trick, because she gave up her pique and slumped back against the tree in defeat. For long, agonizing seconds, she stared down at a cool covering of green moss growing over a tree root.

Finally her gaze lifted to his. "I have some bad news, Dean. You're not going to like it."

Alarm sank its icy claws into Dean's stomach. He hardened himself, locking his jaw, tensing his muscles, preparing for the worst. Bracing one arm on the tree behind Eve, he dominated her space. *Tell me.*

"Well." Eve looked away, then peeked up at him again. She frowned. "It'd be easier to do this if you weren't glaring at me like that."

He fucking well didn't want to make it easy on her. "Say what you have to say, damn it."

In defiance, she crossed her arms. "It sort of changes your plans for tonight."

The oxygen left Dean's lungs. His plans for the night? That's what made her look so ill?

To be certain they were on the same wave, he asked, "My plans for sex? That's what we're talking about here, right?"

She nodded miserably. "Yes. Mother Nature has come calling."

Mother Nature?

She had her *period*? That was it?

A shock of humor went through Dean, loosening his tensed muscles, lifting the instinctive rage against rejection. He wanted to laugh, and even more than that, he wanted to kiss her silly.

But he wasn't a dummy. He put his other hand on the tree, too, caging her in. Poor thing. Eve looked tired and cranky and ready to hide herself away.

She avoided his gaze, but he could see her frown—and the blush of color on her face.

After choking down his amusement, Dean fashioned an expression of concern. "You're having your monthly?"

"Yes," was her clipped reply.

This close, he could smell the sun-warmed scent of her hair and skin. Combined with her very womanly emotions, it affected him in a wholly sexual way. "And that's making you feel bad?"

Blue eyes came up to clash with his. "Why do you ask?"

Uh-oh. Tiptoe carefully, he warned himself. "It's just that you're not as . . . animated as usual." And you're downright mean, too—but Dean kept that observation to himself.

She slumped with a groan. "If you want the truth, I feel like crap. I have awful PMS. My periods last a week, I bloat, and yeah, I feel drained."

A *week*? Dean felt his own groan struggle to get free. "I'm sorry."

"Me, too." Her voice lowered. She dropped her forehead to his sternum. "I was really looking forward to tonight."

Gently, Dean tipped up her chin. "I'm not the squeamish type, honey. And there are plenty of ways—"

"Forget it." Eyes wide, Eve attempted to shove him away, realized he didn't plan to budge, and settled on thrusting her face up close to his. "I *am* squeamish, but even if I wasn't, I'm not up for it. Trust me on this, Dean, I am not good company."

No sex, huh? To Dean's surprise, he realized that he just plain didn't care. But how to convince her? Being a gentleman about it wouldn't do. She'd tell him to get lost, and he refused to do that.

Again, he tipped up her chin so she looked at him. "You owe me, Eve."

"What?"

"We had a bet, lady. You lost, so I'm coming over." She looked so volatile at that, Dean stepped back out of reach. But he didn't relent. "If you want to be grouchy and sleep, that's okay. I can take it. But you can't cancel on me."

"I meant what I said. No sex."

"I'm not deaf. I heard you. I'll wait until you're ready." Dean held his ground. "But I'm still coming over."

Something, maybe relief, flashed over Eve's face before she crossed her arms and turned her stiff back on him. "Fine," she snapped. "Don't listen to me. Suit yourself. But don't say I didn't warn you."

Dean took in her chiseled posture, the severe stiffness of her shoulders. Even her rejections filled him with warmth, tenderness, and the purest pleasure.

So odd.

He'd be celibate for several days, but the grin came anyway. "You're wasting your time, honey." He bent and kissed the nape of her neck—and felt her shiver. "There's something else you should know about me."

She peeked over her shoulder at him, her brows arched in question.

Dean said, "I don't scare easily."

Their gazes held for a long moment before Eve again turned away.

No, Dean decided, Eve couldn't scare him away—not when he wanted something, and for whatever reason, he wanted *her*. Not just sex. Not any woman.

Eve.

Now. Tonight. And tomorrow.

With or without sex.

And, damn it, he had no reason at all to pick that apart. He'd just go with it and enjoy himself, and in the process, he'd bring Eve enjoyment, too.

WHEN Dean walked into the lobby of the Cross Streets Motel, he saw Roger at the faux marble countertop of the front desk, staring into a computer screen. He knew Roger owned and operated the place, but this was the first time he'd seen him there.

He had a feeling that wasn't a coincidence.

A little slow in the awareness department, it took Roger a good full minute before he felt Dean's stare. When he looked up and saw Dean watching him, he literally jerked. Surprise gave way to determination.

Circling out from behind the counter, Roger headed for him. "Dean. Got a minute?"

Just to be a prick, Dean glanced at his watch. "Maybe one. I need to shower and change and get over to Eve's."

Irritation compressed Roger's mouth for an instant. "I see." He formed a resentful smile. "You two are practically inseparable already."

"You have about forty seconds left."

Green eyes flinched with anger. "Fine. Could we step into my office? It's more private."

Roger started away but had to turn back when Dean said, "Here will do."

Since they stood in the center of the lobby with no chance for privacy, Roger inhaled sharply. He started to rein himself in, but then burst out, "Fuck it." After one big aggressive step toward Dean, he said, "I'll cut to the chase."

"Yeah." Dean folded his arms over his chest and leaned into the wall. "You do that."

"I want to know what you're doing in Harmony, how long you'll be here, and what the hell you're planning with Cam."

Seeing no reason not to tell him, Dean shrugged. "I'm here because Cam invited me. I don't yet know how long I'll be here. But while I'm here, I hope to help Cam get back on track."

"What does that mean, 'back on track'?"

"She's in debt. The house needs work. I haven't entirely thought it through, so I don't know to what extent I'll get involved, but I plan to help her with both circumstances." Dean watched Roger, waiting to see how he'd react to that news.

Visibly frustrated, Roger ran a hand through his blond hair, leaving it less styled, and making himself appear almost human. "I was going to help her," he said more to himself than to Dean.

Right. But for what purpose? Dean wondered. He'd always been a good judge of character, and everything about Roger screamed suspicion. No man who flaunted his money the way Roger did could be trusted to care about and understand the really important things in life.

No man who bullied others would be compassionate enough, gentle and caring enough for his sis—

Whoa. Hold the phone.

Staring at Roger, Dean literally backed away—until he caught himself. No fucking way would he let himself start thinking in terms of . . . He couldn't even form the thought without a lot of wariness.

But, damn it, he had to face facts. In speed-of-light time, he was starting to feel like a . . . big brother.

Well, shit.

Roger gave him a curious frown, and Dean cut him short by saying, "Is that it? Because I have things to do."

Shoving his hands into his pants pockets, Roger forged ahead. "I just thought . . . Well, considering Cam and I will be married—"

"Maybe."

That one word, and the possibilities that came with it, nearly spurred Roger to violence. "We *will* be married," he snarled. "Don't doubt it."

Interesting reaction, Dean thought. Did Roger actually love Cam? Or was he driven by other motives? "Is there a point to this, Rog?"

The shortened name had Roger bristling, but he brought himself under control. "Since we'll be"—his lip curled— "family, I thought you might want to get to know me better."

Dean laughed. "No." Family? *No, no, no.* He would not start interviewing suitors for his sister. If he ever did anything that asinine, he deserved to be blindfolded and stuck in the ring with two of the best Brazil had to offer. "Cam can make up her own mind who she wants to associate with."

"Damn it, man, I'm trying—"

"Dean. Roger. What's going on?"

At that familiar female voice, Dean closed his eyes in dread. But only for a second. He didn't want to miss a thing, not Roger's reaction, and not Cam's reception.

His sister knew he was staying at the motel, but so far they hadn't run into each other. Of course he'd been more away from the motel than in it.

He intended to keep it that way.

Harsh with guilt, Roger spun on his heel toward Cam. "Sweetheart." His smile wouldn't convince anyone. "I didn't hear you there."

Dean smirked at Roger's obvious discomfort. Idiot.

For her part, Cam stood near to Roger with a familiarity Dean couldn't ignore. So maybe they were an item. That didn't mean his sister would actually marry the ass.

Along with a trim black skirt and tailored blouse, Cam wore a name badge. It infuriated Dean.

What type of man had a woman he loved working second shift for him?

Roger cleared his throat. "Cam, honey, I thought you were doing some inventory."

She sent Roger a gentle smile. "Yes, but I finished." She turned to Dean with caution. "How is everything?"

Dean couldn't help but grin. "You lack subtlety, Cam." Without thinking about it, he touched her cheek. "Eve is fine. Don't worry about it."

Chagrined, she smiled an apology. "I know it's none of my business."

It was none of Roger's business, but Dean had no problem with Cam's honest concern for her friend. "It's okay."

"When I left for work, Eve was about to leave, too, and I know you two were still sniping at each other." She bit her lip. "I'm sorry if the work on the roof made it more difficult for you to patch things up."

Dean shook his head. "Stop fretting. There's nothing to patch up. I'm heading over there tonight, just as soon as I shower and change."

Delight relaxed Cam's posture. "That's wonderful. I'm glad to hear it."

"Maybe," Roger offered, "Eve will be incentive enough to keep your brother around longer." He put his arm around Cam's waist. "Wouldn't that be nice?"

"Whatever makes Dean happy makes me happy." Cam dug in her skirt pocket. "By the way, you have a couple of messages. They're on your voice mail in your room, but I also wrote them down." She handed several slips of paper to Dean.

He gave them a brief glance. "Simon Evans, my trainer—among other things." He hoped there wasn't anything urgent that needed his attention. When he first came to Harmony, he'd planned a very brief visit. Simon knew that.

But now . . . Well, he didn't know how long he'd stay; he only knew that he didn't want to leave yet.

"He called three times," Cam prompted.

"Yeah." Dean frowned. "I had my cell off while I was working on the roof because I didn't want to be bothered."

And he hadn't thought anyone would try to reach him anyway. "It's probably nothing." At least, he hoped so. "Maybe a sponsorship offer or something. Those come up a lot."

Restless with wariness, Cam touched his arm. "Dean . . ." She dropped her hand, shifted, looked at Dean, looked away, and finally said, "You won't leave without telling me, will you?"

Like a punch in the heart, her concern struck him. Damn. Did she really think he'd do that? That he'd sneak away without so much as a farewell? Had he given her reason to think it?

Before Dean could reassure her, she rushed into more nervous chatter.

"I'm not trying to pressure you or anything. It's just that with your trainer calling, I figured he might want you back for some reason. And I understand that. You have a very serious career."

A career that she figured was a whole lot more important than any long-lost family?

Her smile trembled. "I'm afraid I'll wake up one morning and find out that you've left as suddenly as you arrived. I'm afraid I won't have a chance to say . . ." Her voice faded. "Good-bye."

"Cam . . ."

Desperate, she moved closer to him. "If you wouldn't mind too much, I'd like your number and address and all that. I wouldn't intrude, I promise. I wouldn't visit without an invitation. But—"

Empathy, affection, and the need to protect, all crashed down on Dean, blinding him and stealing his tongue. He couldn't get a single word choked out, so instead he went with his gut and lifted Cam off her feet in a forceful bear hug.

It was the most uncommon thing, how it felt to hold a sister. Good, but not a routine type of good. He put his nose in her hair and inhaled, and it all seemed familiar and yet very, very strange. Somehow comforting. And reassuring.

Cam's affection worked like quicksand, sucking him in until he knew struggling wouldn't help at all. In fact, it'd make things worse.

Voice gruff, Dean said, "I won't disappear, Cam. I promise."

She gasped, then whispered, "Dean, *please*."

He lifted his head—and saw Roger's anxiety and anger. Well, hell. He had Cam compressed against his chest tight enough to asphyxiate her. Unlike him, she wasn't made of muscle and thick bones. In comparison, her frame was small and delicate.

Roger wanted to attack him. Dean saw it in his eyes, in the way he breathed and how he held himself. Dean would almost relish a reason to put the bastard out with one nose-crunching blow.

But Roger only snarled, "For God's sake, you're cutting off her air, man. Let her go."

Having already loosened his hold, Dean tilted Cam back. "I'm sorry, hon. You're okay?"

"A few broken ribs, that's all." Her wicked, teasing smile showed a strong resemblance to Jacki that Dean hadn't before noticed.

After Cam smoothed her clothes, she reached up to cup Dean's face. "Do you mean it? You'll let me know before you leave Harmony?"

His sister was a demonstrative woman, a natural nurturer. A woman who enjoyed physical contact. Dean thought of her with Roger, and it plain didn't sit right with him.

"Yeah." He met Roger's gaze with a clear warning. "You'll know."

"Thank you." She put her arms around his waist and this time, it seemed a natural thing to return her embrace.

ONLY one young man stood at the counter in the lobby when Dean went out the doors an hour later, freshly showered and changed into clean clothes. He assumed Roger had gone home, and Cam likely had duties elsewhere. He felt a reprieve at avoiding more emotional conflict with her.

Once outside, the hot, humid air closed in on Dean. The crunching sounds of his soft-soled shoes on the gravel lot echoed through the darkness. Security lights, stationed near the entrance to Roger's establishment, failed to reach the far end of the lot, leaving many cars cloaked in heavy shadow.

Because Dean always parked away from other cars, the Sebring presented a lone, hazy structure, barely visible against the overgrown weeds and untended shrubs from the convenience store behind it.

As he crossed the lot, Dean dialed Simon Evans. His trainer picked up on the fourth ring.

"Evans here."

Dean started to reply, and a slight noise and a shifting in the shadows snagged his attention. Vague, maybe even part of his imagination, it still triggered his senses, putting him on alert. His gaze scanned the area, peering through the thick cover of darkness.

Nothing.

Evans hung up on him.

Shit. Dean redialed and this time when Simon answered, he said, "Hey, it's Dean. Sorry for losing you, there."

"Bad connection?" Simon asked.

"Just a distraction." He saw no reason to tell Simon he'd gotten spooked enough not to reply. "I got your messages. What's up?"

"A great deal, that's what. Pack your bags and get on back here."

"No."

Simon hesitated. "What the fuck is this? You don't even want the details before refusing?"

It wouldn't matter. "You're dying to tell me, so go ahead."

With gruesome delight, Simon said, "Desmond broke his hand in the last fight. Shattered a couple of bones. He's out for awhile."

"Sucks for him. What's it have to do with me?"

"That fight drew a lot of attention. Most of it negative."

"Nothing unusual in that." Dean continued to look around the blackened area as he went to his car. He couldn't shake the feeling of being watched. "We've always gotten more than our fair share of bad press."

"And that's where you come in. You're their golden boy. Successful in your own right, polite and upbeat. Clean-cut."

"Clean-cut?" Dean laughed at that. A daily shave and shower was as close as he got to spiffing up. "How does anyone figure that?"

"You keep short hair and avoid piercings. Other than that tattoo you got ages ago, you haven't been inked. You don't smoke or drink and when half the world is caving into steroids, you speak out against their use."

"I did one freaking commercial." Dean shook his head. The twenty-second clip that blasted the use of steroids in sports wasn't played in the States, but it aired often in other countries.

"And you donate to educational pursuits, along with a shitload of other charities."

"It's a tax deduction."

Simon spoke over him. "And you saved that one old lady. We'll be getting mileage from that for years."

Dean locked his jaw. "I hope you're joking."

"It'll be a video of you. Sort of a reality thing where they tail you everywhere you go—"

"No."

"They'll plug in highlights of some of your fights. Thirty-second knockouts and some that went the distance. They'll show you without a scratch and beaten bloody."

"No." Hell no. The last thing he wanted was a camera stuck in his face twenty-four/seven.

Simon let out an aggrieved breath, then switched tactics. "I thought you were going to ring me up once you got settled in."

Dean shrugged. He hadn't settled yet, and he doubted he ever would. Not with the way Harmony dredged up so many mixed memories—some good, most bad. "I got side-tracked with a few things."

"Right." Simon hesitated. "Look, I'm coming to see you."

Dean dug his keys out of his jeans pocket. "What for?"

Leaving no doubt as to his mood, Simon snarled, "Something's going on. You're not acting right."

"I'm fine." If being buried in confusion over two sisters he barely knew was fine. If thinking you heard and saw things moving in the darkness was fine. If—

"You got the shit beat out of you in that last fight, Dean."

"I won."

He snorted. "You moved like a fucking rookie. A dozen opportunities to submit the bastard came and went and you did jack shit."

True. Still . . . he had won. "Gregor's here. I'm going to spar with him."

Stunned disbelief sounded as harsh as cannon blast. "The hell you are!" Simon's voice rose loud enough to break his eardrums. "Do *not* spar with Gregor until I'm there, Dean. I mean it. You'll end up killing him." Simon took a breath, then continued to mutter for a few more seconds, before saying, "I've got a pen and paper ready. Give me the damn address. I'll be there in just a few days."

Well, hell. With everyone following Dean into Harmony, maybe they should do an exhibition. They could put that in their ridiculous video. Eve could set it up. Her family would love it.

Which meant she'd love it.

Not a bad idea.

In fact, the only bad idea was his repeated use of the word "love."

Dean cut his thoughts short, saying, "Do me a favor first, will you?"

"Depends. Crazy as you're acting, I need to hear the favor first."

"Hire someone to do a background check on Roger Sims. He's a local here with a lot of enterprises." Dean named some of the establishments to make it easier to investigate Roger.

"This Roger fellow do something to you?"

"Not really." Staring at the darkness surrounding him, Dean tacked on a silent: *Not yet.*

"Then what's the problem?"

Seeing no real hope for it, Dean said, "He's dating my sister."

More stunned silence, then with dry humor, "That bastard. Want me to have him killed?"

Trust Simon to make light of surprising news. "If you're not going to grill me on my never-before-mentioned family, then can I suggest that you bring some gear with you?"

"Gear?"

"For sparring. If I'm going to do this with Gregor, might as well do it right."

And maybe, just maybe, that applied to everything, Dean thought.

Even that damned "L" word.

CHAPTER 15

MOONLIGHT danced on the surface of the pool water. A warm breeze lifted stray hairs from her face
and teased over body parts exposed by her bikini: her
throat, her belly, and her thighs. Jacki heard the crickets in
the woods beyond. The call of an owl.

And she heard her own heartbeat, fast with trepidation
and anticipation.

Standing close behind her, feeding her senses with his
scent, his masculine presence, Gregor whispered, "It's nice
out here at night."

Briefly, Jacki closed her eyes. And in her mind, she saw
him in his goofy green lizard boxers, a substitute for
trunks. He exuded consummate power. Iron muscles, bold
tattoos, and so much confidence made him dangerous, especially to her common sense.

She had to be insane to put herself in the position of
being alone with him like this.

As if he'd read her thoughts, Gregor's palm moved over
her shoulder, then turned her to face him.

"Everythin' okay, sugar?"

Not even close. Drawn against her will, Jacki moved her bare feet nearer to his. "Why wouldn't it be?"

"Dunno." He caught both her shoulders, restraining her with gentleness. "But you're quiet, and a quiet woman is enough to set my hair on end. It's a bad sign. A very bad sign."

A nervous chuckle threatened. "Really? And why's that?"

"It means you're thinkin' of things." His hands moved up to her throat, rough fingertips rasping against her delicate skin, leaving gooseflesh in their wake. "Probably reasons you shouldn't be here with me. But I'd rather you just go with the moment."

Her heart hammered so hard, it felt like pain. Bravado, Jacki told herself. Be audacious. Be brassy.

Be what Gregor expected.

Tilting her head back, Jacki smiled up at him. "And what would the moment be?"

The dark night couldn't hide the glitter in Gregor's eyes. "This." He bent, and his mouth moved briefly over hers.

Feather light. Cautious. Sweet and easy . . .

For about three seconds.

Then he groaned and hauled her flush to his big body, unleashing all that awesome sex appeal on her.

Having her flesh smashed up against his gave her firsthand knowledge of how he felt burning hot and rock solid. And . . . dynamic. Electrifying.

As her feet left the ground, Jacki braced her hands on his wide shoulders, and she thrilled at the taut, bulging muscles. Oh God, he was so much more man than any man she'd ever known or even imagined.

While his mouth ate at hers, he cupped one big hand under her bottom, lifting her up and into him so that a long, solid erection dug against her belly.

She jerked her mouth free. "Gregor . . . Wait."

Breathing audibly, he rasped, " 'Kay." Two more sucking breaths, then a ragged: *"How long?"*

She could blame nervousness for making her giggle. She was not the giggling kind. These days, she didn't have a single thing to giggle about. "I don't know. I just . . . This is a surprise."

Slowly Gregor lowered her down his body until her feet touched the decorative tiles framing the pool. "What is?"

Jacki flagged a hand around them, showing her helplessness with her feelings. "This. Being here with you and running everything at light speed."

Like a badly wounded animal, Gregor dropped his head back and groaned. Lifting both hands, he scrubbed them over his face.

She'd angered him. Maybe he felt she'd been a tease, led him on.

But she hadn't planned to.

They would have gone out after he finished working with Dean. But then Jacki realized that Aunt Lorna planned to stay out late with her friend, and Cam wouldn't be home until well after midnight. Seeing a movie or having dinner didn't really interest her.

But staying home to swim with Gregor, taking the opportunity to get to know him better, did interest her.

At the time.

Cocking one hip, Jacki folded her arms under her breasts. "Maybe you should leave," she sneered. "I hate hearing a man suffer so dramatically."

Gregor stepped back. He dropped his hands.

Waiting for his irritation, his accusations, Jacki met his gaze directly.

"Sorry."

"Say what?" Jacki stared at him in the darkness.

He made a frustrated sound. "You heard me, darlin'. I'm sorry, damn it."

"You are, huh?"

"I know better than to rush a woman. Y'all like things slow and easy."

"Y'all?" He could be *such* an ass. "Gregor, there's a chance, a slight chance, that this evening can be salvaged."

He went still. "You got my attention."

"But I swear, if you plan to compare me to whatever type females you've been with, it's the very last time we'll talk."

Silence reigned. They watched each other. With comical wariness, Gregor moved in. "Okay. I know I somehow offended ya. I got that much. But can you clear things up for me so I don't do it again?"

When he got close enough to touch her, Jacki held up a hand.

He halted.

But he was so damn big, so imposing, that he might as well have been lying atop her, because she felt him that much.

Her lungs constricted, but she sounded reasonable enough when she said, "For your information, going fast was working for me."

Bending his knees a little, Gregor lowered himself enough to look her in the eyes. "Yeah?"

"It was working too well." She touched his chest; she couldn't help herself. "That's what got to me."

He put his hand over hers and started breathing heavier again. "Could you maybe explain that?"

Jacki took a turn at groaning. "Tell you what. Why don't we swim a little, maybe give you a chance to cool off. You can clear your head and then we'll talk."

She felt his skepticism before he said, "Dream on, darlin'. Alaska couldn't cool me off right now."

"Let's try it anyway." And with that, Jacki turned and made a sleek dive into the darkness of the pool. The tepid water closed over her, caressing places already sensitized by Gregor's attention. When she broke the surface, he was there, grinning at her.

"Hi." He chuckled at her surprise. "You swim like a snail."

Such a big loveable lug . . . *Loveable?* Jackie slicked back her wet hair. "Better?"

"Not a smidge." He tread water easily. "C'mere."

Dangerous. "Why?"

"I wanna touch you."

She shouldn't . . . "Okay."

The second she reached him, he closed his mouth over hers. This kiss proved softer, less invasive—but just as pleasurable. It lulled her. And it didn't take Jacki but a minute to realize he supported her weight in the water.

Lifting heavy eyelids, Jacki saw that he'd eased them to the shallower end of the pool without her noticing. With his legs so much longer than hers, he stood on the bottom when she couldn't.

"I didn't mean to rush you before."

He said that so sweetly, Jacki forgave his cracks about women in general. "It's okay."

"And if I compared you to other women, then that was just stupid."

"I agree."

"You're sure as hell different enough."

"Uh . . . thank you. I think."

"Different is good." His hands settled on her waist. "I took one look at you and felt like I do when gettin' choked out. All blurry and weak in the knees—but determined, too."

That made her smile. "Have you been choked out very often?"

"Nah. I'm pretty good. Not on Havoc's scale, yet. But I'm gettin' there."

Jacki pushed back from him. Her brother again? If this was another ploy to get a match with Dean, she'd drown Gregor. "I do *not*—"

"Yeah." He snuggled her right back up close to his body. "I don't want to talk about him, either."

She would have protested that, but Gregor kissed her again, more with need than finesse, and damn, she loved it.

Everything about him excited her unbearably.

When she wrapped her arms around his neck, he grew bolder, gliding his fingers over her hip.

Mouth still lingering on hers, he whispered, "This tattoo makes me hot."

"Really?"

"Thinkin' of you gettin' it, how you probably squirmed, and how you'll squirm some more when I'm kissin' you right there. . . ."

Oh God. "It's . . . it's a pretty tattoo. Not a sexy one."

"You're pretty." He drugged her with kisses, all the while trailing his fingers gently over her skin. "And sexy."

"Gregor . . ."

His fingertips teased over the crotch of her bikini bottoms, shocking her, thrilling her.

He groaned for her. "Damn, sugar. Tell me you're ready, please. Before I explode."

Jacki wanted to retreat before she embarrassed herself. And she wanted to wrap her legs around him and beg him not to stop.

All she could do was shake her head.

"No?" His mouth left a damp trail along her jaw to her throat to her ear. In a disappointed whisper, he asked, "Not yet, huh?"

She felt like a fool. "I want you, Gregor. I really do."

"But?"

Jacki licked her lips and prayed he wouldn't laugh at her. "I'm a virgin."

He didn't laugh.

He *scoffed*.

Smiling at her, one hand tangling in her hair, he teased her, saying, "Okay, then. Whatever you say, baby. I'm game."

Her blood went cold. "Game?"

"Whatever turns you on." He kissed her—and didn't notice that she remained frozen and stiff. "Should I coax these skimpy bottoms off you then?"

She felt like screaming. Her voice, however, was calm to the point of being frigid. "You can get your hands off me, that's what you can do."

Out of sheer confusion, Gregor released her.

Angry, hurt, and mortified, Jacki paddled fast and hard to the edge of the pool and climbed out.

"Jacki?" She heard him thrashing through the water, belatedly coming after her.

She whirled back toward him, thankful for the darkness so he couldn't see her tears, and she couldn't see his surprise, maybe even his hilarity. "Do you really think I'd lie about it, you big jerk?"

He stunned her by flattening his hands on the edge of the pool and vaulting straight out.

Jacki backed up, but in two long strides Gregor stood in front of her. "It doesn't matter to me."

"What doesn't?"

"If you are or aren't a . . . you know. A virgin."

Jacki laughed with scorn. "You can't even say it."

His unease was palpable. "I said it, damn it."

"But you don't believe it," she sneered right back, "even though I told you I am."

"Okay, fine. You are."

"I wasn't asking your permission."

"Jesus, woman." He towered over her, heaving, furious, frustrated. And desperate. "What the hell do ya want, anyway?"

Jacki didn't have an immediate answer to that. But she knew what she didn't want—and that's exactly what Gregor gave her. She turned her head away.

"Look at you," he snapped. "You reek sex, and you know it."

"*Reek?*"

"And I'll be damned if I've ever seen a virgin with hair or makeup like yours."

Her teeth snapped together. *She* moved closer to him. "Are you saying I dress like a slut?"

"No! God, no." His hand gripped her waist. "I'm sayin' you look like a woman who knows what she wants, and that's what I figured you to be. If you say you aren't, fine. No problem. Doesn't matter."

Jacki snickered. "Right. It doesn't matter now because you see your chance to get laid slipping away."

He threw up his hands. "Hell, yeah, that's part of it."

"The biggest part."

He jutted his jaw toward her. "The biggest part is tentin' my damn soppin' boxers right now, thanks to you." He crowded in until she felt his hot breath when he said, "Care to take a look?"

She did and then wished she hadn't. "Go home, Gregor."

"Home is Nevada."

Jacki's heart clenched so hard, she gasped with the discomfort of it.

"But I told your brother I'd help with the roof, and that's what I plan to do." Gregor snatched up a towel and wrapped it around himself. "*I'm* a man of my word."

He said that with accusation, as if she weren't. "*I'm* not a man!"

"Can't prove it by me." And with that parting shot, he left.

Jacki stood there, rooted to the spot until Gregor disappeared into the dark of the night. She still stood there when she heard his car roar to life, then pull away. He didn't burn out. He didn't squeal the tires.

He was a jerk, but not that kind of jerk.

And he was gone.

With nothing left to do, she picked up her own towel and went inside. Her only comfort was that he said he'd be back to finish the roof.

But as she went up the stairs in the silent, empty house, she wondered how long would that take? Another day, two at the most.

Jacki had always known that she'd be lousy dealing with a sexual relationship. When she acted like herself, men expected things of her. And she couldn't act any other way. It just didn't sit right with her.

So for that reason more than any other, she'd remained a virgin. It wasn't morals or fear or a religious conviction.

No guy had seemed worth the hassle of explaining.

Except that with Gregor, it had felt different.

Apparently she'd been wrong. Nothing new in that. Over the last year she'd been wrong about a lot of things.

Within minutes, Jacki had changed and gotten into bed. But she didn't sleep. She couldn't.

She already missed Gregor, damn it, and he hadn't even left yet.

DEAN had several considerations on his mind as he went up Eve's walkway and knocked on her door. If he knew Simon, and he did, he'd show up sooner rather than later. Only two years older than Dean, Simon had it together in a way Dean couldn't even imagine. He had a steady woman in his life, a place he called home, and family galore.

For Simon, things were black and white the way they used to be for Dean—before Cam had thrown herself against him and acted thrilled to "meet" him.

Now he stayed more muddled than otherwise. He changed his mind faster than a politician, let emotion rule his decisions, and deliberately enmeshed himself with a woman who had nothing in common with his life.

While Dean waited for Eve to answer the door, he suffered a smidge of guilt. He didn't like it. Guilt didn't set right with him. He always tried to do what he considered right, and then he let it go.

But this time, how could he?

As if Cam didn't have enough on her plate, he'd contributed to her uncertainty, allowing her to think he'd leave as suddenly as he'd arrived. Hell, he kept thinking of reasons not to go at all. . . . But he would.

Eventually.

Cam also had additional worry for Jacki because her job—a job she'd taken thanks to him—wasn't the best. And Gregor, a man Dean liked but also knew to be a first-class womanizer, had set his sights on Jacki.

Great job, brother. So far he was batting a big fat zero. The wonder of it was that Cam hadn't told him to get lost.

Again.

Thinking that added to the sting of anger he felt toward Lorna. She'd kept many things from his sisters, important things that they had a right to know. But telling them wouldn't be easy, on him or them.

Not that it was his duty to set things straight.

But it was his *right* to do so, to explain everything to the fullest. When he'd first decided to return to Harmony, he'd planned to explain that and more.

Then he'd met his sisters. His plans no longer felt right. *He* didn't feel right.

With everything else came an instinctive dislike of Roger that constantly churned Dean's thoughts. He didn't like Roger. He didn't trust him. The man was up to something; Dean didn't know what, but he rarely ever ignored his gut reactions.

Somehow he had to figure out how Roger fit into the scheme of things and what he could get out of making Cam dependent on him. Because that's what he'd done. He'd helped her, not enough to get her entirely out of debt but just enough to make her need him. Maybe trust him.

Impatient, Dean again rapped his fist on Eve's door and finally it opened. Half asleep, Eve eyed him, halfheartedly beckoned him in, and then turned away. Her hair hung in a high, loose ponytail. She wore a football jersey two sizes too large—and apparently nothing else.

Well, maybe panties. He couldn't be sure. But definitely not shorts. And definitely not a bra.

Spellbound, Dean stood in the doorway and watched as Eve dragged back to the couch to more or less collapse on it. As she stretched out, he saw a flash of panties sexy enough to tempt a saint.

Nice. Very, very nice.

A noise on the television drew him out of his fascinated study of her soft, sleepy body. He knew those familiar sounds of grunts and blows, the excited voice of the commentator, the cheers of the crowd.

Holding a paper sack in one hand, Dean stepped inside and quietly closed the door behind him. He clicked the lock into place. "You got some SBC tapes?"

"Mark brought them over. He stayed to watch two of

them with me, to make sure I understood, then he left." She kept her eyes on the television screen. "You just missed him."

Thank God for small favors. "How many tapes did he bring?"

"A lot." She waved a hand toward a stack of ten or twelve DVDs sitting on the shelf beside the television. "On the other tapes, I skipped all the fights except yours. For this one I started at the beginning so I've been through the weight classes. Your fight's only been going a few minutes." With one arm folded beneath her cheek, Eve curled onto her side and drew her knees up. "This has been a great distraction. Your muscles look even bigger when you're fighting. Not that there's much fight. You either knock people out or take them to the ground and twist their limbs until they tap out. Neither of your other fights lasted past the first round. It's all rather . . . riveting."

"More blood flow." Dean strolled in and glanced at the TV. "Muscles always pump up during a fight."

She winced. "Good God. What is that man trying to do to your arm?"

"It's called a Kimura." Blindly, his attention on the fight, Dean seated himself near her feet. Without speaking, Eve drew her legs up more to make room for him. "Basically it's a bent arm lock that goes against the shoulder."

"Why don't you tap?"

"He doesn't have good leverage for it. If he was a little more practiced, he'd know it and change his position."

She covered her eyes. "I can't watch."

Dean just smiled. A second later, when the crowd roared, Eve uncovered her eyes and then slowly straightened in her seat.

"What happened? How'd you get on top of him?"

"I told you, I'm good." Dean sat back, and instead of watching the screen, he watched Eve. "Now I'm in what's called the mounted position—which is a good place to be. I can hit him, and all he can do is try to avoid the blows. He can't really hit me back, or at least, not with much force."

When blood sprayed from the other man's nose, Eve gasped. "Your other fights weren't this brutal."

"It's called ground and pound. A good way to take all the steam out of an opponent." The color left her face, so he soothed her, saying, "Don't worry. The ref is about to stop it." He patted her leg, liked the feel of her warm silky skin, and ran his palm up to her thigh.

Though she seemed to pay him no attention, her toes curled.

Enough of that, Dean decided, or he'd forget that this night didn't include sexual satisfaction. "I'll be right back."

Eve didn't answer. The wrap-up to the fight held all her attention.

Pleased with her, Dean carried his paper sack into the kitchen. In the cabinets above the sink, he found a bowl. Hoping that she liked his surprise, he opened the carton of ice cream and dished out two big scoops.

As he walked back into the family room, the DVD ended and Eve turned off the set. "There are always so many famous people there."

"In the audience, you mean?"

"Yeah." She looked stunned. "TV and movie stars, models, athletes."

"It's a popular sport." Dean sat beside her again and, with a flourish, held out the bowl. "Here you go."

Pulling back, Eve stared at the treat. For the longest time she said nothing. Then she whispered, "Amaretto Cheesecake?"

"Yep. There's a whole carton in the freezer if you want more."

Still she didn't take the bowl. "How did you know?"

"Cam told me."

Her gaze lifted to his. "You talked to her about us?"

"I told her you were having your period so my night was ruined, but I didn't want yours ruined, too. I asked her if she knew of anything special I could get you."

Her eyes flared. "Oh, that's just freakin' great." She snatched the bowl out of his hand and scooped up a heaping spoonful. "So now your sister knows we're fooling around. When I barely know you. I can't imagine what she thinks."

Dean laughed. "I was just teasing you."

Mouth full, Eve mumbled, "Oh."

"I told her I wanted to bring you dinner, and she said you'd probably rather have the ice cream."

"Cam knows me so well." As she spoke, she spooned up another heaping bite. "Odds are that she knows we've slept together. I never could keep anything from her." She shoveled in the bite, and her eyes closed in bliss. "Mmmmm. Thank you."

The look on her face as she savored the flavor filled Dean with satisfaction. Voice softened by pleasure, he said, "I'm glad you like it."

She offered the next bite to him, but Dean shook his head. "I'm good."

"You have no idea what you're missing."

Yeah, he did. But for Eve, he'd miss it in silence. He lifted her feet into his lap and examined her toes. She had narrow feet, finely arched, soft and smooth. To keep her toenails painted such a perfect pink, she had to get regular pedicures.

Eve Lavon would be very high maintenance.

Dean had already noticed her love of high-quality clothes, and not once had he seen her in the same pair of shoes. Whether she dressed up or went casual, everything on her coordinated. From her earrings to her lip gloss, her hairstyle to her perfume, she planned every detail. Even now, in a football jersey, she looked pulled together and sexy. The red lace on her panties matched the red on her jersey.

In no time, the ice cream bowl was almost empty. Dean watched her lick the spoon, and asked, "More?"

"Not just yet. Maybe later."

"All right." He could feel her tension, so he rubbed the arches of her feet, stretched out the tendons, worked her ankles.

On a heartfelt groan, Eve tipped back her head and

closed her eyes. "You're turning me into a hedonist." One eye opened. "Is there anything you're not good at?"

As he worked his thumbs down the insides of her feet, Dean watched her toes curl again. "Probably a lot of things."

"Like?"

He shrugged. "I don't think I'm very good at dealing with sisters."

Both eyes opened. "Oh?" Eve sat up a little more. "Why's that?"

"They're not what I expected."

"You didn't expect nice?"

No, he hadn't. In his mind, he'd built them up to be self-ish and self-serving—as if they'd had a hand in booting out a nine-year-old boy. He'd anticipated meeting two pampered, privileged women who he'd find uninteresting and obnoxious.

Instead they were sweet and kind, loving and likable.

Everything sisters should be.

That all sounded melodramatic enough for poetry, so Dean kept the thoughts to himself and instead, he said, "I'm buying Jacki a car."

Chapter 16

Eve's spoon fell out of her hand and hit the bowl with a clatter. Shock widened her eyes and left her soft lips parted. She gulped. "You're buying her a *car*?"

Dean shook his head with impatience. "Not a new car and not anything fancy. Actually she might refuse to drive it."

"No," Eve said. "She won't. She'll be thrilled."

He hoped so. "It's a little Escort four speed. An economy car. It's basic, but solid. It doesn't even have automatic windows." And in his defense, Dean added, "She needs her own transportation, damn it, her own independence, and—"

"Dean." Eve sniveled, her lips trembled, and she covered her face to muffle a sob.

Taken aback, Dean stared at her and realized she was actually ready to cry over it. Looking toward the heavens, Dean fell back into the couch. "Why the hell do women always do that?"

"I'm on my period," she snapped tearfully. "That's why."

Using a baggy sleeve on the jersey, she wiped the tears off her cheeks. "If my emotional outbursts bother you, then you can just leave."

"Why are you always trying to get rid of me?"

She shot back, "Why are you insulting me?"

Not about to retreat, Dean let out a long aggrieved sigh. "I didn't mean the crying, honey. That's just female." He took in her clumped lashes and red nose, then added, "And it's kind of cute."

"Cute?" Her tear-damp face scrunched in anger. "Of all the sexist—"

To avoid an argument, Dean quickly interrupted. "I meant making a big deal out of nothing. The car wasn't that expensive."

"It wasn't?"

"I stopped by the dealership on my way home." Dean felt sheepish—and that was an entirely new sensation for him. "They were still open."

"So . . ." Eve dabbed at her eyes as she carefully picked her words. "You already bought the car?"

"I pick it up tomorrow."

More tears trickled out, and she dashed them away. "Does Jacki know yet?"

"No."

"Does Cam know?"

He shook his head.

"Uh-oh." Swinging her feet out of his lap and to the floor, Eve sat up. After a second of deep contemplation, she turned to him. "Cam won't like it, Dean."

"It has nothing to do with her. This is between Jacki and me."

"Jacki doesn't have car insurance. That is, I'm sure Cam has her insured as a part-time driver on her car, but that's only—"

"I'll take care of it."

She stared at him, and her face started to crumple again.

"Oh, for God's sake." Dean shot to his feet and paced away. "I'm a single man with very few expenses. No kids or home or anything like that. Cam has enough on her plate. It's not a big deal for me to help out a little."

"Buying a car *and* insuring it is not a 'little' help. It's an enormous contribution."

"Not from where I stand." Needing her to understand, Dean explained, "And don't think it has anything to do with being a big brother or any of that other clichéd crap."

"No, nothing clichéd about it," she agreed. "It has to do with you being a good guy."

Dean rolled his eyes. "Knock it off, Eve."

She stared at him in near adoration. "I wish I wasn't on my period."

Surprised, he asked, "Why?"

"Because right now, you're almost irresistible."

That irritated him all over again. "Just because I bought a damn car—"

"Actually it has little to do with the car, so don't get defensive." While appearing to mull things over, Eve smoothed the hem of the shirt over her knees. "It's not any one thing, Dean. It's the whole package. The bod and the face, the attitude and confidence, your ability and your honor—"

Honor? Of all the . . .

"I want you, too. A lot." Dean had to stop her before she sainted him. Hell, if he wasn't immune to a blush, he'd be red faced for sure. "But I don't mind waiting until you're more comfortable."

With a wobbly smile, Eve reached out her hand to him. The second Dean reseated himself, she crawled right into his lap and snuggled against his chest. "I'm sorry I gave you a hard time earlier today."

"You're forgiven."

"And I'm glad you insisted on coming over despite my grumpy mood."

"Me, too." Dean meant it. A lot of the unsettled worry he'd carried had dissipated while talking with Eve. "You realize that I didn't tell you about the car to seduce you or anything?"

"I know." Tilting her head back on his shoulder, Eve smiled at him. She slipped her hand around his warm throat to the side of his neck. "Dean?"

"Hmmm?"

"Why did you tell me?"

Hell if he knew. But talking with Eve was easy. She knew his sisters, cared about them, and expected him to do the same. Unlike Gregor, she wouldn't harass him about assisting Cam.

No, she just cried over it.

Making a big production out of rearranging her pony-tail, Dean smoothed it down her back. Eve needed an answer, so he cupped her cheek, touched her eyebrows with his thumb. "I guess . . . it was bothering me. What Cam and Jacki are going through, I mean."

"What are they going through?"

He looked away from her insightful gaze. "Hell, I don't know. It's just that I always figured—that is, I assumed—that they had the better bargain after our folks died. Not that Uncle Grover was bad. He wasn't. I cared a lot about him."

"You loved him."

Dean nodded. He felt no shame in his feelings for Grover. "And respected him and liked and admired him. He was a hell of a role model. Fair without thinking about it. Considerate almost by accident."

"Honorable," she said with conviction.

Dean frowned at her. "Grover was strong as a horse and determined to have things his own way, but never by force or abuse."

"Hmmm. Sounds like someone I know."

To keep her from singing his praises again, Dean picked up her hand and examined her fingers. So delicate and feminine, but with a woman's strength.

He imagined them wrapped around his cock, squeezing, stroking, and lust twisted through him. Feeling her warm, soft weight in his lap, her gentle breaths, Dean knew it'd be easy to change her mind about lovemaking during her monthly.

But he wouldn't.

Lacking a rationale that he could easily discern, Dean wanted her to know that he could enjoy her company with or without the benefit of sex. Dropping his head back on the couch and closing his eyes helped him to stay focused on their conversation.

"When I compare Grover with Lorna, it torments me, because I have to admit that I've lived with things backward in my mind."

"That's not true."

"I had the bargain," he insisted. "I always felt like I'd been kicked out. Now . . . now I feel like I abandoned them."

"Dean." Eve squirmed around on his lap, making Dean's teeth lock, until she could kiss his chin. "Don't think that Lorna was all bad. She wasn't." With a gentle touch, Eve brought his face down to hers. "Cam and Jacki had whatever they really needed."

"Not love." *And not me.* His hands clenched. "They didn't have affection, either." That resounding fact was made utterly clear every time Dean witnessed Lorna with them.

"I don't know. Lorna's an odd duck. On the surface, she might seem to care mostly about appearances and her own comfort."

"With Lorna, I'm not sure there's anything below the surface."

Eve poked him in the ribs. "She took Cam and Jacki to the doctor when necessary. They never missed a dental appointment. They might not have had the newest fads in clothes or makeup, but they were always decently dressed and clean." She gave him an encouraging smile. "That has to count for something, right?"

With every word Eve spoke, Dean felt more pained. He put a hand to Eve's back and rubbed. "Sometimes, in the countries where we worked, the nearest doctor was a day's drive away. Only in the case of an emergency did you bother with a doctor."

"Somehow I can't imagine you being ill very often."

"I rarely am. I think I built up a great immune system." Without even realizing it, Dean's hand had wandered from Eve's back to her hip. He raised it again. "If I went to the dentist, it was because I had a toothache. And clothes were things you bought when there were too many rips to keep them together."

Eve made a wry face. "Huh. Well, maybe that explains your choice of wardrobe now."

Because he wore ragged jeans and a faded black SBC shirt, Dean laughed. "Comfort will explain most of what I do."

"Right. Like getting the crap beat out of you in the ring?"

Pretending to dump her off his lap, Dean listened to her squeal, then righted her again, saying, "Smart-ass. I catch a few punches here and there. That's unavoidable. But they pay me well to fight because I fill the stands."

She looked dubious, and damned if Dean didn't feel defensive again.

Other than negotiating a new contract, he *never* discussed money with anyone, mostly because he didn't allow a dollar sign to define him as a fighter or a man. He'd grown adept at avoiding a direct reply to media inquiries, and anyone daring enough to ask out of sheer nosiness got rudely put in place.

But this time, before Dean could censor himself, the words came out. "I get a quarter of a million just to step in the ring."

Eve's jaw dropped.

"Winning gets me more, and as I told you, Eve, I usually win."

When she finally found her voice, Eve gasped. "I had no idea."

"I noticed."

She shoved back from his chest to glare at him. "I wasn't asking about your personal finances."

"No, you were just assuming a lot." He gave her a look. "All of it bad."

Her gaze skipped over him, and she relented. "Okay, so you dress for comfort. I believe it."

Damn it, did she have to sound so sarcastic. "It bothers you?"

"No. Why should it?"

Even the less-than-astute Roger had noticed they were fast becoming an item. "You're a regular fashion plate, honey, and I'm far from it. That's why."

"So?"

"You're seen in public with me."

Her absurd look of confusion wouldn't fool anyone. "But it's not like we're married or anything. We're not even really all that involved."

Her denial of a real relationship had Dean stiffening with unreasonable affront. In a cold whisper full of challenge, he said, "You don't think so?"

"Of course not." As if she mistook his mood and wanted to reassure him, Eve patted his chest. "Don't worry, Dean. I won't forget that you're here for a visit only and that you'll be taking off again soon."

"I don't know when I'm leaving."

She just smiled. "But you know you're not staying. So I won't complicate things, I promise."

"Damn it, Eve—"

"I'm enjoying you a lot; I won't lie about that. While you're here, I hope to see you more. But I won't make the mistake of falling for you."

"You won't, huh?" He'd have to see about her determination to keep him at arm's length. If he put his mind to it, he could get her to—*What the hell was he thinking?*

Dean scowled at her, though his irritation was mostly self-directed because of his gut reaction to her lack of interest.

"No, I won't. You don't have to worry about me trying to change you in any way. How you dress is none of my business and I know it." After she said that, she dared to smile and touch her fingertips to his collarbone in an innocent caress that set him on fire. "Besides, no matter what you wear or don't wear, you look pretty darn hunky to me."

Shit. Dean knew he needed to get his mind on other things ASAP. His physical need for Eve was hard enough to resist. Now he wanted to seduce her into admitting it was *more* than physical for her.

Because it was more than that for him.

He hadn't known her long enough to feel the way he did. The rational part of his brain told him that, but every other inch of his body, psyche, and soul insisted that time frames didn't matter one iota. Not this time.

He knew part of his fascination with Eve might be her close relationship to his sisters. She had an inside track with Cam and Jacki; already she knew them better than he ever would, guaranteed by a shared history that he'd missed.

But Dean was smart enough to know that not just any woman would have drawn him so easily. From the moment he'd spied Eve standing there in Roger's bar he'd felt the chemistry. Just as she had. From the jump, he'd wanted her, and having her hadn't made the craving go away. If anything, knowing her intimately had only intensified things.

Catching Eve's playful fingers, Dean held her hand flat on his abdomen and asked something that had been bothering him for a while. "Does Cam know how our parents died?"

The question stumped Eve. "What do you mean? They died in a car wreck, right."

"That's all Cam knows about it?"

Growing more concerned, Eve said, "Why? What else is there to know?"

"She's never said anything more to you?"

"Dean." Eve scooted off his lap before he could stop her. "I'm not in a tolerant mood today, as you already know. Stop playing around and tell me what's going on."

Dean ran a hand over his hair. Should he tell Eve before Cam and Jacki knew? He could trust her not to say anything. That wasn't the point.

Thinking aloud, Dean said, "I'm not even sure they

should know. I mean, it's not a nice story for a daughter to hear." He turned his head toward Eve, and said by way of question, "I can't imagine that either of the girls remembers much about our parents?"

"No. And with almost all the photos missing, they didn't have any visual reminders to grow up with."

"That might be a good thing." In fact, perhaps that was Lorna's reasoning for removing all the photos. Could she have altruistic motives after all?

No. Dean didn't think so. "Some people aren't cut out to be parents."

"Meaning Lorna?"

He shook his head. "You know I was nine years old when my mother and father died."

"A very young boy."

"Not mature by any stretch," he agreed, "but old enough to remember my friends, the games we played and the scuffles we got into. Unfortunately I can't recall much other than a few brief smiles from my mother. My memory is of a beautiful woman who didn't look or act like a mother."

Eve settled back into the couch and listened quietly.

"She hired people to care for Cam and Jacki and only involved herself enough to dictate how they were dressed, so that her friends would go on about how cute they were."

"What about you?"

"Boys were a father's responsibility." He shrugged, remembering his mother's sentiments. "But Dad was the type who enjoyed the image of a family man, and not the family itself. When he wasn't working, he was golfing with his business buddies, making connections. That sort of thing."

"As you said, you were only nine when they died. It was an awful time, losing your folks, being removed from your home. Maybe you aren't remembering it exactly right."

She sounded hopeful and sad. Dean smiled. Eve had said she wanted children someday. He instinctively knew she'd be a loving, caring mother. Seeing her interaction with her own family shored up that impression, and then there was her close, caring relationship with Cam.

"Because your parents are so close with you, it probably seems impossible to you for a mother and father to be so detached. But that's how it was. I *do* remember a lot of it, and what I don't remember was there in photographs and letters. Anything that wasn't real clear to me, my uncle helped me with."

"And you don't think he might have a skewed perception of things?"

"No." Dean touched her face—and unburdened himself. "My mother was having a long-standing affair. My father found her in bed, in our family home, with another man. I was out playing with friends, but Cam and Jacki were there, supposedly down for a nap with the nanny watching over them."

"Dear God."

Dean dropped his hand. "According to the nanny, there was a lot of screaming. The man left . . . and my mother went with him."

Eve sat there, speechless.

"I guess my father wasn't ready to let her go. Or maybe he was too angry to let her lover just walk away. He drove after them, both cars were going too fast, and that's how they wrecked. Ironically, though my parents were in separate cars, they both died." Dean shook his head. "Mother's lover didn't."

Her face pale, her hands twisted together, Eve whispered, "Cam and Jacki have no idea."

"I figured as much, but I wasn't a hundred percent certain. Lorna knows. She could have told them." He shrugged. "She and Grover were at the house together after the funeral when the man showed up."

Eve's hand slipped into his. In a voice tinged with anger, she asked, "Where were you?"

"Sitting on the couch." The corners of Dean's mouth lifted with the memory. "Grover had been explaining to me that I was coming with him, that I wouldn't be staying with my sisters. He was doing his best to make it sound like an adventure when this loud, enraged guy barged in without knocking."

"Jesus, Dean." Eve curled into him, putting her arms around him, squeezing him tight.

She wanted to comfort him, not excite him. Since returning to Harmony, he'd had more unique experiences with women than in all his years away.

They were good experiences.

With good reason, it had been years since Dean relived that day. He hated the memories, how they always brought back that hollow sickness and the awful sense of being lost and scared. "I remember that the guy was shouting about my father killing my mother, though I didn't really understand what he meant. He kept saying that without her, he had nothing to live for."

"The selfish bastard."

Dean realized that Eve was crying again, but this time in anger. Her emotions really were on a roller coaster, and he wasn't helping.

Best that he get through the rest of the story in a hurry. "Grover was impressive as hell. He charged across the room and shut the idiot up with a Superman punch that knocked him out cold."

"Superman punch?"

"Sort of a flying blow. A short jab with the momentum of your body behind it." His description didn't really do the power punch justice, but Dean didn't know any other way to explain it. "After that, Grover opened the door and dragged the guy out, down the porch steps, and to the curb. He left him there. When he came back in, he still looked pissed. He told Lorna to go take care of Cam and Jacki."

"And she did?"

"Oh yeah. In two seconds flat, Grover and I were alone. He squatted down in front of me, and I remember he looked damned mean, but I wasn't afraid. Not of him. He told me to ignore the man because he was no more than a drunken idiot and that I should never listen to anything a drunk said. He told me that I was going with him, and that he'd take care of me."

"Pretty blunt," Eve said.

"Yeah, but you know, I felt better, at least for a little while. Instead of worrying about the future, I was anxious to get a chance to ask Grover about fighting."

"Did you get to say good-bye to your sisters?"

"No. We left right then. Grover told me that anything I needed, he'd get for me." Dean shook his head, remembering how fast everything had changed and how different his life became that day. "When we got to Grover's car, that guy was still lying in the street, and his face was all bloody."

Eve's mouth compressed. "Well, I can't feel sorry for him. He got what he deserved."

Dean laughed without humor. "That's how I figured it, too. He was married with a child as well. Grover assumed he left his wife, but didn't know for sure."

"That's an awful story, Dean."

"Yeah, I know." He brushed the backs of his fingers over her cheek. "Is it a story that Cam and Jacki should hear?"

"I don't know."

"There was money left to them, Eve. Plenty to last them both through college." Dean sat forward with his elbows on his knees. "It doesn't make any sense that they'd be strapped for cash like this."

Almost by rote, Eve rubbed a hand over his back. "My mom thinks Lorna squandered too much of the inheritance on her own indulgences. But it's not like she's dripping in diamonds or layered in furs. Some people just aren't very good at managing money."

Looking back at her, Dean said, "I'm good at it."

Her chin lifted. "Me, too."

The challenge in her tone nearly made Dean smile. "I noticed that right off. Not many single women your age could afford such a nice house."

"Oh. Well . . . thank you." Flustered, Eve frowned at

him. "I think Lorna probably tried, but she went from being a thirty-six-year-old single woman to the caregiver of
two babies."

"That sounds a lot like Cam talking."

"She's said it many times. Cam's defensive of Lorna,
of anyone she cares about."

And that now included him.

"It's getting late," Dean said, "and I'm done strolling
down memory lane." He lifted Eve into his arms. "Time for
bed."

"What are you doing? I can walk."

"I like carrying you." As he started toward her bedroom,
he nuzzled against her neck. "I can smell the scented soap
and lotion from your bath. It's nice."

"It's supposed to be soothing."

"Right. I feel real . . . soothed."

Eve wrapped her arms around him and rested her head
against his shoulder. "I hate what you went through."

"It was a long time ago. I probably shouldn't even have
brought it up." He reached her bedroom and kicked the
door shut behind him.

"You wanted to know if Cam or Jacki had heard the history. And Dean, I'm glad you trusted me enough to tell me
about it."

Very slowly, Dean let her slide down his body until her
feet touched the floor. Hands at her waist, he smiled down
at her. "You ready for bed?"

"I need a few minutes." She went on tiptoe to kiss him,
then left for the connecting bath.

Bemused by how he'd opened up to her, Dean watched
her go. It didn't escape his notice that Eve listened while
he talked, contributed her own thoughts, but didn't push
him when he wanted to let it drop.

In more ways than he could count, Eve Lavon was one
special lady.

While he heard water running in the bathroom, Dean
went out to his car and retrieved his overnight bag. As Eve
stepped out of the bathroom, Dean waved his toothbrush at

her, said, "My turn," and closed the door on her expression of surprise.

After brushing his teeth, Dean took off his shirt and jeans. He folded them and put them in his overnight bag, and left the bag, with his shoes, by the bathroom door.

When Dean stepped back into the darkened bedroom, he could make out Eve's form already in the bed, under the sheet, and seemingly asleep. He sensed that having a man stay over was new to her, so he understood her need to hide. But he wouldn't encourage it.

"I can't see a thing." He opened the curtains to let in the moonlight. "That's better." No reply. "So how did your appointment go today?"

Finally Eve peeked out at him. "Okay." Her gaze touched everywhere, lingering on the front of his boxers. "I got the job."

Dean went to the other side of the bed, lifted the sheet, and stretched out along her back. Sliding one arm under her pillow and the other over her waist, he settled in. "That's good." He kissed her ear. "Anything interesting?"

"A wedding."

Dean paused. "Really? You do those, too?"

"I do it all," she bragged.

"Hmmm." To keep her from shying away, he put one hand over her belly and eased closer to her until his groin nudged firmly against her bottom. "Good to know."

She snickered. "That's not what I meant."

"So what kind of wedding will it be?"

Looking at him over her shoulder, she asked, "You're really interested?"

Unable to help himself, Dean kissed her again. "Why wouldn't I be? You're a very interesting woman."

Suddenly she twisted to face him. "The bride has no idea what she wants, and the groom doesn't trust himself. They gave me free rein to do as I please."

Even in the darkness, Dean could see the glitter of excitement in her eyes. "You like that idea, huh?"

"Sure. If I can't plan the perfect wedding for me, I may as well plan it for someone else."

Damn, having Eve this close was nice. And stimulating, but he could ignore that for the pleasure of holding her. "So tell me the plan, honey. What do you consider the perfect wedding?"

CHAPTER 17

E VE couldn't believe Dean wanted to discuss this. Most men shied away from any talk of weddings or white dresses or happily ever after.

Not Dean Conor. Nothing made him uncomfortable.

Except the love of his sisters.

Eve scooted to sit up in the bed and turn on a lamp. Dean didn't complain. He just propped his head up on his palm and waited.

"They don't want a big wedding. They only have fifty people invited."

"What about you? How many would you want at your wedding?"

Without hesitation, because she'd already given it lots of thought, she said, "I have thirty on my side who'd need to come. But the size would depend on the groom's relatives and friends."

He grinned. "Can you imagine a bunch of guys like Gregor in tuxes?" The grin expanded into a laugh. "I'd either have to limit it to family alone or invite a hundred tattooed warriors."

Fascinated with how easily he joined her in the planning of the fantasy wedding, Eve said, "I'm not into tuxes. I think it's too formal."

Dean trailed one finger down the length of her leg. "And here with the way you dress so nice and are always so polished, I figured you for a formal gal."

"On occasion I like to dress up as much as any other woman. But for a wedding, I always thought it'd be nice to wear something comfortable and floating and soft, instead of yards of stiff lace. White, for sure. But maybe something in ultra-soft eyelet cotton. Ankle length." She closed her eyes. "Instead of roses, I'd carry daisies and carnations. And instead of a veil, I'd weave some of those same flowers into my hair."

While looking more at her legs than her face, Dean murmured, "Sounds really pretty to me."

Picturing it in her mind, Eve pulled her legs up and put her crossed arms on her knees. "Bridesmaids could wear similar dresses in a rainbow of pastel colors. Daffodil yellow and sea-foam green and sky blue. The groomsmen could wear beige cotton drawstring pants and soft cotton tunics and . . ." She caught herself and laughed self-consciously. "A little out there, huh?"

Voice gone husky, Dean said, "I could see it."

She made a face. "Well, that'd be my idea, and while I like it, I wouldn't foist it off on my new clients."

"Why not?"

She shrugged. "Because weddings are very serious things to most people. I like my job and don't want to get a rep as a hippy nutcase. And besides, that's my wedding. I'm saving it for me."

Dean said nothing for several moments, then he held a hand out to her. "Come here. Let me hold you."

"All right." She turned off the light and, feeling stiff and silly, rested back down beside him. "I suppose for this couple, I'll arrange something low-key but traditional."

Dean spooned her. "Tuxes and stiff lace, huh?"

His body heat, spiced by his unique scent, surrounded her. "With the wedding march and orange blossoms. It's what they want, just not too elaborate. I can handle it."

"Whatever you arrange, I know it'll be perfect."

Eve bit her lip. "Thank you."

His mouth touched her shoulder. "How're you feeling? Okay?"

It surprised her to realize it, but she felt like her usual self. "Actually I feel fine."

"Good." His hand settled on her belly. "I'm glad to hear it."

Eve hated to say anything, but she didn't see how she could avoid it. In their current close position, she could feel his erection.

"Dean . . ."

"Shhh." His fingers stroked her stomach, then stilled. "Don't worry about it."

He had to be kidding. "But you're hard."

"Yeah, I know. It's not really something I'd miss. But trust me, it's not a problem."

Eve turned to face him, displacing his hand so that it naturally settled on her hip. "You're sure?" She could barely make out his features in the dark, but she saw the whiteness of his teeth when he smiled.

After stroking back her hair, he kissed her forehead. "If it was an issue, I'd go take care of it and then come back to you."

Words failed Eve. Her shock must have been obvious, because Dean laughed.

"Everyone does it, Eve."

But not everyone *talked* about it.

His evil grin practically lit up the room. "You know it's true, honey. The only people who say they don't are liars and people with really bad memories."

To hide her face, Eve curled into him. "Let's get some sleep."

Dean laughed again. "I can't believe you're being so shy about something that's perfectly natural."

By way of an answer, Eve pretended to snore. And thankfully, for her peace of mind, Dean gave her a squeeze, turned to his back, and pulled her into his side. "Good night, sweetheart."

Sweetheart. That sounded so nice coming from him.

She didn't say anything. But she did kiss his chest, close her eyes, and enjoy his closeness. Right before she fell asleep, she had the unsettling thought that Dean Conor could be a cure for PMS.

Too bad he didn't plan to stick around indefinitely.

WHEN Eve awoke the next morning, a weak sun struggled to shine through a haze of clouds. She sat up, felt groggy from such a deep sleep, and looked to the other side of the bed. It was empty.

Straining her ears, she heard Dean's voice and assumed he was on the phone. After a quick trip to the bathroom, she made her way into the great room.

Dean paced the floor with his cell phone to his ear. "It's the two tires street-side. No, not slashed. But the valves are cut off, so they can't just be refilled. Definitely deliberate." He lifted a thick wrist and looked at his chunky black watch. "Thanks. That'll work. See you then."

The second he hung up, Eve said, "Someone let the air out of your tires?"

He turned with a smile. "Hey, babe." With only a few long strides, he reached her. "I'm sorry. Did I wake you?"

"No. I had to be up any—" A yawn took her by surprise, and he smiled while she covered her mouth. "Sorry. I'm not quite awake yet."

"You have an appointment today?"

"In a few hours. But it usually takes me that long to get it together."

With that familiar gentleness she now craved, he ran his knuckles along her cheek. "How can a woman look so damn good first thing in the morning?"

When she started to speak, he put his thumb to her lips. "It was a rhetorical question, so don't bother telling me that your hair needs to be brushed or that your eyes are puffy."

"All true."

Gaze warm and intimate, Dean whispered, "And you still look good enough to eat."

Sensation went through her, making her eyes heavy. "It's way too early for you to do this to me, especially when I can't take advantage of it."

"Sorry." He gave her a quick perfunctory peck on the forehead. "Coffee's already made."

"Bless you." Eve hurried around him toward the kitchen, but said again, "Someone vandalized your tires?"

"A kid's prank, maybe. The car service should be here within half an hour, but I'll still be behind by the time they get the car ready to go again."

As she poured steaming coffee into an oversized mug, Eve offered, "I can give you a lift to Cam's if you want. I can be ready by the time the car service gets here."

Dean pulled out a chair from the table and straddled it. "I don't want to rush you."

She didn't tell him that after such a great night's sleep, she felt ready to take on dragons. Taking a quick shower and doing a speed job on her makeup would be a piece of cake. "No problem." Mug in hand, she started back out of the room, but paused to say, "Naturally your coffee is perfect."

"Something else I do well?"

"The damn list is becoming endless."

EVE surprised Dean by getting ready in just under half an hour. And of course, she looked incredible dressed in a classy crocheted halter top, with brown gauchos and matching slide sandals, finished with several pieces of delicate gold jewelry.

Cam and Gregor stood outside, eyeing the cloudy sky with concern. The second Dean stepped out of Eve's car, Gregor chucked down the rest of his coffee, handed the empty mug to Cam, and strode out to meet him. He passed Eve on her way to chat with Cam, but spared her no more than a nod.

"Your sister is already gone."

Gregor barked that disclosure like an accusation, making Dean frown. "Yeah, so?"

"Cam says she took her aunt shoppin', but I know that's not it. She's avoidin' me."

"Why?" Dean asked with a raised brow. "What'd you do now?"

Amazingly enough, impotent color rushed into Gregor's face and neck. No words came to him until, in a low voice, he snarled, "Fuck you, Havoc," and stormed away toward the backyard.

Huh. Dean watched Gregor go, wondering what *had* he done? The more he thought about it, the tenser he got. A few minutes later, feeling mean, Dean started after Gregor with the intent to confront him, when he heard a curse and a terrible clattering crash.

Cam and Eve shared a look with Dean, and a second later they all rounded the house at a sprint.

Gregor lay sprawled on the ground, the ladder partially covering him, a visible knot rising on his forehead.

Incredulous, Dean stopped near his feet. "Did you fall off the roof?"

Gregor stopped rubbing his head to glare at Dean. "No, I did not fall off the roof." Furious, he threw the ladder to the side and sat up with a few winces and groans. "The damn rung broke."

An awful foreboding went through Dean. "What are you talking about?"

"The tenth or eleventh rung up. Thank God I wasn't all the way to the top." He picked grass off a bloody scratch on his arm. "The wood snapped beneath my foot and that threw me off balance. I tried to grab for the gutter, but I didn't make it. I went sailin', and the ladder came down with me."

While both Eve and Cam fussed and fluttered over Gregor, Dean bent to the broken rung, examining it. His simple check left him frowning. The ladder rung hadn't broken thanks to age or wear and tear. No, given the orangey stains left behind, it seemed more likely that someone had used a rusty saw on it, chewing almost completely through the wood. It needed only a little pressure—or Gregor's two hundred and seventy-five pounds—to snap it in half.

The purpose being . . . that whoever used the ladder would fall.

Deliberately sabotaged? Like his tires?

Dean remembered seeing a shadow, perhaps a human shadow, near his car when he left the motel. But he'd been talking with Simon and despite the warning in his gut that told him to pay better attention, he'd dismissed the incident.

Until this morning when he found his tires vandalized.

And now this.

If it hadn't been for the two things combined, he could have written either off as a prank. If it wasn't for the deliberate destruction to his car tires, he could assume both he and Gregor were targets.

No doubt about it: Someone had wanted him to fall.

Last night in the hotel lobby, Roger had been peeved with him. And he'd been absent when Dean left the hotel.

Not only that, Roger had known that Dean was going to see Eve.

Roger didn't like him—that much was clear. But did he dislike him enough to destroy his property and attempt to cause him physical harm?

Given Gregor's banged-up body still supine on the dew-wet ground, the possibility couldn't be ignored.

But why?

Horrified, Cam brushed off Gregor as he lumbered to his feet with a few winces and complaints.

"I'm fine," he told her, intent on looking at the ladder himself.

In a sympathetic whisper, Cam said, "But your poor head."

Dean peered at Gregor's melon and dismissed Cam's concern. "It's just a goose egg. He's had worse."

"I'll get you some ice," Eve offered.

"Don't bother." Gregor tapped his knuckles against his crown. "Dean's right. I'm not hurt. I've got a skull like tempered steel. It just pisses me off that I fell."

Cam twisted her hands together and looked from one man to the other. "This is terrible. You could have been killed."

"From that itty-bitty fall? No way." Joining Dean, Gregor bent to examine the ladder. In two seconds flat, he came to the same conclusion as Dean. "Well, I'll be damned! I think—"

Dean gave him a quick hard look. "That the wood was rotted? I agree."

Not being a complete dummy, Gregor frowned but held his tongue. "Yeah. Uh, right."

Dean nodded. He didn't want to say anything to anyone just yet. He'd have his answers, in his own time and in his own way—without tipping off the idiot responsible.

"I should have checked the ladder myself," Cam fretted. "I'll go buy another one right now."

"No," Dean said. "This one will do."

"But if the wood is rotted—"

"It's sound everywhere else. We're almost done now, so we'll just avoid that rung."

The sound of a car parking out front drew Gregor's attention. His face hardened with resolve. "Dean's right. We'll be done in no time at all." And with that, he slammed the ladder back up against the side of the house and went up to the roof.

Shielding his eyes, Dean stood at the bottom of the ladder and looked up. "I hear Jacki."

"Yep." Gregor pulled a kerchief from his pocket and tied it around his forehead.

"I thought you wanted to talk to her."

"I did—before she pissed me off by avoidin' me. Now I don't know if I do or not. Besides, if she wants to talk, she knows where to find me."

"You sound like a bitch."

"Fuck you, Havoc." Then, chagrined: "My apologies to the ladies." Gregor turned his back on them all and went to the roof peak to work.

Sighing, Dean faced the women. Cam bit her lip, more to keep from chuckling than from affront at Gregor's language. Eve glanced at her watch, impatient to make it to her appointment.

To his sister, Dean said, "Don't worry about it. Gregor's just letting off steam. I have a feeling he and Jacki will work it out."

"I'm not in the least worried. I know a love-struck man when I see one."

"Gregor?" Surely she wasn't serious.

"He's fighting it, I'll give you that. But it won't help one bit. If Jacki wasn't my sister, I'd almost feel sorry for him. He doesn't stand a chance." She leaned closer to whisper, "But Jacki doesn't know that yet, and it might be best if you don't tell her."

"If you say so."

Cam glanced at Eve, smiled, and said, "I have some things I need to do inside, so I'll leave you two to say good-bye."

The second his sister left, Dean pulled Eve close. "When will I see you again?"

"I won't be back to my place till around seven tonight." She toyed with the neck of his T-shirt. "You're coming over tonight?"

"Yes." Dean kissed her—and didn't want to stop. "And tomorrow night. And the night after that."

Eve nodded, but said, "I'll still be . . . unavailable."

"And I'll still enjoy your company."

A beautiful glow came over Eve. "All right then."

"Promise me one thing."

Eve tipped her head. "Okay."

"Be extra careful."

When she frowned in confusion, Dean considered things. Someone, probably Roger, wanted to hurt him. How best to do that, than to hurt Eve?

The thought terrified him and made up his mind.

He caught Eve's arm. "Let me walk you to your car. There's something I need you to know."

CHAPTER 18

❧

A few hours later, after a lot of progress, Dean pulled off his gloves and looked toward Gregor. They'd worked in near silence, and for Gregor, that wasn't even close to normal. "It won't take much more for us to finish up here. Let's take lunch a little early. I have something to do."

Without looking up, Gregor said, "If you want," and he finished hammering in a nail. "Anything important?"

Dean shrugged that off. Gregor's silence had been so unnerving that it was a relief to hear him speak. But he wanted to tell Jacki first. "You coming in?"

"I dunno." He started hammering another nail. "You go on and I'll think about it."

"Suit yourself." The last thing Dean wanted to bother with was a sulky fighter.

A few minutes later, when Dean opened the sliders and walked into the house, he saw both sisters in the kitchen. Jacki sat cross-legged in a chair, her knees sticking out at an odd angle while she chatted with Cam. She looked . . . adorable. As quirky as he now knew her to be.

Nodding every so often, Cam stood at an ironing board set up between the kitchen and the laundry room. She had a whole stack of clothes to go through.

It didn't matter that she'd worked through part of the night and then got up early. There'd be no idle time for Cam. She wouldn't allow it.

Odd how they each felt so familiar in such a short period of time. Like he knew them, *really* knew them, when such a thing wasn't possible.

And yet . . . he could have said word for word how the next few minutes would play out. He knew what Jacki would do and how Cam would react. He knew what would motivate each of them.

It was his own motivations that remained murky and troubling.

Rather than hold back any longer, Dean said, "Hey," to get their attention.

Almost in unison, the sisters looked up and smiled at him with welcome.

Jacki unfolded herself from the chair. "You look hot. Want something to drink?"

He nodded. "Just ice water would be good."

Cam put aside her iron. She shook out a freshly pressed shirt, hung it neatly, and then crossed the room toward him. "How's it going on the roof?"

"We'll be done today."

"Really?" That stopped her in her tracks. "Well. That's wonderful." She had a difficult time getting her mouth to smile. "I had no idea you'd accomplish so much so quickly."

Dean knew exactly why she sounded so odd. He wished for some way to make this easier on her, but he knew that Cam herself would make that impossible.

And sure enough, she said, "I can't thank you enough. If you'll just tell me how much I owe you, I'll repay you right away."

No time like the present, Dean thought. He planted his feet and looked her right in the eyes. "I won't take your money, Cam."

He might have given her a grave insult for the way she reacted. She sucked air into her lungs, forced a stiff, stilted smile, and stared right back. "Of course you will. I won't let you—"

"You can't very well stop me."

The truth of that brought out her temper. "I don't need charity."

"It's my house, too, remember?" Dean pulled out a chair as if he hadn't a care in the world, when inside, his heart wanted to break for her. He sprawled in his seat and let out a tired breath. "You said so yourself."

Cautiously, her gaze darting between brother and sister, Jacki set an ice-filled glass of water in front of Dean.

"Thanks."

"No problem."

In the coldest voice Dean had heard from Cam so far, she said, "Had I known that you wouldn't let me repay you, I'd never have agreed to this."

Gently Dean said, "I didn't ask your permission, hon."

Fury colored her cheeks.

"Cam, sit down."

Arms tightly crossed, she shook her head. "I don't want to sit."

"All right, then stand. But you're not going to like what I have to tell you."

Fascinated, Jacki seated herself across from Dean, propped her chin in her hands and waited.

"From what I understand, Roger has helped you with some improvements and repairs."

"Where," she demanded, "did you hear that?"

"From Roger himself, when I ran into him at the realty office where Eve's mother works. He also told me that a lot more repairs need to be made."

Caution warred with anger in her eyes. "That's why I'm selling."

"To Roger."

She shook her head hard. "No. Never."

Stumped, Dean stared at her. "But I thought that you two were—"

"Engaged, I know." Finally she pulled out a chair and sat down. "But you see, Roger thinks to do the same as you— swoop in and save poor little me. Only I'd rather save myself."

Save herself from what? Financial debt? "If you plan to marry him, Cam, then it's only natural that he'd want to help out."

"I won't ever get married as long as I owe so much. I wouldn't feel right about it. The debt would always be between us. That's not what marriage should be. It's definitely not what my marriage will be."

A guilty flush took Jacki's breath. Avoiding making eye contact with anyone, she straightened from her slouched position and stared down at her hands.

Dean noticed, but Cam didn't.

He decided he'd talk with Jacki about her reaction. Soon. But not just yet.

"After I sell the house and get out of debt, then I can get married."

"To Roger?"

"Yes. Probably."

Dean hadn't expected this wrinkle. "Do you love him, Cam?"

She started to shake her head, but then suddenly stopped. "I think so." Her chin lifted. "I've known him forever."

"How long is that?"

"We grew up around here together. Went to school together and all that."

"You're childhood sweethearts?" Dean hadn't realized that Roger grew up in the area. A sudden chill skated down his spine. If Roger had been around that long, then all kinds of things were possible.

"We didn't start dating until high school, but we've always been friends, good friends. I know him better than anyone else does. Even though he tries really hard—sometimes *too* hard—to win Eve over, I know she doesn't understand him, and so she doesn't like him." Cam sent a brief look at Jacki. "And I know you're not fond of him, either, Jacki."

Dean waited for Jacki to deny it, but instead she ducked her head.

Cam didn't appear to mind. "So often I see a side of Roger that others don't see. He's so sweet to me, and so gentle. He always wants to help in any way he can." She looked up at Dean. "He hasn't had an easy life. He's had to work extra hard for everything he has now. He's earned all his success, and I'm very proud of him."

Jesus. Cam made him sound like a saint.

"But that's just it—Roger's done so much for me that it's hard to tell what's in my heart when I also feel grateful to him. And beholden. And . . . and *obligated*."

Dean sat in awe. His sister was one smart cookie. "I see."

"I don't want to confuse my own feelings, and I definitely don't want to confuse his."

Maybe the discussion on other repairs should wait. "I understand."

"Do you?" She looked away at nothing in particular. "You're so independent."

But alone.

Dean *hated* that thought as soon as it hit him. To fend it off, he put a fist on the table. "You told me this house was partly mine."

Wariness brought Cam's gaze back to his. "It is."

"Then I don't want to sell it. And I don't want it to fall down around us. For years you've had the upkeep. Now it's my turn."

Her mouth opened and closed twice before any words emerged. "Don't be ridiculous! I've lived here. It's not at all the same thing."

"I might live here, too." *What the hell was he saying?* "Off and on that is. Around my . . . other schedule." Good God. Now he'd done it.

Jacki perked right up. "Really? You're thinking of being here on a permanent basis?"

"Semipermanent. Maybe." And then, "Shit, I don't know."

Enjoying his obvious confusion, Jacki beamed at him. "Cool. I'd love to have you around more often."

Disgusted, Dean turned from Jacki back to Cam. "Since this is now my home, too, it means I have every right to make any improvements that I want to make."

Confused, Cam said, "I suppose so."

He didn't like her beat-down attitude, but he'd fix that. Somehow. "Good. Then that's settled."

Gregor stuck his head in. He looked at Cam and only Cam. "Any chance I could get somethin' to eat?"

Jacki turned away to present a deliberate cold shoulder.

Manners dictated that Cam try to make up for her sister's slight. "Of course. Gregor, I'm so sorry. I meant to have something ready, but I forgot. I guess I got a little absorbed in my discussion with Jacki. But I can get you a sandwich. Will that do?"

"It'll be fine." Gregor eased in another step. "So what were you two discussin'?"

"Before Dean came in, we were trying to decide how Jacki would get back and forth to work tomorrow."

Gregor stepped the rest of the way in and closed the door behind him. Still without looking at Jacki, he said, "I'll drive her."

Jacki spun around to stab him with a lethal glare. "I'd rather walk," she hissed. "Or *crawl*. Or . . . or be *rolled* down the sidewalk."

Cam made a sound of impatience. "Jacki, for heaven's sake."

Dean couldn't help himself. He laughed. When Cam and Jacki both frowned at him, he rubbed the grin off his mouth.

"You're not going to walk," Cam told Jacki calmly, as much to fill the awkward silence as for any other reason. "You'll take my car and I'll get a ride with Roger."

In for a penny, in for a pound, Dean thought. He cleared his throat.

Cam took one look at him, saw his apologetic smile, and groaned. "What now?"

"I bought her a car."

Cam and Jacki said at once, "Who?"

He nodded at Jacki. "You. I bought you a car." She blinked at him in disbelief. "Nothing all that fancy. A Ford Escort."

Again in unison, the sisters said, "You did *what*?"

Amazing, Dean thought, how their minds formed the same thought at the same time, and verbalized it with such accuracy. Because Cam looked the most volatile, Dean addressed her first. "Jacki needed transportation. I bought her a car. End of story."

"Oh. My. God." For once, Cam looked more inclined to smack him than hug him.

The opposite of her sister, Jacki bubbled right out of her seat with excitement. "What color is it?"

"Silver."

Cam sent Jacki a quelling look before turning the full force of her displeasure on Dean. "You cannot buy her a car."

Jacki's hands landed on her hips. "Yes, he can. He said he already did."

"No." Cam yelled at Jacki in an uncommon loss of control. "He cannot. Dean doesn't owe us anything, certainly not a car. If anything—"

Unwilling to let her say it, Dean rose to his feet. "It's not about owing you." He put his hands on Cam's shoulders before she could retreat out of reach. "I can afford it. I want to do it." He squeezed her shoulders in apology, then added, "And it's got nothing to do with you, Cam."

Cam turned big, wounded eyes on him.

Dean held firm. She needed to learn that she wasn't responsible for her sister. Not anymore. "This is between Jacki and me."

Jacki stepped forward in a massive about-face. "If Cam doesn't want me to take the car, I'm not taking it."

Dean studied her, saw the resolution in her eyes, and felt so much pride at her loyalty toward Cam that it nearly choked him. "Fair enough. But what the hell am I going to do with it, then? It's paid in full. The dealer won't let me return it."

Jacki glanced at Cam with hope.

Still frozen and hurt, Cam shrugged a shoulder at her sister. "He's right. It's none of my business."

Dean gently shook her. "I said it was between Jacki and me. But as her big sister, everything about her is your business."

A calculating gleam put golden lights in Cam's brown eyes. "And you're her big brother, so it's your business as well?"

Thunderstruck, Dean dropped his hands and took a step back. He swallowed. Glanced at Jacki. Did his best to ignore Gregor's hulking presence. "Something like that, yeah."

A smile slowly softened her mouth. "Okay then. Thank you."

Dean had the awful suspicion he'd just been out-manipulated.

Jacki put her hands in the air. "I should probably be offended that the two of you think I need so damn much care, but I'm too curious about the car to mind that much." She grinned. "When do I get to see it?"

Relieved to have that settled, Dean glanced at his watch. "We can head over there now to pick it up. Can you drive a stick?"

Her face fell. "No."

Gregor presented himself to the room. "I can. I'll teach you."

Jacki said, "No—"

"Damn it, Jacki," he burst out, making everyone except Dean jump in startled fright. "I believe you, all right?"

Jacki blanched. In a whisper, she said, "Shut up, Gregor."

He shoved his way further into the room, paying no

attention when he almost knocked over Dean. "Not until you forgive me."

"Believe her about what?" Cam wanted to know.

His gaze on Jacki, Gregor squared his massive shoulders. "Jacki explained to me that—"

"*Gregor!*"

He towered over Jacki. "Well? You gonna forgive or not?"

Impotent fury left Jacki trembling. "This is blackmail."

"Nah, it's desperation." Gregor's eyes narrowed. "With someone as stubborn as you, I'll do what it takes."

Through her teeth, Jacki said, "*Fine.* You're on probationary forgiveness."

He grinned hugely. "I'll take it."

"But if you so much as—"

"I won't." Gregor slung his arm around her shoulders. "Now let's go get your car."

JACKI felt every breath Gregor took. She felt him studying her face. Her body. The heat of his interest burned her.

Gnashing her teeth together, she ground the gears and then exploded, "*Stop it!* Just . . . stop it. I can't concentrate when you're doing that."

He coasted his knuckles along her cheek. "I don't think I've ever had a virgin. God, I can hardly wait."

Molten excitement nearly melted her on the spot. She pushed in the clutch, shoved the gear shift into park, and put on the brake.

That time of night, with the excessive heat wave, the park was nearly deserted. It would have been the perfect place to practice driving, if Gregor weren't so intent on seducing her.

Realizing what she'd done, he looked around and frowned. "You're still in the middle of the road."

Jacki opened the door, got out, and walked away.

"Jacki!"

She kept going, into the wooded lot beside the roadway,

to a picnic table set in a clearing. Brushing off the fallen leaves and dead bugs, she cleared a spot and sat down.

Thirty seconds later, Gregor lumbered through the brush and joined her. "Damn it, woman. I thought you planned to walk all the way home or something asinine like that."

"No." A fuzzy caterpillar made its way across the top of the picnic table. Using a leaf, Jacki captured the bug and set it safely on the ground.

Gregor sat beside her. He was silent for a moment, then said, "I'm not rushin' ya. If you thought I was, well, you were wrong."

"Really?" Jacki felt too wilted in the heat to debate the point with him.

"Yeah, really. I just . . . you're so cute. And sexy."

"Uh-huh."

"And a virgin." He tensed all over. "God Almighty, that's a turn-on."

Jacki couldn't help but laugh. "And naturally you've already decided you'll be my first?"

"Well . . . yeah. I mean, I hope so." He hesitated, and slowly his expression turned into a dark thundercloud. "Won't I?"

She wasn't the least bit intimidated. "I don't know, Gregor."

His muscles all bunched up in tension. In a raspy whisper, he asked, "You're seein' someone else?"

Jacki half-expected him to start beating his chest at any moment. "No."

"You're sure?"

Being droll, Jacki said, "Are you going to start calling me a liar again?"

"*No.*" He relaxed a little. "No, course not. If you say I'm it, I'm it."

Oh, for the love of . . . "I didn't say you were *it.*"

Smug, Gregor pointed out, "I'm the only one you're seein', sugar."

"But that doesn't mean I plan to end my virginity with you."

"Oh."

How a big hulking oaf could look so crestfallen, Jacki didn't know. "You're making me crazy, Gregor."

"Try sittin' where I'm at honey, then tell me about crazy."

On a deep sigh, Jacki swung a leg over the bench so that she could straddle it, facing Gregor. "Look. What I'm saying is that I'm not ready yet. I know that now. And I don't like you pushing me."

A look of insult had him tucking in his chin. "I didn't. I wouldn't."

Jacki rolled her eyes. "No? Then what do you call those hot stares and easy touching and outrageous compliments?"

He treated her to another easy touch, this one to the side of her throat. "That's your fault, darlin', not mine. If you weren't so irresistible . . ."

She slapped his hand away. "That's exactly what I'm talking about."

"I'm levelin' with ya, damn it. I don't expect you to just shove down your pants or anythin'. . . . Well, unless you wanted to."

Jacki inhaled, but Gregor rushed on before she could vent.

"But you are sexy. So sexy, you're making me crazy. Good crazy. I can take it. I *wanna* take it. Hell, you need a month? Fine. I'll last a month." He caught both her hands and kissed her wrists. "But I can't *not* touch you or look at you. That's askin' too much."

His words rang with so much raw sincerity, Jacki believed him. And maybe that's why she blurted, "I'm built like a boy."

One brow slowly lifting, Gregor glanced at her lap. "Come again?"

She jerked her hands free and slapped at him. "Not *there*, you ass. That's as average as any other woman." Jacki flattened her hands over her chest. *"Here."*

Gregor looked at her hands, licked his lips, and looked some more. "There?"

Exasperated, Jacki grabbed one of his big hands and lifted it to her chest. She pressed his palm against her less-than-A-cup boob—and heard his ragged groan.

"Why the hell are you groaning?"

Mouth open to accommodate his fast, heavy breaths, Gregor dragged his gaze from where his hand very gently cuddled her, up to her face. He swallowed audibly. Gaze smoky, face flushed, he rasped, "You are so fucking soft."

"I'm *flat*."

"I can feel your nipple all puckered up and tight and I think I just might come in my pants."

Jacki stared at him. "You're serious?"

He swallowed again, but kept his gaze glued to hers. "You wouldn't wanna help to that end, would ya? I mean, one little touch from you—*no*. No, you said you weren't ready, and by God, I'll wait."

"Gregor . . ."

He snatched back his hand and was gone from the bench seat in the blink of an eye.

Stunned, Jacki watched him storm away.

But he didn't go far. Just far enough to stand there with his back to her while he sucked air hard and fast. "We should go."

"I was thinking of getting a boob job."

Gregor whirled around so fast, he nearly tripped himself. A variety of expressions went over his face in rapid succession until determination landed and stuck there.

Somehow, in one big stride, he reached her again. Holding her by her upper arms, he lifted her off her feet until she reached eye level with him. "What the hell are you talkin' about?"

Such a vehement demand. "I know I'm lacking in the rack department, Gregor. It's always bothered me. A lot. It's one reason I avoided guys for so long."

He looked at her chest, his nostrils flared, and then he pierced her with his black-eyed gaze. "Good. I'm damned glad, 'cuz now that I know I'll be first, I can't bear the thought of some other bozo havin' you."

Hanging there in his grip, Jacki let out another long breath of exasperation. "You really are hung up on that 'being first' thing, aren't you?"

"You have no idea."

Jacki didn't know what devil prompted her, but she heard herself saying, "Roger offered to pay for the surgery."

Confusion pinched Gregor's brows together over his nose. "What surgery?"

"The boob job."

Slowly he lowered her to her feet, but still held on. "He did what?"

Uh-oh. Okay, so now she knew the difference between Gregor's irritation and very real anger.

And this was pure red-hot anger.

"He's Cam's fiancé, you know?"

"What the hell does that have to do with anything?"

"Well, Roger said that he knew being flat bothered me. I guess I'm sometimes obvious."

"I didn't know it."

She snorted. "Where women are concerned, you're about as astute as a wooden block."

"Or maybe," Gregor said through his teeth, getting all tense and pissed off again, "it just never occurred to me that a hot little number like you would have some hare-brained hang-up over something that doesn't matter worth squat."

Wow. He said an awful lot there. "'Doesn't matter worth squat'?" Never had Jacki heard that goofy saying. "Never mind. The point is, it does bother me, and Roger said he wants to make nice with me, to get closer to Cam, so he offered to hook me up with a plastic surgeon that would do the surgery real cheap, and then Roger even offered to pay him."

"I'll kill the bastard."

Jacki made a face. "You're not going to kill anyone, Gregor."

"Yeah. I am." After releasing her, he started away for the car.

He sounded so serious that Jacki suddenly got nervous. "Wait a minute!"

Gregor kept on going. "If you don't want to walk home after all, haul your little ass over here and get in the car."

Of all the nerve! Jacki ran to get ahead of him, then planted herself in front of the passenger door. "I will not allow you to—"

He lifted her, set her aside, and opened the door.

He put the keys in the ignition and, growing desperate, Jacki scrambled onto his lap. "Damn it, Gregor, I'm serious."

"Me, too. Deadly serious. That prick has no business even noticin' your body, much less commentin' on it, and no way in hell should he make you think you need some quack surgery."

With her draped all over him, Gregor turned the key and started the engine.

Very real panic set in. "Gregor, *please*!"

He paused. He stared at her in a long, edgy silence before finally saying, "Please what?"

Suspicion niggled. Had he just pulled a fast one on her? He no longer looked so volatile. But Jacki couldn't be sure. "Please don't overreact."

He waited in silence.

But really, Jacki liked his defense of her, especially over something that had caused her so much insecurity as a woman. "Please don't go pick a fight with Roger."

"You know you don't need any damn surgery?"

"I know you don't think I do. But," she said with emphasis, "if I decide I ever want it, I'll do it just the same."

"Works for me. Long as it's what you want and not something you think you need."

How sweet. "Okay."

Gregor wasn't done. "What's it to you if I mess up Roger's face? I got the impression you didn't like him much anyway."

"I don't. Or that is, I didn't. But I just found out that Cam actually loves the jerk and that changes everything."

"She told you that?"

His surprise mimicked her own. "Yeah. I know. Insane but true. I guess there's something about Roger that I've missed."

"The snake skin? The sharp teeth? What?"

Jacki flattened her mouth. "I shouldn't have told you about his offer."

That fierce frown snapped back into place. "You should have told me sooner."

Okay. So maybe it was time to push a little. Jacki tilted her head, and asked, "Why?"

To her surprise, Gregor didn't shy away. He looked at her, cupped her face, and kissed her hard. Long. Wet and deep.

Relaxing against him, enjoying him, Jacki kissed him back.

He eased away from her and touched his nose to hers. "That's why. Something's goin' on between us. Something big."

Hope blossomed. "You think so?" For her part, Jacki knew she was already half in love with the big lug. Maybe more than half.

Gregor nodded. "I know so." He put his hand over her breast again, gently caressed her, then with visible resolution, lifted her to sit in her own seat. "Tomorrow, next month, or next year, I will be the first, honey. Count on it."

Hands shaking, smiling all the way to her heart, Jacki fastened her seat belt. "Okay."

At her reassurance, Gregor shook off his anger. "You're not doin' any dumb surgery, are you?"

"No. I'd already decided against it, because I know Cam would see it as her debt, too."

"Forget the cost, damn it. You—"

"And," Jacki said, stealing his thunder, "I'd already decided that anyone who didn't like me as is was just plain out of luck. I'm not changing."

"Hallelujah." Gregor looked her over, ending his perusal with a low whistle. "You're temptation enough as is."

"Thank you. Now what about Roger?"

Gregor put the car in gear and pulled away from the edge of the road. "I'll let Roger off the hook this time—after I explain to him that you're mine."

So possessive. "You won't hurt him?"

"Nah. It'd be too much like kickin' a puppy. I wouldn't feel right about it."

That wasn't his sentiment moments ago, so Jacki decided to be perfectly clear. "Good to know, because I couldn't really care about someone who was the type to go pounding on people just because they did something annoying."

His eyes narrowed. "Fightin' bothers you?"

"Bullying bothers me." She tilted her head. "I would love to see you fight, though. Not on a tape, but live."

Gregor mulled over the idea. "That can be arranged. In fact, the idea of keepin' you close to hand suits me just fine." He flashed her a grin. "Better odds on me bein' around when you decide you've spent enough time chaste, and you're ready to cut loose."

Jacki laughed with him—but truthfully, she was ready right then. Now all she needed was the right moment to tell him.

CHAPTER 19

T HE sun sank low in the sky, sending a crimson tide over the horizon. Dean applied the last dabs of tar to hold down the loose corners of the shingles around the vents. He'd just wiped his hands clean and started to stand when he felt someone watching him.

Trying to look nonchalant, he scoped the area around him and saw no one. But he felt it. No doubt about it.

Prickles of unease went up his spine. He thought about the broken ladder rung, his destroyed tires, and he refused to take any chances. Utilizing caution, he went down the ladder, all the while paying attention to his surroundings.

The house was quiet and empty. After a phone call from Roger, Cam went off to work early. With Dean's blessing, Jacki and Gregor left a few hours before, supposedly so Jacki could practice driving the stick. Dean figured they both had more than manual stick instructions on their minds.

The idea of Gregor with his sister had grown on Dean, especially after seeing how Jacki affected him. And as long as Gregor remained with Jacki, Dean knew she'd be safe. In light of recent events, that counted for a lot.

Not long after everyone else had left, Lorna returned to the house. Her displeasure at finding only Dean there was extreme.

Crazy old broad.

In shrill tones, she demanded to know how long he'd be, and when she realized she'd be home alone with him for several more hours, she made another hasty departure. Dean should have felt guilty for running her out of her home; Lorna looked more tired than usual, and he guessed his intrusion, along with the financial difficulties and house problems, were starting to take their toll on her. She wasn't a young, resilient woman and suddenly, things weren't going her way.

But Dean felt no real guilt at all. If anything he hungered for an opportunity to tell Lorna what he thought of her and her parenting skills. It was just as well that she'd left, because despite her sour personality, his sisters cared about her. And that would make it difficult for him to vent as he wanted to.

Concealing himself in the shadows of the house, Dean checked his watch. Eve would be home by now, and he pictured her as she'd been last night, curled on the couch in comfy clothes, all warm and soft.

Just thinking about her got his heart pumping a little faster. He found himself smiling. In anticipation. In pleasure.

Earlier he'd told Eve that he wanted to move in with her, to be nearer to her in the case of a possible threat. After explaining about the ladder, she'd taken his request at face value and agreed.

Deep down, Dean figured they both knew it was an easy excuse, and both intended to use it anyway.

Eve understood that for now, he didn't want anyone else to know about his suspicions. Not that he didn't trust his sisters, but the fewer people who knew, the less chance there'd be for Roger to find out. And as Dean's number one suspect, he wanted Roger as much in the dark as possible, to make it easier for him to trip himself up.

As Cam's best friend, Eve had a problem with that, but she promised anyway.

Dean made quick work of putting away the tools and the ladder, cleaning the area, and locking up the house. Still sensing watchful eyes, he headed to his car, which now had four brand-new tires. Once inside, he turned on the air and called Eve.

"Hello?"

The mellow, almost lazy tone of her voice had Dean smiling. "Hey. You hungry?"

"Mmm. I don't know. What are you thinking?"

Dean wanted nothing more than to crash on the couch with her, but he said, "We can go out if you want. I recall promising you a few dates."

"I plan to hold you to them."

"Or I can bring something home."

That word *home* hung between them with some silent but stirring meaning.

After a moment, Eve said, "If you want to go out, I can throw on jeans."

Meaning she didn't have anything on right now? A mental picture formed, teasing Dean and adding a gruff tone to his voice. "Whichever you want."

"You really don't have a preference?"

"No," he lied.

"Then let's just eat here. I've been watching another of your fights, sort of in slow motion. Do you think you could teach me some moves?"

Anticipation dulled Dean's other senses. "Yeah," he said, dragging out the word, savoring the thought. "I can do that."

His phone beeped with an incoming call. Dean ignored it.

"I'll go by the hotel first to grab some things and shower. What should I pick up?"

"Surprise me." The phone beeped again, and Eve said, "Are you getting a call?"

"I'm ignoring it."

"It might be Cam or Jacki."

He glanced at the lighted number and said, "It's probably not."

"Who is it?"

"I don't know. I don't recognize the number."

"Dean, check it. It could be important."

Her nagging didn't annoy him. Just the opposite—it somehow made their relationship feel more official.

"Whoever it was just hung up. Don't worry about it. If it was Jacki or Cam with a problem, they'd call you next, right?"

"Probably."

Dean glanced in the rearview mirror, still saw no one, and put the car in drive. "I'll be there soon, okay?"

Voice soft, Eve said, "I'm looking forward to it."

ATOP the hill behind his hotel, Roger dropped down to sit alone in the dirt and dead leaves. Night insects began stirring, but he paid no attention to them. It didn't matter that he'd gotten mud on his shoes or that his suit pants had snagged several times on sticker bushes.

Nothing much mattered at all, not anymore.

His time had about run out. If he really wanted to change anything, he'd have to do it soon.

But how? He'd tried, and he'd failed.

Squeezing his eyes shut, Roger remembered Cam's reaction when he'd again asked her to marry him. He'd rushed things, he knew that now. But what else could he have done when all his plans were crumbling around him?

He saw Cam's sweet but sad smile. He saw the sympathy in her eyes. Even before she said no, the refusal began echoing in his head.

Walking away from her had seemed his only option. Cam called after him, but he didn't want to hear her assurances, her excuses. Not anymore.

Her goddamned brother had changed everything.

Bastard.

Leaning back against a tree, Roger stared at his hotel at the bottom of the hill. From his vantage point, he could see the lot filled with cars, the lights as they came on automatically, one by one. He saw cars driving by, people coming and going.

He knew what he had to do.

Rage, disappointment, and regret burned in his veins. He hadn't wanted to do it, not ever. But Cam literally left him with no choice. All his life, he'd been fucked by those around him. Cheated of what was rightfully his, of what he deserved. What he wanted.

Not again. Not this time.

He had his back to the wall. He had nothing more to lose.

WHEN Dean came out of his hotel room, he found Gregor propped against the wall, waiting for him.

Before he could ask any questions, Gregor said, "About damn time," and fell into step beside him. "I would've knocked, but I couldn't remember which room was yours."

"Something wrong?"

"If you consider your sister gettin' surgery wrong, then yeah."

Dean turned so fast that Gregor bounded back in surprise. "What the hell are you talking about? Jacki's sick? Hurt?"

"No. Shit. Calm down, all right? I didn't mean to scare you."

Scare him? He'd more than scared him. Dean frowned at that and mentally collected himself. "What surgery is she getting?"

"She's not. Not now anyway."

His patience run thin, Dean said, "Gregor," in a way that spurred the other man to spit it out.

"Roger was goin' to pick up the tab on a boob job for her."

Of all the things Gregor could have said, that one left

Dean's brain scrambling to decipher. He didn't even want to think about Jacki having boobs, for God's sake. But for Roger to be involved, for him to have suggested . . .

Dean started away with a purpose. "I'll kill that son of a bitch."

"No way, man." Gregor hurried to catch up. "If anyone gets to kill him, it'll be me."

Dean didn't slow down. "Then why the fuck are you here bothering me?"

"Jacki made me promise I wouldn't."

Dean barked a laugh. "That's your problem. I didn't promise jack shit."

Grinning ear to ear, Gregor said, "Hey, that's right. Well, hold up then. At least let me watch."

They made it to the lobby and found it empty. Again.

Dean stormed up to the front desk and banged on a small bell until a young man presented himself. But he didn't know where Cam or Roger might be, and Roger didn't answer his page. The young man offered to take a message, and Dean declined the offer.

Frustrated, Dean ran a hand through his hair, considered his options, and came to the crazy conclusion that maybe he should discuss this with Eve. She knew Jacki better than he did. She'd be rational about it, instead of emotional, which he knew he damn well was.

On that thought, Dean stalked from the hotel, totally forgetting that Gregor dogged his heels.

"Hold up, will ya?"

Dean stopped, closed his eyes, and slowly turned. "What now?"

"I wanna know what you're plannin' to do."

"I don't know yet." Dean continued on to his car—this time parked closer to the building, under a bright lamp. And then, with accusation and annoyance, "What the hell was Jacki thinking?"

Gregor rolled a shoulder. "That she needed a bigger rack to get a guy's interest, I guess."

Dean stared at him.

"She's not real endowed in that department, not that I mind at all, but she didn't know that—"

"Forget I asked." Head spinning, Dean unlocked his car door.

As if he hadn't spoken, Gregor leaned back on the car and continued. "I told her she was already sexy as hell."

"Gregor—"

"You bein' her brother and all, you probably don't see it. But she's hot."

"Do you want me to kill you, too?"

Gregor shook his head, but he couldn't hide his smile. "I reckon she's convinced, because she said she'd forget about that whole cuttin' and addin' plastic business."

Good God. "Not another word."

"You know, I'd like nothin' more than to see old Rog flattened like a bug, but it did seem important to Jacki that I leave the man intact."

A safer subject. Dean started to relax. "Yeah. Cam's probably in love with Roger, and that'll make him important to Jacki, too."

"Damn, Havoc. That's real astute of you."

In a killing mood, Dean turned on Gregor. "Are you trying to egg me into a fight?"

"Nah. Course not. But that's exactly what Jacki said." He grinned. "I guess you know her pretty good now, huh?"

Dean started to tell Gregor what he could do with his observations when an insect, probably mammoth in size given the noise it made, buzzed right past his ear. He cursed, swatted at the bug, and a second later Gregor landed against him full force.

Taken off guard, it was an easy thing for Gregor to throw him to the ground. But it wouldn't be so easy for him to keep him there.

Dean reacted instinctively. He went with the momentum, turning as they landed to reverse the position so that he was on top. He under-hooked Gregor's thick arms, put the boots in on his legs, and effectively left Gregor with no way to move.

Staring into Gregor's eyes at close range, Dean calmly demanded, "Are you out of your fucking mind?"

Gregor struggled against him and said with a gasp, *"Gunshot."*

Confused, Dean frowned at him—and a bullet hit the ground right next to them, sending up a spatter of gravel and . . . blue paint. "Oh shit."

Together they rolled out of the way and behind Dean's car.

Dean already had his cell phone in his hand when Gregor said in disgust, "Damned annoyin' kids."

"Kids?" Dean asked, while waiting for a cop to answer his call.

"Doncha think? I mean, it's paintball, right?" Gregor shook his head. "Don't mind tellin' you, it scared the shit out of me. I thought it was a real gun, with real bullets. And that first shot damn near took off your ear."

"If that's your way of explaining why you jumped me, no explanation is necessary."

Gregor pulled on his ear. "I was just sayin' . . . Hey, listen, no more shots."

Dean gave him a look. "Maybe that's because we're hiding, so they don't have a target." Finally the police answered his call, and within ten minutes, a cruiser showed up, lights and sirens blaring. People left the hotel to investigate the commotion.

And still Roger didn't present himself.

But how could Dean point the finger at him without more evidence?

More?

Hell, he had none. Not really. Because of that, Dean left it to the cops to figure out what they could while he called Eve to let her know he'd be late and why. He ended his call just in time to see Gregor whispering into his own phone.

"Jacki?"

Gregor nodded, said a few things more, and finally said his good-byes. "Too bad Cam doesn't have a cell phone. You could call her, too."

No cell phone? That was news to Dean. His surprise must have shown, because Gregor elaborated.

"I asked Jacki for her number, but she said that neither one of them had a cell. They don't like monthly bills."

Dean put his hands on his hips and walked away. It wasn't that they didn't like monthly bills, but rather that they couldn't afford them.

If he hadn't been so busy trying to keep Cam and Jacki at arm's length, maybe he'd have known that. Then he could have . . .

His thoughts tripped up at that point. Cam already resented the money he spent on the roof and car, and he still intended to do other repairs to the home's interior.

How the hell would he have convinced her to keep a cell phone and let him pay the monthly bill? And why did he want to so badly anyway?

But Dean already knew the answer to that.

They were his sisters.

Twenty years had passed, and yet, not a single day over all that time really mattered. Not anymore.

Maybe family was like that. Cam had never doubted their connection. From jump, she'd claimed him and expected him to allow her to do so.

He'd fought it, but now Dean had to admit that Cam had won.

Damn but he wanted to talk to Eve about this.

Officer Ramsey, a veteran of twenty years, stopped to talk with Dean while his partner spoke with the crowd.

"We checked around the area, but you know how it is. All we found were a few spent paintballs. They were probably shot from somewhere up the hill. The shooter would be able to see you two down here beneath all the security lights, while keeping himself well hidden in the dark."

"Cowardly bastard," Dean muttered, convinced more than ever that Roger was behind the attacks.

"You think it was kids?" Gregor wanted to know.

The cop shrugged. "Doesn't matter. It's still a serious assault. One or both of you could have been killed."

Gregor scoffed at that. "From a toy gun?"

Dead serious, the cop stuck his clipboard under his arm and launched into a lecture. "In my day, it was BB guns. I knew a lot of boys who got hurt by those things. A few even blinded. Now the paintball gun has taken over as the lethal weapon of choice for kids."

"Lethal?" Gregor asked.

"Over three million of the damn things were sold in our country this year. But just because they use compressed air instead of gunpowder to launch their projectiles doesn't make them any less powerful than a regular firearm. And because people consider them toys, they don't take near the precautions they should."

"I didn't know," Gregor said, looking suitably chastised.

"You want some statistics? I got statistics coming out my ass." Ramsey held up a finger. "The muzzle velocity of a paintball gun can range from around a hundred and fifty feet a second to twelve hundred feet a second. For traditional firearm pistols, it's seven hundred and fifty to fourteen hundred feet a second."

Dean whistled. "Not much difference."

Another finger went into the air. "There're over twenty thousand serious injuries and approximately four deaths every year."

Gregor rubbed the back of his neck, ill at ease with the rebuke.

A third finger went up, accompanied by a hard stare. "Most of those injuries and nearly all the deaths are kids under the age of fifteen."

Feeling for Gregor, Dean clapped the cop on the shoulder. "Must be tough to deal with."

"You can take that to the bank. I see parents all the time who want to argue that they're toy guns. If I had my way, they'd be off the market. Then we wouldn't have to deal with shit like this." He indicated the splattered paint in the hotel's parking lot.

Gregor cleared his throat. "What's the chance of catchin' the kids who did this?"

"Slim to none, and unfortunately, Slim's outta town. We don't have any witnesses and not much in the way of evidence. The shooter or shooters are long gone. And I can't very well shake every kid in town who owns a paintball gun. But I'll be watching, and if I come up with anything, I'll let you both know."

Dean shook his hand. "We understand. Thanks for coming out so quickly."

"I only wish we could do more."

As the officers left, Dean looked toward the hotel.

Truthfully he was sort of glad the cops couldn't nail anyone in particular.

He wanted to deal with Roger himself.

WHEN Dean finally made it home, Eve was starved. She took one look at him as he walked in and put her arms around him. Odd how her grumpiness just evaporated away the second she touched him.

He did his best to hug her back, considering he held a bucket of chicken and a bag of side dishes.

"Hey," he said, "you okay?"

Eve leaned back to look at him. "You crazy man. Of course, I'm okay. I'm offering you comfort from your lousy day."

That sexy grin she'd grown to adore made him look less tired. "Comfort, huh?" He stepped back to eye her head to toe. "Look at you. Is it possible for you *not* to look sexy?"

Eve smiled. She'd chosen the white and pink striped cami with matching floral boy shorts just for him. "I had the flu once." She took the food from him and started for the kitchen. "I was sweaty with a fever, throwing up every ten minutes, and felt too lousy to even comb my hair. Trust me, it was a very ugly thing."

"I wish I'd been here to help you."

Her heart did a small flip. Yeah, Dean would have helped. And knowing him now, she didn't think he would have minded her icky appearance all that much. He was so earthy, so natural about life and the trials that came with it, that he probably just rolled with the punches on everything.

"You know, after the day you had, we could have just thrown together peanut-butter-and-jelly sandwiches. You didn't have to stop for food."

"I wanted to."

When she reached up to the cabinet to retrieve two plates, Dean put his arms around her and hugged her from behind.

Nuzzling against her nape, he whispered, "I missed you."

And her heart did another flip. If he kept that up, she'd be dizzy and breathless in no time. Plates in hand, she turned in his arms and smiled to soften what she'd say next.

Dean looked at her and sighed. "Okay, what is it?"

His intuition surprised her, but she didn't doubt it. "I think you should tell Cam what's going on."

"Not yet." He kissed her nose and took the plates from her to carry to the table.

"But this is getting out of hand. Messing with your tires was one thing. Causing a fall from a ladder, shooting at you—you could have lost an eye!"

"Or worse, I know." Dean opened the bucket of chicken and inhaled. "I'm starved."

"Dean," Eve said with exasperation. "She's your sister. You have to trust her."

"No," he said, glancing up at her. "I don't."

"Well, you should!"

"She thinks she's in love with Roger." He took silverware from a drawer and put it on the table. "She won't be unbiased about any of this."

It was nice, Eve thought, how Dean just automatically worked with her to do what needed to be done. He wouldn't be a man content to sit in front of the television while others—especially a wife—worked around him.

And that was about the most dangerous thought she'd had yet.

"I know. She told me." After getting two bottled drinks from the refrigerator, Eve sat at the table. "But Cam isn't a woman who takes love lightly."

"Meaning?"

"Meaning she doesn't just think it. She *is* in love with him."

Dropping into his seat, Dean complained, "Here it comes."

Eve frowned at his sarcasm, but she didn't hold back. "I doubt Cam could love a man capable of what you're suggesting."

"I knew it." Now visibly irate, Dean scooped a heaping pile of potato salad on her plate and set it down in front of her.

Eve eyed the mound of food—enough for two grown men—and shook her head. "You knew what?"

"That you'd take a woman's perspective on this."

"That might be because I'm a woman. But you realize I can say the reverse, that you're taking a man's perspective on it."

"Which is?"

"You don't like Roger, you don't want your sister to marry him, so he has to be the villain in this scenario."

Dean finished chewing a big bite of chicken, swallowed, took a drink, and then pointed his fork at her. "Actually I'm taking the logical perspective. People rarely do things without motives."

"Everything that's happened to you isn't necessarily related."

"I don't believe in coincidence. Not three in a row."

Eve stopped to regroup and rethink her strategy.

"I see the wheels turning," Dean pointed out. "But I'll warn you now that I'm not easy to manipulate."

She waved that away. "Could we compromise?"

"In what way?"

"Let's give it just a few days. If nothing else happens, you'll tell Cam about your suspicions. You'll trust her enough to also be logical and to know a good man from a bad one." She smiled sweetly. "After all, she had you pegged from the get-go."

To Eve's way of thinking, Dean pondered her suggestion far too long. She was just about to throw her chicken bone at him when he conceded.

"All right. I've got someone checking into Roger's background, and until I hear from him, I don't want to jump the gun anyway."

Eve sat back and gave him a blank stare. "I hope you're joking."

"Not even a little. But there's another reason, too. I'd already decided that you know the girls better than I do."

"Girls?" she teased, raising one brow as if affronted.

"Women. Sisters." He shook his head. "Cam and Jacki. I'm getting to know them, but I feel like I'm missing a lot of the pieces. I figure between hanging out at the house to do the rest of the repairs and talking with you, I'll have a better idea of how to handle them."

"Handle them?"

Dean eyed her as he dug into a second piece of chicken. "You keep repeating things I say."

"Only the stupid things."

"Are you going to eat or not?"

She looked down at the small dent she'd made in the food he'd put on her plate. "I have eaten. I'm just not a glutton. There's no way I can consume all this in one sitting."

"Sorry about that. Finish up with what you do want, and I'll show you some moves."

"You sure you feel up to it?"

"Definitely." Sensual promise glittered in his brown eyes. "Got any preferences?"

Without hesitation, Eve said, "I want to learn how to do an arm lock, rear naked choke, and the Kimura."

That slow grin appeared again. "You have been watching fights, haven't you?"

"And learning a lot. Once you've taught me a few things, I plan to give that brother of mine the surprise of his life."

The phone rang while Dean was still laughing. As Eve excused herself to answer it, she thought how nice it was to see Dean like this, teasing and relaxed. His laughter made her smile from the inside out.

Her smile died as soon as she heard Cam's upset voice.

After talking to her a few minutes, Eve offered to drive to her house. They had consoled each other many times, and no man, not even a well-meaning brother, would change that.

But Cam knew that Eve was with Dean, and she insisted that she only wanted to go to bed.

Eve returned to Dean with a frown.

"Anything wrong?"

Probably too many things to count. "You aren't going to like it."

"Let me hear it anyway."

Rather than drag out the inevitable, Eve propped an elbow on the table and explained what she knew. "Roger asked Cam to marry him. Again. Cam refused. Again. This time Roger didn't take it that well."

Half out of his seat, Dean asked, "What did that bastard do?"

"Not what you're thinking. He didn't yell at Cam or harass her. He left. Just walked away." And Eve couldn't help but feel a little sorry for him. "Cam said he looked brokenhearted."

Dean snorted at that.

"A few hours later, she got a handwritten message from him." Eve understood Dean's reaction, because not that long ago, she had despised Roger, too. He always came across so pushy, so controlling—a total mismatch for Cam.

But through Cam, Eve was beginning to see Roger differently. If Cam loved him, and she did, then he couldn't be all bad.

"The note said he was taking a few days off and would get in touch with her when he returned. Cam's a little frantic, and feeling guilty for not explaining herself to him. She doesn't know where he went, and he's not answering her calls."

Dean stood and went to the window to stare out at the darkness. "When was this?"

He looked so lost in thought, Eve came up to lean against him. "About an hour before someone shot at you." He said nothing, his thoughts contained inwardly. Eve nudged him. "What are you thinking?"

With an ease of familiarity, Dean's arm slipped around her shoulders, and she fit herself against his side. "That this sudden trip of his is a cover-up. That he must be planning something more." He finally looked at her. "I just don't know what. Or why. And until I do, I'm not going to rest easy."

CHAPTER 20

WITH Roger gone missing, the next three days went by without incident. Still Dean couldn't stop worrying, and he made a point of spending time with Cam and Jacki. They worked on the house together, shared lunch, and went swimming. In terms of strengthening their relationship, each day felt more like a year. In no time at all, he had memories of his sisters, some newly built, and some shared from their animated stories of growing up with crazy Lorna as a guardian.

Cam told tall tales on Jacki, making her most recent antics sound harrowing and nerve-wracking—which was probably how Cam had viewed them, being she was the motherly sort.

For her part, Jacki mimicked Cam, giving the impression of a schoolmarm or a staid librarian.

Neither woman took offense; instead they laughed at each other. They were open and honest with their affection, confident in the love they shared. Dean both envied their closeness and relished it.

When he left himself unguarded, he felt a part of it.

If Cam hadn't been so out of sorts, her usual good spirits gone missing, their time together would have been perfect. Not that Cam complained or pouted. Her pride would never allow her to do that.

But Dean noted that her smiles weren't as bright, and they never reached her eyes. He wanted to talk to her about Roger and his suspicious absence, but damn it, he didn't know how, not without upsetting her more.

Cam wasn't the only sister causing him concern. The other worry had to do with Jacki—more specifically how Gregor watched her every move with a look that all men recognized. Dean hated to admit it, but he'd become a stereotypical big brother after all, and it hadn't taken all that much to get him there. His resolve to remain unattached had been no match for his sisters' warm, infectious charms.

All his life, Dean had prided himself on knowing his own mind. He accepted who he was and what he wanted. He faced his weaknesses and understood his strengths.

But around Jacki and Cam, he didn't know his own mind. What he thought he wanted changed each day that he spent with them. His future, once neatly laid out, no longer appeared so appealing. He liked being with Jacki and Cam, but he hated the way it weakened him.

Spending his evenings with Eve helped. He'd taught her several moves, and sometimes when they grappled, she surprised him. Not that she came close to getting the better of him, not even for a split second, but she had good speed, and she remembered every little detail.

When Eve lost, as she always did, she got even by alternately teasing Dean for his growing preoccupation with his sisters and urging him to get even more involved. Her attitude made the upheaval less startling and more natural.

If Eve had her way, he'd move back to Harmony and live under the same roof with his sisters, discussing with them everything from their monthlies to bra sizes to the latest fashions.

Eve claimed that siblings should be able to share everything and to count on each other no matter what.

Because she had that relationship with her brother,
Dean trusted her knowledge on the subject. But that didn't
make the reality of strengthening iron bonds any easier,
when he'd always considered himself a free man.

"When will you fight again?" Sitting on the floor, her
back against the wall, Cam watched as Dean repaired the
ceiling in Lorna's room. Her idle chitchat should have been
a nuisance. With other women—women who were not of
the sisterly sort—he'd had little interest in learning all
about them. But with Cam he savored the easy camaraderie
growing between them.

For the most part, Lorna had stayed out of Dean's way.
Today she kept close, constantly peering into her bedroom
where he worked with an expectant scowl. She probably
hoped to catch him pilfering through her jewelry or searching her closet. Dean knew she would leap at any opportunity to validate her low opinion of him.

At Cam's question, Lorna lingered, watching him and
waiting to see what he'd say.

"Simon wants to set something up. A special promotional program. I don't know that much about it yet, but I
think it'd be like a reality series or something." Dean applied compound mud over the repaired holes in the ceiling.
When it dried, he'd sand it smooth and then paint it to
match the rest of the room.

"A reality series about you?"

He shrugged without taking his attention from his task.
"Given what Simon told me, I'm guessing that cameras
would follow me around while I trained for six weeks or so
and then record the fight the night of the tournament."

Lorna came further into the room, her expression and
tone hopeful. "When is this fight? Does this mean you'll be
leaving us soon?"

"I haven't decided yet." Dean enjoyed disappointing
her. "But even if I did go, I'd still come back. Didn't the
girls tell you?"

Cam cleared her throat. "When would Simon orchestrate this special program?"

Her attempt to change the subject fell flat. So Cam hadn't mentioned his plans to Lorna? He wasn't surprised, knowing how Lorna would react.

Lorna snapped to attention. "Young lady, have you kept something important from me?" Her tone and appearance seemed more panicked than angry. "What has this meddling interloper done now?"

Knowing *he* was the interloper, Dean stepped in to spare Cam from defending him or taking the heat of Lorna's temper. "I've decided to move back here for good."

The old gal's jaw nearly hit the floor. *"What?"* she screeched in a shrill voice. And then with more strength, she shouted, "No!"

Actually Dean hadn't made any such decision at all. It wasn't like him to bluff, but he couldn't resist the prime opportunity to gig Lorna.

Unfortunately Cam didn't know it was a bluff, and she shot to her feet in excitement. "You're serious!"

Dean would have regretted the impetuous statement, but Cam hadn't sounded so elated since Roger split and that made his bluff an actuality.

He wasn't about to disappoint Cam.

"Yeah." Stepping down from the ladder, Dean smiled at her reaction. "Why not?"

She launched herself at him, crying, laughing. "Dean, that's wonderful! I can't believe Eve didn't tell me."

His arms went around her as if he'd been hugging her his whole life. "That might be because I haven't told Eve yet."

Finally pulling herself together, Lorna narrowed her eyes and curled her lip with hatred. "And just why would you tell that girl anything at all? She's not family. She's nobody. She—"

Still holding on to Dean, Cam said, "Because he's in love with her."

This time, Dean's jaw dropped. Hearing Cam blurt out

a deeply hidden thought like that sucked all the air from his lungs.

Cam just poked him in the side and continued grinning. "Oh, come on, Dean. Did you think I wouldn't notice something *that* noticeable?"

The same arguments he'd given himself now spilled out to Cam. "I haven't known her long enough to be in love with her. And you haven't known me long enough to make that type of assessment on my feelings. Far as you know, I could behave the same with every woman."

A dimple showed in her cheek. "Is that so?"

The automatic "yes" died on Dean's tongue. From the onset, his determination to have Eve had helped blunt the transition back into his hometown, his past, and his sisters' lives. He hadn't just wanted Eve, he'd *craved* her.

That hadn't changed. It didn't matter if he was with her or away from her. The desire remained, always.

And why not? Eve was attractive, she wanted him, too, and she had character traits that would draw any man.

Frowning, Dean thought of Tiffany, the groupie in his room when he'd first awakened from his last fight. A beautiful woman. Cheerful. Sexy. More than willing. Tiffany even shared a love of his sport.

Yet he'd had no problem sending her on her way.

"No," Dean admitted, "I don't feel the same about all women."

"You don't look happy about it."

"It's unsettling, if you want the truth."

"I don't see why." Cam's smile gentled. "Love isn't on a time line, you know. When it's right, it's right."

Had Eve confided in her? The thought intrigued Dean. "You think it's right between Eve and me?"

"Almost from the moment she met you, she's been connecting with you in a way that I haven't seen from her before. I think it's great."

In a tone that barely sounded human, Lorna whispered, "I don't see what's so great about it."

Dean glanced at her, and even he was taken aback when

he saw that she was nearly beside herself with unmasked hurt and fury.

Startled, Cam reached for her. "Aunt Lorna—"

"No!" Lorna jerked back and then pleaded with Cam. "Can't you see that he's taking over? It's all calculated and devious. Already he ran off your fiancé. Doesn't that matter to you?"

Cam eased away from him. "Dean had nothing to do with that, Aunt Lorna. Roger and I just need to work out a few things."

"Right." So much scorn dripped from her words. "And just how can you work out anything when Roger is *gone*?"

Cam lifted her chin. "He'll be back."

But she didn't sound convinced of that.

"You should never have allowed Dean to drive him away. Roger would have saved us all financially." Lorna's rant became barely coherent. "He offered. He wanted to help. He's rich and kind. An excellent catch. Yet over and over again you've turned him away. Then you beg *this one* to stay?"

The accusation in Lorna's tone strengthened Cam's position. "Of course I want Dean to stay. He's my brother. He's your nephew."

Filled with loathing, Lorna's gaze swung to Dean. "I wouldn't claim him then, and I won't have him now."

Cam gasped, but Dean just folded his arms, wondering how far Lorna would go. Would she finally say why she despised him so much? What could a nine-year-old boy have done to earn such enmity?

"That's enough," Cam said.

But Lorna refused to retreat from her position. "You're being an utter fool, girl. You can't trust him. I know how Grover raised him in his image. Oh, Dean will play the benevolent big brother just to worm his way in, but then he'll call in the debts and kick us all out to the street corner. You wait and see."

Cam looked at Dean, maybe hoping for him to defend himself. But Dean had no intention of doing so. He didn't owe Lorna any explanations at all.

"You're just like them," Lorna claimed with glee, charging forward to close the space between them. She shook a measly fist in his face. "You were already too old for me to change, but the girls were still babies, untainted by them."

Cam looked between Dean and her aunt with confusion. "Them who?"

From the beginning, Dean had wanted Lorna to admit to his parents' failings, but now . . . he couldn't bear the idea of upsetting Cam.

"Shut up, Lorna."

"You wanted them to know," she accused. "You threatened to tell them yourself."

"I've changed my mind."

"Well, that's too bad for you!"

Cam raised her voice to demand attention. "Tell us *what?*"

Shaking all over, Lorna turned on her. "Your parents were immoral drunks." Righteous in her fury, Lorna pressed her fist to her chest. "I tried to protect you from that. It's why I sent him away." One manicured finger stabbed toward Dean.

It didn't matter what she said about him, Dean decided. Cam had faced enough realities in her life. If possible, he wanted to protect any illusions she had about their parents.

"That's enough, Lorna. Drop it."

As if she hadn't even heard him, Lorna raged on. "That's why I've been strict with you, why I never indulged you in any way. You have your parents' blood running through your veins, so I couldn't allow alcohol to ever—"

"Shut up, damn you." Dean started forward, to do what he didn't know.

Cam stopped him with a hand on his chest. "It's all right, Dean. I already knew. Jacki, too."

Dean stared at Cam in shock. She stood tall and proud, so strong yet sympathetic toward her aunt. His pride for her doubled.

Lorna went pale. "No." She shook her head. "I got rid of everything. The letters, the photos—"

"Me," Dean added.

"But not the memories." Cam tipped her head with sympathy. "People talk, Aunt Lorna. It was inevitable that I'd hear things."

"That can't be true." She shook her head in denial. "I took care of everything. *Everything*. There's no way. Tell me you're making it up."

"I didn't want to distress you." Cam reached for her, but again, Lorna fended her off.

"You're lying." She blinked hard at Dean. "*He* told you, didn't he?"

"Dean didn't have to tell me." Despite Lorna's rejection, Cam took her hands. "It doesn't matter about our parents, Aunt Lorna. Jacki and I had you, and we appreciate all you did for us."

"Yes." Lorna breathed a little easier. "Yes, you had me. You'll always have me." She tried a smile that barely shifted the distraught lines of her face. "You won't let Dean ruin everything."

Good God, Dean thought. What the hell did Lorna expect him to do anyway?

"You're wrong about Dean," Cam insisted. "He's a good man. I know you did what you thought was best, but you should never have sent him away."

"No, I shouldn't have," Lorna murmured in agreement, her gaze unseeing. "That was a mistake. Now he's back, and he wants revenge."

"Revenge?" Cam frowned with worry. "Nonsense."

"He hates me. How could he not? He'll throw me out, I tell you."

From the doorway, Eve announced, "Of course Dean won't kick anyone out. He loves his sisters. Given half a chance, he'd probably even grow fond of you, Lorna."

With Lorna's every word, Dean had grown more uneasy. He did despise Lorna, and worse, he pitied her. Combined, they made a very uncomfortable feeling in the pit of his stomach. Now at the sight of Eve, he relaxed. "Hey."

She smiled brightly at him. "Hey yourself."

Something seemed different about her. Or maybe that was celibacy making him feel that way. Dean hadn't even come close to getting his fill of Eve, and then she'd gotten her period, and—

Eve walked to Cam. "You okay?" she asked softly.

Dean looked at his sister and belatedly noted her pallor. "Cam?"

What had he missed? One moment Cam had been reassuring Lorna, well in charge of the situation, and now she looked far too vulnerable.

Big tears welled in her eyes. She dashed them away with an impatient hand and met his gaze. "Is Eve right?"

Confusion swamped Dean. "About what?"

"Oh, for God's sake, girl." Lorna patted Cam's hand. "Don't fall apart now. Roger will have you back. He'll help all of us with this mess if you just allow him to."

Cam shook her head at that. "Dean? Do you love us? Jacki and me, I mean?"

That's what had her all tearful?

Before Dean could find his voice, Gregor said, "Great timin' on my part, don't ya think, Havoc?"

Annoyed at the intrusion, Dean turned his attention to Gregor—and found Simon standing in the doorway. Next to him, Jacki gawked.

Eve glanced at Simon, looked away, and immediately jerked her gaze back to him again. "Oh my God."

Blinking away her tears, Cam asked of no one in particular, "Who *is* that?"

Amused, Dean shook his head. Simon always got that reaction from the fairer sex. At thirty-one and with a mixed martial arts record of thirty-five wins, one draw, and only one loss, he still looked as pretty as ever. No cauliflower ears, scars, or outrageous tattoos for Simon.

He stood six feet, two inches tall and weighed 205 pounds, all of it ripped muscle. Naturally swarthy, with dark brows and dark chest hair, an imposing manner, and a clean-shaven head, Simon grabbed attention wherever he went.

The baldness was not an accident of nature; long ago Simon had removed all the hair from his head, and now it had become his trademark look. For some reason, his lack of hair only made women comment more often on his dark brown eyes.

Thanks to the ladies, Simon didn't get a kick-ass nickname like "Havoc" or "The Maniac." Early in his fighting career, the female fans dubbed him "The Sublime."

And it stuck like glue.

"Ladies," Dean said, noticing that even Lorna had gone speechless and slack jawed, "the man you're all drooling over is Simon Evans, my trainer, manager, producer, and any other job that comes up."

Ignoring Dean's reference to the attention he drew, Simon looked around the room. "Who's related to Havoc?"

Both bug-eyed and twittering, Cam and Jacki snuck their hands tentatively into the air.

"Aha." Propping his fists on his hips, Simon nodded. "I get it now."

"Get what?" Gregor wanted to know.

"Havoc's tattoo."

Alarmed at the direction of Simon's thoughts, Dean warned, *"Don't,"* but he was too late.

"Three vines," Simon explained, tipping his head toward Dean's biceps. "Two of them real dainty with rosebuds, one all covered in thorns."

Gregor said, "So?"

For years the other fighters had heckled Dean about his tattoo, curious as to what meaning, if any, inspired the design. Not once had he ever laid claim to any muse beyond the ignorance of youth.

And now Simon planned to expose him.

Hoping to miss this little unveiling of truths, Dean began gathering up his tools.

"It's Dean and his sisters," Simon announced.

Shit, shit, shit.

As he felt the burn of curious gazes, Dean's heart landed in his stomach.

"And now that I've seen his sisters," Simon clarified, "I know exactly which vine represents Dean."

At that point, Dean would have walked out, but Eve, Cam, and Jacki blocked his way. They had that *ooooh* look that women sometimes got when they thought a man did something that they all found endearing.

"It's nothing," Dean ground out. "Don't make it into something, because it's not."

"Nothing at all," Cam whispered, still smiling in that sentimental, touched way.

For her part, Jacki grinned wide enough that he could see her damn molars. "I'm glad you got the tat before you met me, otherwise I might have been the thorny vine."

Grinding his teeth together, Dean saw Eve watching his sisters like a proud mother, and that, more than anything else, left him livid.

Shoving the half-empty bucket of compound mud at Eve, Dean shouldered past his sisters.

He paused by Simon only long enough to ask, "You heard anything yet on that business I asked you to check into?"

"I'm expecting a call soon."

"How soon?"

"Anytime now."

Dean nodded. If Roger had anything to hide, he'd find it. "Let's go, Gregor."

"Go where?"

Stepping into the hall, Dean said, "To a gym. I already scoped one out."

"You did?"

"Yeah. And now that loud-mouthed Simon is here, we can get that promised sparring out of the way." He didn't wait to see if anyone followed him or not.

He was too embarrassed.

He even had the awful suspicion that his face might be red.

As Dean strode away, he heard Gregor say, "Well, hell, Simon. I don't want to spar with him now, when he's in this crappy mood. He'll kill me."

"Idiot, he's going to kill you anyway." Simon started after Dean. "But that's the best way for you to learn."

"How," Eve demanded from close behind, "can Gregor learn anything if he's dead?"

Wanting to put distance between them all, Dean bounded down the stairs, reached the kitchen, and . . . wondered where he should go next. He didn't want to just walk out on Eve. The backyard looked private, but he'd have to wait for her to lead her there. He looked at the laundry-room door, the family room . . . well, hell. He stopped in the middle of the floor.

He didn't run from anyone.

Okay, he'd never run from a *man*. But sisters were no different, at least not in that respect. Running was chicken-shit, no matter who chased you off.

He had no reason to be embarrassed. He'd been four-teen when he got the idiotic tattoo, and in the fifteen years that followed, he'd never gotten another.

Everyone made melodramatic, foolhardy mistakes in their youth.

While waiting for the others to catch up, Dean leaned against the counter, crossed his ankles, and pondered his new circumstances.

Did Eve love him? He hoped so, because Cam was right—he loved her. He more than loved her. He needed her.

Somehow his life had turned upside down on him.

Like the Pied Piper, everyone followed where Dean went. Within seconds, the kitchen overflowed with bodies, and the din of various conversations filled the air.

Lorna continued to mutter, more to herself than to any-one else. Cam and Jacki, while still sneaking rapturous glances at Simon, discussed the idea of Dean moving in. Gregor warned Simon that Jacki was off limits so he might as well not get any lurid thoughts, and Simon told him to go screw himself.

Only Eve came close and that was to say, "You have to tell your sister about Roger. It's been three days, and he's not back yet."

"Nag, nag, nag." God, he adored her.

She frowned at him. "Are you really going to fight Gregor?"

"Sparring is not fighting, but yeah, I am. I need to let off steam and there's no better way than pounding on Gregor's hard head."

Eve touched her fingers to his chest. "Oh, I don't know about that. I can think of a better way."

Dean froze. "What does that mean, Eve?" He caught her teasing fingers and held them still. "And don't toy with me woman."

Eve laughed in delight and leaned closer to whisper in his ear. "It means I'm once again available for intimate activities."

Darkness closed in. The voices in the room receded. His awareness of others faded away.

Still holding her hand, Dean pushed away from the counter and started toward the sliding doors.

"Dean," she whispered, frantically trying to pull her hand free.

"I only need a minute." Less, maybe.

Half in embarrassment and half in laughter, Eve hissed, "You're just going to have to wait."

"Can't." Dean got the sliding doors open and—

"Where do you two think you're going?" Lorna demanded.

Dean stopped dead in his tracks. He swallowed. Hell, he had a jones, so no way could he turn and face two sisters, a trainer, Gregor, and Lorna.

Eve laughed. "We aren't leaving. I just have a few things I need to say to Dean. We'll be back in one minute, I promise."

In a stage whisper, Gregor said, "More like half an hour, I think."

"I think you're right," Simon said. "Havoc lacks subtlety. I'll have to work on that with him."

"What are you talking about?" Lorna demanded to know.

Eve groaned and propelled Dean beyond the door, over

the deck, and across the yard toward the woods. She kept going until the voices could no longer be heard.

They reached a large tree and Dean spun her around so her back was against it, then he caged her in. "Thank you."

She fended him off with both hands flat against his chest. "Don't even think it."

Her puny resistance was like nothing to him. "I'm thinking it, Eve. Sorry."

That made her laugh again. "You're incorrigible."

"I'm so hard, I'm dying here."

"Poor baby." Eve went on tiptoe to kiss him. She looked so pretty that Dean wanted to steal her away. "I can cancel some afternoon appointments if you'd like to meet me back at my house in a few hours."

His groan rumbled out as a deep complaint. "Hours?"

"Sorry, but I have a few things this morning that can't wait."

She really did look sorry—for herself and him. That helped Dean get it together. He glanced back toward the house and saw several people standing at the patio doors, watching them.

"I suppose I can't even cop a quick feel with that nosy audience there."

Eve peeked around him, saw the same thing, and shook her head. "Nope. Besides you have to tell Cam about Roger and—"

"Eve . . ."

"—and you need to decide what to do about Lorna. I hate the thought of her making Cam more miserable just because Cam doesn't hate you."

"How about I just kick Lorna to the curb, as she expects me to?"

"No. And that's not funny." Eve again glanced at the house. "Dean, why didn't you tell me that your trainer was drop-dead gorgeous?"

"Because men don't talk that way."

She tilted her head at him. "You don't mind that I think he's gorgeous?"

Dean grunted. "You and every other woman." He gave her a quick kiss. "No, I don't mind. You're not blind, after all. But you're also not the type to get involved with two men at one time."

"So I'm a sure bet, huh? Is that what you're telling me?"

Dean laughed at her show of mock insult. "You're honorable."

"That sounds better." She sighed with regret. "I do have to go. Promise me you'll talk to Cam."

"You weren't here to know, but Lorna has given her a hard time all day. I think she's had enough thrown at her for now."

"Excuses, excuses." Eve knotted her hand in the front of his shirt. "She has a right to know what you're thinking, so promise me."

Reminding himself that Eve knew his sisters better than he did, Dean nodded. "All right, if it's that important to you."

"Thank you." She lingered, looked at his hand on hers, then up into his eyes. "About your tattoo—"

Dean released her. "Not up for discussion."

"Okay."

"I mean it, Eve."

"I know." Her eyes twinkled as she fought a smile. "But is Simon right?"

Shoving his hands on his hips, Dean turned and walked off three steps, then stalked back. Of course she didn't let it drop. When Eve had something on her mind, he couldn't dissuade her. "Yeah, he's right. And that's enough on the subject."

"But it's so—"

"Do *not* say sweet." There was only so much he could tolerate.

The teasing left her eyes, and instead he saw something much deeper there as she said, "How about noble?"

Noble? Dean cocked a brow in surprise. "Is that supposed to be a joke?"

Eve slowly shook her head. "Any fourteen-year-old boy who cares so much for his sisters, even after not seeing them for five years, that he'd want a permanent reminder of them on his body where it could never be lost or stolen is very, very noble."

Damn. Dean stared at Eve in wonder. Would she always see the best in him?

He hoped so.

Knowing he had to lighten the moment or he'd start to declare himself, Dean started toward her. "You know what I think?"

"What?"

He'd almost reached her. "I think you just want to get laid, so you're showering me with compliments."

Laughing, Eve started backing away toward the house. "You're right. I do." Forestalling any comment he might make about that, she glanced at her watch. "Two o'clock, okay?"

Resigned to waiting, Dean nodded. "I'll be there."

"And I'll be waiting." She turned and hurried away.

CAM stood at the front door and watched that gorgeous hunk of manhood leave with Gregor and Jacki. Even from the back, he could steal her breath away. From the top of his perfectly sculpted head down to his large feet, Simon Evans was a man guaranteed to delight the female senses.

Someone should have warned her. One moment she'd had her head lost in the heavy discussion between Lorna and Dean, and then suddenly he was there, shocking her speechless.

She'd never seen anyone like him. He was simply . . . beautiful. But in a very masculine way. When he looked at her, she could barely breathe, much less speak. And when he moved . . .

Shivering, Cam took one last lingering look and then forced herself to shut the door. She pitied any woman who got involved with that one. She certainly wasn't brave enough, but then, Roger—even with his imperfections—already had her heart.

If only he'd come back to her.

Refusing to leave her alone with Dean for some ridiculous reason, Lorna paced the floor behind Cam. Her aunt acted as though Dean were a malicious villain.

The way Lorna had turned up the insults, doing her best to blame Dean for past and present problems, infuriated Cam. At the same time, her aunt seemed especially fragile during any mention of the past, which kept Cam from speaking her mind. Aunt Lorna had given up much to raise them. At the time of her parents' deaths, her aunt had been a much younger, single woman with no ties or commitments.

Cam couldn't forget that, any more than she could give up a brother she'd just reclaimed.

Thank God Roger had already told her the stories circulating around town about her parents. It had been an unpleasant shock to discover that her parents were far from ideal caregivers. But Roger, always having her best interests at heart, had known that being forewarned would make it easier to deal with the resurgence of old truths.

It made sense now, why Lorna had removed all photos and memories of her parents, why she detested drink so much, why she'd always been so rigid. Her parents had caused a very ugly scandal and then left Lorna to raise two children among the rumors, speculation, and gossip.

No, Cam corrected herself, they'd left her *three* children.

But Lorna had ruthlessly cast Dean aside.

Appearances meant everything to Aunt Lorna, so it must have been excruciating for her to face down the neighbors, to answer the nosy questions and ignore the rude stares. Yet she'd stayed and done her best by them. Not a great job, but not an awful job, either.

Normally Lorna took immaculate care with her hair and dress. But lately she looked almost haggard. It worried Cam and made her heart ache. Her aunt was even more insecure about her position in the family than Cam had ever guessed.

Dean poked his head into the room. "If you have a minute, I'd like to talk to you." He glanced at Lorna. "In the kitchen. I made some sandwiches. We can talk over lunch."

Rather than address that, Cam said, "Your friend is very handsome."

Dean gave her a lazy smile. "So I've heard."

"He's a striking man," Lorna murmured, still pacing restlessly. "You have more friends than I assumed."

"And that bothers you?" Dean asked.

Cam didn't want them to start sniping at each other again. She loved Dean, but where he was young and vital and independent, her aunt was nearing sixty, and very afraid for her future. "Dean . . ."

"Your parents had friends," Lorna said low. She looked up at Dean, her narrowed eyes adding extra crow's feet to her face. "Unfaithful, lying, lewd friends."

"Aunt Lorna," Cam said by way of reprimand. "You can't compare Dean to our parents. He's nothing like them."

Lorna's posture stiffened. "Maybe not."

Her admission surprised both Dean and Cam.

"It does seem you're different," Lorna continued. "Stronger. More resolute. But the fact remains, if you hadn't come back, the past might have stayed buried."

"No." Cam refused to let Lorna fool herself. "Something like that never goes away. The uglier things in life have a way of always resurfacing, usually when you least expect them."

Lorna actually smiled. "It appears you're right about that."

Again Cam felt shocked. Was Aunt Lorna finally coming to grips with Dean's role in the family? God, she hoped so. "Please don't let it bother you, Aunt Lorna. It's best that we all know and deal with it now."

Nodding, Lorna turned to Dean. "I shouldn't have blamed you. It's my fault, really. I didn't handle the situation as I should have."

His confusion plain, Dean spared a glance at Cam before replying to Lorna. "Cam and Jacki are pretty wonderful. You raised them, Lorna. That counts for a lot."

"Yes, yes it does. Thank you." She laced her fingers together in front of her and cocked her head in a curious way. "There was an awful lot of love talk today."

Cam bit her lip.

Dean said plainly, "Cam and Jacki are very easy to care about."

"And Eve?" Lorna came two steps closer to Dean. "Is it true that she factors into your plans to stay?"

Remembering Lorna's disparaging remarks about her friend, Cam answered ahead of Dean. "Eve is a very beautiful person, Aunt Lorna."

Lorna absorbed that with a lot of thought. "I suppose to be your good friend, she must have many redeeming qualities."

That was as close as Lorna had ever come to being kind toward Eve. Cam blinked in surprise, and then she smiled.

Dean loved her and Jacki, and he wanted to move back home. Her aunt was softening. Finally things were coming together as they should.

If only Roger would return, Cam knew her heart would be full. But at least for now, she had hope for a happy resolution. "Let's all go eat. I'm starved."

Lorna fell into step beside them. "If Dean has something to tell you, I want to hear it, too."

"Sorry," Dean said. "But I need to talk to Cam alone."

"No." Lorna took up a stubborn stance. "Whatever other problems we've suffered, Cam is still my niece. As you already said, I raised her, I care for her. Whatever you have to tell her, you can say with me here to protect her."

Cam didn't blame Dean for wanting to exclude Lorna. He had valid reasons to resent her.

Sometimes Cam resented her, too.

But for the sake of avoiding further hostilities, she agreed with her aunt. "It's all right, Dean. I don't mind if she stays." Cam pulled out a chair and seated herself.

With a shrug, Dean followed suit, but Lorna remained standing.

"This isn't about our family history, Cam." He looked grim, and that worried Cam. "It's about Roger."

"Roger?" She shook her head in confusion.

"He's a saint," Lorna declared. "A *saint,* I tell you. He's taken care of us, assisted us in times of need—"

"He tampered with my tires," Dean informed them. "He's the one who cut through that rung on the ladder, probably hoping that whoever stepped on it would fall."

Cam couldn't get a single word out.

Dean took her hand. "And he shot at me."

"*Shot* at you?" Cam gave a nervous laugh of disbelief. "But, Dean, Roger doesn't even own a gun."

"Not a regular gun, maybe. But this was a paintball gun. And trust me, it wasn't a damn toy. It was powerful enough that if one of the paintballs had hit me in the head, it could have killed me."

"But . . ." None of it made sense to Cam. She turned to Aunt Lorna, who stood there in shock as well. "This doesn't make any sense."

"I'm sorry, Cam." Dean gently squeezed her fingers. "I know it sounds crazy, but I don't know who else it could have been. Roger knew I was going to see Eve the night my tires were destroyed in front of her house. He knew we were working on the roof, and he has access to your home, so getting to the ladder wouldn't have been a problem. And it was at his hotel, where Roger would know my whereabouts, that Gregor and I were shot at."

Refusing to even think of Roger doing such a thing, Cam shook her head. "There has to be some other explanation."

"On the surface, it all sounds like circumstantial evidence. And when Roger comes back, I'll be willing to talk to him. But he left town right after the last incident."

"Because I refused to marry him."

"Or because I called the cops."

Lorna stepped behind Cam and put a hand on her

shoulder. "I think you should go, Dean. You've upset her enough."

"No." Trying to pull herself out of the fog, Cam patted her aunt's hand. "This is Dean's house, too, remember."

"One thing at a time, hon." Dean stood. "Promise me that if, or when, Roger contacts you, you'll let me know."

"I don't know. . . ."

"I'm not going to attack him, I promise. I just want to talk to him. If I'm off base, then Roger can clear this all up in no time, and I'll gladly apologize to him. But until then, I want to know that you're not alone with him."

To her disbelief, Aunt Lorna agreed with Dean. "It wouldn't hurt to be cautious, dear. And once Dean talks to him, we can put this nonsense to rest."

"All right. I'll let you know if I hear from him." Cam prayed that would be soon. She couldn't bear the thought of Roger never returning to her.

Dean nodded in satisfaction. "Now." He clasped his hands behind his back. "Since I'll be moving to Harmony, and because I intend to handle any financial difficulties you've had, I'd appreciate it if you'd show me all your records."

Cam looked up at Aunt Lorna. "Aunt Lorna has always taken care of our money, so you'll have to work with her on that."

"I'm good with numbers," Lorna said.

Smiling, Cam agreed. "It's been very helpful to us, not to be bothered with bill paying and balancing budgets and all that." Cam prayed that Dean would understand. Her aunt needed a solid role in their lives, one that gave her importance and allowed her to contribute.

"I can walk you through everything," Lorna said. "Just let me know when you're available."

To Cam's relief, Dean nodded. "How about tomorrow afternoon?"

Lorna nodded. "That would be fine."

"Thanks." Dean bent and put a kiss to Cam's cheek. "I need to get going now."

Concerned that her aunt might have run him off again, Cam said, "What about lunch?"

Dean winked. "I'll grab something on the road. Today I'm getting my stitches out, and then I have a date with Eve."

"Oh." Cam grinned, too. "Well, then, I'll probably see you tomorrow afternoon."

CHAPTER 21

❦

BEFORE Dean made it completely up the walkway, Eve had her front door open. She must have been waiting for him.

She'd changed from her work clothes into a casual T-shirt and jean shorts. Her hair hung loose down her back. Her feet were bare, and Dean could see that she'd skipped wearing a bra.

After one look at the anticipation on her face, Dean knew it'd be a very close thing.

He didn't slow his approach, didn't say a thing. When he reached Eve, she threw her arms around his neck, and Dean backed her into the house, then kicked the door shut behind him.

Catching her beneath the bottom, he lifted Eve up and she wrapped her legs around him. Locked together, he walked them into her bedroom.

Other than their heavy breaths and an occasional soft moan or sound of pleasure, the room was in silence. For the longest time, Dean held her against him, kissing her, gliding his hands over her back, that lush bottom, lower.

Eve arched against him and freed her mouth. "I can't wait."

"You don't have to." He lowered her feet to the floor and skimmed the shirt off over her head. With an arm behind her, he pressed her upward and took one nipple into his mouth.

Her fingers clenched in his hair.

She smelled of soap and lotion and of Eve, a combination guaranteed to make him nuts. When he switched to the other nipple, she groaned and then attacked the snap on his fly.

Dean caught her hands. "No, honey. Not yet."

"Dean—"

"Shhh. Trust me." Still holding her hands, he walked her backward to the bed. When her legs bumped into the mattress, he urged her to lie back while he came down over her with his knees braced on either side of her hips. He kissed each of her palms—then pressed her hands above her head.

With a submissive moan, Eve turned her face to the side and closed her eyes.

Taking his time, Dean surveyed her body. She was so pretty, so sexy. But more than that, she was his. And he'd known it almost from the moment he spotted her in Roger's bar.

Leaning down, he kissed a trail over her soft skin, from her shoulder to her right breast, her ribs to her hip bone. Eve squirmed, but otherwise stayed still. Utilizing slow precision, Dean moved to her right side and peeled away her shorts and panties.

His hands resting lightly on her waist, he said, "Open your legs for me."

She did, but not far enough to suit him. Dean lifted her left leg until she bent it, then pressed it outward, leaving her sprawled and open and so very tempting.

Breathing deep and slow, Dean teased his fingers from the inside of her knee, up, up, until he touched her silky lips, now wet and hot, softly swollen. Easing himself down on an elbow beside her, he watched her face while he fingered her.

When a careful touch made her shiver, then moan, he smiled. "You like that, don't you?"

"I like you."

Carefully Dean worked two fingers into her, as deeply as he could. "Do you more than like me?" She started to reach for him, but he said, "No. Stay still and just let me enjoy you. I feel like I've been waiting a lifetime."

Her lashes lifted, and she stared at him with smoky blue eyes. "Yes."

"Yes what?"

"I more than like you."

At her admission, tension gripped him. Dean took her mouth again, sinking his tongue in just as he worked his fingers in her. He could feel her muscles tightening around him, and he withdrew, then worked a third finger in. Her excitement slicked the way, dampening his hand, filling the room with her scent.

Her breaths came faster, hotter.

Unable to resist any longer, Dean leaned away from her, met her disappointed gaze, and lifted his fingers to his mouth. His eyes closed at the taste of her, then opened again so he could see her every expression.

Face flushed, Eve watched him with excitement.

"I want more, Eve." He bent to kiss her belly. "I want everything." He moved lower.

Eve pressed her legs apart, taut with anticipation.

Clasping her knees, Dean opened her wide, and after one mind-numbing look, he covered her with his mouth.

She cried out at the contact, cried out again when his tongue curled around her, stabbed into her, licked deeply and softly over her.

Knowing he'd lose it any second now, Dean put her legs over his shoulders. Using his fingers to open her a little more, he drew her distended clitoris into his mouth and suckled softly.

In seconds she was coming, riding up against his mouth, twisting on the bed. Her hands again locked in his hair as she ground out a climax, crying, moaning, then sinking slowly back to the mattress. Little aftershocks kept her trembling. Her skin was dewy, warm.

Dean reared back and shucked off his jeans. Eve lay there, spent, smiling, and content. He barely had enough forethought to find a condom before he pressed into her, clenching his teeth against the incredible pleasure of it.

The first stroke took him deep, and he locked her close to his heart, holding her too tightly but unable to loosen his hold.

Eve wrapped her legs around him and made soft, soothing sounds in his ear. Dean rode her hard, nearly violent in his need, but she stayed with him, moving with his rhythm, and when he threw his head back and shouted out a release, Eve stroked his chest and watched him.

After collapsing beside her, his limbs still throbbing and his cock still wet from her, Dean knew he wanted to do it again. Every night, maybe a lot of days, for the rest of his life.

At almost nine, the phone rang. Languid from repeated lovemaking, Dean watched as Eve crawled out of the bed, naked and rosy from head to toe, thanks to his beard shadow. She lifted clothes and hunted through sheets and blankets in the destroyed bedroom before finally locating the phone beneath a chair.

"Hello?"

Dean watched her face, the way her lips moved when she spoke, the tilt to her head, how her slender fingers tucked her tangled hair behind her ear.

Getting knocked out was nothing compared to this.

He loved her so damn much, it hurt all over, sharper than any physical pain, more consuming. His unending desire for her was like a live throbbing in his heart, his head, his muscle and sinew. Even after repeated lovemaking, he needed to breathe her in, taste her again, touch her and hold her, and just be with her.

So many things that she'd said or done affected him deeply. Rather than think him foolhardy at fourteen, she'd labeled him noble. From the beginning, she'd known how he would react with his sisters, when he hadn't had a clue.

She'd expected a lot of him, all of it good.

How could he not love her?

As Eve spoke into the phone, Dean paid little attention to the words. He was only aware of the feelings flooding through him, so full of clarity for the first time since returning to Harmony.

When she hung up, he watched as she crossed to his side of the bed and seated herself on the mattress. "Dean?"

"Hmmm?" He reached up and touched her breast. Not because he wanted to make love again, although he did. And not because she was naked.

She was so damn sexy, she stole his breath, but even that didn't factor in. He touched her because he could, because she was his even if she didn't know it yet.

"That was Lorna." She frowned as she said that.

"Anything wrong?"

Her gaze met his, and he knew the answer before she spoke. "Roger called and asked Cam to meet him at the hotel. She left already."

Dean shot upright on the bed. "She did what?"

"Lorna said that you told Cam to call you before meeting with Roger, so she wanted you to know."

Dean was already off the bed and hunting for his jeans. "Son of a bitch."

Eve helped him in the search. "Do you really think there's any danger?"

"I don't know." Fuck. Where was his cell phone? His wallet? "I need my keys, damn it."

His urgency rubbed off on Eve. "I'll come with you."

Dean grabbed her shoulders. "No. I don't want you anywhere near Roger. I have a bad feeling about this."

"But—"

"Not now, Eve." He released her and stepped into his pants. "Not this time."

He found a shirt and yanked it on over his head, then shoved his feet into untied athletic shoes. Turning, he found Eve scrambling into her own clothes. "You're not going."

"You're not my boss."

Dean paused, determined to make her see reason. Only there wasn't any time. He drew a breath, striving for patience. "Usually I think this pushy need you have for butting into my business is cute."

Eve paused, staring at him in disbelief and hurt.

"This time, there's nothing cute about it. Be smart, will you please? You're holding me up, when Cam could be in danger."

"If you really believe that, call the police."

"And tell them what? That I suspect her fiancé of foul deeds? Don't be dumb."

Her back went stiff. "Dumb?"

Hell, he hadn't meant to insult her, but he did not have time for this. "Damn it, Eve—"

She bent, picked up his keys, and tossed them to him. "Go." She dropped to sit on the edge of the mattress. "I'll be here when you get back."

That sounded more like a threat than a promise, but Dean nodded and trotted out the door. "Thanks."

He'd apologize for the "dumb" comment when he returned. Surely she already knew he didn't mean it that way.

By the time Dean pulled into the hotel parking lot, he'd put most of his worry about Eve from his mind. She was a reasonable woman who wouldn't hold one misstep against him. Would she?

Then he saw Roger. And Cam and Jacki. And Gregor trying to get to Roger . . . sort of. If Gregor had really wanted Roger, Cam and Jacki couldn't have held him off.

Dean jerked the car into PARK and stalked toward them. "Back off, Gregor."

Gregor yelled, "He still thinks Jacki should get a boob job."

Roger, more irate than worried, said, "I do not. I said if she wanted one, I'd help her."

Jacki smacked at Gregor, shoved against him, even pinched him once. But Gregor just kept easing closer to Roger in an intimidating fashion.

Frantic, Cam met Dean halfway. "Please call a halt to this, Dean. Please."

Rigid, Dean gave one nod. He reached Gregor, caught him by the back of the neck and yanked him away.

Gregor hadn't been expecting that.

He actually fell on his ass. An instant later, Jacki was there beside him, seeing if he was hurt.

"Where'd you go, Roger?"

"Nowhere." Roger straightened his clothes, still seething. "I just needed some time to think, so I stayed in my house for a few days."

"Convenient," Dean told him, "that while you're playing hooky, someone is trying to shoot me."

"I'm in no mood for your ridiculous accusation, man, so back off."

"The hell I will."

Roger squared off with him. "So you want to settle this in private?"

"Yes."

That startled him, probably because Dean had previously refused to fight him. But Roger didn't back down.

Grim and determined, he started to agree—until Gregor got back on his feet and planted himself between them.

"C'mon, Dean, you don't really want to kill him."

Cam said, "No, he does not. Now knock it off, Dean." And to Roger, she said, "I won't have you fighting my brother."

Roger looked at her askance and marginally complied.

"Look, Cam told me what happened and what you think. But it wasn't me."

Shoving Gregor to the side, Dean demanded, "Then who else?"

On the explosive edge, Roger snarled, "How the fuck should I know, you arrogant ass." He came chin to chin with Dean. "I imagine you've got enough people pissed off to make a baker's dozen."

Dean gave an evil smile. "You're not seeing my sister alone. I don't trust you."

Cam threw up her hands. "I thought you weren't that kind of brother!"

"I wasn't." He glanced at her, chagrined. "But I am now."

"Well, that changes things," Gregor said with a shrug. "Go ahead and smash him, Dean. He has it coming."

Roger dropped his head, laughed hoarsely, and then raised his face to see Cam. "I haven't slept much in the last few days. But Lorna left a message on my machine, saying that you had something important to tell me, so I'm here. If you'd just spit it out now, I could get away from this over-bearing ass of a brother you have."

Cam blinked at him. "But . . . Aunt Lorna told me that you have something you have to tell me."

Roger locked his jaw. "I do. But your brother has refused us any privacy, and I'm afraid I'll insist on it before I make you hate me."

Hate him? Dean studied Roger and wondered what was going on now.

Cam deflated. "Oh Roger, I could never hate you. I wish you'd believe that."

He turned away and stared into the night.

Cam touched his arm. "I love you, I really do. I just can't marry you yet."

"Not last year. Not now." Roger shrugged off her hand. "And no time in the future."

"I didn't say that."

Dean suddenly had the awful suspicion that they were

at cross-purposes, and he tired of it. "She won't marry you as long as she owes you money."

Roger jerked around at that. He looked at Dean, then stared at Cam. "What's he talking about?"

Embarrassed, Cam ducked her head.

Dean answered for her. "She doesn't want financial debt to come between you. And that makes me wonder why the hell you're so determined to keep her in your debt."

Confused, Cam shook her head. "Keep me in your debt?"

"I feel like an interpreter, for God's sake." Dean sighed. "Roger's keeping you in his debt by paying off stuff that's insignificant, but holding on to loans that you can't immediately pay off. I know he forks over money to Lorna left and right."

Cam stared at Roger. "You do?"

"No offense, honey, but your aunt is sometimes difficult to tolerate."

Dean smirked. "And it's easier to give her money so she can absent herself?"

"Yes."

"That doesn't explain why you've kept Cam in your debt."

Roger looked from Cam to Dean and back again. He leaned back against the brick wall of his hotel. "It's easy enough to figure out. The only way I know for sure that I can keep her is to keep her in debt. As long as she owes me, she won't cut ties with me."

Gregor snorted. "Now ain't that fuckin' sweet as molasses?"

Jacki slugged him harder this time. "Gregor, will you shut up?"

"Not until he explains why the hell he thought to comment on your body one way or the other."

Cam looked rather curious about that one, too.

Running a hand through his hair, Roger shrugged. "I saw her worrying about it."

"You did?" Jacki asked.

"You were looking at the roof, where he"—Roger indicated Gregor—"was working. Then you'd look at your . . ." He nodded at her chest. "You've never made any pretense of liking me. I saw that your lack of curves bothered you. I thought that maybe solving the problem for you would be a good way to ingratiate myself to you. You'd get what you wanted, and I'd gain your gratitude."

"This is incredible." Cam shook her head as if dizzy. "You actually thought that would endear you to anyone?"

"Other than Lorna, everyone important to you dislikes me."

"I don't need anyone's approval, Roger."

That seemed to set him off again. "Well, good for you." He sneered. "But nothing else I've tried has worked! I figured getting in good with the people you care about couldn't hurt."

Cam went nose to nose with him. "This is insane. I already told you that I love you."

"Then marry me, damn it!"

"All right!"

Silence fell.

Until Roger dropped his head forward on a groan. "I don't believe this." New tension gripped him. "Now that your aunt is ready to expose me, you finally say yes."

Dean still felt that something wasn't right—and it centered around Roger. "Expose you for what?"

"I suppose it doesn't matter anymore. If I don't tell you, Lorna will." He cast an evil eye on their audience, accepted that no one was about to budge, and turned back to Cam. "I told you about your parents, how they drank too much, how your mother and father were unfaithful to each other."

And suddenly Dean knew. He closed his eyes, calling himself a dozen times a fool for not figuring it out sooner.

"Yes." Cam watched Roger, her heart in her eyes.

Dean wished for some way to spare her. "You're the son."

No one understood except Roger. "That's right."

"I remember Grover told me that my mother's lover had a family." Dean recalled the story as if it had happened yesterday. "When my mother died, the guy she'd been cheating with was so grief stricken, he left his wife and kid."

"He was a drunk, always depressed over something,"

Roger said in a toneless voice. "I had just turned eleven when everything changed. Your parents died, and my life fell apart. Not a whole lot of difference, except that you all still had family."

Cam bit her lip, and her eyes grew teary. "You didn't?"

Roger shook his head. "After my father disappeared without a word, my mother cried for a month. She barely noticed me, she was so busy cursing my dad one minute and praying for him to come back the next. Finally she just gave up. I came home from school, and she was gone, too, just like my dad. The only difference was that she left a note, saying she wouldn't be back." He half laughed. "Dad didn't even do that much."

Cam started to touch him, but Roger moved away. "People found out, of course. That's why I got shuffled off to a foster home, then another one and another one."

"I'm so sorry," Cam whispered. "I had no idea why you had grown up in foster homes."

Roger's hands fisted, his shoulders tensed. "I've lost everything I ever wanted." He turned to face her. *"I didn't want to lose you."*

"You won't."

He laughed. "Lorna told me how you'd feel about me. She told me you'd never be able to look beyond the shame of being with me. If everyone else in town realized who I was, the gossip would never end. You have to admit, it's one hell of an irony for me to fall in love with you."

As if no one else existed, Cam looked at Roger and said softly, "It doesn't matter."

"I was going to tell you," he said. "I took a few days off to work up my nerve. I'd tried everything to win you over, and when I realized it wasn't going to happen, that you'd never marry me, I figured I owed you the truth at least."

Gregor stared at everyone in confusion. "If you were eleven when all that happened, doesn't everyone around here already know who you are?"

"No. I lived a few counties over, and when I went into the foster program, I was away for a few years. By the time

I came back, I had a new name and I'd changed a lot. From grade school to junior high, some boys become men."

Cam reached for him. Roger tried to dodge her, but Cam wasn't an easy woman to shake off once she set her mind on offering comfort.

Dean knew that for a fact.

Hugged up to Roger's chest, Cam said, "I don't understand why you wanted to meet me here to tell me this."

Roger finally put his arms around her, his cheek to her head. "I didn't." He hugged her tight. "You're the one who wanted to meet here."

Cam leaned back to frown at him. "No. Aunt Lorna said you were here, and you needed to see me." With an apologetic smile, she told Dean, "I'm sorry I didn't call you. Lorna and I agreed that it really wasn't necessary. I knew Roger couldn't be the one doing those—"

Roger stiffened. "Lorna."

Dean's heart almost stopped. "She called me, Cam, to tell me you were coming here."

"But that doesn't make any sense. She told me not to call you."

"She called me, too, she knew that I've been at home—I thought she told you that's where I was." Roger said. "Your aunt knows how I feel about you, and she's the one who encouraged me to loan you money, to keep you indebted to me so you couldn't walk away from me. Today she told me that you needed to talk to me, so that I should meet you here."

Bewildered, Jacki said, "But why?"

"You have money," Dean told them with sudden realization.

"Plenty," Roger agreed. "I found out some time ago that you had a sizeable inheritance. Your aunt has diverted funds and hidden them for herself. She hates the thought of Dean being here, poking around and uncovering what she did with your finances. She was in charge of it until you turned twenty-one."

"I'm twenty-three now," Cam pointed out. "No one has notified me of any inheritance."

"Because your aunt had full control for so long, she's been able to cover it up."

Jacki crossed her arms over her chest. "You knew this and never told Cam?"

"Lorna told me that if I did, she'd reveal my secrets. I didn't want to lose her."

"Idiot."

Roger paid no mind to Jacki's insult. He kept all his attention on Cam. "I figured that once I convinced you to marry me, I'd tell you everything then."

"Jacki's right," Cam said. "You should have told me."

"I know that now. I'm sorry. For a lot of things."

"But I'm wondering," Gregor said. "What's the old bird up to, sending everyone here to meet?"

Cam suddenly stumbled away from Roger. Her hands to her mouth, she said, "Oh no."

"What is it?" Roger asked.

"Dean . . . after you left today, Aunt Lorna tried to convince me that you didn't really care about Jacki or me. She said she knew the truth, that the only one keeping you in Harmony was—"

"Eve." The word barely whispered out of Dean's mouth before he turned and started running.

Behind him, Gregor yelled, "Should I call the cops?"

And Roger, right behind Dean, shouted, *"Yes."*

DEAN barely killed the engine before he jumped out of his car and hit the ground at a run. Without knocking, he charged into Eve's house. "Eve!"

No answer.

Strides long and heavy, he looked in Eve's bedroom, through the great room, and finally trotted into the kitchen. He drew to a halt.

Eve sat in a chair, her head pulled back by the fist Lorna had twisted in her hair. A long butcher knife, the blade bloody, swung back and forth as Lorna paced behind Eve.

CHAPTER 22

⁂

Dean saw the blood on Eve's arm and prayed the cut wasn't too serious.

"Lorna?"

She jerked, adding pressure to Eve's hair.

"Dean? You aren't at the hotel, bludgeoning poor Roger to death?"

"No. I'm here."

"That's unfortunate." Almost in apology, Lorna said, "I threw away the paintball gun when I saw that you'd called the police. I'm not sure how the whole fingerprint thing works and I knew it would look suspicious for me to have it after what happened."

Dean watched her closely. "I assume your prints wouldn't be on file."

"No. Of course not."

"If you have a suspect, you can take prints and see if they match."

"Oh." Lorna considered it. "I suppose I should dispose of the ladder, too, then. I just never considered it. I'm not that type of person, you understand. I don't have a criminal mind. Other than Roger's father, I've never physically hurt anyone."

Dean had started to ask her about his tires, too, but she effectively threw him off with that disclosure. "Roger's father?"

"Grover left that piece of trash on the curb in front of the house. But that wouldn't do. I couldn't take over the parenting of two young girls with the evidence of their black past right there for all the neighborhood to see. Surely you understand that?"

With an eerie calm settling around him, Dean leaned in the door frame. He kept his stance deceptively casual, but given the opportunity, he'd be on Lorna in a heartbeat. "What did you do with him?"

She smiled. "I brought him in, of course. I got him coherent, and then I promised to take him to see your mother. I convinced that miserable idiot that she wasn't dead after all."

"And then you killed him?"

"He killed himself by living a disreputable life!"

Dean couldn't look at Eve. Not yet. "How did he die, Lorna?"

"It all worked out for the best." The hand holding the knife rested on Eve's shoulder. Chortling as if delighted with herself, Lorna said, "I waited until night, after Cam and Jacki were asleep. I gave him a bottle of whiskey to fortify himself during the drive, then I drove him to a dirty little lake located well out of town."

"He got drunk again?"

Lorna nodded. "I realized the man was an alcoholic. To tell you the truth, he made more sense inebriated than he did when sober."

Dean waited as she sorted through the memories.

"After he was good and drunk, I told him your mother was hiding, waiting for him. I had planned to just leave him out there, but we were standing near the edge of the lake when he fell and didn't get up again." She shrugged. "I don't know if he hit his head or just passed out."

"So you helped him into the water?"

"Yes." She looked up at Dean, her gaze vague and dull. "For all I know, he's still there." Suddenly her hand tightened on Eve's hair with a vicious yank. "Why didn't you just leave town as you should have? Everything would have been so much simpler."

Eve gasped, and that small sound almost stopped Dean's heart.

Think, Dean. He had to calm himself. He'd seen more than his share of blood—but always on big, muscular men who paid no attention to it. Blood caused from sport, not from a deliberate attempt to cause pain.

Not on Eve.

Roger wouldn't be too far behind him, and surely, Gregor had already called the police. They were liable to blaze up with lights flashing, sirens full blast.

Would the commotion push Lorna over the edge?

Carefully Dean stepped away from the wall. "Lorna, I think Eve's hurt."

"It's just a little slice." In her own defense, Lorna explained, "She tried to take my knife from me."

Eve whispered, "I'm sorry, Dean. She took me by surprise."

He shook his head at her. Maybe if Eve stayed quiet, Lorna wouldn't think too much about her or the passing of time. "The money doesn't matter, Lorna."

Her gaze shot up to his. "Ah, so you know about that?"

"Roger told me."

"That ingrate." Full of affront, she shook her head. "He's been a vast disappointment."

"It doesn't matter, Lorna. You deserved the money."

"I really did," she agreed.

"And I have enough of my own. More than Roger, in fact." That was a lie, but Lorna wouldn't know it. "I can take care of everyone, including you."

"You'd do that for me?"

"I owe you for taking care of Cam and Jacki all these years. All you need to do is put the knife away."

"I can't." She paced again, as far as the length of Eve's hair would allow. "This girl is wrong—you'll never care about me. Your parents didn't. They liked Grover, but they thought I was a bore. I heard them say so. A bore and a prude and unwanted."

Jesus. She was still hurt over something twenty years old? That thought gave Dean pause. He hadn't wanted to admit it, but until his sisters and Eve had made everything right, he'd been hurt, too.

But not like this.

Not the way he'd be hurt if he lost Eve.

"They designated you to care for their children, Lorna. That means they respected you an awful lot."

"Ha." Lorna actually laughed. It was a dry, crackling sound tainted with madness. "They burdened me with them because they didn't have anyone else who'd take them in."

Dean prayed that neither Cam nor Jacki would ever know of those particular words leaving Lorna's mouth.

He took a careful step forward. "Lorna—"

The knife flashed high into the air. All laughter gone, Lorna said, "If you move again, I'll have to stab her."

Eve's lashes fluttered with fear. Her knuckles turned white as she gripped the seat of the chair, sending crimson blood trickling down her arm to drip onto the floor. She licked dry lips and tried to be brave, but she hadn't led the same type life as he had, and this was too hard for her.

What the hell should he do?

"You're only here because of her," Lorna reasoned. "If she's gone, you'll go away, and everything will be the same."

"I'll take her away," Dean promised. "She and I will both leave."

Lorna curled her lip. "You take me for a fool?"

"No." Suddenly behind and to the side of Lorna, Dean saw a slight movement.

Simon.

How Simon had entered the house so silently, how he'd even known where to find them, Dean didn't know. But his heart pumped hard and fast with exhilaration. Eve would be okay now.

To keep from giving away Simon's position, Dean looked at Lorna and only Lorna. "You're okay, Eve." Simon was almost within reach of her. For a big man, he moved without making a sound.

"I know." Eve stared at Dean, taking or giving comfort, he wasn't sure.

Lorna laughed, a little less certainly this time. "She's cut, Dean. She's . . . bleeding." Her nose wrinkled and she struggled to swallow. "I can smell the blood. I didn't realize that. How you do this barbaric stuff all the time is a mystery to me."

"I don't cut people, Lorna."

"Not with a knife, no. But I watched a few of your fights. You make people bleed. You use your elbows, your fists, your—"

"Cutting someone isn't as effective at stopping them as other means, Lorna. For instance a blow to the liver will make even a grown man drop. It's the most crippling pain imaginable." He looked at Eve. "You remember me telling you that just last night, don't you, honey?"

"Yes." As if choreographed, Eve's elbow flashed back against Lorna in a solid strike—right into the liver.

Eyes gaping, mouth open, Lorna released Eve with a gasp—and Simon knocked the knife from her hand, probably breaking her wrist in the process.

Soundless in her pain, Lorna collapsed to the floor.

In a heartbeat, Dean scooped Eve up and away from the chair, close to his heart. She cradled her injured arm and squeezed closer. "Dean?"

"Shhh. I've got you now." He went to the sink for a dish towel and managed, one-handed, to wrap her arm.

Eve swallowed and nodded. "Thank you." With her head tucked under his chin, she said, "I love you, Dean."

Jesus, he wanted to howl. She was upset so he couldn't, *wouldn't*, put too much stock in those words. But still it felt damn good to hear them. "I love you, too."

She drew a shuddering breath, wiped her cheeks on his shirt, and straightened. Looking back at Lorna, she whispered, "God, that was awful."

"She's not just mean," Dean said, "she's insane."

Simon picked up the knife, then knelt over Lorna to check on her. "It's all right, old girl. Slow, shallow breaths. That's it. Hang in there. Help's on the way."

Curled on her side, wheezing in pain, Lorna made a sad, pathetic sight. Having suffered a few liver blows of his own, Dean almost sympathized with her. Almost. "Is she hurt bad?"

"Nah. She'll be all right. Your lady's elbow didn't do any real damage, just took the fight out of her. But I broke her arm." Simon glanced up at Eve and said, "Good for you."

"Dean taught me a few moves."

Simon lifted one dark eyebrow. "Did he?"

"What are you doing here?" Dean asked him.

"The short story is that I got the info you wanted on your future brother-in-law. I tried to find you at the hotel to fill you in, and instead I ran into Gregor and your sisters. They told me what had happened, and that Roger had already clued you in to his background."

"Gregor stayed with my sisters?"

Simon nodded. "He's being real heroic and protective."

That thought both rankled and relieved Dean at the same time. "I'm glad to know she's safe."

"If you say so." Simon grinned. "Roger's out front, by the way. I told him that if the cops showed up, make them come in quietlike. I didn't know what might be happening in here, if anyone had a gun or not."

"That's why you didn't wait for the cops?"

Simon eyed Dean. "I couldn't have you getting yourself killed. I've got too many big-money deals lined up, and they all include you."

Knowing Simon as well as he did, Dean discarded all mercenary motives and kissed Eve's forehead. "Let me see your arm, honey."

"It's okay." But Eve lifted it for his inspection.

Dean loosened the towel. The bleeding had already stopped. "I don't think you'll need stitches."

"Good." She rolled in her lips and struggled to regain her composure. "She came in here, saying she had to talk to me about you. I told her fine, but that I wouldn't let her insult you. We came into the kitchen for coffee, and she . . . attacked me."

Dean smoothed back Eve's hair. "Thank God you'd gotten dressed."

"Yeah." She put her forehead to his. "There is that."

Simon helped Lorna to sit up. She looked dazed, blank, and much older than her fifty-seven years.

Still holding the big knife, Simon rubbed his forehead with the back of his wrist. "I'd say you owe me, Havoc."

"More than you realize."

"Wrong. I'm not blind. That's why I'm sure you'll do the project I mentioned." Simon smiled with satisfaction. "Afterward you can return to your lady."

Dean looked at Eve, hugged her again, and said, "Yeah, I'll return to her."

Seconds later, backup rolled in. As a precaution, Roger had not only called the police, but he'd also asked for an ambulance. He came to stand by Dean as authorities tended to Lorna and then, under police supervision, took her out of the house to a waiting ambulance.

Not at any time did Lorna look lucid.

Simon strolled out to answer what questions he could.

"Cam is going to be devastated." Roger closed his eyes and put his head back against the wall. "Despite everything, she cares for her aunt."

With Eve in his arms, Dean now had a better understanding of Roger's fear over losing Cam. And realizing that his parents' irresponsible actions had also affected Roger put a different slant on everything.

Finally he could understand some of Roger's actions.

"I should go to Cam," Eve said.

"No." Tightening his hold on Eve to keep her in place, Dean stationed himself beside Roger. "She has Roger. He can handle it for now."

Roger didn't reply.

Dean moved around in front of him. "I've got my hands full here, Rog, and I'll be more than a little pissed if you force me to knock some sense into you."

Roger opened his eyes and scowled. "This changes everything, damn it. I never told Cam about her aunt. If I had, none of this would have happened. It's my fault—"

"Don't be a martyred idiot, okay? We don't have time for that shit right now. *No one* realized Lorna was really nuts, not even my sisters. If those closest to her didn't know, how could you?"

The epitome of a beaten man, Roger looked at Eve's arm and winced. "I'm so sorry, Eve. Damn sorry."

"Go to Cam," Eve told him, and it was clear that she'd also softened toward Roger. "She loves you. And Dean's right, she needs you now."

"I don't know." He moved away from the wall, hopeful. "You really think she'll be able to forgive me?"

Without hesitation, Eve said, "Yes. She loves you."

As a precaution, Dean added, "If you disappoint her, I will have something to say about it."

A tired smile lifted Roger's expression. "I suppose you want me to marry her?"

"The sooner the better."

After a fleeting grin, Roger clapped Dean on the shoulder and headed off. Dean felt confident that he'd go to Cam, and that eventually, his sister would be okay. She was resilient and strong and he had great faith in her.

Dean touched his forehead to Eve's. "Things have happened awful fast."

"Light-speed fast," Eve agreed.

"My whole life has changed."

Blue eyes soft with worry, Eve watched him. "And?"

Dean smoothed back her hair. "I have to leave, honey. I need to settle some things, make some decisions—"

Eve put a finger to his mouth. "I don't know what will happen with Lorna, but even with Roger in the picture, Cam will need me here."

"Yes."

"Summer is a busy time with my business. I have a lot of events lined up."

"Your work is a priority."

"And speaking of priorities, my family . . . my family is *here*."

"My family, too."

Eve put her head back on Dean's shoulder. After a heavy moment of silence, she said, "You take care of whatever you need to, Dean. But know that when you come back, I'll be here waiting."

Two months later, Dean knocked on Eve's door. He felt ridiculous in khaki slacks and a black polo shirt, especially with new bruises on his face and a bouquet of mixed wildflowers in hand. The time he'd been gone had dragged out with one complication after another. Instead of eight weeks, it felt like a year since he'd seen her and touched her. His whole body ached with the need to make love to her, but he wouldn't. Not right away. He had a lot to say, a lot to explain.

A lot that he wanted to share.

While away from Eve, he'd forced himself to give her some space. He'd only called a few times. Mostly they talked about Cam and how she was dealing with Lorna. Strangely enough, it made Dean feel better to know that Cam had Roger at her side.

Jacki had stuck by her sister until after Dean finished his stint with the reality series. Then, the night of the fight in Atlanta, she surprised Dean by showing up in the audience. When he won, he could have sworn he heard her cheering.

Impatience growing, Dean rapped on Eve's door again. Eve called out, "Hold your horses," and seconds later, the door opened and there she was.

At her first sight of him, her face lit up, then went cautiously blank. "Dean. I didn't know you were back in town."

He pressed the flowers into her hand. "I think I owe you these ten times over."

"Flowers?"

"You said you like them mixed, right? Wildflowers?"

"They're beautiful."

Determined to get it all said before his control broke and he ravished her, Dean said, "I also owe you some dates, as I recall. But they'll come later."

"They will?"

Hearing whispers behind Eve, Dean girded himself for disappointment. "Your family is here?"

"Yes." Eve absorbed the sight of him, head to toes and back again. "All of them."

Voices approached, and then they were all there in front of Dean, drawing him inside with enthusiasm.

Eve stepped back helplessly, the flowers clutched to her chest.

Recaps of his fight, of how fascinating the special promo had been, rang out. As Ted pumped his hand in congratulations, Dean's tension eased.

It wasn't so bad seeing Eve's family. If all went well, they'd soon become his family, too.

Perching on the edge of his seat, Mark said, "You dodged every punch that maniac threw and then drilled him with a jab each time. How the hell did you do that?"

"The other fighter telegraphed his moves," Eve said, remembering what Dean had told her. "He loaded up before every punch, putting all his weight on one leg. If he hadn't kept trying for a knockout blow each time, he'd have been more successful."

Dean grinned with pride. "That's right."

She held up the flowers. "I'll go put these in water."

More questions rang out, but as soon as Eve returned,

Dean reached out a hand to her. When she took it, he pulled her onto his lap.

To Eve's mother, he said, "I'm sorry, Crystal."

She tucked in her chin. "For what?"

Anticipating Eve's reaction, Dean tightened his hold. "For not going through you when I bought my house here in Harmony."

Surprise widened Crystal's eyes. "You bought a house?"

"Only a few blocks away, actually."

"A fixer-upper?" Eve wanted to know.

"No." Dean looked at her and had to kiss her. But with her family all watching, he kept it brief. "It's practically new, actually. Maybe twice the size of yours, with an acre lot. It's nice."

Eve blinked in surprise and bemusement. Finally she shook her head as if to clear it. "So you plan to stay around?"

Aware of her brother grinning, her father smiling, Dean kissed Eve again, lingering a little more this time. "I'm staying."

Crystal asked, "Have you furnished it yet?"

He shook his head. "If Eve marries me, then it'll be up to her if we live here or move to my place. And if we move to my place, she might want to help me pick out the furnishings."

Eve went mute.

"If you're marrying Eve," Mark asked, "why would you want another house?"

"So Eve would know she had choices." Dean touched her lips with his thumb. "And that I had choices, too."

Smile quivering, Eve asked, "But you chose me?"

"Yes. And I hope you choose me, too."

Ted cleared his throat. "I suppose we should give you some privacy."

"I don't mind," Dean told him, and he meant it. Because Eve had gone quiet, he chucked her under the chin. "Did you know that Jacki is leaving Harmony?"

She shook her head.

"She and Gregor are moving in together. Gregor swears they'll get married just as soon as Jacki agrees, but Jacki doesn't want to get in the way of him fighting."

"Would she be in his way?"

"Of course not. Gregor will convince her of that soon enough."

"Cam and Roger plan to stay here," Eve told him. "But they'll take a long honeymoon once things are settled with Lorna."

It was an unfortunate situation, but Lorna hadn't spoken since the day of her arrest. She ate very little and spent most her time staring into space. It seemed she would just waste away.

Officials thought she might be too incompetent to stand trial. Dean still considered her a danger, not just to herself, but to others as well. It relieved him that Lorna stayed in an institution, constantly monitored.

Thinking of how close he'd come to losing Eve, he lifted her arm and kissed it. "You're okay now?"

Her voice as low and soft as his, she said, "Not even a faint scar."

Crystal turned all business. "Okay, time for us to go."

Mark and Ted had a million questions, but Crystal was a formidable woman and had them out the door in less than two minutes.

Standing at the closed door, Eve said, "You've run off my family again."

Dean took her hand and led her back to the couch. "I like your family."

"They like you."

Smiling, Dean pulled Eve down onto the couch with him. Moving over her, he took her mouth in a long, leisurely kiss that left her clinging to him and breathing fast. He almost got distracted enough with that to put off other, more important things.

But he knew he couldn't.

Stretched out over Eve, he said, "My khakis are getting wrinkled."

Eyes dreamy, she licked her lips and stared at his mouth. "I noticed the clothes."

"Did you now? And do you like them?"

She ran her fingers over his shoulders while pretending to think about it. "I told you once that you look good, no matter what. You don't have to change how you dress to suit me."

"Are you sure about that? Because I will if it matters. That is, if it matters a lot."

She grinned. "It doesn't. Not at all."

Letting out his breath, Dean said, "Good, because I only bought one pair."

She tried to kiss him again, but Dean dodged her. "I did buy one other thing though."

"What's that?"

"Not a ring, if that's what you're thinking. You have great taste, and I thought you might want to pick that out yourself."

She looked a little disappointed, but said, "We'll be picking out a ring?"

"Definitely." Dean sat them both back up. He rolled his sleeve up above his biceps and showed Eve the enhancement to his tattoo.

Her lips parted.

Added to the vines was a single three-dimensional daisy, shadowed to look as if it grew in the sunshine.

Dean tipped up her chin. "You said you wanted daisies at your wedding, so I thought—"

She threw herself against him, knocking him back down on the couch. "I missed you so much."

Dean held her, but he had to finish. "I wanted you to know that I'm here for *you,* Eve. I love my sisters, and I want them in my life. You're a part of them, a part of Harmony." He tried to sort his thoughts, to make it clear for her. "But even if you weren't, I'd still want to marry you. If I'd met you in the audience, I think I'd have wanted you. If I still didn't know my sisters, I'd want you. Even if—"

She put her fingers over his mouth. "All you have to say is that you love me."

"I love you."

She settled against him. "I love you, too, and that's all that really matters."

Dean relaxed. "What would you think of me opening a gym here?"

Stiffening her arms, Eve raised herself above him. "Here? In Harmony?"

"To be near you."

"But . . ." She couldn't seem to grasp the concept. "You're not going to continue fighting?"

"I don't think so. At least not for a while."

"But you're so good at it."

He cupped her behind and grinned. "I'm good at loving you, too."

"Oh, Dean." She kissed him silly. "I don't want you to give up fighting for me."

"Don't think that, okay? I'm redirecting myself, which is something I've been considering for awhile. I love the sport too much to leave it completely, and if I got a really good challenge, I might be lured out of retirement. It happens. But for now I want to teach. I'm even better at teaching than I am at fighting, and I know I'll make one hell of a coach." Half under his breath, he said, "God knows, Gregor needs work."

Eve suddenly laughed.

Enjoying the sound, Dean turned her beneath him, got comfortable, and asked, "What's so funny?"

"Oh, I was just thinking. . . ." She wrapped her arms around him, the picture of a happy woman. "It sure will make things interesting, having Havoc in Harmony."

"I hope so," he told her. "Because with you here, I don't plan on leaving again anytime soon."